PRAISE FOR *THE WATER AND THE WILD*

"*The Water and the Wild* is a debut children's fantasy that feels akin to the British childhood favorites I grew up reading—The Chronicles of Narnia, *The Dark Is Rising*, and *Alice in Wonderland*. So introduce your child to a modern classic in the making or read it yourself in nostalgic remembrance." —Jill Hendrix, Fiction Addiction

"Engaging. Imaginative." —*Kirkus Reviews*

"Humorous descriptions and vivid creatures. Should keep many readers intrigued." —*Publishers Weekly*

"An exciting journey full of obstacles and fun action." —*VOYA (Voice of Youth Advocates)*

The
Doorway
and the
Deep

K. E. Ormsbee

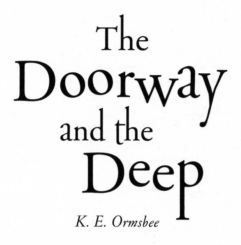

chronicle books · san francisco

Library of Congress Cataloging-in-Publication Data:
Names: Ormsbee, Katie, author.
Title: The doorway and the deep / by K. E. Ormsbee.
Description: San Francisco : Chronicle Books, [2016] | Sequel to: The water
and the wild. | Summary: Even after escaping from the Southerly Kingdom,
Lottie Fiske has returned to the magical Albion Isle, despite the fact that she is a
wanted criminal there, because she is seeking answers about her abilities, and her
parents—but war is threatening Limn, and the answers she needs seem to lie in the
Northerly Kingdom, along a road full of dangers.
Identifiers: LCCN 2016000984 | ISBN 9781452136363 (alk. paper)
Subjects: LCSH: Magic—Juvenile fiction. | Orphans—Juvenile fiction. |
Friendship—Juvenile fiction. | Adventure stories. | CYAC: Magic—Fiction.
| Orphans—Fiction. | Secrets—Fiction. | Friendship—Fiction. | Adventure
and adventurers—Fiction. | GSAFD: Adventure fiction.
Classification: LCC PZ7.O637 Do 2016 | DDC [Fic]—dc23 LC record
available at http://lccn.loc.gov/2016000984

Manufactured in China.

Design by Amelia Mack.
Typeset in Jannon Antiqua.

10 9 8 7 6 5 4 3 2 1

Chronicle Books LLC
680 Second Street
San Francisco, California 94107

Chronicle Books—we see things differently. Become part of our community at www.chroniclekids.com.

To Kenneth and Ann Ashby,
who gave me summer days on the farm
and to George and Betty Ormsbee,
who gave me bittersweet Irish ballads—
I love you.

References to poems are marked with a 🍂.

Find a complete list of the poems referenced on page 408.

"To unpath'd waters, undream'd shores, most certain
To miseries enough; no hope to help you,
But as you shake off one to take another;
Nothing so certain as your anchors."

—WILLIAM SHAKESPEARE, *THE WINTER'S TALE*

CHAPTER ONE

Sharpening Lessons

A RED APPLE TREE grew in the heart of Wandlebury Wood. It was a burst of color in a land of white. Its roots sank deep into the earth, so deep they reached other worlds altogether. Though the bark was grooved by the grinding of time, it showed no sign of decay.

A solitary guard hovered beside the tree, though there was little activity to keep him busy these days. Since the Plague had come to Wisp Territory, there had only been two travelers to emerge from the apple tree's trunk: a girl with a periwinkle coat, and a boy with a slight cough.

Not five minutes' walk from the red apple tree was a place known by its current residents as the Clearing. Here, set apart from the surrounding forest, three yews grew from an expanse of white grass, canopied by silvery fabric and strings of globed lights. Autumn was in the air, and hard gusts of wind often blew through the Clearing, causing the fabric to billow, the lanterns to teeter, and the long white grasses to whisper amongst themselves. Such a wind was blowing now, on the cusp of a new dusk. It was whipping up the lemony hair of a girl who stood upon the branch of one of the yews.

"Trouble's missing," she said.

"Urgh," the tree replied.

Lottie Fiske peered into the tree's hollowed-out trunk. She had just learned in the past week how to keep her sneakers balanced on a yew branch without toppling over.

"Fife?" she called.

"Something is talking. *Why* is something talking?"

A plume of black hair appeared in the trunk hole under Lottie's nose. Fife blinked up at Lottie, his eyes bleary in the glare of the setting sun.

"Um," said Lottie. "Good evening."

"Shhh," said Fife, flapping a hand at Lottie's mouth. "The talking. Make it stop. So . . . loud."

"I need to talk to Oliver," said Lottie. "Trouble's gone—"

"—missing," Fife finished. "Huh. Did you check your pockets?"

Lottie gave Fife a dirty look.

"What? It's funny."

"He was in my pocket when I went to sleep, and when I woke up he was gone."

"Wait. He's just been gone for a day?" Fife snorted. "That hardly qualifies as missing."

"But you don't understand! He left without my permission. Gengas aren't supposed to do that."

"Yeah, but Trouble's *trouble*. Didn't Ollie tell you that the first rule of training is to remain cal—"

"I AM REMAINING CALM."

"Lottie?"

Two glowing eyes, bright yellow with concern, appeared behind Fife's mane of hair.

"Lottie," Oliver said again, his voice hoarse from sleep. "Why are you shouting?"

"I wasn't—Fife, *stop laughing*."

Fife just laughed harder, his shoulders shaking as he floated out of the yew. He turned a double somersault and landed in a thick patch of mud at the tree's base.

"Quit worrying!" he called up. "You'll feel much better about the whole thing once you've eaten some breakfast."

"I'm confused," said Oliver, rubbing his eyes. When he lowered his hand, his irises had dimmed to a groggy gray. "What's the problem?"

"Trouble. He flew off, and he hasn't come back."

"Has he done that before?"

"Of course he hasn't! Don't you think I would've told my own genga trainer if Trouble was misbehaving?"

"You didn't tell me about the candy incident."

"Ooh!" shouted Fife. "Don't forget the green paint incident. That one's a classic."

Lottie sniffed proudly. "I had complete control of those situations."

That wasn't true, and both Lottie and the boys knew it. The last time Trouble had misbehaved, they had all nearly been banished from Wisp Territory. It had taken several hours of heated discussion between Mr. Wilfer and Silvia Dulcet to sort things out.

It was a tricky position to be in, having to depend upon the generosity of the wisps. But Iris Gate, the Wilfers' home in New Albion, was a charred husk and now belonged to King Starkling. Lottie, Fife, and the Wilfers were wanted criminals on Albion Isle—now more than ever after their escape from the Southerly Court. In the end, Silvia Dulcet, Fife's mother and the Seamstress of the wisps, had offered them shelter.

Mr. Wilfer remained one of the most revered healers on the island, so Silvia had struck up a deal with him: she would provide a home for him and his guests if Mr. Wilfer would work on a cure for her people's plague. The arrangement had been, in the words of Fife, "very symbiotic or some such crap."

These arrangements were made while Lottie was still back on Kemble Isle, staying with Eliot at the Barmy Badger. Mr. Walsch had taken his son to see the doctor a few days after Lottie's return from Albion Isle. It had been an eventful visit, and Lottie had spent the entirety of it grinning from ear to ear.

It was impossible, the doctor had said. *Unprecedented. Unbelievable.*

The doctor had gone on to use several other big words beginning with "im" and "un," but the long and short of it— all that *really* mattered—was that Eliot Walsch had made a remarkable recovery since his last visit, when that very same doctor had said, "Two, maybe three weeks to live."

"The disease is still present," said the doctor, "but Eliot himself is in excellent health, considering. I simply can't explain it."

Lottie didn't mind that the doctor had no explanation. She had one of her own.

She had a keen.

With the touch of her hands, she could heal others.

She had healed Eliot.

So Lottie's status as a wanted criminal hadn't deterred her from returning to Albion Isle. She still had a good deal to learn about her keen, and, according to Mr. Wilfer, if she wanted to be the best healer she could be, she needed to train. Lottie did want to become a good healer, but more than that, she wanted to make Eliot Walsch better for good.

Eliot's father had been wonderfully understanding about the whole thing. He wasn't like other adults—people like Mrs. Yates who didn't believe in magic and thought there was only one proper way to do things. Mr. Walsch believed Lottie's story about another world—an Albion Isle just on the other end of an apple tree's roots. Not long after that doctor's visit, Mr. Walsch sold the Barmy Badger and moved to a cottage south of New Kemble. It was a humble stone house, much smaller than the Barmy Badger had been. But in its backyard grew a whole grove of apple trees—some green, some red, some yellow. Lottie, who knew full well the precious value of an apple tree, thought Mr. Walsch could not have chosen a better new home.

On the pale October morning when Lottie and Eliot pulled the silver bough of one of those trees, Mr. Walsch hugged them tight and bid them goodbye.

"When you get a chance like this, kiddos," he said, "you must take it."

Eliot promised Mr. Walsch he would send a letter home every day, using a certain copper box Lottie had retrieved from the stump of her apple tree in Thirsby Square. He and Lottie both promised to return in a month's time for Thanksgiving dinner and the winter holidays.

And so Lottie and Eliot had come to live in Wisp Territory, where Lottie fell into a steady routine. At dusk, she sharpened her keen with Mr. Wilfer. In the hours just before dawn, she trained her genga with Oliver. The space of time between, she spent with Eliot and the others, exchanging stories, playing games, and going on what adventures they could within the confines of Wisp Territory.

This particular morning, according to her routine, Lottie should have already been eating her breakfast in the Clearing. But this morning, Trouble was missing.

"Lottie," said Oliver, "I wouldn't worry too much. Trouble is your genga. He's got to return to you sooner or later."

"Yeah," said Fife. "If he doesn't, he'll die of loneliness."

"Not helpful, Fife," said Oliver.

Lottie felt ill.

"You look pale," observed Fife. "Breakfast is definitely in order."

Adelaide and Eliot were already out of their yews. Eliot sat cross-legged in the long grass, bent over his sketchbook, his left hand smudged black with charcoal. Lottie was used to finding her best friend in this posture. Today, working under lantern light, Eliot was sketching Adelaide. She sat across from him, hands folded in her lap, lips pulled up in an aggressively pleasant smile. Since Eliot's arrival in Wisp Territory, Adelaide had made it clear that she considered Eliot to be *refreshingly refined*. Lottie thought what this really meant was that Adelaide had a bit of a crush on him.

Since Lottie had first arrived in Wisp Territory, she had lived here in the Clearing. Like the glass pergola, where Silvia and her royal entourage resided, this place was set apart from the plagued wisps living under quarantine in the surrounding territory. Silvia had designated the Clearing as a safe haven for Lottie and her companions, though Lottie didn't think this was so much an act of kindness as it was an attempt to keep them under her watch. Silvia saw Lottie and the others as helpless children—"babes in the wood," she'd once called them—who couldn't look after themselves. This would've bothered Lottie more, perhaps, if the food Silvia provided at the Clearing's dining table were not so good.

As usual, the low, long birch table was decked with an assortment of foods: wild cherries, blue-speckled eggs, nuts, berries, pink honey, and paper-thin bread that the wisps called wafercomb. Lottie's stomach grumbled at the sight of the spread. Maybe Fife had been right, she thought, and all she really needed was a stomachful of food to put things in perspective.

It had been difficult at first to grow accustomed to breakfast at sunset and supper just before sunrise. But after a little while, Lottie had actually come to like the wisps' nocturnal lifestyle. She missed sunshine, but Wisp Territory looked its best in the dark, lit by the warm gold of lanterns and haunted by shadows.

Lottie took her usual seat at the table, next to Eliot. He put away his sketchbook and cast her a grin.

"Thank goodness," he said, reaching for a fistful of hazelnuts. "I'm starving."

Lottie wanted to point out that Eliot could've gone ahead and eaten without her, but she was well aware Adelaide considered such behavior "unrefined."

"There's only one thing more unrefined than eating before everyone is present at the table," Adelaide had said once, "and that's showing up *late* to breakfast."

This morning, however, Adelaide didn't seem to mind her companions' tardiness. Her eyes were glimmering with excitement, and the moment the others were settled, she said, "Autumntide comes soon!"

Fife made a gagging noise.

"I passed the pergola yesterday," said Eliot, "and I overheard the guards talking. They said there's going to be cider and music and dancing. Sounds fun, right?"

"It sounds like it might actually be a civilized gathering," said Adelaide. "The Seamstress is said to wear the grandest ball gown for the occasion. I hear she takes the whole year to sew it."

"Hm," said Oliver. His eyes were a nondescript brown.

Fife looked like he'd swallowed his tongue and that it had gone down quite the wrong pipe.

"What's wrong with Autumntide, Fife?" Lottie asked.

"Yeah, what's wrong?" said Eliot. "It kind of sounds like Halloween. Halloween is my favorite."

"First off," said Fife, "I have no idea what Halloween is, but it sounds idiotic. Second, Autumntide isn't some grand party like the Southerlies think."

Adelaide's nose crinkled. "Well, certainly it couldn't be like a *proper* Southerly party. Wisps don't have the resources to—"

"Ada, have you ever actually been in Wisp Territory for Autumntide?"

"What a stupid question," said Adelaide. "You know I haven't. And for your information, I'd rather not be here at all. I'd rather be safe at Iris Gate, in a clean room, next to a well-tended fireplace, drinking proper tea and doing home-work for Tutor. But since that isn't possible, I'm trying to make the best of my circumstances."

Adelaide looked very proud of herself. Fife said some-thing under his breath that sounded a lot like "ridiculous."

"Well then, *you* tell me, Ollie," said Lottie. "What's so bad about Autumntide?"

"There are poems about it," he said.

"Good poems, or bad?"

"Uh." Oliver's eyes flickered to an unsettled pink. "Poems about death."

Lottie felt Eliot's shoulder tense against hers.

"They're just stories, though," said Oliver. "Right, Fife?"

Fife nibbled on a berry. He said nothing.

"Stories about what?" Lottie pressed.

"Well," said Oliver, "the legend goes that at Autumntide, the whitecaps come out and, um, 'paint the ground with snowy blood.'"

"'Snowy blood,'" said Lottie. "You mean, *wisp* blood?"

Adelaide let out a high-pitched laugh.

"Whitecaps," she said, "don't exist."

"Sorry," said Eliot. "What's a whitecap, exactly?"

"Something that doesn't exist," Adelaide said helpfully.

"Does too," said Fife.

"Oh, and I suppose you've seen one?"

"No. But I have seen the ground painted with snowy blood. Every year, at least one wisp gets killed. Everyone knows to be extra careful around Autumntide, but there's always some stupid type who goes out and gets themselves, well, *whitecapped*."

"Yes, but what *are* whitecaps?" asked Lottie.

"They're short," said Fife. "They've got four legs, four arms, four fingers on each of their four hands. And their eyes—"

"Let me guess," said Adelaide, rolling her own eyes. "There are four of those, too."

"No, ten," said Fife, matter-of-factly. "And solid black, like pots of ink, so you don't ever know where they're looking. They hibernate underground, but every year, around this time, they come to the surface and feed with their four rows of teeth. For whatever reason, there's something about wisp blood that drives them crazy. They're wild about it. It's said that, before they feed, they dip their cloth hats in the blood of their victims as part of their killing ritual; that's where the name whitecap comes from. I don't believe someone has to die *on* Autumntide, but wisps have to be extra careful this time of year."

Eliot was shaking. Lottie looked over in alarm, concerned that he was frightened or, worse, feeling ill.

He was laughing.

"Sorry," he said, lowering his hand from his mouth, "but *whitecap*? It's such a funny name. Sounds like a procedure you get done at the dentist's."

Adelaide said, "Everyone in New Albion says whitecaps are just something wisps made up to frighten sprites."

"Well, that doesn't make sense, does it?" said Fife. "Considering it's wisps they're after."

Adelaide shrugged. "Well, if they *do* exist and they *do* only drink wisp blood, the rest of us don't have anything to worry about, do we?"

"Maybe not," said Fife. "Or maybe they only drink wisp blood because only wisps have ever been around. It's not like we're used to sprites hanging out during Autumntide. I'd assume you're all fair game."

"Would you stop already?" said Adelaide. "You're just trying to scare us."

"Whatever!" Fife threw his hands in the air. "All I'm saying is that chances are someone's going to get drained clean this season, and it's not going to be me."

"Can we talk about something else?" said Oliver, pushing away his plate of wafercomb. "I'm losing my appetite."

"I should go," said Lottie, shoving her remaining wafercomb into her mouth and shouldering her satchel. The dark was coming on fast now that the sun had set. "I'm going to be late for training."

Adelaide sighed loudly. She crossed her arms. She was clearly waiting for someone to ask her what was wrong.

Fife, Oliver, and Lottie ignored her.

Eliot asked, "What's wrong?"

Adelaide shrugged. "Oh, nothing. It's just, I think we're all very aware of the preferential treatment a certain someone is receiving."

Lottie chewed uneasily on her wafercomb.

"Adelaide," said Oliver, "don't be like that. Lottie needs more tutoring time than us. She's really behind."

Oliver was smiling reassuringly, but his words stung. Lottie knew she was behind. Most sprites started sharpening when they were six years old. She was nearing thirteen, and she had only just begun. In three years, she wouldn't be able to sharpen anymore. And though she would never admit it to the others, Lottie had begun to fear that she was so far behind she would never catch up by her sixteenth birthday.

"I wouldn't phrase it like *that*," Fife said. "You can't be behind in something if no one's really ahead of you. And there's no one else like Lottie to compare her to."

Lottie could see Fife's tongue peeking out from his lips. He was using his keen on her, trying to flavor his words to make her feel better.

"Yes, but just because she's so unsharpened doesn't mean the rest of us should suffer," said Adelaide. "Father didn't have a spare second all last week to work with me. And anyway, he's not even properly trained to help sharpen a hearing keen. If Tutor were here—"

"But Tutor isn't here," Oliver said, "and sharpening isn't really the priority right now."

"Then what is?" Adelaide demanded.

"*Ad-uh-laide*," said Fife, throwing his hands up. "I dunno if you've forgotten, but we're trying to keep clear of a *crazy and murderous king*."

Lottie cast a glance at Eliot. He looked uncomfortable, as he always did when anyone brought up the king who had tried to kill Lottie and was still hunting her down.

"I think I'll head out with Lottie," he said, getting to his feet.

Adelaide stopped glaring at Fife and turned to Eliot. "What? But that will be boring for you."

"Nuh-uh." Eliot threw an arm around Lottie's shoulder. "I'm just a plain old human, remember? All this magicky stuff still fascinates me."

Adelaide made a face but said nothing.

"I'll see you all later today," said Lottie.

As she and Eliot were walking away, Oliver called out, "Lottie?"

She turned, and he smiled, his eyes a deep navy.

"Don't worry too much about Trouble," he said. "Wait and see. He'll be back in your pocket by dawn."

"Clear your mind."

It was the third time Mr. Wilfer had given Lottie the same command. She winced in frustration, closed her eyes, and tried again. Her hands were clasped around a smooth stone the size of her fist. Mr. Wilfer called the stone a training token, and in the past few weeks of training, he had instructed Lottie to hold it, focusing all her thoughts on its presence, and do nothing more than clear her mind. It had become an extremely tiresome exercise.

"I *am* clearing my mind," Lottie grumbled, gripping the stone harder.

"If your mind were clear," Mr. Wilfer said, "then you would not concern yourself with conversation, and your grasp would be relaxed. *Clear . . . your . . . mind.*"

Lottie inhaled deeply, from her stomach, like Mr. Wilfer had taught her during her first lesson. Slowly, she crept into the deep, white space of her mind, where thoughts and memories could not touch her. She continued to inhale deeply, exhale loudly. In, out, in, out. The whiteness expanded, and a calm cold descended on her limbs.

Then memory grabbed her, tearing into her calm with sharp talons.

Grissom stood before her, Northerly vines winding up his body, constricting around his chest, turning his enraged face an unnatural shade of purple. Two words rang like an echo in the air: *Vesper Bells.*

Lottie shrieked. She threw the training token with wild force.

"I can't," she said, opening her eyes. "I *can't!*"

Beyond Mr. Wilfer, Eliot sat wide-eyed, one hand in midair, clutching the stone Lottie had hurled.

She blinked. "Did—did I throw that at you?"

Eliot dropped his hand. "Um, yeah? But I'm okay."

Mr. Wilfer was rubbing his temples, his back to Lottie.

She was afraid to say anything, afraid that Mr. Wilfer was

upset and—far worse than upset—disappointed. Lottie made a careful study of her shoes, then of Mr. Wilfer's front door.

Mr. Wilfer did not work inside the glass pergola, but just beyond it, inside a cottage made of tightly woven willow reeds. According to Silvia, the house was created as a resting place for Northerly visitors—traders, diplomats, and friends of court—who were too spooked by the prospect of sleeping in the yews. Mr. Wilfer had converted the cottage into his laboratory, where he spent most of his time poring over old books and mixing strange ingredients in vials, in an attempt to find a cure for the wisps. Lottie's sharpening lessons took place outside the cottage, in a small clearing of chopped grass and two fallen yew trunks.

Lottie now sat on one of the trunks and buried her chin in her hands. Beside her, Eliot whistled a pop song Lottie had heard on the radio back in the human world.

"Eliot," said Mr. Wilfer. "Please. If you're going to be a spectator, you must be a silent one."

Eliot promptly hushed up. Mr. Wilfer crossed to where Lottie sat.

"Don't take it out on Eliot," she said. "It's me you should be mad at. I can't do it, Mr. Wilfer. I've been trying the same stupid thing for a month now, and I just *can't*."

"You can," said Mr. Wilfer. "You simply don't have the patience."

"I'm patient!" Lottie snapped.

Mr. Wilfer raised a brow.

"Fine," Lottie muttered, defeated.

"I understand. Of course you'd like your keen to sharpen faster. What happened with Eliot was rather . . . unprecedented."

Mr. Wilfer and Lottie had already spoken at length about what had happened that night at the Barmy Badger, when Lottie had given way to what she'd thought was one of her "bad spells" and healed Eliot in a way that shocked the doctors back home—in what even here in Albion Isle was considered a very rare display of power.

Lottie had not had a single bad spell since that night. Now, for the first time, she found herself longing for one. She'd stubbed her toe on purpose. She'd upset herself thinking about Pen Bloomfield, her worst enemy back at Kemble School. She'd purposefully tried to get lost in plagued parts of the wood, surrounded by the odor of disease. These all proved to be terrible experiences, but not one of them had brought on a bad spell.

"That is the way with all keens," Mr. Wilfer had explained at their first lesson. "They have a flair for the dramatic. When they first appear, they're bright and showy. When Adelaide turned six, she asked me where the loud music she heard was coming from. It was from ten blocks down, in the concert hall, where the Southerly Boys Chorale was putting on a concert. Even now, Adelaide can't hear a full ten blocks away. It only happened that once, you see, at the very onset, when her keen made itself known. After that, Adelaide began sharpening with her tutor. It took her years to develop her keen. She couldn't even hear into the next room until she turned eight.

"When you were little, you were *fighting* the pain of your keen. You saw it as something bad, something to be afraid of, not to embrace. You'd been healing yourself for years, but your keen longed for a bigger outlet. When you made Eliot better, your keen did the work for you. But now things are different. Now *you* must be the one to work."

In the days after she'd healed Eliot, Lottie had dared to think that everything would be magically better. She'd thought that all she would have to do in the future was wait for a bad spell, then hold Eliot's hand until, one day, he was completely healed of his illness. She hadn't thought she would have to practice.

She certainly hadn't thought the practice would be so hard.

"This is a frustration every sprite endures," Mr. Wilfer now said, patting Lottie's shoulder. "To know what you are capable of without having yet attained it. But you mustn't get discouraged. I can sense your impatience, Lottie. As long as you are discontented with your progress, you won't be able to move forward with your sharpening. The first step is—"

"I know, I know. A clear mind."

"A clear mind is a *content* mind—one devoid of impatience. Without it, training is useless."

"Then training is going to be very useless today, Mr. Wilfer." Lottie sighed. "My mind isn't anywhere close to clear."

Mr. Wilfer frowned and asked, "Is there something bothering you?"

Lottie wanted to tell Mr. Wilfer that Trouble had run away and that she was worried about him. But if Lottie told Mr. Wilfer that, he would think she was even more of a failure. *Real* sprites didn't lose their gengas.

"No," she said. "No, it's just a bad mood. And I don't want to waste your time. I know you're very busy helping the wisps, and I already feel guilty."

"Guilty? Whatever for?"

"Adelaide's right: I'm stealing time from her and the boys. They need to sharpen their keens, too, and you're the only tutor they've got here."

"Yes," said Mr. Wilfer. "Yes, that's true."

Lottie focused on her hands, clasped in her lap. She was trying to beat down a familiar feeling.

Useless, said an unwelcome voice inside. *You're* useless.

"I've been trying to keep the five of you safe," said Mr. Wilfer. "That will always be my priority. It is a difficult thing, Lottie, to see my children ripped from their home. I desire for them to have the best training, to want for nothing. That is impossible here, and the fact constantly troubles my heart. But it should trouble *my* heart, not yours. This is not your doing. King Starkling alone is to blame for his actions. Our current circumstance is his fault, and it is partially mine, too. It is an adult matter, Lottie. There is nothing for you to feel bad about."

But it's my matter, too, Lottie wanted to say. *It is my world and my keen, and I am allowed to feel bad when things are a mess. I am allowed to want to make them better.*

"You must be patient with your keen," said Mr. Wilfer. "Guilt will only impede you."

"So what do you suggest I do?" Lottie asked, irritated.

"I suggest that you rest. Perhaps I have been pushing you too hard. Perhaps it's too much strain, too soon. Your time will be better spent if you *breathe,* then begin anew."

"Rest," said Lottie.

She didn't like the sound of it. She hadn't really rested for a long time—not since the day she had first traveled through the roots of the apple tree in Thirsby Square.

"Rest," repeated Mr. Wilfer. "No work. Not even genga training with Oliver."

That, at least, thought Lottie, would be an easy instruction to follow, considering she currently had no genga to train.

"How long?" she asked.

Mr. Wilfer scratched his bearded chin. He said,

"Let's give it till your return from Kemble Isle, after your holidays."

"*What?*" Lottie jumped up. "But that's weeks from now! Weeks I could be sharpening."

"Weeks of training that will serve no purpose if you are in the state you're in now."

"But—"

"Lottie. This is better."

Lottie's teeth clamped down, the only barrier that kept her angry protests from tumbling out. She got to her feet with arms crossed, glaring at Mr. Wilfer.

"You're right, you know," said Mr. Wilfer. "I haven't been able to spend as much time with my children as I would like. Rest for you means extra training for Adelaide and Oliver. That *is* what you'd like, isn't it?"

"Yes, of course," said Lottie. Though she wanted to say, *Not like this.*

"Spend the time with your friends instead. No more training here, and no exercises while you're back in Kemble Isle. You will be better for it, I promise."

"Fine," said Lottie. "*Fine.*"

And so sharpening lessons came to a close.

Eliot joined Lottie as she readied to leave and pressed something into her hand. It was a candy. Not just any candy—a sweet-so-sour. He winked, and the ache that had been growing in Lottie's heart softened.

Mr. Wilfer was straightening his robe and black satin collar. He looked nervous, and that could only mean one thing: he had an appointment at the glass pergola.

"Mr. Wilfer?" said Lottie. "Is it true what the wisps say about Autumntide? Should we be afraid?"

"There's no need to be frightened," said Mr. Wilfer, "so long as you don't go wandering too deep into the wood. They're said to only come aboveground in the daytime, so I suggest you turn in before sunrise and stay put in your yew until dusk."

Lottie's eyes grew wide with interest. "So they do exist?"

"Whitecaps? Of course they do, nasty brutes. Who's been telling you differently?"

Eliot grinned and said, "Your daughter."

"You shouldn't let it get you down," Eliot told Lottie on their walk back to the Clearing. "I'm sure the others had trouble when they first started sharpening."

"Yeah, when they were *little kids*," said Lottie. "I'm almost thirteen. I should already know how to control my keen, not be sitting around holding rocks and trying not to think."

Eliot went quiet, his green sneakers plodding on the powdery white path in a soft *tup-tup-tup*.

In a voice so low she didn't think Eliot could hear, she said, "I need to make you better."

"You heard Dr. Gupta," said Eliot. "I *am* better."

"Not *all* better. He said the symptoms had improved, but the illness was still there. You're still sick. I see you hiding your coughs sometimes."

"But it's not anywhere as bad as it used to be. I'm walking around with you in a magical world, aren't I? I disappeared inside an apple tree. I hang out with sprites and wisps every day. I'd call that an improvement on lying around in my deathbed."

It was the first time Eliot had ever said the "d" word out loud in Lottie's presence. It was easier to admit it now the danger had passed. But the fact remained: Eliot had been *dying* just weeks ago.

"You saved my life, Lottie," said Eliot. "That's more than enough. I don't have to be entirely better. I mean, maybe it's impossible to be one hundred percent normal. Maybe the sickness is just as much a part of me as the color of my hair or my bad eyesight. I'm okay with that."

"You're just saying that to make me feel better," said Lottie.

"Maybe," said Eliot. "Or maybe I'm really okay. Anyway, we should be focusing on the positives here. A rest from sharpening means more time for adventures! We still have a few days before we go back to Kemble Isle. Now we can hang out all the time. It'll be like one long snow day."

Lottie smiled. During the month he'd been in Wisp Territory, Eliot's enthusiasm for Limn hadn't diminished one bit; if anything, it had grown, fueled by poetry-laden conversations with Oliver and portrait sessions with Adelaide. Every day, Eliot was bursting with new information. ("Did you know that wisps first float when they turn ten?" and "Ollie says some sprites can taste the weather. *Taste weather.* Imagine!")

Even when Lottie was most frustrated by Trouble's mischief or her inability to *clear her mind*, Eliot always managed to chase away the cloudy thoughts with a bright word or two.

They reached the Clearing, where they found Oliver sitting on an uncurled yew branch, reading a book. A white finch circled above his head, warbling mournfully. Lottie frowned at the sight.

"Why is Keats so sad?" she asked.

Oliver turned a page without looking up. "I'm reading something sad."

"Lord Byron," said Eliot, reading the words embossed on the spine. "What're you reading sad poetry for?"

"Same reason I read happy poetry," said Oliver, closing up the book and tossing it inside the yew trunk. He hopped off the branch and landed gracefully in the long grass.

"You're through early," he observed.

"Mr. Wilfer was busy," said Eliot. "He had to leave for a meeting with the Seamstress."

Lottie stared at Eliot. His lie had been as smooth as one of the Seamstress' satin gowns. Lottie was grateful. She didn't want to revisit the subject of what a failure she'd been at sharpening.

"I see you've found Trouble."

Lottie started. Oliver was looking at the left pocket of her periwinkle coat, and something was indeed moving beneath the tweed fabric. Lottie reached inside. Her fingers curled around a bundle of feathers.

"Trouble!"

She tugged him out with a relieved cry.

Trouble cheeped and rustled his black feathers, settling into Lottie's palm.

"Where have you *been*?" Lottie demanded.

Trouble tilted his head. He chirruped, unperturbed. Then he swept from Lottie's hand and joined Keats in his circular dance.

"That's super rude, Trouble," Eliot called. "She was worried about you!"

Lottie, however, was distracted. There was something else in her pocket that had not been there before—something cold and hard-edged. She pulled it out.

It was a key. It was small, just the length of her index finger, and looked like an ordinary house key. It was only when Lottie turned it over that she saw the little black diamond embossed on its top.

CHAPTER TWO

A Key to Nowhere

"THE MARK of the Northerly Court."

Fife gawked at the key in his hand, poking at the black diamond etched into brass.

"This is the weirdest thing," he said. "What unsavory characters has Trouble been hanging around?"

They were all sitting inside the boys' yew tree, circled around the pillowed floor. Lottie had called them there to discuss the appearance of the strange key in her pocket.

"Trouble was gone for less than a day," said Lottie. "He couldn't have just flown into Northerly Territory and back again. Could he?"

"Gengas can be quite fast," said Adelaide.

"Or it could be from spies in these parts," said Oliver.

"What, like those Northerlies, Roote and Crag?" said
Fife. "Or Dorian Ingle? *The Barghest?!*"

"Fife," said Adelaide, "I swear to Titania, if you go into
another one of your Barghest frenzies . . ."

Adelaide was referring to Fife's recent obsession with the
fact that the fiercest beasts in all of Albion Isle had made
a vow of obedience to the Fiskes. This led to Fife getting
very worked up about the possibility of Lottie commanding
a whole army of Barghest and developing a special howl that
could be heard across the Isle. Adelaide called these Fife's
"Barghest frenzies." He indulged in one at least once a week.

Lottie found this interest unsettling since she could not,
in fact, call any Barghest with a special howl and since she
had no idea how to even find the particular Barghest who
had helped her escape the Southerly Court. Since she'd
returned to Limn, there had been no sign of the Barghest—
or of the Northerly spy Dorian Ingle.

"Maybe," said Eliot, "Trouble just found the key lying in
the dirt somewhere and thought it looked pretty?"

The others exchanged glances.

Fife said, "Doubtful."

"There wasn't anything else in your pocket?" Adelaide
asked. "No note, nothing to explain the meaning of the key?"

"Nothing," said Lottie. "What I can't make out is if
Trouble just found the key, or if . . ."

"If what?" asked Eliot.

Lottie let out a shuddery sigh. "If someone *else* summoned Trouble? Is that possible?"

"Of course not," said Adelaide. "No one can summon a genga other than the genga's owner. They respond only to the exact timbre of your voice."

"That's not entirely true," said Oliver. "There are some keens—"

"Ugh!" Fife tossed the key from his hand, as though he had been burned. "Stop talking like that, Ollie. Splinters are the worst."

Eliot frowned. "Splinters?"

"Sprites who use their keens for *illegal purposes*." Fife lowered his voice dramatically. He wiggled his fingers and made an eerie whistling sound.

"Like what?" Lottie asked, rubbing at her goose-fleshed arms.

"Impersonating other sprites," said Oliver. "It's against Southerly and Northerly law, but there are some keens that can do it. Mainly taste and touch. They say some splinters can alter their appearances. Others can imitate another sprite's voice. Even summon their genga. It's possible."

Lottie's eyes widened. "You mean someone else out there could be impersonating me?"

Lottie had the sudden, uncomfortable sensation of being naked, though she was very well bundled up in three layers of clothes.

"It's possible," Oliver said again, "though I don't know why a splinter would use their keen just to send you a Northerly key to nowhere."

"It's not a key to nowhere," Eliot said. "We just don't know where the *where* is yet."

"Well, it's nowhere I'd like to go," said Adelaide. "You should throw it away. Or bury it."

"Have you asked Trouble about it?" said Oliver.

Lottie nodded glumly. "He won't listen to me. Every time I've tried to ask him where he's been, or where he found the key, he just flies off."

"So we don't know where it's from," said Fife, "and we don't know what it's for. Talking about it won't change anything. I guess we just wait and see if anything else weird happens."

Fife looked a little too excited about the prospect of something weird occurring again.

Lottie felt protectively at her coat pocket, where Trouble was currently sleeping. She tucked away the Northerly key in her other pocket. She did not intend to follow Adelaide's advice and bury it. She didn't trust the key, and Lottie thought it better to keep things she didn't trust close by, where she could keep an eye on them.

Lottie's first day of "rest" wasn't restful. She slept, but her dreams were nightmares—as they often had been since her return to Albion Isle. Fife had explained that bad dreams were common in Wisp Territory. It was something in the air, something unseen, that crept into the ears and wound around the brain and turned even the cheeriest dreams to bleak, black mist.

Lottie once asked Mr. Wilfer if there was a remedy to the nightmares.

"There are remedies," he replied, "but they can be extremely addictive. Dreams are a delicate, dangerous business. Other healers might disagree with me, but I don't dabble in anything that so strongly alters the workings of the mind."

This had sounded very noble and impressive at the time, but after nearly a month's worth of bad dreams full of choking Northerly vines and unfriendly Barghest with bared teeth, Lottie was weary of sleep. She no longer looked forward to sinking her head into the pillow, even after a full and tiring night. She dreaded that moment just before unconsciousness, when her thoughts turned nonsensical with disconnected words and impossible images.

This time, her nightmare was worse than usual. In it, she was back in the throne room of the Southerly Palace, surrounded by dark tapestries and shelves full of strange-looking bottles. Her feet were dragging her toward the throne, where King Starkling sat smiling lazily at her. As Lottie came closer, the king's deceptively young skin began to bubble and split, revealing a thick, tar-like substance beneath. He smiled wider, revealing blood-coated teeth.

"Tsk, tsk," said Starkling. "Not sharpening, I see. This is hardly the time for a vacation when there are *only two, maybe three weeks left to live.*"

Lottie emerged from the dream with a shriek, waking Adelaide. Her skin was damp, her shoulders trembling. She apologized, sure that Adelaide would be angry at the disturbance. But then Adelaide did something entirely unexpected. She found Lottie's hand in the dark, and she wrapped her cold fingers around Lottie's wrist.

In a soft voice, she said, "It's okay. I have them, too."

"What are they about?" Lottie asked.

There was a long silence. Finally, Adelaide said, "My mother."

Lottie remained quiet, unsure of what to say.

"I wasn't even two years old when she passed," Adelaide said, "so it's quite impossible that I could remember her. But—it's silly, I know, it's not as if it's really possible—but I dream I remember her *voice.* I remember a song she would hum as I fell asleep."

"It's not silly," said Lottie. "Sometimes I think I can remember my parents' faces, even though the image is just from the picture I have of them."

"No, but it's not like that," Adelaide said impatiently. "I hear her voice like a real, *true* memory. I hear the melody."

Then Adelaide hummed. It was a gentle sound, one that took Lottie off guard; she wasn't used to hearing gentle things from Adelaide. The song was sad, though there were no words to make it so. Its drooping melody made Lottie feel as though she had lost something, something she could never reclaim and never replace. And though it was sadness that carried her to sleep, Lottie had no more nightmares that evening.

That week, the forest turned golden. In a single day, the yew needles fell from their branches to the earth, transformed by death to a glittering yellow. The grass, too, faded from pure white to the color of cream. Late autumn had settled on Wisp Territory, thick with cold and the scent of smoke. Lottie was glad she and Eliot had packed sweaters, mittens, and warm boots. Now more than ever, she made use of her periwinkle coat and green scarf.

Resting was difficult work, Lottie discovered. She spent nearly every hour of the next two days with Eliot, and though

Mr. Wilfer had told her that her presence alone improved Eliot's health, she still noticed when he coughed extra loud or overlong, and each time her heart spasmed with guilt. How was she going to make Eliot better if she wasn't even trying to improve her keen? What if he got worse again, and this time she couldn't heal him?

Trouble, at least, was better behaved than usual. He kept close by Lottie and did not squawk obnoxiously or nip at her fingers or peck about her belongings—all of which he'd been wont to do before. It was as though Trouble sensed Lottie's anxiousness and, out of sympathy, had become less of a nuisance. This evening, the eve of Autumntide, Trouble flew serenely overhead as Lottie, Eliot, and Oliver walked down a path to the Clearing.

They had just paid a visit to the red apple tree, where Eliot had sent his weekly letter to Mr. Walsch, all under the watchful eye of the wisp guard. In just two days, Lottie and Eliot would use the tree to return to Kemble Isle for Thanksgiving. Still, Eliot insisted on sending his letter.

"I promised I'd write weekly," he said. "Dad might worry."

Lottie had once asked Fife why more wisps didn't simply come and go between Limn and the human world. Fife had looked at her as though she'd grown an extra nose. He had laughed. And then he had asked, very seriously, "Why would anyone want to go to the human world?"

"There's folklore in Limn about the sort of people who live there," he'd said. "Nasty stories about bad witches and wars and torture. Not to mention, magic isn't at large there anymore. Who would want to visit *that*?"

"I think Father was right," Oliver said. "Rest has been good for you, Lottie. Trouble's much better behaved now than he ever was during our lessons." His eyes turned cloudy gray. "Maybe I'm a bad teacher."

"You're not," Lottie assured him. "Not at all."

She meant it, too. As frustrating as her genga lessons had been, Lottie was certain she'd never met a more patient person than Oliver Wilfer. She was also grateful to Oliver for befriending Eliot so readily. It seemed that the two boys had an endless supply of things to talk about. Eliot rambled about painting, and Oliver about poetry, and sometimes they talked so long on their walks that even Lottie got bored.

Adelaide never joined them on these walks because she claimed that anywhere beyond the Clearing and the glass pergola was "unsafe."

"What she really means," said Fife, "is she doesn't like the stench of Plague."

Fife didn't come on walks either, but only because he was too busy assisting Mr. Wilfer as he tended to ailing wisps and worked in his cottage laboratory, trying to invent a cure for the Plague. Every dawn, Fife arrived at supper with slumped shoulders but full of new healing terms he'd learned that day. "Did you know that fresh-scraped lichen can soothe a cough?" he'd ask with a full mouth, berry juice running down his chin. And "Today, Mr. Wilfer showed me how to best sew stitches around joints!"

"At least Fife is doing something productive," Adelaide would say, which wasn't meant as a compliment to Fife but a complaint that her father never seemed to have enough time for her.

But the past two days had been different. Mr. Wilfer had more time to devote to both Adelaide's and Oliver's sharpening, and if Adelaide was still upset, she couldn't possibly blame Lottie anymore.

"Look!" said Eliot.

A red banner, notched at its bottom, was staked in the middle of their path. Just past it, only twenty paces beyond, stood another banner, this one light umber.

"I guess they're decorations for Autumntide?" said Lottie.

Oliver shook his head. "I think they're wards."

"Wards?" asked Eliot.

"Against whitecaps."

"*Oh.*"

Lottie and the boys walked on, passing banner after banner, which bore no symbol, no mark. All were alternating shades of crimson and orange.

"Kind of creepy," said Eliot. "I don't think I like Autumntide after all."

Conversation petered out after that.

In the Clearing, they met Fife and Adelaide for supper. Adelaide was beaming. "Father and I had the most tremendous breakthrough today! I was able to achieve *transference*. Transference, already!"

Adelaide looked like she was expecting high praise, but Lottie had no idea what she was talking about.

"Uh," said Eliot. "What's transference?"

"It's pretty rare," said Fife. "It means passing your keen along to someone else. Just temporarily, mind. But not many sprites can do it."

"You mean, you can make other people hear from far away, like you?" Eliot asked.

Adelaide blushed, grinning more widely than ever. "Yes, that's what it means. It can only be with one other person, and I have to touch that person for it to work. It's a thin connection right now, but the point is that I *did* it. Tutor told me that I wouldn't be able to until I was sixteen, if at all. Seems he was wrong!"

"That's wonderful, Ada," said Oliver, pouring a goblet of water for himself, then for Eliot and Lottie.

"All I needed was some individualized attention," Adelaide went on, turning to Lottie. "If only my sessions could be like that *all* the time."

Lottie bristled. She was glad Adelaide had been able to spend time with Mr. Wilfer, but all the same, she couldn't help feeling jealous. Here Adelaide was having a *breakthrough* after only two days of concentrated sharpening, and Lottie couldn't even keep her mind clear.

"Just imagine," said Fife. "Imagine all the rulers who'll want you by their side, passing on all the foreign secrets you overhear."

Adelaide wrinkled her nose. "I don't intend to be used for political purposes."

"Well, what else are you going to do? Anyone with a hearing keen like yours becomes a spy, or a diplomat, or *something* political."

"Politics are distasteful," said Adelaide.

"But with your keen," Fife pressed, "you could save lives. You know, if you used it for good."

"Sweet Oberon, Fife, why do you even care?" Adelaide said, her voice going shrill. "It isn't as though I could go into politics if I wanted. I'm a traitor to the Southerly Court. We all are. We don't belong to anyone. No one will *want* us."

An unpleasant silence wrapped around the table. This was not something they talked about. No one ever mentioned New Albion here. They didn't talk about how sometimes, on walks through the forest, wisps would spit at their feet or call out rude comments about Southerlies. It was as though they had all silently agreed never to mention those things. Now Adelaide had broken the unspoken rule.

"Um. The wafercomb is extra good tonight," said Eliot. "*Yum.*"

"Mmm-hmm," said Fife. Snickering, he threw a hazelnut at Oliver, who threw a walnut back, and the tension fizzled away, forgotten.

As they ate, the Clearing turned lighter with the first rays of sun.

"It'll be day soon," said Oliver. "We ought to get back to our trees before—well, before anything happens."

"You too, Oliver?" Adelaide sighed.

"As 't were a spur upon the soul," quoted Oliver, "a fear will urge it where to go without the spectre's aid."

"Ugh," said Adelaide. "I thought I could count on you at least to not hold to such silly superstitions."

"Your father believes in whitecaps, you know," Eliot said.

Adelaide went red in the face. "He does not."

"He told us so," said Lottie, exchanging a smile with Eliot. "He said we should be careful, or the whitecaps will gobble us up."

"Technically," said Fife, "whitecaps don't gobble. They suck and slurp."

"Technically," said Adelaide, "whitecaps do none of the above, because *they don't exist.* Now, I'm off to my yew but only because I'm tired of listening to so much stupidity, not because I believe in monsters."

"I didn't believe in things like sprites and wisps a few weeks back," said Eliot. "Sometimes you get proven wrong."

Adelaide tossed her hair. "I'm never wrong. Coming, Lottie?"

Lottie thought Adelaide was being ridiculous, as usual. All the same, the sun *was* on the rise, and she was thinking about what Eliot had said. Sometimes you did get proven wrong, and Lottie reasoned she'd rather climb into a yew with ridiculous Adelaide than have her blood drained from her body by a drove of fanged whitecaps.

"Coming," she said, waving goodbye to the boys. "See you tonight."

"If we're still alive," said Eliot.

Lottie knew it was only a joke, but her heart skittered at the very idea of Eliot not greeting her in the morning. She pushed the thought from her head and ran to catch up with Adelaide.

Lottie still hadn't lost the wonder she felt every time she watched a yew branch uncurl from a splintery whorl. The sight was equal parts beautiful and terrifying. In fact, Lottie thought, the same could be said of the wisps themselves.

"Oh, look!" cried Adelaide.

The last of the yew needles were falling. This was not the way Lottie was used to seeing leaves fall back in Kemble Isle—slow and sporadic, almost imperceptible until the day she realized no leaves remained on the branches. This was something else. It was a sudden flurry of golden needles, whipped about by wind, turning circles and pinwheeling and catching in Lottie's hair. It was a honey-tinted snowfall.

Adelaide giggled. It was the first time Lottie had heard her giggle since she'd come to Wisp Territory.

"It's *beautiful*," Adelaide breathed. "The loveliest sound, too. There's nothing so nice as the sound of leaves landing on the ground."

"You're lucky you can hear it so well," said Lottie. "It must be nice."

Adelaide hopped up the branch of their yew, and Lottie followed her into the dim, warm, hollowed-out trunk. The curling branch sealed them back inside, safe from any intruders—whitecaps included.

"I didn't know things like that made you so happy," said Lottie.

She liked this side of Adelaide—when she wasn't busy complaining or arguing with Fife.

"Autumn's the season I love best," said Adelaide. "Back in New Albion, we have the loveliest festivals. When I was little, Father would take us to the pumpkin patches, and Oliver and I could get *three* pumpkins apiece. Father would call me his itty-bitty squash."

Lottie's smile grew. Adelaide's disappeared. Her eyes went wide, like she'd just realized a huge mistake.

"You *cannot* tell Fife that," she ordered. "Or Eliot."

"Eliot wouldn't make fun of you, though."

"I just don't want him to know. It's private."

"Then I won't tell anyone," said Lottie. "Promise."

The girls changed into their nightclothes and, as was their routine, curled up in blankets on opposite sides of the trunk. It was a strange arrangement if Lottie really stopped to think about it: no bed, no chairs, no table, just one wide cushion inside a giant yew tree. Yet for all its strangeness, it was comfortable. It almost made up for all the nightmares.

Almost.

Lottie woke to Adelaide jabbing angrily at her stomach.

"Make him stop," Adelaide groaned. "He's been going on for minutes straight."

Lottie's hand shifted to the pocket of her nightgown. Trouble was still safely bundled inside, but he was squawking with shrill persistence. He wriggled against Lottie's fingers as she pulled him out.

"Trouble, hush," she said, stroking his feathers. "*Hush.*"

Trouble did not hush. His squawks only grew louder. And he had been doing so well these past few days!

"What's wrong with him?"

"I don't know," said Lottie, continuing to stroke Trouble. She drew him nearer and placed a comforting kiss atop his head. "Trouble, it's all right. Shhh."

Adelaide rummaged on her side of the trunk. There was a flurry of violet feathers. Lila, Adelaide's own genga, perched on Lottie's shoulder and gave one sharp chirrup.

Trouble stopped squawking. He went deathly still and quirked his head toward Lila.

Lila chirped again. This time, Trouble bowed his head. He gave a contrite coo.

"What just happened?" Lottie asked Adelaide.

"I asked Lila to calm him down. She's good at it."

Adelaide whistled, and Lila returned to her outstretched finger. She patted the bird once, then tucked her out of sight. Lottie looked to Trouble. His chest puffed in and out slowly, as though he were sleeping. Gingerly, she tucked him back into her pocket.

"Thank you," she told Adelaide.

"Mm-hm." Adelaide was pulling a brush through her long, brunette hair in measured strokes. "But you really need to learn how to control him. No one respects a sprite who can't command her own genga."

Adelaide didn't need to tell Lottie that. It only made her feel worse.

"Don't say anything to Oliver about this," said Lottie. "Please? He'll think I haven't learned a thing from our lessons."

"Well, have you?"

Lottie took some time to think this over. Really, she'd taken a good deal of time in the past month to think about it. Owning a genga was nothing like owning a pet—or at least what Lottie had imagined owning a pet would've been like, had Mrs. Yates not been strongly opposed to the very existence of domesticated animals. And "own" wasn't the right word at all. Lottie did not feel she owned Trouble any more than she owned Eliot or Adelaide. And while Lottie did feel Trouble belonged to her, she also felt she belonged to Trouble. He seemed to be in better spirits when she was happy, lower spirits when she was sad, and particularly rebellious when she was feeling . . . well, *troubled*.

Oliver had once told Lottie, "We call it genga lessons, because you can teach your genga to do some things: carry objects, deliver messages, fetch help. But in plenty of ways they're *un*teachable—not because they're stupid, but because they're too smart. They're part of us, and we're part of them, but we're completely separate, too. We've got our own plans, and they've got theirs. And sure, they'll help us out more times than not, but there are times they're going to insist on their own way."

Lottie tried to remind herself of this on a daily basis, especially when Trouble did something like steal a tube of Eliot's paint to squirt on someone's head. But as much as Lottie told herself this behavior was normal, that she was learning, that Trouble would sometimes insist on his own way—she couldn't help but notice that no one *else* seemed to be dealing with this sort of genga-related difficulty.

"Yes," Lottie finally replied. "I've learned lots of things. I just haven't had a genga since I was born, like the rest of you."

Adelaide shrugged. "Well, come on, then. It's past sunset, and I want to see Fife's face when he realizes he's been believing a bunch of piskie tales."

When the girls emerged from their yew, the first thing Lottie noticed was that all the branches were completely bare. The ground was a blanket of pale gold needles and cream grass, bathed in sunset light. Adelaide inhaled deeply.

"Do you smell it?" she said. "Heavenly."

It did smell heavenly—a perfect mixture of aging bark and sun-crisped leaves.

The boys were already out. Fife and Oliver sat atop the Clearing's dining table, talking. A lantern sat between them, throwing shadows on their faces.

Eliot was sitting in a thick pile of yew needles, grabbing handfuls, then opening his fingers to sift them out again. When he caught sight of Lottie, he gave a whoop.

"Happy Autumntide!" he called. "Whatever that means."

"So!" said Adelaide, poking Fife's shoulder. "No reports of a gruesome death by whitecap, are there?"

Fife made an ugly face. There were blue circles beneath his eyes. It looked like he hadn't slept a wink.

"I hear they're serving spiced cider at the pergola," said Oliver. "Anyone interested?"

Eliot jumped to his feet. "Cider. Yes."

It was decided. They set out for the glass pergola, Oliver leading the way with lantern light. Unfortunately, this new excursion did not stop Fife and Adelaide's bickering.

"I slept exceptionally well last night," Adelaide said. "I didn't keep myself up fretting about an imaginary monster."

"Neither did I," said Fife.

"You're just not willing to admit you were wrong."

"Good thing *you* never have that problem," Fife growled.

Oliver tried to distract them by loudly reciting a poem entitled "Stopping by Woods on a Snowy Evening."

Eliot and Lottie shared a look. Eliot was straining his mouth very hard in an attempt to not look too amused by the fighting.

"Thank you," he said, "for not contradicting every other word I say. Seems exhausting."

"Very," Lottie agreed. "I wonder why they haven't just agreed to never talk again."

"*What?* What fun would that be? Look at the two of them. You can see how much they're enjoying it."

Fife and Adelaide *did* seem very bright-faced about the whole thing.

They rounded a thick stretch of yew trees and arrived in the clearing of the glass pergola. A great table stretched in front of the pergola steps. It was surrounded by members of the Wisp Guard and of the nobility, all mingling and murmuring amongst one another. None of the plagued population of wisps were allowed anywhere between here and the Clearing. These were all the remaining healthy members of the wisp race—those privileged or important enough to have afforded an inoculation from the Southerly Court, back when the Southerly Court had still traded with the wisps.

Some wore silver circlets, others bronze, others glass, according to ranks that Lottie still didn't quite understand. Lottie was used to seeing these wisps clothed in pale robes, sashed with ivy. But today, the noble wisps were not dressed in their usual soft spectrum of colors. They were all wearing black.

Eliot scratched his nose uncomfortably. "Did we not get the memo?"

"It looks like a funeral," said Lottie.

All eyes turned to Fife, who had gone very still. His hair, which always stuck up in an impressive defiance of gravity, now particularly seemed to be standing on end.

"Oh, sweet Oberon," he said.

Oliver's calm blue eyes shifted to green. "Fife, what is it?"

"Oh, Oberon, no. *Nooo*."

Adelaide backed away from Fife, as though afraid he might spontaneously combust.

"Is he broken?" Eliot asked Lottie.

"What's wrong, Fife?" asked Lottie. "I'm sure there's still cider left, if that's what you're worried about. Look! Cynbel is ladling some out right now."

At that moment, Cynbel looked straight at Lottie from across the clearing. She'd forgotten that, though wisps did not have keens like sprites, they still had exceptional hearing—especially Cynbel, the captain of the Wisp Guard.

A terrible memory bloomed in Lottie's mind. It was the day she had broken Mrs. Yates' sewing machine after running a dishcloth under it, just to see if it would work. Mrs. Yates had been enraged. She'd called Lottie a stupid, worthless child and then threatened, for the first and only time, to send Lottie to an orphanage on the mainland. Lottie tried to push the memory out of her head, but she couldn't with Cynbel's eyes still fixed on her, dragging the images out. This was the very worst thing about wisps—their ability to stop her cold with their eyes alone.

Cynbel's hard gaze finally shifted from Lottie over to Fife. Then Cynbel smiled. It wasn't a nice smile.

"Cynbel, that imbecile," Fife observed. Then, "It isn't a funeral. Wisps wear black as a sign of reverence."

"Um," said Eliot, making a valiant attempt to follow, "so does that mean they're being reverential or whatever to Autumntide?"

"No," said Fife. "It means my uncle's back."

CHAPTER THREE

Ground Painted with Snowy Blood

"I THOUGHT the Tailor was searching for a cure in the northern territories," said Oliver.

Fife looked like he'd swallowed a live fish. "Yeah, I thought so, too. So did everyone. But the guy loves surprises. Come on, I'm investigating."

Fife motioned for them to follow. He skirted around the congregation of black-cloaked wisps and closer to the wood. The five of them edged along the River Lissome in single file, ducking behind a line of trees as they made their way closer to the glass pergola. Fife floated inches above the ground. He waved at the others to be quiet as they approached a narrow doorway carved into one of the pergola's courtyards.

"Isn't Fife royalty?" Eliot asked. "Why do we have to sneak into the place?"

"Fife was born *to* royalty," said Adelaide. "That isn't quite the same thing."

"Also," said Oliver, "you might recall how we're not exactly in a good way with Cynbel."

"That's all my fault," Lottie admitted, thinking of what was now called the green paint incident. "Well, mine and Trouble's."

"He didn't like us before that," Oliver said.

"Mother and Uncle will be having a private conversation," said Fife, "so we can't very well go tromping into the pergola right in front of Cynbel and a whole court of wisps. Good news is that spiced cider has a rather *calming* effect on wisps when drunk in large quantities." A wicked smirk stretched to Fife's dimples. "And they *always* drink it in large quantities. As long as we're careful, we shouldn't have any trouble sneaking in while the lot of them are otherwise engaged."

"Why are we sneaking in the first place?" asked Eliot.

"Because," said Lottie, "the adults aren't going to tell us what the Tailor's arrival is really about. That means we have to find out for ourselves. Isn't that right, Fife?"

"Just so," said Fife.

"Maybe," said Eliot, "the Tailor came back because he was tired? Living away from home can be exhausting."

Lottie looked up sharply. Though Lottie missed nothing about her former life in New Kemble, she knew that the letters exchanged between Eliot and Mr. Walsch weren't a substitute for the father and son seeing each other in person. At least she and Eliot were heading back to Kemble Isle the next day.

"That's not why he's returned," said Fife. "Uncle doesn't give up easily. Whatever news he's brought back with him has got to be big. That's why we're going to find it out."

With that, Fife floated through the courtyard archway.

By now, Lottie had seen inside all the courtyards of the glass pergola. Some contained statues, others fountains, still others weapons. The most important courtyard contained the Great Lantern of the wisps and was accessible only by members of the Dulcet family.

The courtyard they now stood in was, in Lottie's opinion, the ugliest of them all. It was overrun with ill-tended vines and thorny plants, and there was no bench to sit upon, nor fountains to listen to, nor statues to contemplate. It looked like a gardening project gone wrong, then forgotten. As a result, no one ever visited this courtyard. Lottie supposed that was why Fife had brought them there.

"Right," Fife said, crouching at the entrance of the glass pergola proper. "This close enough for you, Ada?"

Adelaide shut her eyes, her upturned nose wrinkled in concentration.

"It's faint," she said. "They're in your mother's private quarters. Stay quiet, the rest of you."

Lottie heard a snicker. Eliot's eyes were watering from laughter.

"Sorry," he squeaked out. "I'm still getting used to it. It's *funny*. She's like a comic book character."

Adelaide kept her eyes closed, but color burst in her cheeks.

"What's funny," she said, "is that you're the only one *without* a keen, Eliot. Now hush up and let me concentrate."

Eliot nodded obediently, though he covered his mouth and continued to laugh silently.

Adelaide remained quiet. She frowned, faintly at first, then harder. At last, she shook her head, annoyed.

"This is stupid," she said. "He's talking about some new collection of robes he bought in Thistlebram. Nothing more."

"No," said Fife. "He didn't come home early just to chat about thread counts. He came back with important news."

"Maybe we missed it," said Eliot, who had since recovered from the shakes.

"*No*," Fife said. "No, this kind of news is the news you don't just mention and forget. It's the kind of news that requires immediate action. Like an invasion of Wisp Territory or a cure that's faster than Mr. Wilfer's. Something *big*. It *has* to be."

"Fife," said Oliver. "Maybe the Tailor just wanted to come home early, and that's all. Home-keeping hearts are happiest, for those that wander they know not where are full of trouble and full of care."

"That's certainly what it sounds like," said Adelaide, "which means we've been doing all this juvenile snooping for nothing. You're his nephew, Fife. If you're so convinced something's wrong, ask him yourself."

"What an excellent idea!" Fife cried, clapping Adelaide on the shoulders. "Why didn't I think of it? Oh! Yes! Because, unlike some people, I don't have sponge cake for brains."

Adelaide shoved Fife away. "You're so uncivil."

"Ooh, ouch. Fifth me."

"I can't believe y—*wait!* Where are you all going?"

The others, led by Lottie, were leaving the courtyard and heading back into the wood, the bickering Fife and Adelaide hurrying to catch up.

"I'm telling you all," said Fife, "something is off. Something's not right, and I'm not going to shut up about it until we—*sweet Oberon, what is that?*"

Fife's yelling was unnecessary. The others had already reeled to a halt and were staring ahead at something in their path. Oliver's lantern light poured over a mound, dark and motionless. It was covered in something pale and slick.

White liquid—*blood*—was pooling around what Lottie was now sure was a dead body.

"I told you they existed! I *told* you! *The whitecaps strike again!*"

Fife was airborne. He flapped his arms frantically, face blotchy with panic.

Adelaide pressed her hand to her head and said, "I think I'm going to be sick."

"W-what do we do?" Eliot asked. He looked ready to puke at Lottie's feet.

Lottie shook her mind free of the sight.

"We tell someone," she said. "We have to *get* someone. Oliver?"

Oliver was still and silent, but Lottie knew this did not mean he was unreachable. It meant that, though he was paying attention, he was also thinking hard. Now, he looked to Lottie with resolve in his black eyes.

"Cynbel," he said. "I'll fetch him."

He ran back to the glass pergola.

Though he had stopped shouting, Fife was still hovering in a frenzy above Lottie's head.

"No one believed me! 'Stuff and nonsense, Fife,' you said! 'Just a myth,' you said! Now some wisp—so stupid to wander out at dawn—and now he's—he's *dead*, and—wait. *Is* it a he? Maybe a *she*, and, Puck's wings, it smells grotesque."

Lottie had never seen Fife as hysterical as this. She barely avoided getting conked in the head by one of his flailing feet. Clearly, the one person who best knew what to do in this situation was in no position to help. She sucked in a cold breath, steeled herself, and approached the bloodied circle of grass.

Adelaide gasped. "Lottie, *no!* Don't *touch*—"

Lottie knelt beside the motionless body. She could make out legs, curled inward, and shoulders, hunched tightly together. After another steadying breath, she pushed at the shoulders until the body lurched onto its back, revealing the wisp's face.

Lottie recognized him. He was one of the Wisp Guard. She had seen him before, patrolling the pergola and the surrounding wood. Lottie wondered if he had simply been doing his duty when the whitecaps attacked.

Then she felt it. The wisp's thumb brushed her wrist, ever so slightly.

"He's still alive!" she cried to the others.

Frantically, Lottie pushed away the wisp's heavy cloak. Something sharp caught at the hem. Lottie tugged it back to reveal a large spearhead, made of black metal, lodged into the wisp's side. Her hands came back slick with blood.

Fife hovered her side. He was no longer in hysterics, but he was still shaking badly.

"This can't have happened long ago," he said, "or he would've lost all his blood by now. Come *on*, Spool."

Fife held a yellow kingfisher. The genga was quivering,

clearly unnerved by the bloody tableau before it. Fife stroked her back reassuringly. Spool gave a nervous twitter, then puffed up her chest and, with a cough, produced a filmy vial from her beak. Hurriedly, Fife unstoppered the vial and poured its contents—Piskie Juice—on the wisp's wound.

"What else do we do?" Lottie asked. "Should we try to take the spear out?"

"*NO!*" Fife threw himself between Lottie and the body. "Oberon, Lottie, that is the very *last* thing you want to do."

"Well, I don't know!" Lottie said, feeling panic seize her for the first time. "I'm not a healer apprentice like you!"

"Yeah, well you're an actual *healer*!"

Lottie shrank at Fife's words. Tears pricked her eyes. He was right: if anyone should be useful at a time like this, it was her. Healing was her keen, yet here she was, stooped next to a wisp who desperately needed healing, and she could do nothing. What good were her stupid lessons now?

"You shouldn't even be touching him," Fife said, too distracted to notice Lottie's wet eyes. "You being half-human."

"What's that supposed to—"

Lottie was interrupted by the arrival of Cynbel and several members of the Wisp Guard. Oliver was leading them. Hastily, Lottie blotted her eyes.

"He's still alive," she said, as two of the guards pulled her and Fife from the body. "He needs help right away."

A flutter of white wings zipped past.

"Keats will fetch Father," Oliver said. "He'll know what to do. Lottie, your *hands*. Fife, her hands!"

"Yeah, yeah, I know," Fife said, uncorking yet another filmy vial that Spool had produced. "Ada, make yourself useful, would you? Get her cleaned up with this."

Though she looked terrified to come anywhere near the bloodied body, Adelaide snatched the vial from Fife.

"Come on," she said, tugging Lottie's shoulder. "Get away from them. You too, Eliot. It's not safe for you."

Lottie stumbled after Adelaide to a clean patch of grass, where Adelaide sat her down and ordered her to hold out her hands.

"Keep them cupped tight," she instructed. "Don't move. Just let the salve do its work."

Then Adelaide poured out the contents of the vial— something sludgy and teal-colored. The sludge moved in strange ways across Lottie's skin, crawling up against the tug of gravity. It sizzled, but it did not burn, and as it slowly evaporated, it left her skin entirely clean of wisp blood.

"You okay?" Eliot asked, his hand on Lottie's knee. "Does it hurt?"

"No," she said, "but, Adelaide, what do you mean, it isn't safe? What's wrong with wisp blood?"

"Hasn't anyone ever told you? Wisp blood makes humans fall into deep sleep. Too much, and—"

Cynbel's shouts drowned out the rest of Adelaide's words.

"Take him to the infirmary immediately!" he was barking to the other wisps.

"I don't think he should be moved," said Fife. "If you just wait for Mr. Wilfer, he'll tell you the same—"

"Quiet, halfling," Cynbel said. "You're no healer."

"I'm *telling* you," Fife argued. "He shouldn't be moved. He's losing too much blood as it is."

"Take him," Cynbel ordered the guards.

Four floating wisps hauled up the body. As they did so, blood gushed from the wisp's chest and spattered to the ground. They carried him off, leaving a trail of white in their wake, and Lottie remembered the line of poetry Oliver had quoted days earlier: *paint the ground with snowy blood.*

"As for you," said Cynbel, turning on Fife. "You keep forgetting that your place in these woods is precarious. Wilfer may have authority here, but you do not."

Fife floated to Cynbel's eye level, his face purple with anger. "*You* seem to keep forgetting that I'm a Dulcet."

Cynbel smiled without humor. "You may be a Dulcet, but you will never have authority over *me*. Go tell ghost stories with the other children."

As Cynbel floated away, Fife called him a long, sibilant word Lottie did not recognize but that caused Adelaide to gasp.

"What?" said Fife, shrugging. "That's precisely what he is."

Oliver's brow was stitched in troubled thought, his eyes a deep yellow.

"Fife," he said. "Whitecaps are supposed to drain their victims of blood, right?"

Fife nodded.

"Drain them *entirely*?" Oliver said.

Again, Fife nodded.

"What are you saying?" Lottie asked Oliver. "You don't think this was whitecaps?"

Fife didn't look too happy with this development.

"Who else could've done it?" he asked. "Who else would kill some random wisp on Autumntide?"

"I don't know," said Oliver, "but you yourself said the wound had to be recent, and it's been nighttime for a while. The whitecaps are only supposed to come out in the day."

"They could've overslept."

"What about the spearhead?" said Lottie. "It was in the wisp's side. Do whitecaps use weapons like that?"

Fife licked his lips. "The stories say they just use their bare teeth."

"Four rows of teeth, right?" Lottie said. "Wouldn't that leave marks all over the wisp's body? I didn't see any."

"Who else would want to kill a wisp guard?" asked Eliot. "Does this kind of thing happen a lot?"

Eliot looked nervous. The color had gone out of his face. Lottie hadn't seen him so pale since back in September, when he had been gravely ill. She wrapped her hand around his.

"Of course not," she said, looking to Fife for confirmation. "Does it?"

"Wisps are dying here all the time," said Fife, "but from Plague, not murder."

"Why are we still standing around?" Adelaide nodded uneasily at the bloodstained grass. "It smells foul, and I feel terrible. And for all we know, whatever attacked the wisp could still be close by."

"Ada's right," said Oliver. "We shouldn't be here."

Together, they headed for the pergola, following the bloody trail the Wisp Guard had left behind. Eliot, whose mittened hand was still entwined with Lottie's, gave a sudden cough. Then another, dry and staggered. Then another.

"Eliot?" said Lottie. "Are you okay?"

Eliot nodded, but he coughed again, a series of jagged barks. Then, just as quickly as it had come on, the attack subsided.

"I'm fine," he said, wiping at his watering eyes. He smiled sheepishly at the others. "Just swallowed the wrong way. It's the cold air, that's all."

They continued on their way, but Lottie didn't stop staring at Eliot. She knew those coughs.

She knew it wasn't just the cold air.

CHAPTER FOUR

The Tailor of the Wisps

THE CONGREGATION of wisps was gone from the glass pergola. The table sat vacant, strewn with half-drunk cups of spiced cider. Only a few black-cloaked wisps remained, and they stood at a distance, speaking in low tones. The air was full of jittery unrest.

"Shouldn't we get inside, too?" said Adelaide, casting a nervous look around.

"Why ever do *you* want to go inside?" Fife asked. "What is there to hide from? I thought whitecaps were make-believe."

Adelaide paled. "I didn't say it was a whitecap. I just think we should be in our yews, where it's safe."

"Fife," said Oliver. "Look."

He pointed to a wisp guard floating at the entrance of the pergola. The guard was staring straight at Fife.

"Son of Silvia," she called. "Your presence is requested in the Royal Bower."

For a moment, Fife looked confused. Then his face hardened into a sneer.

"Oh, *is* it?" he said, hands on his hips. "Fancy that."

"You and your friends," said the guard, who either had not picked up on Fife's unpleasantness or did not think it worthy of attention. "The Wilfers, the Heir of Fiske, and the human. You have all been summoned to appear before the Seamstress and the Tailor. Come."

Fife looked ready to argue. He looked ready to refuse.

"Come on, Fife," Oliver said. "Don't be difficult. Not at a time like this."

"I wasn't going to," muttered Fife, which everyone knew was a lie.

They followed the guard into the pergola. She led them down its long hallway, passing courtyard after courtyard. The River Lissome flowed alongside them, cutting a path through the center of the glass floor, and the soft splash of moving water echoed against the walls.

"Should we be freaking out?" Eliot whispered to Lottie.

"I don't know," she whispered back.

She had no idea what the Seamstress and Tailor could possibly want from the five of them at a time like this, but she had a creeping suspicion it couldn't be anything good.

They reached the threshold of the Royal Bower. Its frosted glass doors were closed.

"Wait here," the guard instructed before slipping inside and shutting them out.

"All that sneaking around for nothing," said Eliot.

"Can you hear anything?" Fife asked Adelaide.

"I'm trying," she said, closing her eyes. "Hold on."

After a long silence, she said, "Father is there, too. It's the three of them. That must've been why Father didn't answer Keats, Oliver. They're talking about—" Her eyes fluttered open. She looked at Lottie. "They're talking about *you*."

"What about me?" Lottie asked, startled.

"It's about your keen. The Tailor is asking Father about it. About if it can be used to cure the wisps. Here. Take a listen for yourself, if you'd like."

"How—?" Lottie began, but she then remembered what Adelaide had said the day before about transference.

"I need your hands," said Adelaide. "Both of them."

Lottie held out her hands. Without hesitation, Adelaide took hold of them and pressed her thumbs deep into the centers of Lottie's palms.

"Be quiet," she said. "Concentrate."

Lottie did just that.

The voices sidled into her head, growing louder, and louder still. The first words she could clearly distinguish were Mr. Wilfer's.

". . . an impossibility. Believe me, there is no sprite better qualified to assess her innate abilities."

"Such a high opinion of yourself, Moritasgus."

This voice Lottie did not recognize. It sounded dusty, as though it had just been brought out of storage after a long period of disuse. This, she reasoned, must be the Tailor.

"What I say is true." Mr. Wilfer sounded angry. "I cannot help that you are displeased with it."

"We have discussed it before, Lyre," said a glassy, child-like voice—Silvia's. "The girl is of no use to us. Moritasgus is doing all he can to find a—"

"Is he?" interrupted the Tailor. "I don't know what spell these sprites have cast over you, Silvia, but I will not be taken in so easily. What does he have to show for himself after a month of eating *our* food, sleeping under *our* protection?"

"Medicine cannot be rushed," said Mr. Wilfer. "I swore my best efforts to your sister, and I always honor my oaths."

"Really? Will you honor your oath to us the same as you did to Starkling?"

"Enough!" cried Silvia.

There was silence.

Then Mr. Wilfer spoke again. It sounded like he was choosing each word carefully. "I will tell you what I told Silvia:

I've been training the girl this full month through. She's started the sharpening process extremely late. Even if she continues to train at an accelerated pace, I don't believe she will ever be able to heal the masses. Her keen is rare, yes, and covetable. But it is limited. From what I can tell, she can only heal on a case-by-case basis, and only then if she's developed an empathetic connection to the patient."

"Then what good is she to us?" said the Tailor. "To any of us? Heir of Fiske, indeed. She might as well belong to one of the worthless houses—a Spivey, or an Outeridge. I'll tell you what the trouble is: she's been contaminated by human blood."

"Without human blood," said Mr. Wilfer, "she would never have developed such a unique gift."

"*Unique?* It is little better than useless."

"Would you call your own nephew useless?"

"Certainly not. I have no nephew."

Silence followed, then was broken by Silvia's irritated voice.

"What is it, Wren? Have you fetched them?"

"Yes, m'lady," said the voice of the wisp guard. "They're just outside."

Lottie pulled her hands out of Adelaide's.

"That's enough," she said. "I don't need to hear more."

"What's wrong?" asked Eliot. "What did they say?"

"Nothing," she said. "It's nothing."

Adelaide had heard everything, Lottie realized, embarrassment hitting her like a hot splash of water. She expected Adelaide to look smug, but she didn't. She looked sad. She looked *sorry*, as though she had been the one to tell Lottie that her keen was little better than useless.

"Lottie—" she whispered.

The doors to the Royal Bower swung open. The guard named Wren reappeared and motioned them to walk through.

"The Seamstress and Tailor will see you now," she said.

They entered the bower. Lottie had not set foot in this place since her first visit to Limn, when she, Oliver, Fife, and Adelaide had been on the run from the Southerly Guard. Some things were as she remembered them: the large weeping willow, its bark and leaves a pure white; the gauze awnings overhead; the vastness of the bower. But something had changed. Maybe it was that Silvia did not look anywhere near as regal as she had that first meeting. She floated before the willow tree some six feet in the air, reclining as though she were lounging upon a sofa, drumming her fingers along her jaw like an impatient child. Mr. Wilfer stood at the tree's base, arms folded and brow darkened.

Next to Silvia floated a tall, thin figure with the longest black hair Lottie had yet seen on a wisp. His chin was sharp, his cheekbones high, and his nose bent in two separate places. It was a severe countenance, made more severe by its frigid eyes. Lottie had never before been so vividly reminded of how *inhuman* the wisps were. Unlike his sister, the Tailor of the Wisps sat in midair with perfect posture, the same as if there had been a solid throne, not mere air, at his back.

Despite the fright Lottie felt at the sight of Lyre Dulcet, she could still see it: he looked very much like Fife. Or rather, she thought, Fife looked very much like his uncle.

"*Curtsy,*" a voice hissed.

Lottie realized she'd been staring far too long at the Tailor of the Wisps. Adelaide was bent low in a delicate curtsy, her eyes burning up at Lottie, urging her to do the same. On her other side, Oliver was bowing, and even Eliot was making his own sloppy attempt at a show of reverence. Lottie grabbed the edges of her periwinkle coat and stooped into her own curtsy. When she rose, she noticed Fife standing cross-armed, defiant. His lack of deference hadn't gone unnoticed.

"What do you mean by this?" Lyre demanded of him. Lottie saw spittle fly from his mouth as he spoke.

"I'm a Dulcet, same as you," said Fife. "And I'm a sprite, which means I don't owe you a bow."

"Your friends, too, are no wisps, yet they have appropriately chosen to show veneration to their hosts."

"Oh, but you're not my host, *Uncle,*" Fife said, smiling. "You're family."

Silvia stopped drumming her fingers. She was looking hard at Fife, her eyes watering. "Cynbel has informed us that you were the one to find the body," she said.

"We all did," said Fife. "And believe me, I wish we hadn't. It was a nasty sight. You're going to have to find me a therapist, Mother."

"The Guard think it was the work of whitecaps," Silvia went on. "Cynbel, however, reports that the guard's body was pierced by a spear. Is that true?"

"Yeah," said Fife. "I told you, it was nasty."

"See?" Silvia said to her brother. "That is not in keeping with whitecap behavior."

"That's what I was saying," Oliver whispered excitedly to Eliot.

"What does that mean?" asked Lottie.

"It may mean nothing," said Silvia. "Whitecaps are not known for their consistency or cleanliness. But if the guard yet lives, we may find out more about his attacker."

"Shouldn't Mr. Wilfer be helping him?" asked Fife.

Lyre's face darkened. "Are you suggesting, *child*, that we wisps cannot tend to our own wounded?"

"I'm just saying, Mr. Wilfer is pretty qualified for the job."

"As is the healer of our Guard," said Lyre. "And Mr. Wilfer's presence is required here. He does not have the freedom to choose his patients. We decide whom he attends to."

Fife looked ready to start shouting, but he said nothing, only hovered a little higher off the ground.

"The point of this audience," Silvia said, "has nothing to do with this morning's unfortunate event. It concerns news that my brother has brought back from the Northerly Court. News concerning the Southerly King."

Something plummeted deep within Lottie, turning her bones gelatinous. The mention of Starkling brought with it the remembrance of her vivid nightmare: the king's fair skin bubbling like tar, eyes wide with rage, teeth red with blood.

"What kind of news?" Fife asked.

"The Northerlies," said Lyre, "have discovered a way to destroy Starkling."

"Whoa," said Eliot. "*Destroy* him?"

Lyre's gaze jolted to Eliot. His upper lip pulled up in distaste.

"What is *this*?" he asked Silvia.

"A human," she said.

Lyre said nothing more on the matter, but for the next several minutes, he continued to look as though he were suffering from indigestion.

"I have spent these past months in the company of Rebel Gem, leader of the Northerly Court," said Lyre. "Two of the court's spies have attempted to assassinate the king before, using common poisons that had no effect on him. However, Northerly healers hypothesize that

Starkling can be brought down by a plant that grows only in the Wilders. It is called addersfork. It is rare and blooms only at the end of autumn. It is the deadliest poison on our Isle, and it is, I believe, our best chance of destroying the Southerly King once and for all."

"Let me get this straight," said Fife. "You went off to the North to find a cure, and you came back with *poison*? How's killing off Starkling going to help the wisps who are dying?"

"Still your tongue, Fife," said Silvia. "Do not be impudent."

"There is no cure to be found in the northern territories. There hasn't been for years."

Lottie was taken off guard by the sound of Mr. Wilfer's soft voice. She lowered her gaze to where he stood.

"Northerly healers manufactured a cure," he continued, "but used up the vital ingredients years ago. The Plague was eradicated in the North, but now there are no remaining ingredients in the Isle for the cure they invented. There has been little research into another cure that can make use of ingredients still in existence. That task has fallen to me."

"And a shoddy job you've done of it," said Lyre. He turned to Fife. "If you want an explanation for why wisps are still dying, boy, ask your precious healer here."

Fife looked close to bursting, but still said nothing.

"I may not have found a cure in my travels," said Lyre, "but I lighted upon the next best thing. Too long have the wisps lived under Starkling's embargoes and threats of invasion. It was due to his extortion that my people could not afford inoculations—when there were still inoculations to be had. Long has he wanted us weak, and dead. He's been wearing us down, readying to strike and take Wisp Territory for himself. My people deserve justice. Starkling will suffer for what he has done."

"That's all good and well," said Fife. "Everyone wants the king dead. But why are you telling *us*?"

Lottie wondered this, too. They had never before been invited to the Royal Bower or been privy to Silvia or Mr. Wilfer's conversations. Why were the adults now freely sharing their secrets?

"They want something from us," said Oliver. He was studying Lyre with cold blue eyes. "That's what it is."

"Not from *you*," said Lyre, "but from the Fiske girl, yes."

"What?" said Lottie. "Why me?"

"I believe the addersfork will destroy Starkling," said Lyre, "but the place it grows is dangerous terrain. None but Northerlies know how to cross over the Wilders, and fewer still know where to find this addersfork. Rebel Gem has offered to retrieve the plant for me in return for something else."

Lottie's throat felt dry. "You mean *someone* else."

Lyre produced a thin smile. "Rebel Gem is under the impression that *you* are a far greater asset than addersfork,

Miss Fiske. I'm not sure if you're aware, but the name of Fiske has caused quite a stir up North. Rebel Gem thinks your presence alone would be a great boon to the court."

Silence circled around the bower, and Lottie finally understood.

"You think—you think you can just *force* me to go north?"

"My brother and I do consider it rather fortuitous," said Silvia, "that the Heir of Fiske resides in our territory."

"Fortuitous?" said Fife. "That's rich. You can't just give Lottie away to Rebel Gem, like she belongs to you. You haven't even asked if she'd like to go."

"In the end," said Lyre, "it does not matter whether or not Miss Fiske wants to go. She's a fugitive, and she's a guest in my court. Unless you all wish to fall into the hands of the Southerly King, you must rely entirely on me. And if I say you must go north, *you will go north.*"

"But I *can't!*" Lottie shouted. "Eliot and I are going home for Thanksgiving. Silvia said we could use the apple tree to go back to Kemble Isle. We had a deal."

"Little girls with unsharpened keens aren't in a position to make deals," said Lyre. "Things have changed. I refuse to let you use our apple tree."

"So, what?" said Fife. "Lottie's supposed to forge her way to the Northerly Court all alone, just in time for winter?"

"Of course not!" cried Silvia, throwing her hands up. "Fife, darling, *really*. As though we would ever send an honored guest northward unprotected! We've discussed the matter at length with Moritasgus. The Northerlies intend to do all they can to make Lottie's journey safe and worth its while. Rebel Gem has personally arranged for comfortable lodging in the Northerly Court."

"Moritasgus also informs us," said Lyre, "that none of you are particularly happy with your arrangements here in Wisp Territory. As outlaws, you have no fellow sprites to help you sharpen your keens properly."

Lottie felt certain she heard a sneer in Lyre's voice as he said the word "keens."

"The Northerly Court is full of sprites who can help you along in your training," said Silvia. "Rebel Gem has offered you the full protection of the court, just as I have extended my protection here."

"Is that all true, Father?" asked Oliver. "Is that what you want for us?"

Mr. Wilfer looked tired. "I've long felt uneasy about your situation here," he said. "I can think of no better opportunity for you to advance your studies. I think you should be back amongst other sprites. Though I will of course leave it up to you."

"*You* may leave it to them, Moritasgus," said Lyre, "but I do not allow halflings and *other folk*"—here he cast a look at Eliot—"to reside in my territory."

"Hey!" cried Eliot. "But Mr. Wilfer made a deal with the Seamstress."

"He made a deal with her," said Lyre, "not with me. Silvia can play by her rules while I'm away, but *my* rule has been, and ever will be, that there is no room here for outsiders. We wisps have enough troubles as it is without interference."

"Yeah," said Fife. "Troubles you want *us* to help with. And when exactly do you plan on booting us out of here?"

"Tomorrow," said Lyre. "I promised Rebel Gem an immediate transaction."

"*WHAT?*" roared Fife.

Lottie blinked in shock. This news was so sudden, so wholly unexpected, that she'd yet to sort out half its meaning. Travel to the Northerly Court? All she knew of Rebel Gem were the fractured mentions she'd heard from the Barghest and from Roote and Crag, the two Northerlies she had met on her journey to the Southerly Court. She had certainly never heard of a place called the Wilders. And what about *Eliot?*

"What if we do go?" asked Fife. "How're we supposed to travel north, on bare Barghest back?"

"Nothing so uncivil," said Silvia, who hadn't seen the excitement in Fife's face when he asked the question. "Lyre has brought back with him an ambassador from the Northerly Court, sent directly from Rebel Gem as a gesture of hospitality. He's been taking a rest after the long journey, but I've requested Wren to fetch him. Ah! And what magnificent timing, for here they come."

Silvia motioned to the bower doors, where Wren stood guard, her face impassive.

"Go on, then," said Silvia. "Show him in."

Wren opened the bower door and announced, "The honored ambassador from the North."

In walked a young man with shaggy black hair and muscled arms. His gait was confident as he strode toward the willow tree, then stooped in a bow. When he lifted his face, Lottie saw the three metal rings that pierced his nose.

The honored ambassador from the North was none other than Dorian Ingle.

CHAPTER FIVE

Iolanthe

"DORIAN," said Lyre. "I didn't think Northerlies acknowledged royalty."

Dorian Ingle smiled broadly at the Tailor of the Wisps. "I wasn't bowing to you. I was paying my respects to the Heir of Fiske."

Dorian turned his smile on Lottie. Warmth creep-crawled into her face.

"I'm not royalty," she said. "Not even close."

"No," said Dorian, winking at her. "But you possess the courage of the Fiskes. I haven't forgotten that so easily from our last encounter. Lottie Fiske, it would be my honor to serve and protect you on your journey north."

"Yeah, and what about the rest of us?" said Fife. "Will it be your *honor* to protect us, or are you just flirting because Lottie's so nice to look at?"

Adelaide gasped. Oliver's eyes went pink.

"You're a forceful one, aren't you?" said Dorian, sauntering closer to Fife. "The Tailor warned me about you."

"I can't imagine what he said, considering he doesn't know me at all."

Dorian snorted. "Well, listen up, Little Dulcet. It will be my privilege to escort *all* of you safely to the Northerly Court, without regard to parentage or prettiness."

Lottie blushed. She turned to avoid Dorian's gaze, but also because she had something to say to Mr. Wilfer.

"I can't go," she said. "I won't."

"It's been a month," Eliot piped up timidly. "My dad's been really understanding about everything, but he'd be so upset if I didn't come back for the holidays."

"Then let the human child return to his home, where he belongs," said Silvia. "There's no need for Lottie to follow."

"There's every need for me to follow!" Lottie cried. "I have to stay near Eliot. I keep him well. Tell them, Mr. Wilfer."

"It's true," Mr. Wilfer said. "If she and the boy were to part, I fear it would be detrimental to his health."

"That is not our concern," said Lyre.

"Well, it's *mine*," Lottie said. "I can't go on this great errand of yours if it means traveling north tomorrow. I promised Eliot I would go home with him for the holidays. We'll be there for weeks. I *promised*."

"That's terribly inconvenient," observed Dorian, who had pulled a pipe from his breast pocket and was now lighting its contents.

"It's impossible," said Lyre. "I told Rebel Gem I would send you to the Northerly Court straightaway."

"Well, maybe you should've asked my permission first!" Lottie shouted.

"Easy now," said Dorian, puffing out a cloud of orange smoke. "No need to get riled up. Maybe Lottie just needs some time to consider."

"There's nothing to consider," Lottie snapped. "I go home with Eliot tomorrow."

"Have you told her, Lyre?" Dorian asked. "How Rebel Gem has offered to train her in person?"

Lottie grew still. "*Rebel Gem* wants to help me sharpen my keen?"

"A very qualified teacher, too," said Dorian. "Has anyone ever told you how similar Rebel Gem's keen is to your own?"

Lottie shook her head. She suddenly felt as though her neck wasn't properly attached to her body.

"That shouldn't change anything," she said quietly.

"Maybe it shouldn't," said Dorian. "But it's something to consider, isn't it?"

"Tailor," Mr. Wilfer spoke up. "Seamstress. You've given the children a heavy piece of news. I think it best to grant them time to think it over."

The brother and sister exchanged a glance. Silvia gave a slow, solitary nod.

"They can think it over, if that gives them comfort," said Lyre. "But regardless, the Heir of Fiske must be ready to depart in one day's time. No later."

"Don't worry," muttered Fife. "We'll be out of this rotten dump soon enough."

⊷

They were assigned four guards for the journey back to the Clearing. Though Lottie knew Lyre had only sent Wren and the three other guards to ensure that she and the others didn't try to escape, she was secretly grateful for their presence. She still couldn't shake her fear of whitecaps or the memory of that wisp guard slumped in a pool of blood.

Fife talked the whole way back.

"We don't even get a say in the matter. If we don't go of our own free will, that Dorian fellow will probably kidnap us and haul us to the Northerly Court anyhow. Wouldn't be surprised if the Tailor's sold us all into slavery."

No one replied, but no one really needed to. Fife was content carrying on the conversation with himself.

When they arrived at the Clearing, Lottie said, "We should talk it over."

So they all crawled into Lottie and Adelaide's yew, and only after the guards had left and the yew branch splintered back into place did everyone start to speak.

"Father seems to think it's a good idea," said Oliver.

"Yes, well, he was forced into it by the Tailor," said Fife. "Uncle probably threatened him with disembodiment."

Oliver shivered. "Whatever the case, it isn't fair Lottie and Eliot are being backed into it."

Adelaide was crying. "This isn't what I meant when I said I wanted proper tutelage! What kind of qualified teachers can there possibly be in the North? They're all barbarians!"

"I dunno what's left to discuss," said Fife. "They've made our decision for us."

Eliot looked over nervously at Lottie.

"Don't worry," she whispered for only him to hear. "I'm going home with you. Nothing's changed."

Though something *had* changed. Lottie had promised Eliot she would return home. He missed his father, and Lottie knew Mr. Walsch must miss Eliot terribly, too. And she couldn't possibly let Eliot go home on his own. He coughed even when he was with her. What would happen if she left his side?

And yet.

Rebel Gem had offered to train her. *The* Rebel Gem, leader of the Northerlies, had a keen like her own. The memory surfaced in Lottie's mind: the bloodied wisp guard who had struggled for life while she looked on, powerless, unable to help or heal. She wasn't getting anywhere under Mr. Wilfer's instruction, but what if she could make better progress with Rebel Gem?

Then her memory threw up the awful, unwanted image of the Southerly King's cold eyes as he crushed a helpless boy's genga in his hand, a crowd cheering, *"Fifthed! Fifthed!"*

"Do you think the Tailor's plan would work?" Lottie asked. "Do you think if the wisps get hold of the addersfork, they can really kill him?"

"Who knows?" said Oliver. "But it sounds like the only plan they've got."

"*Lottie* is the only plan they've got," corrected Adelaide. "But it's unjust for the Tailor to banish the rest of us up North when we've nothing to do with this silly scheme."

"Come on, Adelaide." Oliver's eyes turned a green as coaxing as his voice. "It won't be that bad. I bet the Northerlies aren't nearly as uncivil as you think. Some of the most powerful sprites in history have been Northerlies— Fiskes included."

Lottie perked up at this. In all the ruckus and confusion, she'd forgotten the fact that her mother was a Northerly.

Her mother had probably visited the Northerly Court, too. The thought made her heart lurch.

"I'll go," said Adelaide, sniffling, "but I won't go happily."

"What about you, Lottie?" Fife asked. "Are you really going back to Kemble Isle? The Tailor isn't going to take kindly to that decision."

He didn't sound accusatory, but he did sound upset.

"I'm really sorry," Lottie said, "but I have to. I care about all of you, and about Albion Isle, but Eliot is—I mean, Eliot could—he could—"

"No one's angry with you, Lottie," said Oliver. "You don't have to explain."

Lottie wanted to say, *But I'm angry with* myself.

"How long will you be gone?" Adelaide asked.

"Nothing was definite," said Lottie, "but we'd planned on staying several weeks at least."

"How will you even get back here is what I want to know," said Fife. "The Tailor's hardly going to let you come waltzing back through his silver-boughed tree after you refuse to cooperate with his plan."

"I don't know," said Lottie. "I don't *know*. I need to talk it over with Mr. Wilfer."

"You'll figure something out," said Oliver. Then, in a tone of voice Lottie knew all too well, he said, "You are the master of your fate; you are the captain of your soul."

Though Adelaide had stopped crying, a heaviness still hung over the tree after the boys had left for their own yew.

Adelaide lay on her back, squinting up at the chandelier. "I've been thinking," she said. "I keep trying to work out how things could've happened differently. How the pieces could've fit in other places so that none of this ever came to be, and my world was the same as before, and Iris Gate was ours again, and Father was the king's right-hand sprite. I would still have my daily lessons with Tutor, and I could walk down to Gertrude's Dress Shop and look at the newest patterns to arrive. It's impossible, but I think about that." She tilted her head to Lottie. "Is that terrible of me?"

"No," Lottie said softly. "I used to think that way all the time, back in New Kemble. I thought that way about my parents. Sometimes, I still do."

"Hm," said Adelaide. "Well, coming from you, that's not much of an assurance that I'm not insane. No offense."

"Oh no," said Lottie. "Of course not."

Even though Adelaide had just insulted her, Lottie couldn't help but smile at her for making a comment that was so—well, so very *Adelaide*.

It wasn't long before Adelaide had dozed off. Lottie waited until she was quite sure she was fast asleep. Then she laced her boots, took a lantern from its peg, and left the yew. She had questions for Mr. Wilfer, and those questions couldn't wait until a new dusk.

◆

Lottie may have grown accustomed to waking at dusk and going about her daily tasks throughout the deep of night, but that hardly meant the shadows of Wisp Territory didn't still unsettle her. Tonight, the wood was far more deserted than usual, and the thought of a blood-draining whitecap—or something else—made Lottie shrink and shiver every time the wind blew too strongly or a branch swayed too close to the path. Though Trouble was flying ahead of her, Lottie could barely make out his black body in her lantern light.

Mr. Wilfer had still been in conference with the Tailor, the Seamstress, and Dorian Ingle when Lottie and the others had left the Royal Bower. She hoped that by now he would be back at his cottage. If anyone could help stop the anxious twisting inside her stomach, Lottie felt sure Mr. Wilfer could. He was a healer, after all.

The only entrance to Mr. Wilfer's cottage was a tall door decorated by wood-carved vines. Lottie knocked once on the door, then waited, hoping for Mr. Wilfer to be in. She did not want to walk farther still to the glass pergola, especially not past the place where they had found the bloodied body of the wisp guard.

The door creaked open. Mr. Wilfer poked out his whiskered face.

"Lottie!" he said, opening the door wider. "I thought you might come. Though alone? I told you the wood is dangerous right now."

"I know," Lottie said dismissively, "but this is urgent."

Mr. Wilfer showed her inside. The cottage was cheery, lit by a half dozen hanging lanterns. Two tables stretched across the room, strewn with glasses and vials, herbs and flowers. There were other, stranger sights, too: a plate of half-eaten French toast, a collection of shoestrings of varying lengths, a jar filled with pink pebbles, a box of used birthday candles, and a fluffy pile of what looked a lot like cotton candy. Mr. Wilfer was wearing a pair of leather gloves, and he held a strainer in one hand.

"Please," he said, motioning to a pair of wooden chairs in the corner. "Have a seat."

Lottie sat as Mr. Wilfer set down the strainer and peeled the gloves from his hands.

"I hope I haven't interrupted something important," she said.

"It's no matter. Just another experiment. I'm trying to capture my own hiccups."

"Is that an ingredient in the cure?" Lottie asked, wrinkling her nose. She still hadn't gotten used to the idea of how Mr. Wilfer made medicine—with giant scrapbooks and ingredients like limericks, watch hands, and violin strings.

"It's a theory of mine," Mr. Wilfer said. "We'll see how it turns out."

"I guess you know why I'm here," said Lottie.

"I believe I do. Though I must warn you, dear, there's no easy solution to the decision you face."

"Limn does mean very much to me," said Lottie. "It's just that Eliot means the most."

"I see."

"Are you disappointed in me?" Lottie asked.

"Disappointed? Why ever would I be disappointed?"

"Because I'm a Fiske," Lottie said. "Fiskes are supposed to be great and noble and do important things, and now I won't even go on a trip north when I'm asked."

"Lottie," said Mr. Wilfer, "as a halfling, you belong to the human world as much as to ours. Neither I nor any of your friends can fault you for having split loyalties."

"But I feel like they do fault me," Lottie said. "And what about the Tailor? Won't he try to stop me going back?"

"He should never have made that deal without consulting you," said Mr. Wilfer. "You and you alone have the right to choose your steps. All the same, the Tailor is powerful, and you are in his territory. I fear he might try to send you north by force. If he's going to change his mind, he'll need some convincing from a persuasive party."

"You mean you?" Lottie guessed.

Mr. Wilfer smiled tiredly. During the time she'd known him, Lottie had discovered that Mr. Wilfer was always suffering from some degree of tiredness.

"Lyre might be the Tailor of the Wisps," he said, "but I am the only healer at his disposal—the only chance of a cure for the Plague. He knows that now more than ever, after returning empty-handed from the Northerly Court. I have no small degree of leverage."

"Are you close to finishing the cure?" Lottie asked.

"It's coming along slowly. Since the vital ingredients used to make sprite inoculations are long gone, I've been forced to invent an entirely new recipe. Some ingredients will take time to produce. Some I may be wrong about. There's one ingredient that may not even exist."

"What is it?" Lottie asked.

Mr. Wilfer settled back in his chair, the wood groaning beneath his weight. He clasped his hands across his stomach.

"There is a fable," he said, "concerning Queen Mab, the first of the new order of sprites and your ancestor."

Lottie leaned forward. "Yes?"

"It's said that Queen Mab had a fascination with the human world. This was back when there were far more silver-boughed trees, and when sprites and humans freely traveled between the two worlds. Queen Mab was also said to be barren, and she longed for an heir to carry on her line. One day, when she was roaming a human wood, she came across a cabin, and in that cabin was a newborn babe. The moment she set eyes on the child, Queen Mab fell in love. She decided to steal the baby in the dead of night, while his parents slept."

"That's awful," said Lottie.

"That was also the opinion of her husband, King Aldrich," said Mr. Wilfer, nodding. "He insisted the queen return the child to his home, but Queen Mab was entranced by the human boy. Then something happened that Queen Mab could not prevent: the child grew ill. She realized it was impossible to keep a human baby alive in Limn. She was forced to return the child to his parents. Afterward, she was inconsolable. She wept for weeks and weeks. Then, one day, she dried her tears and returned to her throne, and she vowed to do nothing but good from that day on."

"And she became very famous," said Lottie, "and had poems written about her."

"Yes, indeed. And as it so happened, many years later, Queen Mab discovered that she was not, in fact, barren. She gave birth to a daughter, and so the Fiske line continued."

"Good news for me," said Lottie, smiling.

"Good news for you," said Mr. Wilfer. "But the matter

of note in this story is the queen's tears. That is the one ingredient I've lost the most sleep over."

Lottie frowned. "Queen Mab's *tears*? But that's impossible! She lived hundreds of years ago, didn't she? Who would be standing around to collect her tears?"

"Then you see the source of my frustration," said Mr. Wilfer.

"Well, I'm sure you'll figure it out," said Lottie. "You weren't the king's right-hand sprite for nothing."

Mr. Wilfer's expression darkened. "No," he said. "No, indeed."

Lottie studied the floor, which was nothing more than hard-packed white soil.

"Mr. Wilfer," she said. "What happened to that human baby—that's what happened to my father, isn't it? He stayed so long in Limn that he got ill."

Mr. Wilfer gave a slow nod.

"And that's what will happen to Eliot," she said, "if he stays in Limn for too long. I've noticed it already. His cough has gotten worse."

"I've noticed it, too."

"He and I have to get back to Kemble Isle," said Lottie. "But if we do, will the Tailor let us return?"

"I've no idea," said Mr. Wilfer.

"Well, why can't you just tell him I'll go north after Eliot and I get back in a few weeks?"

"Lyre is working under a hard-pressed timeline," said Mr. Wilfer. "Many say King Starkling plans on invading Wisp Territory. Or something even more terrible. So in Lyre's mind, time is of the essence."

"And in *your* mind?" asked Lottie.

"I've learned from experience that you shouldn't give credence to fearful rumors. And yet, I know Starkling. I do believe him capable of anything. He's long been at work on a secret project—one that not even I was privy to during my time as his right-hand sprite. I wouldn't put anything past him."

"So you think it's right, what the Dulcets are doing? You think the addersfork will work?"

"Using addersfork is a risky business," said Mr. Wilfer. "It's dangerous enough to obtain, and the actual process of administering the poison . . ." Here Mr. Wilfer flinched, his face clouding over. "But Lyre believes addersfork is the only foolproof way to kill Starkling, because it is the only poison that can be used remotely."

"You mean," said Lottie, "it's not something you'd have to slip into Starkling's food or tea? You could just poison him from afar? Like—like voodoo?"

Mr. Wilfer raised a brow. "I'm not familiar with this *voodoo*, but yes, that's the general idea. If the components of the plant are extracted properly, all one needs is a *part* of the person to be poisoned—a hair, a tooth, a fingernail clipping—and the work can be done. This appeals to Lyre since he has no wisp spies in the Southerly Court. And, truth be told, very few Northerly spies remain. After Dorian Ingle exposed his own allegiance by rescuing us from court, the king has been especially vigilant."

"So the addersfork really could work," said Lottie. "Which means I really could do my part to make things better for the wisps."

"Yes," said Mr. Wilfer. "Though you should not be coerced into it the way Lyre intends. And just because the Dulcets *can* use the addersfork does not mean they *should*. For my part, it's simply not an option. As a healer, I swore to help, not harm. I refuse to participate in the extraction process, should it come to that, and I'm not particularly proud of the Northerly healers who suggested the use of addersfork in the first place. I consider them a disgrace to our practice."

"I *do* care about what happens on Albion Isle, you know. It's just Eliot—"

"I understand," said Mr. Wilfer. "If I were given the choice between the well-being of the Isle and the health of my dear departed wife . . ."

Lottie went still. Mr. Wilfer had never once mentioned his late wife. Lottie had only learned about her through Fife, and even then she had been warned never to bring up the topic around the Wilfers.

Mr. Wilfer shook his head, as though bringing himself out of a daydream.

"I may not be able to convince the Tailor," he told Lottie, "but I will do my very best."

"Thank you, Mr. Wilfer," said Lottie, getting to her feet.

"Try to rest easy tonight," said Mr. Wilfer, walking her to the door. "You worry far more than any twelve-year-old ought."

Lottie fetched her lantern from its peg at the threshold. Outside, the world had grown blacker. It was the dead of night, and dawn was as far off now as the dusk before.

"I will accompany you," said Mr. Wilfer, taking down his own lantern.

"I'll be fine," said Lottie, even though the fright she'd felt before was creeping back in. "I got here in one piece, didn't I? After all—"

Lottie was interrupted by the sound of a terrific *thump*, just feet from where she stood. She jumped back with a yelp.

"Who's there?" she called, though her mind was already whirring fast with images of blood and bone. *Whitecaps.*

The shadows were moving—something gray against the black. Then came voices.

"It's us! It's only us!"

Mr. Wilfer shone his lantern into the shadows.

"Oliver?"

Oliver lay sprawled on the ground, covered in white dirt, bits of yew needles caught in his curly hair. It looked as though he'd fallen. Lottie shone her lantern upward to reveal Eliot sitting in the curve of a yew branch, Fife beside him. Oliver, too, must have been sitting there until the *thump*.

Lottie offered Oliver a hand, but she realized a moment too late, after she'd already knelt, that this was of course impossible; his touch would burn painfully into her skin. She retracted her hand immediately, but Oliver had seen the gesture. As he stumbled to his feet, unassisted, his eyes turned black.

"What on earth are you doing?" Lottie called up to Fife and Eliot. "Were you spying on me?"

"Eliot said you'd sneak out," said Fife. "And of course you *would* when there's a bloodthirsty murderer at large. We weren't going to interfere or anything. We just wanted to be sure you were safe."

"All three of you?"

"None of us wanted to be left out," said Eliot.

"I think," said Oliver, hobbling a step forward. "I—I think I've hurt my foot."

Mr. Wilfer placed the back of his hand to Oliver's forehead.

"You've sprained your ankle," he said. "Come inside. I've something for it."

Oliver followed Mr. Wilfer into the cottage. Fife, meantime, floated down from the yew tree.

"You could've helped him," said Lottie, pointing to Eliot, who was struggling with his own descent, feet scuffling to stay afoot on the branch below.

Fife shrugged. "He's fine."

"Yeah," called Eliot. "I'm fine! Fife isn't any better than me just because he can float."

"That's right," Fife said, tossing his hair. "I'm not better because I can *float*; I'm just *inherently* better."

Lottie laughed, but a part of her was worried. She'd heard the little jabs that Eliot and Fife had exchanged in the past weeks, and she'd begun to worry that it wasn't all in jest. She had a horrible suspicion that they didn't get along.

Eliot eventually made it down, and Lottie hurried over to catch his hands and say in a whisper Fife couldn't hear, "You'll see your dad tomorrow."

The way Eliot smiled at that made the twisting in Lottie finally stop.

When Mr. Wilfer and Oliver emerged from the cottage, Oliver was no longer hobbling. The blue stain of medicine rimmed his lips.

"Better?" asked Fife.

"In perfect health begin," quoted Oliver, "hoping to cease not till death."

"Now, straight back to the Clearing," said Mr. Wilfer. "All four of you. No diversions, do you hear? It's not safe out of doors until the Wisp Guard has made a more thorough investigation of the attack."

"Has he said anything?" asked Eliot. "The guard who was attacked? Can't he tell them what really happened?"

"I expect he could," said Mr. Wilfer, "if he were still alive."

"He died?" whispered Lottie.

"I visited the barracks after our meeting," said Mr. Wilfer. "There was nothing anyone could've done to prevent it, myself included. He'd lost far too much blood already."

"But he wasn't drained," said Oliver. "That's the thing. Whitecaps are supposed to drain their victims *entirely*. And then there's the matter of the spear . . ."

"The Seamstress and Tailor are looking into it," said Mr. Wilfer. "It's not a matter that concerns—"

"*Children*," Lottie said loudly, a scowl on her face.

"Back to the Clearing" was Mr. Wilfer's reply.

The four of them set out, leaving Mr. Wilfer behind at the cottage door. There was far less excitement in the air than there had been moments earlier. Lottie didn't doubt that the boys had followed to look out for her, but she suspected they also must've wanted more information about the day's events. Now they had been sent away with nothing to show for their efforts.

At least, thought Lottie, *I've made my decision. I'm leaving with Eliot, whatever the cost.*

They walked two across down the path—Eliot in step with Oliver, and Lottie with Fife.

"Are you really that angry about heading north?" Lottie asked him.

"Not nearly so angry as I'm acting," he said.

"I would go, too, only—"

"Yes, yes, I know," said Fife. "Eliot's top priority. Anyway, you can't just let the Tailor sell you off to Rebel Gem."

"When I heard he banished you, I didn't believe it," Lottie admitted. "I didn't think anyone could be that cruel. But now that I've seen the Tailor, I—well, he really doesn't like you, does he?"

"Oh, you caught that? Good eye, Lottie."

Fife's tongue was peeking out the corner of his mouth. Lottie knew he was using his keen to affect their conversation, but she could still tell, however cheery his tone, that Fife was sad about something.

"I'm sorry," she said.

Fife tucked his tongue back in his mouth. He frowned into the darkness.

"The worst of it," he said, "is that I *want* to go up north. I want to see the Northerly Court. I never have, you know. But it's all got a bad taste now, because I *have* to go."

"So you're not upset about leaving?" As she asked it, Lottie felt a pang in her chest that felt a lot like jealousy.

"Are you kidding?" said Fife. "I've been itching to leave. Following Mr. Wilfer around has been informative, I guess, but it's not exactly how I imagined it. He's distracted all the time, and he never explains things clearly. Honestly, he's a terrible teacher."

Lottie was shocked. She hadn't ever heard the others speak ill of Mr. Wilfer. She wondered at Fife's words. All this time, at every sharpening lesson, she'd just assumed she was a bad student. She'd never considered that Mr. Wilfer might not be a very good teacher.

They were just approaching the part of the path that banked off toward the red apple tree when Oliver and Eliot stopped ahead.

"Shh!"

Oliver waved for everyone to be quiet. There were voices in the wood—at a distance, but coming closer. These voices could not belong to wisps, who spoke only in smooth syllables. They were rough and full of grit. One shouted an order. Then someone screamed.

It's the whitecaps, thought Lottie.

Oliver nodded away from the voices, into the wood. They hurried into the cover of the trees and crouched behind a thick yew. Fife blew out his lantern. Lottie blew out hers. They sat in the dark, waiting, and Lottie became aware of just how hard and fast she was breathing.

"Should we run?" whispered Eliot, who was crouched next to Lottie, his hand resting on her shoulder.

"No good," Fife said, peeking around the yew's trunk, then hiding himself again. "Whitecaps can smell fear, and they're stupidly fast."

"Well, we can't just stop being afraid," said Lottie, "and if they're going to smell us out all the same, I'd rather have a head st—"

Her words were drowned out by another scream, broken and anguished.

When the sound let up, Lottie could make out words. A woman was speaking nearby, on the path. Lamplight appeared in the darkness, only a few good strides from where they were hidden, and lit the silhouettes of four figures. Three were standing on the path, surrounding the fourth, which was stooped before them, head hung low.

"A lone guard at the silver bough?" said one of the figures. "Your Seamstress should take better care of what precious gifts she has left. The last time wisps were this careless, they lost a certain Lantern."

"I'm not afraid to die," said the stooped figure. "Take my life like a true sprite, Iolanthe, and may Robin Goodfellow curse you to the Fifth Sea."

"Pretty speech," said the woman addressed as Iolanthe, "but it's not cowardice that stays my hand. I've dirtied up my sword with enough white blood today. You're going to be my messenger."

"I'd rather die," said the wisp, though his voice faltered.

"Don't be difficult," said Iolanthe. "I haven't the time for it. You will tell your Seamstress and Tailor that this is only the beginning. Starkling will raze this wood to the ground, one yew at a time. There is nothing your people can do to stop us, so if you wish to die in peace, you won't stand between our axes and your rotting homes."

The two other figures dragged the wisp to his feet and heaved him into the dark.

"Go on," called the woman. "Tell Silvia that Iolanthe sends her regards!"

Lottie expected the wisp to argue, to shout back, to fight. But this time, he merely floated away in an uneven sputter. He was headed down the path in the direction of the glass pergola.

The woman named Iolanthe turned to her companions but said nothing. Lottie wondered if she was merely thinking, or if she was looking at something, or if she was listening—

Listening.

What if this Iolanthe *knew* they were here? What if she, like Adelaide, had a hearing keen? Lottie wanted to warn the others, wanted to tell them to ready their feet to run, but she didn't dare breathe loudly, let alone speak.

Then Iolanthe moved, sweeping back a long cape and removing something hidden beneath—a jar of some sort.

"Is the silver secure, Julian?" she asked.

"It is, your reverence."

"Then keep close, both of you."

Iolanthe dug a hand into the jar, and Lottie realized what it was just as Iolanthe threw the powder into the air. She was using Royal Piskie Dust.

"The Southerly Palace!" Iolanthe shouted, each consonant sharp-edged.

The dust swirled around the three silhouettes in a lazy circle. Then the silhouettes were no more; they'd vanished into the darkness. All that remained was the light powderfall of remaining Piskie Dust.

There was a *crack* of a match strike and the sudden appearance of light as Fife relit his lantern.

"Come on," he said, rising up and floating toward the path at an alarming speed.

No one asked questions. They ran after Fife. Lottie knew what he feared, for she feared it, too. But it couldn't be. That couldn't possibly have happened.

They ran hard down the path, following the white dirt offshoot that led to the red apple tree. One of the Wisp Guard was always posted in this clearing, but there was no guard tonight. Lottie had known there wouldn't be. That guard had been the fourth silhouette.

"Sweet Oberon," whispered Fife.

At his feet, cast in ghostly lantern light, were the splintered remains of the silver-boughed tree.

CHAPTER SIX

Northward

THEY RAN for the glass pergola, even though Lottie knew running did no real good. The wisp guard Iolanthe had sent would no doubt reach the Royal Bower before them and tell the Seamstress and Tailor the terrible news.

Oliver headed in the opposite direction, toward Mr. Wilfer's cottage.

"Adelaide," he said, breathless. "I have to tell Father, and we've got to get Adelaide."

Lottie, Fife, and Eliot kept heading toward the distant, bluish light of the Great Lantern. Once they'd reached the pergola's entrance, they ran down the long hall toward the Royal Bower, Eliot slipping every so often on the cold glass floor and Lottie righting him each time. They found the doors to the bower flung open. The place was abustle with movement and shouts, and so many wisps were floating in so many directions, Lottie ducked a few times out of instinct. Silvia and Lyre were floating low at the willow tree's base. Standing opposite them were both Dorian Ingle and a sweaty, bug-eyed wisp who was talking frantically and, every so often, hiccuping between syllables.

". . . hewn down the silver-boughed tree," he was saying. "Came from nowhere. Used dust, I think. Took my sword. Cut me off. Didn't have the chance to fight. Couldn't raise the alarm. I didn't think they'd *cut it down*."

The words slapped Lottie hard, like a physical blow. She was forced to acknowledge what she'd been trying so hard not to: the silver-boughed tree had been hacked to pieces and was now an unusable heap of bark and fallen red apples. Eliot could no longer reach Mr. Walsch. Eliot and Lottie couldn't go home. Not that way.

"Children!"

Silvia had finally noticed them. She waved for the jabbering wisp to be quiet.

"We saw some of what happened," said Fife, panting. "Or, well, *heard* it, more like. What I'd like to know is who in Puck's name is this Iolanthe?"

Dorian's easy countenance was gone. He was scowling up at the willow tree as he said, "She's Starkling's new right-hand sprite."

"What was she doing here?" Lottie asked. "She's not allowed in Wisp Territory, is she? And it's not like you and the Southerlies are at war."

"We are now," the Tailor said darkly.

Silvia burst into an ear-piercing laugh. "Really, Lyre! We don't have enough healthy wisps for a skirmish, let alone war. Iolanthe knows we're powerless to fight back, as does Starkling. He ordered this destruction knowing full well that we cannot retaliate."

"But *why*?" demanded Lottie. "You haven't done anything to the Southerlies. You're plagued as it is. Why would he do something like this?"

The guard hiccuped. "I heard them whispering as they dragged me from the apple tree. They said Starkling's trying to build a *gorge*."

Lyre and Silvia both started at this.

"What?" said Lottie. "What's a gorge?"

"Nothing that concerns you little ones," said Silvia.

"You know what this means, Seamstress," said Dorian. His voice was urgent. "They're no longer safe here."

Silvia nodded. She turned to Lyre and said, "They must leave."

"Wait," said Eliot. "Who's 'they'?"

"Us," said Fife. "They can't protect us anymore, so we've got to evacuate."

"But," said Lottie, panic sweeping inside her, "but—but *Eliot*."

"The silver-boughed tree is gone, Fiske," said Dorian. "You can't go home that way."

"But we *promised* Mr. Walsch," Lottie said. "He'll be worried. He'll be so frantic. We can't just—"

"It's gone," Fife said softly. "You don't have a choice anymore."

"There is a silver-boughed tree in the Northerly Court," said Dorian. "I feel that bears mentioning."

Lottie turned to Eliot. "I'm so sorry," she said.

"Hey," said Eliot, forcing a smile. "We'll get home. If that means going north first, then we'll go north."

"CHARLOTTE GRACE FISKE!"

Lottie turned at the sound of her full name, yelled with enough force to knock a hat off a head.

Mr. Wilfer and Oliver had entered the Royal Bower, accompanied by a fuming Adelaide.

"What do you mean by sneaking off like that?" Adelaide yelled. "I was worried senseless about you when I woke, and then for Father to come barreling in with news of a tragedy, and I thought—I *thought*—"

Adelaide threw her arms around Lottie and burst into a sob. She choked out, "We're *friends*. Friends stick together. They go places together."

Lottie, startled as she was, put her arms around Adelaide. "I'm sorry," she said. "I thought you wouldn't want—"

"You didn't ask me. You didn't ask me if I wanted to come along!"

She cried into Lottie's shoulder, and though Lottie felt very bad about Adelaide's current emotional state, she was also a tiny bit pleased. Adelaide had the funniest ways of telling Lottie she cared about her.

While Adelaide sopped Lottie's shoulder with tears, Silvia brought Mr. Wilfer and Oliver up to date on the current state of affairs, the most pressing of which was Dorian's suggestion that they leave for the Northerly Court that very moment.

"Oh, but surely not," Adelaide said, letting Lottie loose. "We haven't had any time to prepare!"

"You mean," said Fife, "you haven't had time to brush your hair and pack your nicest dresses."

Adelaide shot Fife a murderous glare. "Some of us actually *care* about our appearances, you slovenly snippet."

"Thank Titania you do, sweet Ada. It's hard enough to look at you as is."

"Seamstress and Tailor," said Dorian. "Moritasgus. I'm formally requesting permission to lead the expedition north immediately, before any more Southerly soldiers infest this wood. Rebel Gem will provide far more protection than your yews can now afford."

"But it's nearly dawn!" Adelaide wailed. "We haven't even had a full day's sleep."

"No, my dear," said Mr. Wilfer, "Dorian is right. You must set out as soon as you can."

"What about Lottie and Eliot?" asked Oliver, anxiously yellow-eyed.

"They will find safety in the Northerly Court," said Dorian, "and access to our own silver-boughed tree, if that's what they desire."

Adelaide, now aware this was an argument she wouldn't win, gave a moan of exasperation. She sat on the ground, legs crossed in a surprisingly unrefined way, and though Lottie thought Adelaide looked a little ridiculous, she felt a lot like doing the very same thing.

"That settles it," said Silvia. "Off you go, to the North."

It was dawn by the time they set out. Wisp Territory had never been very bright, even in the daylight, so dense were the branches and leaves overhead. But now that the yews had lost their needlelike leaves, Lottie's face was kissed with far more sunlight than she'd seen in a long month. She was tired, and her legs were already weary from walking through the plagued part of the wood, past sickly wisps and putrid stenches and cries for help that tore at her heart. She was tired, but she gained strength from the light. She had almost forgotten what it was like to rise with the sun.

Lottie and the others had been allowed to return to the Clearing and pack their belongings, all under the watchful eyes of Cynbel and three of his guards. These guards, along with Silvia, Lyre, and Mr. Wilfer, now followed them to the edge of Wisp Territory and the start of Wandlebury Wood proper. Lottie had traveled through the wood once before, but that had been far off the main path in an attempt to avoid the Barghest and the Southerly Guard.

"We'll travel by foot for a day's time," said Dorian. "Then we'll take the River Lissome north. Provided we aren't tracked and provided the weather holds up, it won't be too daunting a journey."

"Don't worry," said Fife. "Ada will make it plenty daunting."

Adelaide didn't hear Fife; she was too busy crying in her father's arms. Oliver, too, stood by Mr. Wilfer, his eyes dull gray. Lottie turned away, leaving the Wilfers to their private goodbyes. She checked the contents of her satchel: a flashlight from home, clothes, a bag of sweet-so-sours, and, of course, her favorite green scarf. She couldn't shake the suspicion that she was forgetting something important. In a sudden panic, she checked her pocket. Her fingers grazed feathers. Trouble gave a sleepy chirp and turned over, out of reach.

No. She wasn't leaving anything important behind.

Except, of course, the silver-boughed tree.

Eliot hadn't cried or raised his voice or even mentioned the fact that his trip home had been brutally canceled by a group of ax-wielding Southerlies. Still, Lottie felt the loss deeply, and she knew Eliot did, too. Mr. Walsch would have no way of knowing where they were and why they hadn't arrived for Thanksgiving supper. Lottie had searched on hand and knee for her copper box in the ruins of the apple tree, but it, too, was gone. Maybe Iolanthe and her guards had taken it, thinking it was important. Maybe they'd thrown it into the wood and trampled it underfoot. Whatever the case, their remaining connection to Mr. Walsch was gone, and Lottie only knew that the sooner they got to the Northerly Court, the better.

"Ready?" she asked Eliot.

Eliot was checking the inside pocket of his jacket. There was a thick stack of papers threatening to burst the seams of the pocket's lining—all letters from Mr. Walsch that Eliot had received during his time in Limn. He patted the letters once, then closed and buttoned his jacket.

"Ready," he said.

Adelaide slipped out of her father's arms, looking miserable. "I still don't see why *we* have to leave."

"Because the Tailor hates you," Fife said, giving his uncle a pleasant wink.

Lyre didn't acknowledge the gesture. "Travel swiftly," he told Dorian. "No unnecessary stops."

"Fife, dearest," said Silvia, drawing her lips into a dramatic pinch. She knelt beside her son, arms outstretched. Fife backed out of reach.

"Yeah, yeah," he said. "You'll miss me ever so much. You'll weep salty tears into your pillow each night."

Silvia drew back. Her eyes welled with hurt, but she said nothing more.

"Stay together," said Mr. Wilfer, who was speaking to Oliver, but loud enough for all to hear. "Remember, under no circumstance should you split company."

Lottie cast a weak look at Mr. Wilfer. He seemed to understand.

"You will get home, Lottie," he said. "Your friendships can see you through anything. Don't forget that."

"Beg pardon," said Dorian, "but daylight's burning. Let's be on our way."

They entered Wandlebury Wood. Only Adelaide looked back, just once, to wave goodbye to Mr. Wilfer.

"Good riddance," said Fife. "I'm already walking lighter."

But Lottie was certain she had seen a tear clinging to the cheek Fife turned to the shadows of the wood.

They walked for hours. Since her first visit to Limn, Lottie had grown far quicker on her feet. That skill came in handy now. Dorian set a good pace, too—not nearly so fast as she was used to walking with Fife floating ahead. Today, Fife floated behind, the very last of the company. Lottie walked in step with Adelaide. Oliver and Eliot trailed Dorian, singing a song that Eliot had taught Oliver:

> *"What though on hamely fare we dine,*
> *Wear hoddin grey, and all that;*
> *Give fools their silks, and knaves their wine;*
> *A Man's a Man for all that:*
> *For all that, and all that,*
> *Their tinsel show, and all that;*
> *The honest man, though e'er so poor,*
> *Is king o' men for all that!"*

The singing carried on until someone yelled, "Saints and goblins! Would you two finish already?"

The boys stopped their singing and turned, wide-eyed, toward Fife.

"I've never heard anything so blasted obnoxious in my thirteen years, five months," Fife went on. "And anyway, we're supposed to be on the run from Southerlies. Shouldn't we be trying to stay inconspicuous? You'll back me up on this, won't you, Ingle?"

"It would probably be wise," said Dorian, "if you boys didn't sing."

"Well, what else are we supposed to do?" asked Eliot. "We've been walking for ages. We've got to do *something* to keep entertained."

"Then talk about the weather," said Fife. "Or sing something that makes sense."

"It's Scottish," Eliot said. "My father taught it to me. He lived in Glasgow for a while."

"Well, I don't like it," said Fife, "whatever the blazes *Scottish* is."

"It's Robert Burns," said Oliver in a coaxing voice. "I've read you plenty of his stuff, Fife. You really liked it."

"Maybe I was only pretending to like it because you wouldn't shut up about it."

Oliver's eyes turned an injured gray.

"What's the matter with you, Fife?" said Adelaide.

"He's not in a good mood," said Eliot. "Clearly."

"That's no reason for him to take it out on us," said Adelaide. "If you don't have anything nice to say, Fife, then—"

"Oh, *shut up*," said Fife, floating above their heads. "Come on, let's just keep walking. And no singing this time, if you please."

Dorian, who seemed relieved that the bickering had resolved itself without his intervention, resumed the lead.

"Children," he muttered to himself.

Lottie scowled at Dorian's back, though she was angrier still at Fife for giving them such a bad reputation. She wasn't sure why, but she wanted Dorian Ingle to think well of them. Just because they were young didn't mean they weren't smart. Lottie quickened her steps so that she was in stride with Dorian. "What's a gorge?" she asked.

Dorian raised a brow at Lottie but said nothing.

"That wisp guard said Starkling's trying to build a gorge. I know Silvia said it's none of our business, but if we're traveling all this way just to bring Starkling down, I think we've got a right to know what he's up to. So tell me: what's a gorge?"

Dorian arched his brow higher. After a moment's pause, he spoke.

"Gorges are illegal," he said. "They're dangerous and rare and highly volatile. That's why Silvia didn't want to discuss it."

"All right, but you still haven't told me what a gorge *is*."

Dorian scratched his jaw. He said, "In order to make a gorge, you have to hack off a silver bough from an apple tree—like I said, very illegal. But as you might imagine, the silver of a silver bough is precious. Magical. If you siphon the silver out, you can use it to create a portal—a gorge in the ground that leads anywhere you'd like, anywhere at all. Unlike a full apple tree, which is used to travel between worlds, a gorge only has the capacity to travel *within* a world.

So, for example, you could create a gorge between your front door and the entrance to the Southerly Court—a convenient little portal, as it were. It's a fine idea, perhaps, but as it requires killing apple trees, which are rare enough as it is . . . well, you can understand the concerns."

"Why would Starkling need a gorge, though?" said Lottie. "He's king. Why can't he just use Piskie Dust to get where he wants to go?"

"That's the question, isn't it?" said Dorian.

Lottie frowned at him. "Yes, it is."

Dorian said nothing.

"It is the question," Lottie said, "and you know the answer. Only you won't tell me."

"I know *an* answer," Dorian replied. "Just a conjecture. A possibility. And I'm not going to share it with you, because I don't want you getting crazy ideas in your head when they might be completely groundless."

"But I want to—"

"No."

"But—"

"*No.*"

Dorian lengthened his strides until Lottie could no longer comfortably keep up with him. She had a terrible feeling that her attempt to make Dorian take her seriously had only worsened his opinion of her.

As they walked on, Lottie became aware that Oliver and Eliot were having a conversation about impressionist painters from the human world.

"Have you seen his sunflowers, though?" Eliot was saying. "I think you'd love them."

"He's handsome, don't you think?" Adelaide whispered to Lottie.

"Who?" asked Lottie. "*Fife?*"

"What? No, you ninny. I mean Dorian. He cuts quite the rustic figure, doesn't he?"

Lottie stared at the back of Dorian's dark-haired head. She noted his tall stature, his exceptional posture, and the broadsword that hung in a bronze scabbard at his side. Dorian was, Lottie supposed, very athletic-looking. His face wasn't bad, either, though Lottie didn't very much like the nose piercings. Still, she wouldn't call him *handsome*.

Then again, Adelaide had once told Lottie she thought Eliot was handsome, which was even more ridiculous. Eliot was just *Eliot*.

"I guess he looks all right," Lottie said. "But Dorian's a Northerly. I wouldn't think you'd like him."

"He's not a *proper* Northerly," said Adelaide. "He's on their side, but he's from good Southerly stock. You won't find a more thoroughly Southerly name than Ingle."

"If you say so," said Lottie.

She was no longer thinking of Dorian, but of his father, Mr. Ingle. She'd heard just recently from Mr. Wilfer that Mr. Ingle had moved from New Albion to a town called Gray Gully, after King Starkling had put a warrant out for his arrest. Not only had Mr. Ingle harbored fugitives, he was one of Mr. Wilfer's good friends, and his son had turned out to be a traitor to the Southerly Court. Gray Gully, Mr. Wilfer told Lottie, was in Northerly territory, and Mr. Ingle would be safe there. Lottie still worried. She hated to think that the kindly innkeeper was in trouble for something she'd had a hand in.

Lottie glanced back and found that Fife was trailing far behind them, arms crossed, indulging himself in a sulk.

"What's the matter with him?" Lottie asked Adelaide. "He told me he was glad to be leaving Wisp Territory."

"How should I know?" Adelaide said, and then tacked on a long-suffering sigh. "But since you bring it up, I think he's a tad jealous."

This wasn't the answer Lottie had expected. "Jealous? Of what?"

Adelaide raised her brows at Lottie, as though to say, *Don't you already know?* Then she pointed at Eliot.

"*What?*" The idea was so silly that Lottie laughed. "That's impossible."

"What's impossible about it? Just because you're friends with two people doesn't mean they'll be friends with each other. And haven't you noticed," Adelaide added, lowering her voice, "Oliver's been spending much more time with Eliot than Fife these days?"

"That's just because Fife's been busy apprenticing for your father."

"Or it's because Ollie's got much more in common with Eliot than with Fife. Think about it. All they ever talk about is poets and paintings. That's never been Fife's interest. He only talked about subjects like that because it made Oliver happy."

The more Lottie thought this over, the more she realized Adelaide was right. Maybe, she allowed, not all her friends would be the best of friends. But they couldn't be *enemies*. Fife couldn't possibly be jealous of Eliot.

She cast a worried glance at Fife, who caught it and slackened his sulking face. He tipped the smallest of smiles at Lottie.

Fife couldn't be *that* jealous.

Surely not.

"Here!" called Dorian. "We'll stop here to eat."

They settled around a fallen oak tree. Oliver and Eliot unpacked the canvas bags they'd been carrying for the group, each filled with nuts, fruits, and wafercomb. They used the oak trunk as their table. Fife spoke to no one, only munched away on handful after handful of hazelnuts.

"If we keep up our pace," said Dorian, "the river will have wound back to our path by nightfall. We'll board a boat at Dewhurst Dock. I've already sent my genga ahead to make arrangements."

"But we're still in Southerly territory," Lottie said. "Do you think Starkling could have spies posted at the dock?"

"Starkling has spies everywhere," said Dorian. "But docks are different from towns and courts. There are laws and loyalties there that no royal can control. Sailors are governed by the rules of the water, and their only loyalty lies with their crew."

Oliver's eyes turned deep blue as he quoted, "Save I take my part of danger on the roaring sea, a devil rises in my heart, far worse than any death to me."

"Well, okay," said Eliot. "But if that's the case, how can you trust any of those sailors?"

"You're asking the wrong question," said Dorian, breaking a piece of wafercomb. "You *can't* trust anyone, not on the road north. You can only ask whose betrayal will cost you the least."

"I don't like the sound of that," said Adelaide. "Traveling is foul business."

"So is skinning a hare," said Dorian, "but the end result is mighty fine."

"No, it isn't," said Adelaide. "It's disgusting. I don't know how your kind can stand it."

"Forgive me, Mistress Wilfer. I forgot that my carnivorous nature is so offensive to your delicate Southerly sensibilities."

"It's not that hard to remember," said Adelaide, "unless you're dense."

Lottie smiled into her flask of water. She found it funny that, however handsome Adelaide might have found Dorian Ingle, she didn't hold back her usual criticisms.

"Are Northerlies really all that different from Southerlies?" asked Eliot. "They aren't from what I can tell, aside from the meat-eating thing. And, you know, the tattoos."

"We're completely different," said Adelaide, with vehemence.

"He's just curious," said Lottie, defensive. She remembered a not-too-distant time when she hadn't even known what "Northerly" and "Southerly" meant.

"They have different values, the Southerlies and Northerlies," said Oliver. "It's not so much a thing you can put into words."

"Sure it is," said Fife, speaking for the first time since he'd fallen into his sulk. "Southerlies are rich and like the opera. Northerlies are poor and like rolling around in the dirt."

Dorian squinted.

"I'd agree with that assessment, actually," said Adelaide.

"D'you hear that, Eliot?" asked Oliver, eyes a merry blue. "You've witnessed a great phenomenon just now: Fife and Adelaide have agreed on something."

Eliot laughed, and as he did so, Fife's face clouded over. The start of what seemed like a good mood had caved back into a pout. Lottie's stomach sank. Maybe Adelaide had been right about the jealousy thing.

"Hold on, I hear something," said Adelaide. She waved for the others to be still. "Something close, in the wood. An animal."

"It's been tracking us since dawn," said Dorian, unfazed. "Haven't you caught wind of its footfall before now?"

"I—I—no, I haven't," said Adelaide. "And if *you* have, why didn't you say something?"

"I didn't want to send you into more hysterics," said Dorian.

"There!" said Eliot, pointing into the thick of the wood. "I saw something move."

Dorian rose, drawing his sword from its scabbard. Lottie heard it then: a low snarl from the wood. Dorian strode in its direction, sword balanced neatly in his hand.

"Come on out!" he cried. "Show yourself."

The snarling grew louder. Glowing eyes appeared in the dark—two silver pinpricks.

"Wait!" Lottie cried, running toward Dorian. "Wait, *wait!*"

Still, Dorian kept his sword drawn. He threw out an arm to stop Lottie in her tracks.

"It's all right," Lottie said, breathless. "It's a Barghest."

A familiar black shape emerged from the wood. It growled at Dorian, but Lottie knew it meant no harm, same as she knew this was not just any Barghest—it was *her*

Barghest, the very one that had taken her to the Southerly Court and fought valiantly by her side in the Southerly Palace.

Even now, Dorian did not lower his sword.

"Who do you serve, Barghest?" he asked.

The creature stooped into a bow. "Rebel Gem," it said with a voice like metal dragged against metal. "Rebel Gem and the House of Fiske."

Dorian's shoulders relaxed. He sheathed his sword. The Barghest trotted forward, and Lottie fell to her knees by its side.

"It's *you*," she said. "I didn't think I'd see you again, Barghest."

The Barghest let out a wheezing sound and pressed the side of its face against Lottie's palm.

"My fellow Barghest were pleased," it said, "to hear of the return of the Heir of Fiske. I have been sent as a representative to provide protection."

Lottie looked up at Dorian. "Didn't you know?" she asked. "You've met the Barghest before. Why did you draw your sword?"

"You can't be too careful while on the road," said Dorian. "Barghest knows that as well as I do."

Here, the Barghest inclined its head, and Dorian returned the gesture—a sign, it seemed, of mutual respect.

"Splinters roam these parts," said the Barghest.

"They delight in confusing travelers," added Dorian. "Cast their voices, shift the shadows, play tricks on one's senses."

"Oh, please don't talk about them," said Adelaide, shuddering. "It's bad enough we're without hot water and the common niceties of life. The last thing I want to be thinking about is criminals."

"Come on, Eliot," said Lottie, waving him over. "Meet Barghest."

Eliot joined them, grinning. "It's an honor," he said to the Barghest. "Lottie's told me all about you."

"Hello, Barghest," said Oliver, though he made no effort to come closer. His eyes were yellow, and Lottie wondered if he was a little frightened. She didn't blame him; she'd once been terrified of the creature.

"Well, Fife," said Adelaide, "aren't you happy to see a Barghest?"

Fife shushed Adelaide, waving his hand frantically. He looked unsure of himself.

"You remember Fife, don't you?" Lottie asked the Barghest.

It tilted its head in the affirmative.

"Um. Um, yeah. That's me." Fife bowed before the Barghest with utmost reverence. "It's very good to, erm, see you again. Sir. Um. Ma'am?"

But the Barghest was no longer paying attention to Fife.

"News has reached us from the South," it said to Dorian. "Tales brought on the wings of gengas. I came to Wisp Territory to warn you. Then I caught your scent. You've left early, Ingle."

"We know about the gorge Starkling's attempting to build," said Dorian, "if that's what you mean. We've seen evidence firsthand: Iolanthe has cut down the wisps' silver-boughed tree. It was her ax that put the speed in our steps."

The Barghest growled. "Then it is true."

Dorian nodded, then squinted into the sun. "It's past noon," he said. "We need to be moving on."

"So soon?" asked Eliot, and as he did, he broke into a hacking cough. Lottie wrapped an arm about his shoulder

"Can't we rest just a little more?" she asked Dorian. "Eliot's human. He's not used to walking so much, and so fast."

Dorian shook his head. "Sorry, Fiske. The sailors will be expecting us at dusk, and they wait for no passenger."

"I suppose that's in their high and mighty sailor rulebook," muttered Fife, shouldering his satchel.

Adelaide picked up two packs—hers and Eliot's.

"Oh no," said Eliot. "You don't have to—"

"Sorry," said Adelaide, "but I don't waste time arguing after I've made up my mind. Anyway, someone once taught me that you mustn't be too proud to let someone else carry your pack every so often."

"It's no use arguing with her, Eliot," Lottie said cheerfully. "Adelaide's as stubborn as they come."

She and Adelaide exchanged the briefest of smiles.

They set out again on the path. From behind, Lottie heard Fife whisper, "Walking with a real, live Barghest. Someone pinch me, please."

CHAPTER SEVEN

Dewhurst Dock

THEY HADN'T been walking long when the sunlight disappeared and a drop of water splatted on Lottie's nose.

"I don't suppose anyone brought an umbrella?" she asked.

No one had. The raindrops picked up, and soon even the thick branches overhead could not keep the deluge off of their backs. Minutes into the rainstorm, everyone was sopped through. The path became sludgy, and Eliot tripped more often, but Dorian pressed on.

Adelaide took it the worst, snuffling and occasionally saying things like, "If it just weren't so *cold*."

It *was* very cold, and by the time the rain let up, they were all in various states of shivering and sneezing. Their one stroke of luck was that the sun came out soon after and slowly, very slowly, warmed them back up. When its light disappeared again, this time it was due to the coming of night.

"We're close to the Lissome," Adelaide said to Lottie. "I can hear it."

"Hurry up!" Dorian called. "Our ship won't wait on us."

So they hurried up, all the way to a muddy clearing and, beyond it, a large dock. The River Lissome coursed ahead, far wider and swifter than it was in Wisp Territory. They saw several figures mingling along the dock—all men, by the sounds of their voices. As they drew nearer to the flickering dock lanterns, a tall, young man waved to them.

"Ingle!" he shouted, jumping down from a wooden post. "Ingle, my dear fellow, we'd nearly despaired of you showing your sorry face."

Another sailor jogged up to the first one's side. They were both dressed in hide pants and loose shirts, and were boot-clad. They looked to be Dorian's age but they were, Lottie thought, far handsomer. She was glad their attention was fixed on Dorian, not her, or else she felt sure she would've turned red.

"Nash," said Dorian, heartily shaking the hand of a bearded, blond-haired sprite with bright yellow eyes. Then, turning to the other, who had a mound of black curls atop his head, "Reeve. You're a blessed sight, the both of you."

"Was afraid those white-veined scum had cast a spell on you," said the one called Nash. "Or worse yet, the Seamstress had turned you into her personal slave."

"Ha ha," said Fife, his face sour. "You didn't tell us what jokers these sailors are, Dorian."

Nash looked up at Fife, who was floating above his eye level. "Brought one along as a souvenir, did you? How *precious*, Ingle."

"He's not just a wisp," Dorian said warningly. "He's a Dulcet."

"What?" said Reeve, grinning. "*This* is the bastard child?" He grabbed Fife by his right arm, turned his wrist over, and smirked. "Well, I'll be. Looks like a wisp, yet marked like a Northerly. Do wonders never cease."

"Tell us, Dulcet," said Nash, "where did your father run off to after marking you? To the next lass over in Thistlebram?"

"Leave him alone!"

Startled, Reeve let Fife's arm loose. The sailors turned toward Oliver, who stood before them, hands clenched, eyes red.

"Let him be," Oliver said.

Nash pointed at Oliver's eyes. "You. I've heard of you. You're Wilfer's son. The one with a lethal touch. Is it true what they say? Did you really kill a dozen Southerly guards with your bare hands?"

Oliver's eyes turned from red to black. He paled, stammered, said nothing.

"Don't you have any manners?" Lottie demanded, glowering at the sailors. "We haven't even been introduced, and you've already insulted two of my friends." She turned to Dorian. "I won't go anywhere with them if they're going to be like *that*."

Dorian sighed and rubbed his forehead.

"Come on, boys," he said to Nash and Reeve. "Play nice. You shouldn't upset the girls by talking so."

"Upset the *girls*?" Adelaide said, a near shriek. "This has nothing to do with us being girls. It's the boys they're upsetting. It's a matter of common decency. Not that I'd expect much from two Northerlies."

Nash laughed. "What a crew you've brought with you, Dorian. This should be a fun trip."

"Don't worry your pretty face into a pout," Reeve said to Lottie in a babying way. "We don't bite."

"I do," rumbled a voice.

Reeve and Nash jumped as the Barghest crept into the dock light, teeth bared.

"Do you mock the Heir of Fiske?" growled the Barghest. "Do you dare talk down to her, a child of the upper houses?"

"Titania's sake," said Reeve, stumbling back. "You didn't say there would be a Barghest in your company, Ingle."

The Barghest snarled, scraping a paw toward the cowering sailors.

"It's okay, Barghest," said Lottie, setting her hand on his mane.

The Barghest nodded and hid its fangs. Still, Lottie could feel rumbling vibrations under her fingertips.

"The Barghest has offered us its protection," said Dorian. "I trust that won't be a problem."

Nash and Reeve exchanged a look.

"We don't carry *animals* on our ships," said Nash.

"Even if we did," said Reeve, "a creature like that is much too heavy. It'd throw the balance off entirely."

"You're just scared of him!" said Eliot. "That's not fair."

"It's our boat," said Reeve, "so it's our rules."

"Heir of Fiske," said the Barghest, nudging its nose against her elbow, "I do not trust these sailors. I do not think you should travel with them."

Lottie frowned. "But Dorian arranged it."

The Barghest shook its head once, in a jolting way. "There is a foul smell about them. I do not think it safe to be in their company. You can travel north by land just as well."

"But not nearly as quickly," said Dorian. "Look here, Barghest, I'm sorry these fellows have offended you, but—"

"It is not a matter of pride," snarled the Barghest, "but of protection for the Heir of Fiske."

Lottie felt all eyes turn to her. She toed the splintered wood of the dock, uncomfortable. The Barghest's warning made her uneasy. Why did everyone think she needed protection?

She looked at Eliot. He was already struggling so much to keep up with them by foot. And though Lottie didn't like Nash and Reeve, Dorian had vouched for them. Maybe, like Dorian had said, the Barghest was just suffering from hurt pride. Even if Lottie didn't follow its advice, it couldn't hold that against her. It was bound by an oath to obey her, after all.

"I'll be fine," she said at last. "This is the quickest route. It's easiest for all of us."

The Barghest's gaze darkened. "I do not think—"

"Barghest, honestly!" Lottie cried. "I can take care of myself, all right? I'm not totally helpless!"

The Barghest's chest rumbled, but it lowered its head in concession.

"Very well," it said.

Lottie sighed. She placed a hand on the Barghest's head—a silent apology for losing her temper.

"You sure you'll be all right traveling by land?" she asked.

"I have no need to worry for my safety," growled the Barghest. "But you, Ingle. You've sworn to protect them. Do the job I cannot."

Dorian looked offended. "I always see through the job I've sworn to do. I won't start making a muck of things now."

The Barghest kept its glare on Dorian for so long that even Lottie began to feel uncomfortable. Then it turned from the company.

"I will stay as near the river as I can for the first leg of your journey," it said, "before the bank grows hazardous with cliffs and crags."

Before Lottie could thank it or even say goodbye, the Barghest had bounded into the wood and out of sight.

"Well, that sucks," said Eliot. "I liked the Barghest."

"Me too," Lottie said.

And though she didn't say so out loud, though she didn't want to admit it, she did feel less safe with the Barghest gone.

"Well!" said Nash. "Now that we've got that hairy problem sorted, we should be boarding ship."

It wasn't at all the kind of ship Lottie had been expecting—with unfurled sails and a gangplank and a gilded ship's wheel at its helm. It wasn't really a ship at all. A "glorified rowboat" was what Fife called it. There was no mast, only a wide hollowed-out space at the boat's middle. Elevated planks that ran across its ends looked like they could be used for sitting. The entire vessel was made of wood, and painted black.

Like the sign of the Northerly court, Lottie thought. *Like the black diamond.*

"Just wondering," said Eliot, "how exactly does this boat work?"

He pointed at the river, wide and rushing and far more powerful than Lottie had ever seen it before. The current was flowing southward, in the opposite direction they wanted to go.

"There's a reason certain sprites become sailors," said Oliver, looking the boat over with intrigued blue eyes. "They have keens apt for the job."

"That we have," said Reeve, climbing into the boat with practiced ease and offering his hand to Eliot. "No need to look so worried, boy. Take my hand. Steady on."

They boarded the boat, one after the other, and sat where Reeve directed them. Lottie, Eliot, and Adelaide took their seats on one end, Dorian, Oliver, and Fife on the other.

Reeve sat at the back of the boat, his hand on some sort of lever. Lottie didn't know exactly how boats worked, but she was fairly certain Reeve was in charge of something called the rudder, which steered the ship.

Nash was the last to board. With the grace of a cat, he leapt inside and took up a post on the end of the boat opposite Reeve.

"That's that," he said, untying a thick coil of rope that held the boat fast to the dock. "By Puck, it's good to be heading north again."

Now untethered from the dock, the boat began to speed southward, with the current.

Though not for long. Reeve was bent over the rudder. His eyes were closed and both arms were tensed, muscles straining hard under skin.

The boat stopped moving. It lurched, and Lottie grabbed hold of Eliot's shoulder to steady herself. Then, slowly but surely, the boat began floating northward, against the current.

"Very good," Nash called to Reeve, and then his eyes went white entirely, as though they'd rolled back into his head. Lottie bit down her shock as she watched Nash turn and peer into the coming dark.

"What's he doing?" Eliot asked Lottie.

She shook her head in wonderment, answerless.

Adelaide said, "He's the lookout. That's his keen: sight. Most likely, he can see for a full mile ahead of us, even in the dark."

"And Reeve?" Lottie asked.

"Can't you guess?" said Adelaide. "He's controlling the water with his touch. It's a rare gift. He must've had excellent sharpening."

"What're you all blabbing about?" Fife said, floating across the boat to where they sat. "You're not talking about me, are you?"

"No," said Adelaide. "Sit down, would you? It's not safe to hover around a moving boat."

"Tosh," said Fife. "I happen to be very well versed in the rules of floating around bodies of water, and I—"

Lottie didn't want to hear this new argument between Fife and Adelaide.

"I need to talk to Dorian," she announced.

She crossed to where Dorian sat, alone, studying the tree line.

"I don't like your friends," Lottie told him, not minding if the nearby Nash overheard.

Dorian smirked. "'Friend' is a strong word. The three of us sharpened together as boys, back in the Northerly Court, that's all."

"But," said Lottie, taking a seat beside him, "I thought you grew up with your father, in New Albion."

"I did," said Dorian, "for a time. Then he sent me north. He thought I'd get the best training there. Also, I was an asset to the Northerlies for one obvious reason."

Dorian held up his right wrist, showing the white circle branded there.

"That's why you became a spy?" Lottie asked.

"That, and because I could hear so well."

"Fife keeps telling Adelaide she'd make a good spy," said Lottie, "but she says she wants nothing to do with politics."

Dorian glanced at Adelaide, who was still embroiled in the fight with Fife.

"She's a smart girl," he said.

"Do you wish you hadn't, then?" asked Lottie, surprised. "Gotten involved in politics, I mean."

"I don't know anyone who was ever *happy* they got into politics. It's just a way of life for some. A Southerly in the Northerly Court—I *was* politics, incarnate."

"So why do you want to get me involved?" Lottie whispered, staring out at the water. She could just see the tops of their heads reflected below, in the Lissome's ever-changing waters.

"That's Rebel Gem's doing," said Dorian. "And the Tailor's. I'm just an ambassador."

"Do you miss being a spy?"

Dorian was quiet for a long moment. Then he said, "I do. I don't particularly like being in the North. It's painful for me. Though I don't know why I'm telling you this. You wouldn't understand."

"Because you think I'm just a child," Lottie muttered.

Dorian looked surprised. "No. Not at all. I'm just not sure *anyone* would understand."

"What're you griping about back there, Ingle?" called Nash.

"Just engaged in a scintillating conversation with the Heir of Fiske!" he said, throwing Lottie a wink.

Nash turned, eyes rolled back to their normal state. "The Heir of Fiske," he said, his vowels thick. Lottie couldn't tell if he was making fun of her, but the way he stared her down made her uncomfortable.

"I wish everyone would stop calling me that," she said. "It's not like you go around calling people the Heir of Wilfer or the Heir of Ingle."

"You're not at all how I imagined you'd be," Nash said. "All those grand statues of Queen Mab—they don't look a smidgen like you."

"Yeah, well, I bet you don't look a whole lot like your ancestors from a thousand years ago," Lottie said.

"Actually," said Nash, "I've been told I look frightfully like my great-grandfather Coriander."

"So I don't look like Queen Mab," said Lottie, irritated. "Sorry to disappoint everyone."

"You're not disappointing anyone." Lottie was startled by Oliver's soft voice. She hadn't been aware he was listening to their conversation.

"Eh," said Nash. "You're young. Maybe you'll grow into it."

That won't matter much, Lottie thought, *if I can't grow into my* keen. *And even if I do, it's not worth much to anyone.*

Mr. Wilfer's words still stung at her insides. She would never be able to heal the masses, he'd said. She had to develop a "deep empathetic connection"—whatever that even meant.

"A sprite living in the human world," said Nash. "What was that like? Is it true what they say? Is there really no magic there?"

"I don't know," said Lottie. "There's definitely not magic like there is here. But we've got a lot of other things you don't have: cars and televisions and the Internet and . . ." She trailed off, noting the blank looks that Nash and Dorian were giving her.

"I guess it's an all right place," she concluded. "My friend Eliot's father still lives there. That's why we're trying to get back."

"Doesn't *sound* nice," said Nash. "Not to mention, I heard humans killed off all your fairy kind."

Lottie's stomach turned. "Really?"

"So they say. Hundreds of years back, you human lot went squishing them left and right, driving them deeper into the forests. Not much incentive for sprites to go visiting the human world after that."

"No," said Lottie. "I guess not."

"Just as well," said Nash. "We have enough troubles of our own. Plenty of monsters clamoring to eat our flesh here in Limn without us root shooting to another world."

"Come on, Nash," said Dorian. "Now isn't the time for ghost stories. You'll scare the girl."

Lottie gave them a level look. "I don't scare easily."

"What's this?!" cried a voice, causing Lottie to jump.

Fife had floated over and was now crouched beside her.

"Don't *do* that," Lottie said, regaining her breath and balance.

"What?" said Fife. "Did I *scare* you?"

"Oi!" Reeve shouted from the back of the boat. "What's going on up there?"

"Ghost stories!" Fife called back.

"*Ghost stories?*" gasped Eliot. "I love ghost stories."

Fife's smile disappeared. "Of course you do." He rolled his eyes and slouched beside Dorian.

Eliot nodded eagerly. "Lottie and I told them to each other all the time, back at my place. Didn't we, Lottie?"

Lottie remembered. She and Eliot had spent many stormy nights staring out the skylight in his bedroom, telling tales of bloodstains that didn't wash out and strangled waifs who still haunted the streets of New Kemble. Lottie had told Dorian the truth: she really didn't scare easily. But Eliot had a special way of telling his stories that always had Lottie hiding under a blanket by the time it was all over.

"What sort of ghost stories?" asked Oliver.

"Well," said Nash, "the best ones are those about the River Lissome itself."

"Oh, let's *not*," said Adelaide. "I can't think of a more unpleasant way to pass the time."

"If you don't want to listen," said Fife, "just stop up your ears."

"I can't just *stop up my ears*!" shrieked Adelaide, with a wrath so sudden it startled even Dorian and Nash. "You're so *insensitive*!"

Lottie hadn't expected Adelaide to take kindly to Fife's comment (he *was* being insensitive), but even from Adelaide, the reaction was a bit much. Then Lottie caught sight of Fife's tongue peeking out from the side of his mouth.

"You haven't heard the worst of it, Miss Wilfer," said Reeve, grinning. "You Southerlies only tell the prettied-up versions of the stories. We Northerlies have kept them raw and right."

"I bet that down in Fairwind," said Nash, "they say the ghost of Rock Harbor mourns for her true love, not that she murdered him in his bed."

"Hmm," said Reeve. "Or that the Thistlebram witch feeds the local children cinnamon cake, not that she turns them *into* cake."

"Don't forget the splinters," said Nash. "Casting their voices in dark woods, pretending to be your loved ones. Then capturing you and gobbling you up whole."

"And what about Iolanthe?" said Reeve.

Lottie's eyes widened. "What about Iolanthe?"

"You should hear the tales," said Reeve. "They say she's a

splinter of the worst kind. The absolute worst. They say with a single touch, she can transform her skin into any shape in all of Limn."

"Just an old piskie tale, that," said Nash.

"No it isn't," said Reeve. "I've got soldier friends who swear up and down that they've seen strange shapes roaming the Northerly border—a little lost girl some days, or a mewling cat on others. It's Iolanthe, they say, spying for the Southerly King. Or mayhap just waiting around for a poor soul to cross her path so she can—"

"Stop it!" Adelaide cried. "I don't want to hear any of it."

"You heard her," said Oliver, red-eyed. "Both of you cut it out. We've had a long day . . . night . . . *whatever* it is, and the last thing Ada needs is—"

"Calm down, calm down," said Nash. "No need to get in a bramble tussle about it. We were only having a bit of fun."

"We can talk about something else," said Reeve, cheery. "Like what sort of creatures are swimming through the Lissome this time of year."

Lottie wasn't happy with Nash or Reeve, but her curiosity got the better of her.

"What creatures?" she asked.

Nash lowered his voice. "Terrible things lurk under the cold waters up north. Creatures that could swallow down a boat like ours whole. They call 'em ice crawlers. Saw one myself, when I was a boy. My own uncle died in a capsized boat, dragged under in a crawler's jaws."

"They come out in the dead of winter," said Reeve, "sniffing for sailor blood. You don't even hear 'em sloshing until it's too late and they've wrapped their hundred legs around your boat, and *snap!* The hull breaks like tinder."

"Ha!" said Fife. "Brilliant."

Eliot began to cough—stifled at first, then loud and uncontrolled.

"Stop it, all of you. That's quite enough!"

Lottie hadn't meant to scream the words.

She whipped around and found Fife smirking, his tongue touching the air. Heat boiled in her cheeks, but she spent her attention on Eliot first, rubbing his back until the coughs had subsided and he smiled, embarrassed.

"It just happens sometimes," he said. "Nothing to worry about."

Lottie clutched his hand. Though she didn't let on to Eliot what she was doing, she tried very hard to clear her mind, like Mr. Wilfer had taught her. She tried to focus, *focus* on making Eliot better, just like she had that night at the Barmy Badger, when she'd had her last bad spell, and healing heat had coursed through her arms and into Eliot, when—

"Lottie?" Eliot whispered.

Lottie opened her eyes.

"Are you okay?"

"Yes," Lottie said.

No, she thought.

She let go of Eliot's hand.

"I'm fine," he said. "It's just been a long day for everyone. No wonder we're all at each other's throats, right?"

"That's not the only reason," she said, eyeing Fife, who was now suspended in a careless hover at the back of the boat, removed from the others.

Lottie rose and, careful to keep a steady footing, crawled to where Fife floated.

"What's your problem?" she hissed up at him, arms folded tight. "I *know* what you're doing."

"Do you?"

Fife simpered, then slowly stuck his tongue out at Lottie.

"It's childish," she said. "It's not right, messing with people's words like that, stirring up their emotions."

Fife shrugged. "It's only wrong because you noticed it."

"No," said Lottie, "it's wrong because you shouldn't use your keen like that. Some people are trying to sharpen their keens for *good,* and you're throwing a—a keen tantrum."

Fife snickered. "Is that what you call it?"

"I bet it has worse names," Lottie said. "Maybe you're not much better than a splinter."

Fife went still. His hovering cut out entirely, and he landed in the boat with a soft thud.

"Don't call me that," he said, stumbling to his feet. "You don't know what that word really means."

"Sure I do," said Lottie. "You told me yourself: splinters are sprites who use their keens wrongly. That's what you're doing."

"Yeah, well, I can't always help it. I'm still sharpening. I've got less control over it than you think."

"You can keep your tongue in your mouth," Lottie said coldly. "I know you're mad at Eliot for some stupid reason, but that doesn't give you the right to mess with him."

"And just because you've got a crush on him doesn't mean you should treat him better than everyone else."

Lottie stared at Fife. He dropped his eyes. Then, for the very first time, Lottie saw his face turn red with embarrassment.

"I don't have a *crush* on Eliot," Lottie said, casting a frantic glance back at the others, who were luckily engaged in a new conversation. "He's my best friend."

"But you like him best," said Fife. "You only care about him. You were going to go back to your world without giving a flying flip about the rest of us. 'Let Fife and the others go to the Northerly Court. I'm going to trot back home with my *favorite* person, la dee dah!'"

"You said you weren't mad about that."

Fife licked his lips.

"Don't! Don't *do* that. Not on me."

"Everything all right?" called Oliver.

Lottie turned to find that, this time, the entire boat was looking at them. Even from behind her, Reeve was laughing lowly.

"Not the best place for a lovers' quarrel, little ones," he said.

"It's not a—a—" Lottie sputtered. "It's—it's nothing like that at all!"

She wanted to run, to stomp away. But neither of those options was available. Lottie could only keep her back to Fife as she crossed to the front of the boat. She still felt heat switching up her neck and pouring into her cheeks.

"Let me guess," said Adelaide. "Fife's being insufferable."

"Yes," Lottie said. "He most certainly is."

"There's only one cure for all this unhappiness," said Dorian. "It's time we ate."

CHAPTER EIGHT

Monsters in the Dark

THEIR SUPPER, or breakfast—no one could settle on what to call it—consisted of the same food they'd eaten earlier, on the road. Everyone was allotted equal portions of dried berries, hazelnuts, and cheese. Reeve and Nash contributed strips of salted rabbit, which Oliver and Adelaide refused—Oliver politely and Adelaide with more than a few choice words about the foulness of meat. After listening to her tirade, Eliot quietly put back his own portion of rabbit.

"You don't have to do that," Oliver told Eliot. "We don't eat it, but it won't offend us if you do. These extremes shall neither's office do."

"It offends *me*," said Adelaide.

Fife proceeded to chew his meat with noisy smacks and an open mouth.

After they'd finished their food, Nash supplied the company with a beverage called tallis. The liquid was thick and amber, and it smelled of metal. Lottie looked at it questioningly.

"I don't think we're old enough to be drinking this," said Oliver.

Fife downed the liquid in one go.

"Suit yourself," said Nash, "but it's the best protection you've got against the night. Keeps you warm for hours. Your choice if you'd like to fall asleep shivering."

Sleep. The mere thought of closing her eyes buoyed Lottie's heart. She was tired in an all-consuming way that wrapped around her bones and tugged her muscles downward, begging for rest. The scent of her drink didn't strike her as quite so pungent anymore. She sipped it down, and Nash's claims proved to be true: warmth swathed around her arms like a thick blanket. But no—that was a *real* blanket. Eliot had pulled it out of his pack and wrapped it around the both of them.

"Thanks," Lottie said, resting her head on his shoulder.

Then a sour, unwanted thought crept into her head: Fife was probably watching, and he probably thought this meant she *liked* Eliot. *Like*-liked him. But Lottie didn't care. She and Eliot had rested their heads on each other's shoulders since they were eight years old, and she wasn't about to stop now.

"Tallis makes you sleepy," she murmured into Eliot's shoulder.

Eliot yawned in reply.

"I'm turning off the lantern to save oil," said Dorian. "Let's try to get some shut-eye, if we can."

Moments later, the cozy glow of the lantern went out. Lottie's eyes adjusted to the dimmer light of the moon. Across from her, Adelaide was already curled fast asleep, head dropped to her knees. Dorian, too, sat with his head tilted back, eyes closed.

Lottie shut her eyes and concentrated on sounds—the creak of the boat, the wail of wind through the trees on the bank. The hum of conversation had faded into silence, and all was calm. The tallis still hung heavy in Lottie's mouth. The scent of late autumn—dead leaves and crisp water and burnt firewood—filled her senses. Minutes passed like this. Possibly hours. Lottie lost herself in the monotonous calm.

Then there was a scream.

Two bodies scuffling in the dark.

Angry shouts.

The boat heaved to one side, then the other. Lottie sat up, suddenly wide awake.

"Get him, Dorian! I can't—"

Shadows grappled before Lottie. She strained her eyes against the dark to make out the fighters: Dorian. Nash. Oliver.

Oliver's arms were wrapped about Nash's neck; he'd jumped on his back and was holding on tight. Dorian was facing Nash down, his sword drawn.

"Drop it," Dorian shouted. "Drop it, Nash, or so help me, I'll run you through."

That's when the moonlight burst from a cover of clouds and revealed a thin, metal blade. Nash was holding a knife.

There was more movement, more struggle, the sound of a hand slapping across skin. Nash released an anguished scream.

"Drop it!" ordered Dorian.

Nash fell to his knees. Something clattered to the base of the boat.

"Keep hold of him, Wilfer," said Dorian, kneeling to retrieve the dropped knife.

"I've got him," said another voice. Fife was floating behind Nash, holding a bundle of gauze. "C'mon, let's get him tied up."

There were more shadowy movements that Lottie could not make out. Dorian had somehow replaced Oliver and gripped Nash around the neck, placing the point of his knife to Nash's chin.

"Bind him, Dulcet."

Fife wrenched Nash's hands to his back and started tying knots with the gauze. Moments later, he wrapped the last of the material in a triple-knot and nodded, satisfied.

"That'll hold him," he said.

Dorian moved the knifepoint to the hollow of Nash's throat. "You're lucky I don't gut you here and now and feed you to the fishes, piece by piece."

Nash didn't reply. He was sobbing loudly, uncontrollably.

"You're sick, mate," said another voice—Reeve's. He hadn't moved—he couldn't, Lottie realized, or the boat would go careening—but Lottie could see the angered contortions of his face. "You're a disgrace!"

The boat filled with light. Adelaide had relit the lantern.

"What's happening?" she asked. "Would someone kindly explain what's going on?"

"Nash was going to kill her," said Oliver. "I saw him. He gave us the tallis to turn everyone drowsy. He was going to stab Lottie right here, in the dark, while we slept."

Oliver looked horrible. He sat with his head resting on one hand, his eyes a lifeless brown.

Stab her right here, in the dark.

Lottie felt nauseated. She gripped her stomach and tried to breathe in cold air, tried to tell herself that she was *not* dizzy.

Nash was still sobbing hard. He choked out words through the tears. "I didn't *want* to do it. I didn't want to murder some innocent girl, I swear! If you only knew what she'll do to me!"

"Iolanthe," said Dorian.

It wasn't a question, but Nash nodded jerkily all the same.

"Traitor," Reeve growled. "What're you waiting for, Dorian? He'd be long dead by now, under my watch. Slit his throat and throw him overboard. That's the sailors' code."

"I'm no traitor!" Nash said wildly. "If you *heard* the promises she made. If you just heard 'em, Reeve, you'd understand. She's got new ideas. Not Southerly ideas, *new* ideas for the whole lot of sprites."

"She's Southerly scum, you fool!" Reeve barked back. "That's no white circle branded to your skin, is it? And yet you serve the Southerly King's right-hand sprite? Liar! Hypocrite! Traitor!"

"Quiet, Reeve," said Dorian. "It does no good to tell him what he is. I'm only concerned with what information he has."

"I haven't got information, I *swear*."

"Forgive me if I don't believe you after you nearly murdered—" Here, Dorian broke off and turned to Lottie. "I say, Fiske, you all right?"

Lottie felt weak and sick, and she was sure she didn't look much better.

"I—I'm fine," she said. "He didn't hurt me."

"Well, he very well would've if it hadn't been for Oliver," said Fife, who sat hovering cross-legged across from Nash. "I'm with Reeve. I say we dump him into the Lissome."

"Well, Nash?" said Dorian. "Is that the kind of death you want? For there's no chance Iolanthe will have you back after this."

"I'll tell you whatever you want," blubbered Nash. "But I mean it: I know little. Hardly any of us know a thing. I only joined up because she was offering good pay, and my brother—"

"Spare us your excuses," said Dorian, pressing the knife's blade harder against his neck, drawing out a trickle of blood. "Tell us what you know."

Nash's whole body began to shudder.

"I can't *think*," he said. "It b-burns so b-b-bad."

Lottie wondered how she hadn't noticed before now. The splotches of color on Nash's skin were visible in the lamplight. There was a fierce red mark across his jaw, a green bruise on his neck, and two blue handprints across his collarbone. Oliver had hurt him badly.

"What's wrong with him?" Eliot whispered to Lottie.

"He's in a lot of pain," she said.

"You said Iolanthe gave the order," Dorian said to Nash. "Just to you?"

Nash shook his head. "It's Starkling who wants the Heir of Fiske dead. He put Iolanthe in charge of killing her, once and for all. Iolanthe's the one who sent out the assassins."

"Assassins?" Lottie said, her voice bending on the word.

Eliot squeezed her hand, but it did no good. Lottie couldn't feel anything properly.

At last, Nash faced Lottie. His yellow eyes were overflowing with tears. He really did look sorry, but the thought of that knife gleaming in the moonlight made Lottie's stomach turn anew.

"I didn't know the Heir of Fiske would be so young," he said. "Like the rest of them, I hardly believed you existed. It seemed such an impossible thing. So fantastical. It was something I only believed as a tyke, back when me and all the other orphan kids pretended *we* were Heirs of Fiske. Like we could give Barghest orders, tell folks what to do."

"You were an orphan?" said Lottie.

"Oh, don't listen to him," said Fife. "He's just trying to get you sympathetic so Dorian won't off him."

"But why would you pretend to be *me*?" Lottie asked Nash, ignoring Fife.

"Why wouldn't we?" said Nash. "Our village was crammed with a bunch of loons, still convinced a Fiske would show up and demolish the Southerly Court. But we kids at the orphanage had no idea who our parents were. For all I knew, the make-believe could've been true."

"Honestly," said Adelaide. "As though *you* could ever be a Fiske, with a face like *that*."

"No," Lottie said softly. "No, I understand what he's saying. Making up stories you want to be true. I understand that."

She studied Nash, scruffy and dirty-faced—a character she would never have dreamed of meeting back when she'd lived within the confines of Thirsby Square. It wasn't that she'd forgiven this sprite for trying to kill her just moments ago. It wasn't that she trusted him at all. But she *did* understand. She understood that even if Nash was a traitor and an assassin, he might not be so very different from her.

It happened then, with no warning.

Lottie lurched forward and cried out, clutching at her chest. She heard Eliot call her name, felt his hands on her back, but she fiercely shrugged him off.

"I can't breathe," she wheezed.

Her ribs felt like kindling set alight. A tightening sensation wound around her throat. She knew this pain. It was familiar, but she hadn't felt it in more than a month.

"Get her some water," Eliot said. "Give her space!"

Lottie shook her head.

"No," she said. "No, no. I don't need that. It's—"

She lunged for Nash and caught him by one of his bound hands. Startled, he tried to pull away, but Lottie only clung harder.

"No!" she said. "This is how it works."

She shut her eyes. She blocked out the blurred sights around her. She knew this feeling all too well, and she greeted it like she would an old acquaintance. The tightening sensation no longer felt chaotic and uncontrolled. It deepened and stilled, then bent to Lottie's will. This sensation, too, she recognized. She'd felt it once before, by Eliot's bedside in the Barmy Badger.

Lottie grabbed Nash's other hand and held it through Fife's gauze binding.

"Don't move," she said, but she felt so far away from her voice that she wasn't sure if it was a whisper or a shout.

The pain moved within her, from her chest up into her shoulders, then down through her arms and into her shaking hands. Then it cooled, seeping from her fingertips into Nash's skin. Lottie's eyes flew open. She looked hard at Nash and watched as, slowly, the bright splotches of color on his jaw and neck faded away to faint imprints. The colored bruises evaporated from his chest next, turning to shadows of what they'd been before.

Once she was sure she'd passed along everything from her hands to Nash's, Lottie broke their hold and slumped forward with a gasp.

"Lottie!"

Eliot was at her side.

"Are you okay?" he asked.

Lottie nodded. "I—I did it." She looked at Nash, who was still and expressionless. "I *did* it."

"It's true," Nash whispered. "Your keen. It's *true*."

"Watch her!" cried Adelaide. "Dorian, she looks faint."

Lottie sank, her back slamming against the boat's edge. She felt weak all over, like she'd just run for a day and a night. Her breathing still hadn't sorted out to a proper rhythm.

"Oberon, Lottie," said Fife. "What'd you go and do that for? He's the bad guy, remember?"

"Lay off her, Fife," said Adelaide. "Didn't you just see what she did?"

"It wasn't like I *meant* to," Lottie said, pressing her palms against her closed eyelids. "Not at first. It just—happened. I *felt* it, and I knew what I had to do."

When she looked up, she found Dorian giving her a wary look.

"And to think," he said, "those blasted wisps have been hoarding you this whole time."

Nash had begun to cry yet again. Reeve muttered something from the back of the boat about "an embarrassment to the Northerly way of life."

"I didn't want to kill her," Nash was saying. "I didn't know she was so nice a girl. I didn't *know*!"

"If you want to make up for it," said Dorian, "then tell us what you do know. Surely the pain isn't too much for you now."

Nash nodded hastily. "Iolanthe sent messengers into Wandlebury Wood. She offered a reward to any who would kill the Heir of Fiske." He looked at Lottie, and then away. "Far more money than I could ever earn on a sailor's pay. I had my little brother to think about. And I—"

"I'm not asking about your brother," said Dorian. "What do you know about *her*?"

"W-well, Iolanthe may be working for Starkling, but she has her own set of plans, a way of setting things right for all sprites. Many Southerlies aren't happy with Starkling. There are rumors he's not even a true sprite at all, but an impostor from another world. Many say that Iolanthe is better qualified for the throne."

"You're talking about a coup," Dorian said lowly. "But rumors that loud have surely reached Starkling himself."

"Only *rumors*," said Nash. "Iolanthe has proved nothing but faithful to the king. She used to be the captain of the Southerly Guard, you know. And in all those years, she obeyed his every order. Now Starkling wants the Heir of Fiske gone, so Iolanthe has taken it upon herself to see it done. And that's all I know, Ingle, I swear on a piskie's wings. It's all I know."

"Worthless," growled Reeve. "That's what you are."

"I *swear*," said Nash, his voice rising to a whine. "I swear it, Ingle! And you wouldn't gain a thing by cutting me up in front of these poor children, traumatizing 'em for life."

"I don't know what you're talking about," said Fife. "I'd be quite content to watch Dorian dice you up."

"Hush, Fife," said Oliver. "You don't mean that."

"You can stop your begging," Dorian told Nash. "I'm not going to touch you. I'm taking you to the Northerly Court with the rest of us. I'll let Rebel Gem decide what to do with a traitor."

"W-what?" Nash's shoulders shook. "No. *No*, you can't do that!"

"Then which is it?" sneered Reeve. "Death now, or later?"

"You don't understand," said Nash. "My little brother, he lives at court. It'd kill him to see me denounced that way—me, his only kin."

"Then what do you propose we do?" said Dorian. "What's a suitable punishment for a treacherous dog like you?"

Nash was very quiet. Then, meekly, he said, "Just let me off at the next dock?"

Reeve roared with laughter. "Now I've heard it all! I've ruddy heard it *all*."

Dorian shook his head at Nash, disgusted.

"You'll go north," he said. "And as far as I'm concerned, this is your position for the rest of our trip—with your own knife at your throat."

"But you need me," Nash said. "You've got no lookout without me."

"We'll manage," said Dorian. "Meantime, I'm not taking my eyes off you."

"Lottie?" whispered Eliot. "Everything all right?"

For the past minute, Lottie had been struggling to watch what was going on, to listen to Dorian and Nash's talk. But the heaviness that had claimed her eyelids earlier had returned, more forceful than ever. She felt drained all over from the healing she'd transferred to Nash.

"Eliot," she said, reaching for him. "I just need a little rest."

Eliot wrapped an arm around Lottie, then fit himself beside her, so close that their knees and shoulders were touching.

"I'm here," he said.

"That's good," said Lottie, her words breaking into a yawn. She tucked her head against Eliot's shoulder, and he rested his on her tangled hair.

She could hear Nash and Dorian still talking, but she no longer had the strength to translate the sounds into words. Still, her mind was whirring with thought.

She had done it. She had *healed* someone. Mr. Wilfer had told her it would take weeks, even months more before she was ready to use her keen. He'd said she still had to focus on clearing her mind. But Lottie's mind hadn't been anywhere close to clear when she'd healed Nash. She hadn't used Mr. Wilfer's training. She'd done things on her own terms.

Maybe Mr. Wilfer had been wrong. Maybe Lottie was more powerful than he thought. She had to be pretty valuable if Starkling had sent out a whole band of assassins to kill her. And though Lottie knew that thought should have made her tremble with fear, it instead filled her with excitement. She was important in this world. She *wasn't* useless. Maybe, she thought as she drifted to sleep, she'd just begun to discover how useful she really could be.

Lottie was cold, much colder than she'd been when she'd fallen asleep. Even under her periwinkle coat and the new light of sun, she felt goosebumps on her arms. She sat up, blinking against the sunlight, which shone off floating mounds of white in the passing water.

Ice.

They were sailing past *ice*.

The River Lissome rippled past them, spotted with chunks of white sludge. Lottie's breaths emerged as clouds. The air felt fresher in her lungs, but thinner, too. The thick evergreens that lined the riverbanks seemed particularly green. The blue of the sky seemed bluer. And cutting into that bright blue, above the tree line, were the peaks of mountains that had looked very distant before and now seemed close enough for Lottie to reach, pluck, and hold in her hand—an assortment of dark, snow-capped triangles. She wondered just how far they'd traveled during the night and realized they must have sailed not just farther north but far-ther *up*, into a higher altitude. Lottie felt around clumsily at the blanket on her shoulders and discovered that Eliot was no longer by her side.

"Lottie!"

Eliot waved to her from the other side of the boat. He was sitting between Adelaide and Oliver, eating a wedge of cheese. Fife sat in a hover, arms crossed, watching Nash, who had been moved to the middle of the boat. True to his word, Dorian still sat by the prisoner's side, knife in hand. At the back of the boat, Reeve steered them on. Lottie marveled at his endurance. She wondered if learning to stay awake for hours on end, all while using one's keen, was part of the strenuous sharpening Adelaide had mentioned.

"How're you feeling now?" asked Adelaide, joining Lottie where she sat. She offered her a clay tumbler of water and a handful of dried berries.

"Better, I think," Lottie said, taking the water and gulp-ing it down at once. "How long was I asleep?"

"It's nearly sunset," said Adelaide. "You slept the day through. Rather remarkable, given all the jostles and bumps we've had. Reeve says that's because of the ice in the water. And the boys have been talking so loud. I *told* them a hun-dred times to keep their voices down, but . . . *well*."

Adelaide looked over at Fife, who soon felt the gaze of both girls on him. He stuck his tongue out at them.

"At last," he said. "The Heir of Fiske graces us with consciousness."

Lottie rolled her eyes. She wasn't sure she'd forgiven Fife for his behavior earlier.

"It's not much longer," Adelaide said. "We should dock in a few hours, and then Dorian says it's just a short walk to the court gates."

Lottie nodded, but she'd grown distracted by the sight of Nash, who sat with his head turned down, arms still bound. The events of last night were crowding in on her memory, piecemeal.

He tried to kill me last night, Lottie thought. *I could've been* killed.

"We've all been talking about it," said Adelaide, dropping her voice to a whisper. "You healing Nash like that. Where did it come from, Lottie? Was that something Father taught you?"

Lottie shook her head. "No. I can't explain it entirely. I just know it had something to do with Nash. I think it's because I felt sorry for him."

Adelaide looked aghast. "You felt *sorry* for *him*?"

"Well, no, that's not exactly what I mean. I just . . . *felt* for him. And then the bad spell came on, so I did what I did before with Eliot: I took his hands, and I let go. I told you, it's hard to explain."

"It was certainly something to watch. And, well, not that I think that horrible man deserved any kind treatment, but"—Adelaide leaned in closer, dipping her voice even lower—"*thank you*. I know how wretched Oliver felt about those bruises, and he's much better off having seen them healed, you know?"

Lottie ventured a glance at Oliver, who sat talking to Eliot. They were both laughing, and Oliver's eyes were a happy violet—a color Lottie hadn't seen much of lately. She smiled at the sight. Then the boat heaved, and Lottie went tumbling forward.

"What was that?" she asked, righting herself.

"Just ice on the water," said Adelaide.

"Tougher to navigate than it looks," called Reeve.

Lottie looked out at the chunks of ice surrounding them.

"It looks *very* tough to navigate," she said.

The boat shuddered again, but this time Lottie had a better grip and didn't topple.

"Pretty soon, I guess we'll be able to ice-skate to the Northerly Court, huh?" she called to Reeve.

But Reeve was no longer smiling.

"That," he said, "wasn't ice."

"What do you mean?"

"Dorian!" shouted Reeve, ignoring her. "You're going to want to look at this."

Dorian bounded across the boat to where Reeve sat. Nash's knife was still in his hand. He squinted at the horizon, then shook his head.

"It's too early in the season," he said. "It can't possibly be."

"It can't," said Reeve, "but it is."

The boat heaved again, this time sending Eliot flying. He nearly landed in Oliver's lap.

"Steer right," Dorian said, his voice lifting to a shout. "Right!"

"If I veer much farther, I'll run us straight into—"

The boat shuddered once more.

"What can we do to help?" Lottie shouted to Dorian.

"Stay put, and stay silent! Reeve, are you asleep at the rudder?"

"Doing the best I can!" Reeve shouted.

"Whoo, we're going to die," Fife said chipperly. "How'll it be, do you think? Drowning, or the jaws of whatever river monster is boxing us in?"

"Not now, Fife!" snapped Adelaide.

"Aren't you scared?" Eliot asked him.

"Witless," said Fife, grinning.

"You've something wrong with your head," said Adelaide.

"Who of us can swim?" Fife asked. "I know Ollie can, and—well, Ada, have you ever touched a body of water?"

"For your information, I'm a fabulous swimmer, thanks very much."

"I know how," said Lottie, "but Eliot doesn't."

"Right," said Fife. "Well, look, if it comes to it, I can float us out one at a time, and—"

"Brace yourself!" Nash shouted. "It's coming on fast!"

A hard jolt knocked Reeve from the rudder. The boat wavered for a brief moment, motionless on the water. Then they sped backward, fast, into the current.

Reeve didn't try to regain control of the rudder. He reached into his vest pocket and pulled out a rust-colored robin. He put his lips close to the genga's head, whispering something. The bird twittered in reply and then flew to the bank and into the wood, out of sight.

Of course, Lottie realized. Reeve was sending out his genga to alert someone that they were in danger. Lottie shoved her hand into her own coat pocket. It was empty. Panicked, she checked the other one, though she knew that she only ever stored Trouble in her right pocket, not her left. Her heart pattered. Trouble wasn't there. When had he left her? Where could he possibly be at a moment like this?

Lottie's thoughts came to a splintering stop when a sound, low and loud, blasted into the air. She couldn't identify it. It was like nothing she'd heard before. It was so deep and overwhelming that it felt like the sound was in the water and in the trees alike, spinning itself around the boat like a physical *thing*. Just when Lottie thought she could take no more of it, the sound ceased. Then, ahead of the boat, the water broke apart in a great heave, sending waves crashing toward them. Lottie's senses were hit hard with *cold* and *wet*. She was suddenly dripping, and the base of the boat was filled ankle-high with water.

"Hold it off, Reeve!" shouted Dorian.

Reeve was leaning far over the boat's edge, hands plunged in the icy water. He was forming waves, it seemed, but they were small and choppy, not like the massive ones that had crashed over the boat. Those bigger waves had come from something else entirely, something that now towered high above the boat.

It was a monster. Lottie couldn't think of a better word for the massive creature that had emerged from the river. Its body stood as high and wide as a three-story building, broken into thick, fleshy segments, from which poked row after row of spindly legs. Its skin was slick and white. Two large red eyes protruded from the top of its body, which was crowned by a set of short antennae. The monster's mouth was open, baring a row of black, jagged teeth.

Lottie thought of the ghost stories Reeve and Nash had told in the dark. One of them hadn't been just a story.

"It's an ice crawler," Oliver whispered.

The monster's mouth opened wider, and that low sound filled the air again. From where Lottie was crouched, the ice crawler's throat looked infinite.

Reeve was still at the boat's edge, using his hands to whip up waves from the river water, even as the boat sped backward, putting distance between them and the ice crawler. The waves spiked like jagged mountaintops and shot in front of the boat, growing ever higher. Reeve was trying to form a wall between them and the monster.

But it won't do any good, thought Lottie. *That ice crawler is far more solid than a wall of water.*

"It isn't going to hold!" Reeve yelled.

"The boat's going to capsize!" Dorian called to the others. "We've got to get to shore!"

Fife was already hovering above the water's surface.

"Take Eliot first," Lottie said. "*Please.*"

Fife nodded doggedly. "But I'll come back for the rest of you," he said. "I'll take him to shore and come back for you all, I promise. Just hang in there!"

Fife swung his arms around Eliot's middle and lifted him into the air.

"No!" screamed Eliot. "Lottie!"

Lottie's heart stammered, but she said nothing, only watched as Fife and Eliot disappeared into the growing shadows of twilight, through the spray of water on the Lissome.

"Nash," said Oliver, turning to Lottie. "We should loose his bonds."

"*What?*" shrieked Adelaide.

"We're going under," Oliver said. "He at least deserves a chance to fight for it!"

But Lottie didn't need Oliver's reasons. Whatever Nash had done earlier, even Lottie didn't wish drowning on him. She stumbled to where he sat and began struggling against his gauze binding.

"Please," Nash whimpered. "Please help me."

"I will," said Lottie, "but you've got to hold still."

It took several seconds' worth of squinting and tugging, but she found the first of the knots and set about undoing it. The boat juddered. Reeve and Dorian continued to exchange frantic yells. Lottie didn't look up. Setting sights on that ice crawler would do nothing for her concentration.

She loosened the first knot, then the next, and the third. The gauze came free in her hands, and Lottie threw the last of it into the wind. She found her gaze meeting Dorian's, and she saw something there she had not expected: an apology.

"It's all right," Lottie said, not at all sure that Dorian could hear her. "You did what you could."

The current was dragging them at a disorienting speed, and for the moment it had put some distance between them and the monster. Meantime, Reeve's wall of water had grown so high that all Lottie could see over its crest were the stubby antennae of the ice crawler.

At last, the creature had become aware of its escaping prey. It tilted forward and broke through Reeve's wall, shattering it to watery pieces and plunging back into the Lissome. Reeve hung over the boat's side, spent from effort. For a terrifying moment, the monster was nowhere to be seen.

Then the ice crawler burst from the river once more, this time just a foot from the boat's edge. A fresh shock of icy water poured down on them, soaking Lottie's face and forcing her eyes shut. She wiped the water away, freeing her vision in time to see Dorian leap before the ice crawler, sword in hand.

The monster bellowed its air-rippling cry. Dorian lunged forward and drove the blade into the monster's flesh. There was a horrendous *squelch*. Dorian drew the sword out and plunged it again and again. The cries of the ice crawler grew louder, but Lottie didn't know if Dorian's fighting was doing any good; the ice crawler was so big and Dorian's incisions so small. Reeve still hung slumped by the boat's edge, and Lottie began to wonder if he was even conscious. And Nash . . . Nash was nowhere to be seen.

Hurry up, Fife, she thought.

Why didn't we escape to the bank earlier? she thought.

But it was too late for thoughts like those.

Lottie looked toward the tree-crowded riverbank, but she could see no sign of Eliot or Fife. All was turning black in the onrush of coming night.

Then another thought came to Lottie, more horrible than all the rest:

What if the ice crawler could move in water and *on land?*

Water swept over the boat once more. It was up to Lottie's shins, and she realized with horror that the boat had reached its limit. They were sinking—low and low and lower still.

The ice crawler bent its body toward them, its segments folding in on themselves. Several pairs of legs grabbed hold of the boat as though it were little more than a flimsy match-box. The legs clenched, and the wood cracked, and Dorian gave a hoarse shout as he once more ripped his sword across the ice crawler's flesh.

The boat tipped forward into the water. The ice crawler was bringing them down, and Fife hadn't returned from the bank, and Lottie saw now that there was only one thing left to do.

"Come on!" she screamed to the others. "We've got to jump for it!"

She didn't know if they'd heard her. She'd barely heard herself over the ice crawler's bellowing. Lottie looked to the bank. She thought she could see the dim outline of something hovering above the water, but she couldn't be sure. She jumped.

CHAPTER NINE

Blood and Barghest

LOTTIE FISKE was a girl well acquainted with pain. She had fallen out of trees and crashed her bike more than once and been plagued her whole life by bad spells. But no difficulty that Lottie had experienced before now could quite prepare her for the blinding, howling cold that burst into every particle of her body as she plunged into the River Lissome.

When her head came to the surface, all was havoc and a clamor of sounds. The river's current whipped at her legs, dragging them back under the water and, with them, Lottie's head. Her hands and feet had gone numb. She took a frantic gulp of air before she was pulled down. Her coat was heavy, so heavy, and her boots felt like they were made of metal, and why, thought Lottie, did she not think to take them off beforehand?

In the midst of the confusion, she understood with sudden clarity that she might not resurface. The current was too strong to fight. And where was Fife? And what was happening to the others? Then those thoughts scattered to make room for the overwhelming realization that pressure, unbearable pressure, was pushing into her chest, and she could give it no relief—that this pressure would build and build until it burst, and then her thoughts would be no more.

Then, suddenly, relief came. Something wrapped around Lottie's shoulders, and she was no longer being dragged sideways but upward, until she broke from the water into bracing cold air. She breathed deeply, choked in the process, tried to breathe again.

"Hang on," said a voice she knew. "Just hang on!"

Lottie tried to answer, but words coated her throat like thick paste and refused to come out. She was shivering violently, and the arms around her fumbled twice to keep her aloft. Then her back hit solid ground. The world stopped moving. The sounds of rushing water and the ice crawler's bellow weren't so deafening. She thought her eyes were open, but all she could see was blackness.

"Lottie? Lottie, can you hear me? Don't stop listening to my voice, okay? We'll get you warm. It'll be all right. Spool, would you hurry up already?"

A bird squawked. Then came a delicate clinking sound.

"Just *hold on*, Lottie," the voice said again. "Eliot, she's got to drink this. All of it. Watch her closely. I'll be back."

Something pressed against Lottie's lips. She felt a hot liquid trickling into her mouth, filling it with heat and the taste of browned butter. The liquid ran down her throat, and Lottie coughed. Then the heat wasn't just in her mouth, but throughout her body, shooting down her spine and into her arms and legs, filling her with strength and feeling again. She could move. She pushed herself to a sit, and Eliot's face came into focus.

"Where are the others?" she asked, before heaving out a round of watery coughs.

"Fife's gone back for them," Eliot said, steadying her by the shoulder. "How're you feeling?"

"Fife can't rescue all of them," said Lottie. "The boat was going *under*."

Lottie's sight was blocked on all sides by birch trees and evergreens. She heard water close by, but the awful sound of the ice crawler's cries had ceased. The silence filled Lottie with unease.

"We can't just sit here," she said.

She began crawling in the direction Fife had floated.

"Lottie," Eliot hissed, but after a moment's hesitation, he followed.

Lottie emerged through a space in the evergreens at the water's edge. The boat was gone. All Lottie could make out in the moonlight with any certainty was Fife, floating above the water, scanning its surface, calling out, "Ollie? Adelaide!"

There was no response. He sped on, following the current.

"Dorian!" he yelled. "Ollie! Ada!"

"*Fife!*"

The shout came from the opposite bank. It was Adelaide. Fife rounded back sharply.

"Ada? Where are you? Where are the others?"

"They're—no, that is, Oliver's here, but—"

Adelaide's bodiless voice was interrupted by a great explosion of water, just where Fife was floating.

"Fife!" screamed Lottie. "Look out!"

The ice crawler reared out of the river and released another blood-freezing scream. Its mouth hung wide open like a jack-o'-lantern's smile. Its dozens of legs flailed, grasping at the air, and water sloshed heavily as the creature moved closer to Lottie's side of the bank. She remembered then her fear that the ice crawler could travel on land, too.

"Back!" she said to Eliot. "Get back!"

Together, they scrambled into the shelter of the trees. A blur passed by Lottie's face, then tumbled to the ground just in front of her: Fife. Lottie ran to his side.

"I'm okay," Fife said, waving her off. "It's—it's okay."

The ice crawler's cries continued, but they came no closer.

"You heard Adelaide, right?" Lottie said. "She and Ollie are safe. We've just got to wait until the ice crawler moves on, and you can float them to our side of the bank."

Fife licked his lower lip.

"Lottie," he said. "I'm not sure that can happen. I dunno how long that *thing* is going to hang around, and in the meantime I'm—"

"What do you mean?" Lottie interrupted. "We have to find a way to get back to the others. The ice crawler has to move on eventually."

"I don't know what it's going to do," said Fife. "I didn't think ice crawlers even existed until a few minutes ago. But, by Puck, they're real."

Another low bellow sounded from the river.

"Where are we?" Eliot asked.

"We have to be close to the Northerly Court," said Lottie. "Adelaide said we weren't that far off. It's just, I don't know how to get there from here."

"That warming syrup I've given us isn't going to last forever, either," said Fife. His voice sounded odd—threadbare and stringy. "We're cold enough as it is, and wet through. Once the medicine wears off, we're as good as dead."

"Fife?" said Eliot. "Whoa, *Fife*."

Fife had doubled over, hands clutched to his side.

"Are you hurt?" Lottie cried. "Fife, why didn't you say something? How bad is it?"

"It's not worth . . . it isn't even . . ." Fife lowered his hands from his side, and Lottie stared in horror at the splinter of broken wood lodged there. Pink blood soaked his jacket.

"Just a bit of driftwood," Fife said weakly. "I'd fix it myself, but I think it's beyond my skill."

"No," said Lottie. "No, no, *no*."

He was hurt saving me, she thought. *Saving* me.

"Tell us what we can do," Lottie said. "Spool. Where's Spool?"

There was a flutter of yellow wings overhead. Fife's kingfisher flew down and alighted on his shoulder. He chirped loudly, head cocked to the side.

"You carry all his supplies, Spool. You know what he needs. What does he need?"

Spool gave a sorrowful warble. He shook his head.

"There has to be *something*!" Lottie shouted.

"Maybe someone lives around here," said Eliot. "Maybe there's a house or a village. I could go see."

"No," Lottie said. "We need to stay together. Maybe we could send Spool to—"

"Lottie," said Eliot. "Look."

He pointed to a frosted patch of ground nearby. The outline of the warbler was barely perceptible, so dark were his feathers, but Lottie could see his mischievous eyes wink-ing clear enough. Trouble chirped triumphantly.

"But how did you—" Lottie began. "When did you—oh, never mind! Trouble, you have to fly in, or up, or—I don't know, you have to find someone who can help us!"

Trouble chirruped. He sounded annoyed.

"I'm serious, Trouble. This isn't the time!"

Trouble just made a rumbling sound and hopped away, into the shelter of a tree root. Lottie shouted in exasperation.

"Can't *you* do anything, Lottie?" Eliot asked. "Like the way you healed Nash?"

"No," said Lottie. "No, it's not the same anymore. I can't feel it in me."

All the same, she took hold of Fife's hands. He made a weary noise, his eyes drooping.

Clear your mind, Lottie thought. *Clear your mind.*

But she couldn't quiet her raging thoughts. She didn't feel even the smallest twinge of a bad spell. She couldn't heal Fife, and Trouble would do nothing, and they would soon freeze out here, in the middle of a deserted wood.

And what about the others? Oliver. Adelaide. They were freezing to death, too. How Lottie wished they were here! Adelaide would probably be sobbing right now, and Oliver would be quoting useless poetry, but just having them near would've better calmed her mind, would've made her feel that she wasn't so hopelessly alone.

"Listen," said Eliot, jolting up. "Do you hear that?"

Lottie heard. It was a thudding sound. Not a solitary thudding, like a hammer hitting a nail, but many thuds all at once, toppling over each other and growing louder with each passing second.

Lottie's first thought was, *I wonder if that's what an ice crawler sounds like on land.*

Her second was, *There's nowhere for us to go.*

Fife's eyes were shut fast. His breathing was off kilter. If she and Eliot tried moving him, he would lose more blood— just like the guard who had died in Wisp Territory.

The thudding grew louder.

There was nothing to do but wait with bated breath.

The thudding grew *louder.*

"Hey, I know what it is," said Eliot. "It sounds like people running."

"It could be Iolanthe's soldiers," said Lottie. "Maybe they've followed us here."

"Well, if they're going to take us captive at least they'll take us together."

That, thought Lottie, *or they will kill us on the spot.*

Then Lottie heard another sound entirely: a howl. It rang through the wood, its pitch changing, like a melody.

"Not people," she said. "*Animals.*"

"Wolves?" Eliot asked.

Lottie shook her head, her chest trembling with a fragment of hope.

"I think I know what they are," she said, but she didn't dare say it yet.

Another howl rang out, and another. They grew ever louder until Lottie could see movement between the trees.

The first time Lottie had encountered a Barghest had been in a darkened wood, very much like this one. That night, she had been terrified. She'd never seen anything like the hulking frame of the Barghest—built like a wolf, but like a lion, too, yet something else altogether. She was ready now for the sight of these creatures, but all the same she had never seen so many together at once. As they trotted into the splotched moonlight, she found herself terrified all over again. One Barghest was frightening enough, but here were seven total.

Lottie's Barghest was not among them. She knew instantly. These Barghest did not have the dark coat of her Barghest. Their fur was lighter, in varying shades of white and gray. Six of the creatures came to a stop behind the biggest of them—an icy white Barghest, broad chested and heavy flanked. It flashed its fangs, but Lottie knew enough about the Barghest to be certain this wasn't a menacing gesture. If Lottie had any remaining suspicions about the creature's intentions, what it did next sent them all flitting away. The Barghest ducked its head before her in a bow.

"Heir of Fiske," it said. "We have come to give you aid."

"Cool!" said Eliot, who was grinning but also keeping his distance. "That's lucky, isn't it? Aid is just what we need."

The Barghest tipped its head toward Eliot. "It is not luck, child. It was the Heir of Fiske's genga that fetched us hither."

Lottie gaped. She turned to Trouble, who was still roosting quite happily beneath the tree root.

"You!" she said, not sure if she meant it to be a reprimand or a cry of gratitude.

Trouble rustled his feathers with smug assurance.

"Thank you," she said to him. Then, turning to the pack of Barghest, "Thank all of you. We're in a lot of trouble."

"Indeed," said the head Barghest. "It was for such times as these that we Barghest first swore our oath. We will do all we can to assist you."

"Then you've got to help Fife," said Lottie. "My friend, he's badly injured. He needs medical attention right away. Will you take us to the nearest place he can be healed?"

The Barghest lowered its head in assent. It turned to its pack and let loose a series of short, stuttering barks. In response, the pack of Barghest moved. Two padded forward, close enough for Lottie to touch.

"You may ride on our backs," said one. "One of you must travel with the injured boy. You must hold him steady lest he fall."

"I will," Lottie said without hesitation. "It's my fault he was hurt in the first place."

Lottie didn't want to move Fife; she was sure that to do so would hurt him. But she had no other choice. She and Eliot struggled to lift Fife onto the Barghest's back. His body felt limp in Lottie's arms, but he was still conscious, his breaths shallow. Once positioned, he weakly held on to the Barghest's mane.

Eliot climbed atop the other Barghest, but he looked at a loss as to what to do next.

"Clench your legs tight," Lottie said, "and hold on to its mane if you need to."

Eliot still looked uncertain. Lottie climbed atop her own Barghest, behind Fife, and demonstrated as best she could.

"Staunch his wound, Heir of Fiske," her Barghest rumbled out. "Press it closed as best you can."

"Yes," said Lottie. "Yes, yes, of course. Why didn't I think of that? I haven't been thinking at all."

But the truth was, Lottie had been thinking of Oliver and Adelaide. Where were they? *How* were they? Freezing or injured or—no. It was better not to think of that right now. Instead, she focused on the task of unwinding the damp green scarf from her neck and bunching it up. She wrapped her arms around Fife and pressed the scarf against his wound, staying clear of the shard of wood that stuck out from his skin, careful not to drive it in deeper.

"Trouble!" she called.

She heard a sleepy chirp, followed by the flap of wings. She would have to trust that he would follow. But now Lottie *did* trust him. Trouble had found the Barghest. He had very possibly saved them all.

⋙

Lottie had never before felt such weariness.

The arrival of the Barghest had restored her hope, and that was a precious thing, indeed. But Lottie learned soon enough that the presence of hope did not make for an absence of discomfort. She was so uncomfortable in so many places and for so many reasons that they all began to bleed into one all-consuming affliction, and that was *weariness*.

She was weary in her stomach, which had remained unfed for hours. She was weary in her arms, which had struggled against the river current and channeled her keen and now held Fife upright. More than anything, she was weary in her mind from worry. She was worried about Eliot, whom she could hear coughing in the dark. She was worried about Oliver and Adelaide, stranded somewhere on the opposite bank of the Lissome. She was worried about Dorian and Reeve and even Nash, and she tried to beat back an ever-present whisper in her mind that told her they'd been taken down by the ice crawler and were beyond anyone's worry now.

And at every moment, she worried about Fife. Her hands had gone sticky with his blood. With her forehead bent against his neck, she could still feel the faint pulse beating through his veins, but she knew that Fife was in grave danger and that each minute the Barghest bounded on was a minute less in which to save him. Even now, with her hands pressed hard against his wound, she willed on a bad spell like the one she'd felt when she'd healed Nash. Her chest remained frustratingly at peace.

Why, thought Lottie, *could I heal Nash, a kidnapper and a stranger, and not* Fife, *who's actually my friend, who's one of the greatest people I know? Even if he has been acting rotten the past few days . . .*

Surely she felt more of Mr. Wilfer's "deep empathetic connection" to Fife than to Nash. So was it only that she was too tired? Had she worn herself out? Was her mind irreparably cluttered? What was the point of having a keen she couldn't use when she needed it most?

The heat in Lottie's body was fading. Fife had warned that the warming syrup he'd given her on the bank would wear off. In place of its warmth was nothing but damp cold, made three times worse by the whipping wind. Lottie's eyes kept shutting, then snapping open. From somewhere in the back of her mind, she recalled what Adelaide had told her about wisp blood's effect on humans. She'd said that it made them sleepy. Fife was half wisp. Was his blood, now coating Lottie's hands, making her even more tired?

She had no way of knowing how much time had passed since the Barghest pack had first set out. It felt like they had been riding for hours, but Lottie wondered if she hadn't merely slipped into her troubled thoughts the way one does into a dream—where, on the inside of her mind, time passed much more slowly than on the outside.

Lottie's vision was constantly being jostled about by the gait of the Barghest, which made it impossible for her to see anything steadily. But now she could make out several lights bobbing up ahead, and this filled her with a new sense of urgency.

"Hurry!" she cried, unsure if the Barghest could hear. "Oh, please hurry!"

It had been difficult work, holding Fife upright. Now the sag of his weight gave Lottie the most dreadful thought, that this was what it would feel like to hold Fife dead, should they not arrive in time.

The lights grew closer. The trees the Barghest had been so deftly dodging thinned out, clearing the view ahead. They were racing toward a wall made of sharply hewn logs, twice as tall as a grown wisp. The lights—torches atop the wall—shone upon an iron gate guarded by sprites, who held long spears toward the approaching Barghest.

One of the sprites gave a shout. The others raised their voices, too. Lottie couldn't tell if they were calling to the Barghest or to others, unseen, behind the gate.

The Barghest came to a halt before the guards. The shouting stopped, and the head Barghest stepped in front of the pack.

"We bring with us the Heir of Fiske," it growled. "One of her companions is in mortal danger, in need of immediate healing."

"That's *them*, then?" said a voice. "Not much to look at it, is they?"

Tired as Lottie was, those words ripped fresh rage from her.

"It's nothing to joke about!" she shouted, blinking against the torchlight and straining to keep both herself and Fife upright. "What're you all standing about for? My friend needs *help*."

"Don't tell me that's 'er!" cried another guard. "This gangly ickle thing? Nothing but a girl. Did Gem even know what she looked like? Couldn't have."

The head Barghest gave a bone-rattling howl that sent the guard stumbling back.

"Do as the Heir of Fiske commands!" it snarled. "Have you no deference, sprites of the Wolds? Have you no respect left in your bones? Had we arrived in Thistlebram, we would have had a proper greeting.'"

"Calm yourself, Captain Barghest!"

This was a new voice, wholly unlike the others.

A woman appeared amidst the guards, one hand raised in a peacemaking gesture. She wore a long green robe, and her face was hidden in shadow. The guards bowed as she passed. Then the Barghest, too, bent before the woman in green. Lottie nearly lost her balance at the shift of her Barghest's haunches. When she'd recovered, she saw that the woman was walking straight toward her and Fife.

"Do not worry," the woman said, her voice sharp but soothing. "You've found a haven here. I will tend to him."

"Please," said Lottie. "You've got to. You've *got* to."

Black fog bordered her vision.

I'm fainting, Lottie thought.

And the world vanished.

CHAPTER TEN

The Healer of the Wolds

LOTTIE WOKE inside a cave.

Only this cave wasn't a spooky, dank place like the caves she'd seen on television shows about hiking and spelunking. Its walls were a clean ivory color and decorated in velvet drapings. Overhead, the ceiling arched high, bordered on all sides by stalactites—some thick as tree trunks, some thin as freshly formed icicles. They shimmered in the light of an iron chandelier.

Lottie found herself in a four-poster bed, big enough to accommodate four Lotties. She was swallowed in a sea of heavy blankets, and her clothes—periwinkle coat and green scarf and the blue dress she'd been wearing beneath—were all gone. In their place was a nightshift that was blissfully soft on her skin.

For many minutes, Lottie blinked at her surroundings, trying to make sense of them and salvage memories that might tell her how she'd come to be in this place. When that proved unsuccessful, she focused her efforts on the present situation. Though the ceiling here was high, the room itself felt very small. Lottie spied an exit: a narrow opening carved into the wall, just between two tapestries.

"Hello?" she called. Her voice bounced around the room in an eerie trill. "Is anyone here?"

With difficulty, Lottie shoved the blankets off. She slipped out of bed, cautiously setting one foot down, then the other. The floor was uneven, made from slabs of rock, but the rock wasn't cold like Lottie had expected. In fact, it was almost too warm to walk comfortably upon.

"Hello?" she called again, poking her head out the doorway.

Any words she had left to say wilted on her tongue. Lottie was struck dumb by the sight before her. She had never seen a room so vast, so *cavernous* as this. It was ablaze with the roaring firelight of a half dozen fires and, on top of that, two-dozen more iron chandeliers. Stalactites shone overhead in a crowded chorus of sharp edges and sharper points. Some hung so low that they touched the cave floor, forming majestic columns. The walls here, as in Lottie's bedroom, were covered in velvet drapes colored green, gold, and black. Massive bronze racks ran the length of one wall—some stacked with spears, others with swords.

There were people in the room, gathered near the fireplaces. They were dressed in leather vests and thick-furred dresses, and many of them were holding pewter tankards. Still other figures swept through the room carrying bundles of dishware, linens, and occasionally weapons. Lottie was about to call out to one of the sprites hurrying past, but she was stopped short by the sight of a green-hooded figure standing by her side.

"*Wha—!*" Lottie cried out, stumbling away. "How—how long have you been there?"

The hood cast the figure's face in shadow, but Lottie could make out a set of red lips. Those lips turned upward, amused.

"Are you rested now?"

It was a woman's voice. Lottie frowned at its familiarity, and then at last the memories returned to her. She remembered arriving at a gate, remembered the pack of Barghest and Fife's injury and—

"Fife!" she said. "My friend, Fife. I have to see him. I have to know if he's okay!"

"Fife is quite well," said the woman. She placed a hand on Lottie's back that Lottie was too nervous to shake off.

"I've been tending to him myself. He lost much blood on your journey here, but the good thing about halfling blood is that it staunches well. Had he been a full-blooded sprite, and had he not been such a fighter, I'm not sure he would've survived. But as is, he's stable. Still frail, mind, and in need of recovery, but your friend is out of danger."

Relief swept Lottie into a happy haze. She sighed, loud and long. She felt like hugging the woman in green, even though she still had no idea who she was. And then her happiness gave way to another panic.

"Ollie," she whispered. "Adelaide—you've got to send out a search party! All along the Lissome, down south-ward. My friends, Oliver and Adelaide, and—and, oh, Dorian and those Northerlies—and they could be freezing or starving or—"

Memories of the River Lissome and the ice crawler attack came back to Lottie, crashing into her with stinging clarity.

"That's been taken care of," the woman replied. "I sent out a troop of my best soldiers the moment you arrived and your friend Eliot told me the news. More than that, I've sent a half dozen more gengas, including my own, to scout the area. We're doing all we can to recover the others, and I have high hopes we'll find them alive and well."

"Really?" Lottie asked.

"Really." The woman sounded so confident, Lottie wanted to believe her. "And if Dorian Ingle survived that attack, I've no doubt he's doing everything in his power to bring your friends here safely. He always fulfills his duty."

Lottie's heart settled down—not nearly at ease, but a little reassured.

"And how are *you* faring, Lottie?" the woman asked. "You've been my patient, too, you know, these past two days. No girl your age should endure such troubled sleep as you have."

"Two days? I've been asleep that long?"

"You had an extremely strenuous journey," said the woman. "Not to mention, the halfling's blood put you in a deep sleep. Your body was hard at work trying to set things aright."

"Please," said Lottie, "you've got to take me to Fife and Eliot. Oh, and where's Trouble?"

"Trouble?" said the woman.

"My genga."

"Of course! We found him while we were drying out your clothes. He's been flying about the court ever since. He spent many hours by your bedside, too, so there's no need to make that sad face. As to your friends, I can take you there directly. Though are you sure you wouldn't like something to eat first? I don't want to see you waste the strength you've replenished."

"No one else has shown up, then?" Lottie asked, thinking of her Barghest. It had promised to meet them when they docked. Where was it now?

"Just you," replied the woman. "Now, I really advise that we get you some hot foo—"

"No," Lottie said. "I need to see Fife and Eliot first. Then I'll eat or rest or whatever else it is I'm supposed to do."

The woman sighed. Under her breath, she muttered, "How very like a Fiske."

With her hand still on Lottie's back, she guided her through the massive room and toward a hallway—a long stretch of cave free of stalactites, with narrow openings cut into both its walls.

"Where are we?" Lottie asked as they walked. "Who are you?"

"Many know me as the Healer of the Wolds," said the woman, keeping her voice low.

"Wolds?" said Lottie. "You mean the Northerly Wolds? Is that what this place is?"

"No," said the woman, who sounded like she was stifling a laugh. "Goodfellow's grace, Lottie, don't you know where you are?"

"If I knew, I wouldn't be asking you," she said crossly.

It was then that Lottie became aware of an odd phenomenon occurring around her. As the woman in green led them down the hall, those passing by reacted. They moved well out of her way, their heads bent. Some stopped what they were doing entirely to curtsy or bow.

Lottie peered up at the woman, trying to make out more of her concealed face.

"Are you some kind of royalty?" she asked.

At that, the woman really did laugh. "I'm no royalty. I told you, I'm a healer."

A suspicion pinched Lottie's nerves. "Wait. Are we in the Northerly Court?"

"Certainly not the most attractive part," said the woman, "but we're in it, for sure and certain."

Lottie stopped in her tracks. "You mean to say, those Barghest took us straight to the Northerly Court? We were that close?"

The woman turned to face Lottie. She hesitated. Then she raised her hands and pushed back the hood from her face.

Lottie didn't know why the woman wore a hood at all, because her face was a beautiful thing to behold. It was delicate and dark-skinned, and her brown eyes shone like kindled firewood. Her hair was short and curled and colored black.

"I guess," said the woman, "you haven't heard many tales yet about the Northerly Court. Or about Rebel Gem?"

Lottie stood still a moment more.

"*You're* Rebel Gem," she said softly, her certainty strengthening as she spoke the words.

The woman, who really didn't look much older than Lottie, smiled in reply.

"Come along," she said. "I thought you wanted to see your friends."

Lottie walked on.

"I thought you were a man," she said. "Like, a really old man. With a beard."

The woman—could this *really* be Rebel Gem?—snorted in amusement.

"Fair enough," she said. "There are plenty who think that. Most Southerlies do. Plenty of Northerlies, as well."

"But *why?*" said Lottie. "You're the head of the Northerlies. Shouldn't people know who you are?"

Rebel Gem came to a stop outside one of the hallway's door-like openings.

"You'll find what you're looking for through here," she said.

All Lottie's confusion and curiosity were momentarily forgotten. She ran through the opening, into a bedroom much like the one she'd just left.

"Fife?" she said. "Fife!"

For there he was, sitting up in a canopied bed, his black hair askew in every which way.

"Hallo, you!" he said, grinning as Lottie hurried to his side. "We thought you'd fallen under a sleeping spell. Really, we did."

When he said "we," Fife nodded at the other side of the bed, where Eliot sat cross-legged in an armchair, fast asleep. A book rested on his stomach, its spine cracked.

"He's been reading to me, that one," said Fife. "It's frightfully boring, but he's been so good about keeping me company, I haven't the heart to tell him so."

Lottie smiled affectionately at Eliot.

"Here," Fife said, patting the edge of the bed. "Sit with me, if you'd like. It only hurts when *I'm* the one moving."

"Are you in a lot of pain?" Lottie asked, carefully crawling onto the bed's edge.

"It's not so bad," said Fife. "Rebel Gem's been tending to me."

"I know," said Lottie. "She brought me here."

Lottie looked to the dark doorway. She didn't know if Rebel Gem was still there, listening, or if she'd left them alone.

"Okay," said Fife. "I swear, everyone down in Southerly territory says she's a man. Didn't you think she was a *man?*"

"That's just what I was saying!"

"You mean you told her that to her face?" Fife said, gaping. "Sweet Oberon, you're brave."

"I don't know if bravery's got anything to do with it. Mrs. Yates always said I was a very rude person."

"Whatever you call it," said Fife, "I like it."

Lottie cast another look at Eliot. Guessing her thoughts, Fife said, "He hasn't been coughing. That is to say, he seems all right."

"Good," Lottie murmured.

Her mind stirred with the memory of what she and Fife had argued about back on the boat.

"Fife," she began, but he cut her off.

"Look here," he said, "I know what you're about to say, but it's entirely my fault. I was acting like a right loon back there. I was—well, I dunno, I was angry and hungry and an all-around dog about the whole thing."

"I shouldn't have called you a splinter," Lottie said. "And what you said about me was true: I have been only thinking about Eliot."

"That's not—"

"No," said Lottie. "It's *true*. He's been my only friend for so long, I got used to him being the only person I cared about. I think I'm still learning how to be a good friend to *you*."

Fife smiled. "I'd say you're doing a pretty all right job. Eliot told me how you dragged me all the way here."

Lottie laughed. "That's not what happened."

"What I mean," said Fife, "is that you do care, and it was rotten of me to say otherwise."

"So, we've made up then?"

Fife grinned. "We've made up then."

"Lottie!"

Eliot had woken from his doze. He quickly set aside his book and threw himself on the bed, crawling over to where she sat.

"Oi!" cried Fife. "Careful, would you? Mind the invalid."

Eliot wrapped Lottie in a hug.

"I was worried," he said. "Fife and I thought you'd fallen under some sort of—"

"Enchanted sleep," Lottie finished, smiling. "So he told me."

"Have you met Rebel Gem? She's wonderful."

"Eliot's in love with her," Fife said in a stage whisper.

"I am not! I just said she was *elegant*, that's all. Not what I expected, either. I mean, I thought Rebel Gem was some bearded, old guy. And why're you making that face, Lottie?"

"Oliver and Adelaide," she said, new worry springing to her heart. "We were just on opposite sides of the bank, and *now*—now we have no idea where they are."

"We're worried, too," said Eliot, "but Rebel Gem says she's sure they'll turn up all right. She sent out a whole bunch of soldiers and gengas to look for them."

"So she says," said Fife.

"What? You don't believe her?" Lottie asked, dropping her voice, for she still wasn't sure if Rebel Gem was the sort of person to eavesdrop or, worse yet, send spies to eavesdrop on their conversation.

Fife shrugged. "I'm not too keen on authority figures. In my experience, they all turn out to be liars. She'd just better have sent out her best sprites, that's all."

Lottie thought back to that awful night in the boat. She thought of Reeve, slumped unconscious, and Dorian standing tall before the ice crawler, sword in hand. She thought of the burning chill of the water as she'd jumped in and of Adelaide's cries from the opposite bank of the Lissome.

"Yes," she said. "She'd better have sent out her very best."

The three of them had not been talking long when there came a knock at the doorway—though far heavier than a knock ought to have been, and particularly confusing since Lottie knew there was no proper door leading to the room.

"Who is it?" Fife called.

A boy, no older than Lottie, emerged from the shadows outside the room. He was dressed in a vest and long, ratty-looking pants. He carried a bronze staff in one hand; this, Lottie realized, had been the source of the strange knocking noise.

"Didn't mean to interrupt," the boy said, "'s only that supper's being served."

"Don't be shy," said Fife, motioning him to come closer. "It's just Lottie."

The boy's eyes didn't meet Lottie's when she looked at him. He had a tight face, very thin around the cheeks and jaw. His hair was pure white.

"He's been helping take care of me," Fife said. "Bringing in drinks and soups and chocolates. But no cake. They don't make cake up here. Isn't that tragic?"

"Beggin' your pardon," the white-haired boy said to Fife. "Rebel Gem says how you're still to rest, but I'm s'posed to bring *her* to the suppin' lawn."

Lottie didn't particularly like the way the boy said the word "her," as though it were more like the word "grub" or "slime."

"Can't I just have supper here?" she said.

"Rebel Gem insists. You'll be able to visit your friends again soon enough."

The white-haired boy's eyes finally met hers. Lottie recognized their expression all too well; she'd seen it every day back at Thirsby Square, on Mrs. Yates. It was mostly indifference, but there was just the smallest taint of real hatred there, too. Lottie was shocked. She'd never met this boy before. Why would he look at her that way?

"Don't I need to change?" she said, motioning to her nightshift.

"We'll stop by the launderers on the way there, and you can pick up your old clothes. Now c'mon."

The boy was already through the dark doorway when Lottie turned and made a face at the others, as though to say, Do I really have to leave with *him*?

Eliot grinned and shrugged.

Fife said, "Hurry back when they're through fawning over the Heir of Fiske."

Once in the hallway, Lottie found the white-haired boy sprinting ahead of her. She had to run to catch up, and even when she did, he paid her no mind.

"Aren't you charming," Lottie said under her breath.

Rather than waste her time on present company, Lottie turned her attention to her surroundings. They were walking back through the massive, firelit room. There were far fewer people bustling about now than before—all at supper, Lottie guessed. At the thought, her stomach fastened shut as though by tightly drawn laces. Hungry as she should have been, she didn't feel like eating. Maybe it was the idea of arriving at some strange place called the "suppin' lawn" and meeting a bunch of Northerly strangers.

After walking the length of the grand, stalactite-crowned room, they passed into a far narrower passageway. Here, the earth turned moist underfoot. A single splat of water fell on Lottie's shoulder. There were no chandeliers in this passage, but torches instead—and these were few and far between. Lottie got the irrational urge to grab the boy's hand for comfort, but she kept her back straight, taking care that her inhalations and exhalations were as measured as ever. She wouldn't have some Northerly boy she barely knew thinking she was a coward.

Then they turned a corner and stepped through a wide doorway into the dazzling light of the outdoor world. It wasn't the light of the sun, which had already set, but that of candles—hundreds upon hundreds of candles hung in bunches and strung along an open field in swooping arches. With the onslaught of these new sights came a hard gust of autumn wind.

"It's cold," said Lottie, ducking back into the shelter of the cave. "I don't even have shoes on."

"I told you," said the boy, "we'll visit the launderers first." Then, after a moment, he gave a frustrated grunt. "Fine, *I'll* run to the launderers and bring your precious things back, *Heir of Fiske.*"

The white-haired boy ran off, disappearing into the crowded blur of lights and sprites. The laughs and shouts of the sprites mixed in such a dizzying swirl that Lottie wasn't sure if the majority of them were joking or fighting with each other. They moved about in a great open space, which was bordered by stone boulders. Lottie decided that this place must be a sort of courtyard to the cavern from which she'd just emerged. There was grass everywhere underfoot, and not the long white grass of Wisp Territory, but short and deep, deep green.

Through the jostle of bodies, she saw circular stone tables set up in the middle of the courtyard. Piles of food were spread upon the tables, and though many sprites already sat around them, they did not yet eat. Somewhere close by, several fiddles played in time with each other, changing hands in a wild whirl of harmony. A pair of dancing sprites waltzed past Lottie, just inches from her nose.

Confused as she was by the scene, Lottie had to admit it was a glorious sight. She hadn't realized until now just how quiet and colorless life in Wisp Territory had been.

"Here."

Something rammed into Lottie's stomach. Her periwinkle coat. The white-haired boy had returned with her clothes in hand. He dropped her boots unceremoniously at her feet, followed by her scarf and dress.

"Do whatever you want with 'em," he said, "but hurry up, huh? I've gotta deliver you to Rebel Gem before the suppin' starts."

"All right, all right," said Lottie, who wasn't as much concerned with getting dressed as she was with finding Trouble. She checked her coat's left pocket, then the right.

As she'd feared, Trouble wasn't in either. She let out a short groan and then threw the coat over her nightshift, eager for its warmth, buttoning it all the way up to her chin. The tweed was warm and smelled of fresh lavender. Lottie now wished she'd accompanied the boy to the launderers so that she could thank them in person; it had been a long time since her coat had been this clean. She laced her boots on her feet, then stared at her dress and scarf. Though both had been cleaned, they were still stained with faint traces of blood. Fife's blood. Lottie had less of an appetite than ever.

"Burn 'em," suggested the boy.

"I'm not going to burn a perfectly good dress," Lottie said crossly, bunching the clothes to her chest.

"Suit yourself," he said. "Now follow me."

He led the way into the crowd, which was thinning out as more sprites took their seats at the tables. The boy brought her to a table that stood in the very center of the lawn. This table was no different from the others—it was just as large and stocked high with food—but at its far end sat Rebel Gem. When she caught sight of Lottie, her face broke into a smile, and she rose.

"Welcome, Lottie," she said warmly. "You'll sit by me."

The other bodies at the table shifted and murmured and all, without exception, watched Lottie closely as she took the free chair at Rebel Gem's right side. Lottie wondered, just as she was sitting, if she was supposed to curtsy or show some other sign of respect. She ended up making a clumsy bob of her head to the whole table, and she felt very stupid afterward for trying anything at all.

Luckily, her embarrassment was swallowed up by the cessation of fiddle music and the long blast of a horn. The chatter of the crowd died down, and all was quiet on the supping lawn, save for the sound of the wind whistling through the boulders.

Rebel Gem, still on her feet, now climbed atop her chair and threw out her arms. Those sprites who hadn't taken their places at the supping tables now fled to the corners of the courtyard. All eyes were fixed on their leader.

"Friends!" said Rebel Gem, and Lottie marveled that, though her voice boomed loud throughout the courtyard, it still sounded gentle somehow. "This night, we welcome a long-awaited guest to our table. The Heir of Fiske is dining with us."

There came a roar from the crowd so resounding that Lottie's eyes watered.

"Small she may be," Rebel Gem shouted, breaking up the sweep of cheers. "Small and young, but she is a Fiske, so she is one of our own, as all Fiskes ever shall be. Make her welcome, friends. Extend the chalice of goodwill toward our halfling guest!"

Another cheer boomed throughout the courtyard, more shattering than the one before it. Lottie could only stare and swallow, swallow and stare, eyes wide with the spectacle of it all. These Northerlies knew who she was. They were *cheering* for her.

"Stand," said a voice close by. "Stand atop your chair, Heir of Fiske, and show them your face."

But Lottie remained where she was, still as the stone chair she sat upon. Her bones were stiff from shock. She looked around her table at the host of faces. Some looked grim, others jubilant, and two—two dirt-smudged, unkempt faces just across from her—looked very familiar.

"Roote!" she cried. "And Crag!"

CHAPTER ELEVEN

The House of Fiske

"DIDN'T THINK she'd remember us," Crag said for the fifth time that evening. "Didn't think it was possible, one so 'igh up as the Heir of Fiske."

They were well into the second course of supper. The fiddlers had resumed their playing, and the supping lawn was once again filled with the swarming sound of conversation. After Rebel Gem had made her announcement, the eating had begun, and Lottie was grateful that, enthusiastic as the Northerlies seemed to be about a Fiske in their midst, they seemed just as eager to eat the food at their tables.

Supper here was very different from what Lottie had eaten in the South. Gone were the carefully arranged dishes of berries and nuts and stacked wafercomb. At this table, every diner grabbed what he or she wanted and ate without regard to napkins or manners. They carved off chunks of cheese from a wheel, speared slices of meat from a platter, and tore off pieces of thick, brown bread. Every cup over-flowed with what Crag called bramble draught, and which Roote explained to Lottie was a type of ale.

Lottie sipped the ale just once and didn't at all care for its bitter taste, but she did help herself to the cheeses, meats, and breads. After her table had fallen into conversation and removed their attention from her, Lottie found her appetite returning. She hadn't eaten food so rich and heavy as this since her life at Thirsby Square—and then only on very special occasions, like Christmas Eve.

The rest of the company at the table—thirteen altogether—talked to each other with no regard to the girl they'd cheered just moments before. Lottie didn't mind this in the slightest; she was too busy talking to Roote and Crag.

"Why are you here?" she asked them. "I thought you were stationed at Hingecatch as spies."

"That we were," said Roote, "but our post just ran out. Returned today. Never been to the Northerly Court, me or Crag. Never met Rebel Gem. But we were promised a dinner for our service to the court. Then we found such a hulla-baloo going on 'bout the Heir of Fiske we thought we'd be downright ignored."

"Certainly not," said Rebel Gem, leaning into the conversation. "Our court has honored our emissaries time out of mind. We value you immensely, Roote and Crag."

"That's why we're at a fancy table this eve," said Crag, looking around their company sheepishly. "With all the other 'ighbrows and such of the court. We get to sit one night at Rebel Gem's table as thanks for doing our duty in 'ingecatch."

"And what a duty it was!" said Roote, after taking a long swig of ale. "Couldn't be happier to be back in the North, with the fresh wind of the Wolds on my bones. There was a sickly air down in Hingecatch that I didn't much care for."

Someone else at the table called Rebel Gem's attention away, leaving Roote and Crag with a captive audience of one. Crag scratched at his short brown beard. He'd been staring at Lottie this whole while with an attitude Lottie could only call suspicious.

"I guess," she said, "you're a little upset I didn't tell you I was a Fiske when we first met."

"Befuddled, more like," said Crag.

"Confounded," agreed Roote.

"My friends and I were on an important mission," said Lottie. "We couldn't risk telling people who we were. We didn't know who to trust. You understand, don't you?"

"S'pose," said Crag.

"We thought it strange, your company traipsing through the wood like that," said Roote. "But never did I think we'd be sitting with the Heir of Fiske. And to think, Crag sang a whole song about your kin!"

Crag turned red. "Wasn't my best singing, if memory serves."

"I thought it was beautiful," said Lottie.

Though, truth be told, Lottie remembered the song as more depressing than beautiful.

"Anyway," she said, "you shared your food with us and kept us safe, even if it was only for a little while—and all that without knowing who we were. That was very admirable of you."

Crag turned redder still, though Lottie couldn't be sure if it was her words or the ale that was responsible.

"'Twas nothing," Roote said gruffly. "What a Northerly's got, a Northerly shares."

Lottie looked around the supping lawn. That certainly seemed to be the case. The Northerlies around her were passing along plates and jokes alike, and a warmth had settled on this place quite unlike anything Lottie had ever felt before. She wondered if this was a little like what it was to be part of a family—a big family with mothers and fathers, aunts and uncles, cousins and grandparents. She wondered if this was what a proper Thanksgiving felt like—not one where she sat opposite Mrs. Yates at the kitchen table, surrounded by strange-smelling boarders, eating burnt goose.

The thought of Thanksgiving reminded Lottie of Eliot and Mr. Walsch. Dorian had assured Lottie that there was a silver-boughed tree in the Northerly Court. Lottie would have to ask Rebel Gem about it the next chance she got. Though she wondered, now that Rebel Gem had Lottie in her court, would she really be willing to let her return to Kemble Isle? And how could Lottie even think of leaving until she knew Oliver and Adelaide were safe?

"...not chopping, and not rotting from Plague. *Collecting* is what I heard."

Lottie's ears perked at the words being spoken just two sprites down. This was the conversation that had drawn Rebel Gem away, and it had now captured the attention of the entire table.

"Hush, Cliff," said a woman with grooved cheeks and gray hair. She waved for the first speaker—a man of her age with a long beard—to stop talking. "*Hush.* This is hardly conversation for supper, and certainly not one we should be having in the presence of a Fiske."

"How so?" said Cliff, turning to Lottie. "I'd say it's a prime topic for a Fiske."

"Rumors," said the woman. "Only rumors."

"Rumors about what?" Lottie asked.

"*Starkling.*" Cliff spat his name out with distaste. "Spies say he's been making a stockpile of those silver-boughed trees, though no one knows where. Say he's making a world gorge."

"Don't go on, Cliff," said another man at the table. "Nothing but stories, those tales of world gorges. They can't be made. Too dangerous. And unnatural, besides."

"No, I want to know more," Lottie said eagerly.

"Oh, merciful Titania!" cried the gray-haired woman. "Stop filling the child's head with stuff and nonsense. A world gorge, indeed."

Lottie wasn't paying attention to the old woman. She was watching Rebel Gem's face for any shift that might give away her own opinion on the matter. But Rebel Gem's expression had stayed unchanged throughout the conversation, and it remained impassive now.

"I don't see the harm in answering the little Fiske's questions," said Cliff. "Only natural that she'd be curious." Turning his attention to Lottie, he said, "You know how gorges are made, then?"

"From silver boughs," said Lottie. "That's why it's illegal. And they connect one part of your world to another."

Cliff nodded. "Well, some say that if you were to hack away enough silver boughs, harvest enough silver, you could make a gorge that reached not just to another part of Limn, not just to the human world, but *beyond* that—into the *unknown* worlds."

Lottie nodded slowly, uneasy. She remembered what King Starkling had said to her when she'd stood before him in his throne room: *I brought the Plague up from my world*. He had told her that he wasn't from Limn, but he wasn't from the human world, either.

"See," said Cliff, "there used to be all types of trees that led to all types of worlds—way, way back, in the most ancient of times. People say those worlds went bad, and when they did, their trees rotted or were cut down, burned, and erased from all memory. But there are some who've since made it their mission to find those lost worlds again. Legend has it that, should you collect enough silver from silver boughs, you could create a *world* gorge—a passage into one of those dark, unknown places."

"So that's what Starkling's trying to do," Lottie whispered.

"So some say," said Cliff. "So some say."

An agitated quiet settled on the table. Lottie felt a sensation she'd experienced many times since she first arrived in Limn—like those around her were holding a silent conversation she could not understand, nor break into. She looked at her plate of crumbled cheese, her mouth suddenly dry.

"Can't say I like all this talk of bad worlds and rotten kings," said Crag. "Me and Roote, we 'eard rumors enough down at 'ingecatch. Rumors ain't worth a cent, that's what I say. Pay them no mind."

"Excellent advice," said Rebel Gem, and her smile caused Crag to blush fiercely. "On that note, I propose a toast to this table's revered guests. Roote and Crag both served faithfully at their post in Hingecatch for a full year, and for that we honor them."

Rebel Gem raised her chalice. Lottie quickly did the same.

"To Roote and Crag," said Rebel Gem.

"To Roote and Crag!" the table echoed.

They raised their glasses and drank. After that, there was no more talk of the Southerly King or a world gorge.

"I'll confess something," said Roote, leaning toward Lottie. "I thought Rebel Gem was an ol' man."

Lottie smiled. "So do a lot of people, I think. I wonder why everyone is under that impression."

Roote chewed his food thoughtfully.

The night wore on. Aside from Roote and Crag, no one spoke directly to Lottie. Rebel Gem was busy talking to the other guests, and though Lottie tried to catch her gaze several times, Rebel Gem never held it. After a while, Lottie got the impression she was being purposefully ignored, and Roote and Crag soon downed so many cups of bramble draught that they became rather rowdy company.

Lottie sank in her chair, wishing she were back within the comfort of the caves, in Fife's bedroom, huddled in conversation with him and Eliot. She wished that Oliver were here and that he would recite a sonnet with a meaning she might not understand but a cadence that would put her at ease.

She wished Adelaide were here, even if it was only to gape at the bad table manners and wrinkle her nose at the meat on Lottie's plate. More than anything, she hoped Oliver and Adelaide were *safe*.

A chirrup stirred Lottie from her thoughts.

"Trouble!" she whispered.

The obsidian warbler sat perched on the edge of Lottie's plate.

"Trouble, where have you *been*?"

Trouble gave an abashed tweet that sounded, surprisingly enough, like remorse.

"You've got to stop doing that," Lottie said. "I'm worried about so many other people as it is."

Trouble tweeted again, this time in an urgent, excited way. He fluttered up from his perch, and Lottie felt a sharp pain just above her ear. Trouble was tugging at her hair.

"Stop it," she hissed, glancing around the table in embarrassment, only to find that everyone else was too deep in either drink or conversation to notice.

Trouble tugged more insistently, and Lottie had to grit her teeth to keep from crying out.

"All right," she said. "I'll follow you. Just *stop*."

It was only when she rose from the table that she stirred the attention of her dining companions.

"Lottie?" said Rebel Gem. She looked expectant, though Lottie couldn't figure out about what.

"It's my genga," Lottie said, motioning to Trouble, who was still tugging hard at her hair. "I'm afraid he's upset about something. I just need to go calm him down."

Rebel Gem nodded. "Of course. Do what you must."

As Lottie turned away, she was sure she saw amusement dancing in Rebel Gem's brown eyes. Perfect. Now the whole Northerly Court knew that the Heir of Fiske was not only a puny little girl, but also that she had absolutely no control over her genga. What a grand introduction to the Northerlies, indeed.

"Stop!" Lottie said as Trouble tugged her away from the table, out of the winking candlelight and into the shadow of the supping lawn's boulders. "*Stop.* I'm following you now, what more do you want?"

It wasn't until Trouble led Lottie to a narrow crack between boulders that Lottie dug in her heels.

"No," she said. "I'm not going through there. It's dark out, and I don't know what's beyond this courtyard. Anyway, I'm sure Rebel Gem doesn't want me to wander off at a supper that's practically in my honor. It would be really rude. Not that you have any concept of what it means to be—*ouch!*"

For Trouble had nipped at Lottie's shoulder. It wasn't hard enough to pinch through her coat and draw blood, but Lottie had felt it all the same.

"Look," she said. "I'm grateful for what you did back at the river, but I've had enough of your—your *anarchy.* You might be my genga, but I'm your human—I mean sprite—I mean, oh, whatever! You're supposed to obey me, not the other way 'round."

Trouble warbled a vehement string of notes, flapping his wings in protest. Then he rushed past Lottie, into the darkness between the boulders. He did not reappear.

"Trouble?" Lottie called.

As frustrating as he could be, he'd never yet led Lottie astray. She didn't always understand Trouble's behavior, but the last time he'd flown away without her permission, hadn't he fetched the pack of Barghest? Hadn't he saved Fife's life? And though Lottie was angry with him, she was curious, too. Where was Trouble trying to get her to go with such persistence?

"Oh, wait up!" she called, making her decision. "I'm coming, Trouble, just wait for me!"

She looked over her shoulder at the bobbing lights on the supping lawn. The crowd was louder than ever, full of ale and late-night spirits. The fiddles screeched with abandon, not nearly so accurate in their melodies as before. From what Lottie could tell, there was no one looking for her, no one chasing after. She reflected, rather self-pityingly, that she might very well be the least popular guest of honor there ever was. As excited as everyone had been to have an Heir of Fiske in their midst, they had quickly forgotten her existence.

But what were you expecting? Lottie thought. *They must have heard the stories by now, of how you're nothing like Queen Mab and all the Fiskes after her. You can't command people like she could. You're only here as part of a deal between the Tailor and Rebel Gem. You're here because Lyre Dulcet wanted some addersfork to kill the Southerly King. That's all you're good for: a trade.*

It was a terrible line of thinking, made worse still by the fact that Lottie was walking blindly through the dark. She waved her arms in front of her, treading the grass with caution, and as she did so her mind filled with more awful thoughts about what could be out here, beyond the light and safety of the supping lawn: giant cobwebs, perhaps, or deep ravines, or beasts far fiercer than even the Barghest.

"Trouble?" she called. "This isn't funny. If I fall into a hole in the ground, I'll—"

Lottie saw the light then. It had been hidden behind the trees that she was using her hands to feel around and avoid collision. She heard a flutter of wings in her left ear, and Trouble perched on her shoulder. He began singing a cheerful tune.

"Well, I'm glad you're so pleased with yourself," Lottie muttered.

Lottie could see now that the light came from a torch, affixed to a stone wall. No. It wasn't a wall, but the face of something much larger and rounded at its top, crested by crawling moss.

It was another cave.

Lottie stared into its dimly lit mouth. The stone floor had been laid over with paneled wood. Something glittered high across the wall, though Lottie couldn't make out what in the current light. With some effort, she stood on tip-toe and managed to pull the torch free of its mounting. She held a cupped hand to the flame, something she'd seen done in movies, to shield it from any breeze, but after only a few moments of holding it, Lottie could tell this wasn't an ordinary torch. Its flame held steady, no matter how badly Lottie's hand shook.

She stepped into the cave, the heels of her boots clacking loudly on the floor. She raised the torch to make out the glittering on the walls.

It was writing. Golden letters spelled out five words, inscribed in such a flourished style that it took Lottie a good minute to make out their meaning. She deciphered the last word first: FISKE.

Sudden heat filled Lottie, pouring down her throat and straight into her stomach. With a sense of urgency, she worked on the rest of the words until she'd sorted out the full meaning of the inscription:

MOST REVERED HOUSE OF FISKE

Trouble pinched his feet into Lottie's shoulder.

"What is this?" she said.

Her words echoed and circled back to her in sibilant bursts. She moved the torch, casting light deeper into the cave. She could see more lights up ahead, lining a narrowed passageway. She walked on. As she did, Trouble resumed his song, though it had taken a turn from happy to bittersweet. Its notes gave Lottie the impression of dusk after a long summer day.

A draft scuttled through the passageway, prickling the skin on Lottie's knuckles. She was no longer spurred on by Trouble's tweets but by her own burning curiosity.

Most Revered House of Fiske, the gold lettering said. But what Lottie thought, with quickened breaths, was *Most Revered House of My Mother?* It could be that Eloise Fiske had once walked this same path, had seen these same walls, had breathed this same stale air.

The passageway eventually opened wide again, this time onto a bright, white-walled room. Twenty torches, enchanted like Lottie's, burned on the walls. There were tables here, made of dark wood and gilded with gold. On some of the tables sat stacks of books, thick and richly bound. On others sat artifacts, enclosed in glass cases.

"Artifacts" was the best word Lottie could come up with to describe the contents of the cases, for "museum" was the best way she could think to describe the room as a whole.

A row of statues stood along one of the walls, their subjects in varying degrees of glory and proclamation. At their center, a woman most regal held an outstretched scepter toward the room and all its contents. Her body was made of yellowed marble. Lottie knew who she was without looking at the inscription. This was Queen Mab, the first of the Fiskes. To her left and right stood other sprites, all crowned and majestic—two women and two men with first names Lottie didn't recognize but a surname that was her own.

She reached out her hand to one of the statues, a man with a buttoned shirt and a flowing cape. His mouth was fashioned in a jovial laugh, and though Lottie knew his eyes were dead marble, they looked alive in this light. His sculptor had carved the veins of his wrists so deftly that Lottie could've sworn she saw one pulse, ever so briefly, with marble lifeblood.

FORD FISKE, KING OF SPRITES, read the inscription. Was he a distant grandfather? she wondered. Great-great-great-great-great-uncle? And though he was laughing now and would be for all eternity, had he been a happy sprite in life?

Lottie couldn't say how long she spent studying the faces of Fiskes long dead and here immortalized. She might have gone on for hours more had Trouble not peeped loudly from the center of the room, where he'd settled atop one of the glass cases. He peeped again, signaling Lottie to join him.

Reluctantly, Lottie left the company of the statues and crossed to the table. Inside the glass case on which Trouble had perched sat a black cushion, and resting on that cushion was a ring. It was small, fashioned for a very thin finger, and carved entirely of blue stone. Its crest was a thin, flat diamond shape, cut to severe points, and upon this diamond rose a carving that resembled a flowering bud.

"Beautiful," Lottie whispered. Then, "It's so *blue*."

Trouble produced one of his annoyed tweets. He pecked his beak at the glass, drawing Lottie's attention to a metal fixture at the case's front: a keyhole.

"What is it?" she asked. "I'm not going to break it open and steal the ring, if that's what you're after."

Trouble fluttered his wings, clearly exasperated. He hopped from the case to the edge of the table and pecked at Lottie's coat, where her hand rested in her pocket.

And Lottie realized.

She dug her fingers deeper into the pocket and felt the cold, solid form of a key—the Northerly key Trouble had delivered to her days ago in Wisp Territory.

A giddy suspicion overcame Lottie. She tugged out the key.

Trouble was hopping about frantically now, his wings a blur.

It can't possibly be, thought Lottie. *It's too strange.*

But the suspicion dug in deeper, relentless.

She lined the key's grooves up with the keyhole. It was the right sort of key for this sort of slot, but that didn't necessarily mean . . .

The key slid into place without a hint of resistance. Lottie turned it, and there was a satisfying *click.* When Lottie tugged the key back, the case opened as easily as if she had turned a doorknob. Glassy-eyed, Lottie reached in and picked up the ring. It was deliciously cool to the touch and so small, yet so present in her palm.

She held it up to the torchlight, her heart burning with delight.

So beautiful, she thought again. *And so very blue.*

She reached out to touch the carved flower bud, then gasped at a sharp prick of pain in her forefinger. A single bead of blood appeared on the surface of her skin. She'd been cut by one of the harsh points of the diamond setting.

"Careful," said a voice at her back. "That's just as much weapon as ring."

Lottie whirled around.

Rebel Gem stood at the entrance of Lottie's newfound museum, eyes alight not with anger, but interest.

"It becomes you," she said, nodding to the ring.

"I didn't—" Lottie began. "I wasn't going to steal it."

"*Steal* it?" Rebel Gem crossed her arms in a way that made her look very young. Then she drew closer to Lottie. "You couldn't steal it if you tried. It's yours by right."

Lottie frowned. "Just because I'm a Fiske can't mean all this is mine. I mean, surely not. Doesn't it belong to the Northerlies more than me? Aren't you the ones who brought all this here? Who still look after it?"

"No," said Rebel Gem. "That was all the doing of Ford Fiske. That one there." She pointed to the statue Lottie had been most fascinated by earlier. "He thought his family should have a pretty little shrine. They say he carved this place out with his bare hands, and he employed magic from off our shores to keep everything within the cave protected."

"He must not have done a good job," said Lottie, "seeing how I practically broke in."

"Silly," said Rebel Gem. "The enchantment doesn't work on *Fiskes*. That's what I mean: this place was made by Fiskes, so Fiskes have a right to it. I know we Northerlies make a big fuss over your name, but, honestly, I'm not sure there are many who particularly like this cave. They thought it a bit showy, even when it was first carved."

Lottie turned over the ring in her hand, this time careful of its sharp edges. Something new caught her eye.

There was something etched inside the band. It took her a moment to find the beginning of the inscription, but when she did, her heart stuttered at the sight of names she knew as well as her own. *To Eloise,* it read. *All my heart, Bertram.*

Lottie repeated the words in her mind, drawing them deep into her memory, never to let them go.

"This was my mom's?"

"Didn't you know?" asked Rebel Gem. "I thought someone must've already told you about it. And I see you have the key."

Lottie was still staring at the ring, afraid it might vanish should she take her eyes off it. "I've never touched anything that belonged to them. All I had growing up was a photograph."

"Then you should keep it," said Rebel Gem, without hesitation. "No, don't look at me that way, I mean it. What good will the ring do us, locked up in this stuffy old cave? Most sprites would be too frightened to touch it, otherworldly as it is. And, anyway, no one but a Fiske is *supposed* to touch it. That's what Eloise said. She hid the key away after your father's passing, and she only let one other pair of eyes see where. So the story goes."

"What pair of eyes?"

Rebel Gem nodded to Trouble, who was happily perched on the edge of the table.

"Oh." Lottie blinked with sudden understanding. "All this time, I thought someone had given the key to Trouble. But it was just him all along."

"Clearly he thought it was time you had it," said Rebel Gem.

"You said other sprites would be afraid to touch it. Why?"

"It's made of—oh, what do you call it?" Rebel Gem pointed to the engraving bolted beneath the case. "There. *Lapis . . . lazuli?*"

"What's so special about *lapis lazuli?*" Unlike Rebel Gem, Lottie pronounced the words correctly.

"It exists in your world, but not here in Limn. The ring is human-carved, too. A great rarity. Many sprites hold to the superstition that otherworldly items are cursed. Dear Lottie, someone really ought to sit you down and catch you up on things. It's as if you know nothing at all about your parents."

"I don't," Lottie said softly.

"Well, we'll have to do something about that, starting with that ring. Take it. I insist. Take it as a sign of goodwill between the Northerly Court and the Heir of Fiske, hmmm?"

Rebel Gem patted Lottie's back just a little too forcefully and drew out her last words a little too long.

"I'm a teeny bit tipsy," Rebel Gem confided. "But I know what I'm doing. Don't worry, I won't change my mind and apprehend you for thievery come morning. Now, here."

Rebel Gem came closer, and as she did she produced a small, black silk handkerchief from the inner folds of her robe. With it, she plucked the ring from Lottie's fingers, gave it a swift cleaning, and then wrapped it carefully inside the cloth, folding it over twice, then three times.

"Best not to put that in your pocket unprotected. As I said, it's quite sharp. Northerly silk is the strongest fabric on Albion Isle. It will keep that ring from cutting through your clothes."

"*Why* is it so sharp?" Lottie asked.

She didn't want to find fault with anything her father had given to her mother, but she had to admit the design seemed rather dangerous for a piece of jewelry.

"Your father designed it that way," said Rebel Gem. "A small weapon—a last resort, as it were, should your mother need it. She passed through many dangers in such a short life."

Lottie's chest wrenched with sudden pain. She took the tiny silk bundle from Rebel Gem and placed the ring in her pocket. She didn't know if Rebel Gem was telling the full truth, but now that Lottie had found the ring, she wouldn't dare let it go, even if Rebel Gem showed up at her bedside the next day with a legion of Northerly soldiers, demanding its return.

"What are all these other things?" Lottie said, motioning to the glass cases. One contained a bronze crown, another a rusting chalice, and yet another a book so fragile it looked liable to fall apart should Lottie so much as blink in its direction.

"All relics," said Rebel Gem. "Tributes to the House of Fiske, stored here for safekeeping. Can't say that any of them are all that interesting. After all, they're just objects. They can't bring back the Fiskes or their keen."

Lottie turned around slowly. "You know I don't have the keen you're after, don't you?"

"The keen I'm *after*?" Rebel Gem repeated.

"Everyone else seems to be after it," said Lottie. "But you should know, I can't command people like the old Fiskes could. I can only heal them."

"You can *only*?"

Lottie wondered if Rebel Gem's tipsiness was affecting her hearing.

"I've heard all about your keen, Lottie Fiske," said Rebel Gem. "There's nothing *only* about it. A healing keen is a very precious thing. It's a big responsibility, too. I should know."

"You said you were the Healer of the Wolds," Lottie recalled.

"That's one of my names, yes."

"Then you're an actual healer? Like Mr. Wilfer? He told me there aren't many of you left."

"He's right. I'm one of only three Northerly healers, and the other two don't much like to be disturbed, selfish duffers. They only come out to make silly pronouncements about addersfork."

"You don't believe them?" said Lottie. "You don't think the addersfork will work?"

"It might. I sincerely hope it does. Personally, I think the wisps would make better use of their time by strengthening what remains of their guard rather than foraging for lethal plants. But Lyre is fueled by a panic that his people will soon be extinct, and panicked rulers don't make good decisions."

"But you'll do it now, won't you?" said Lottie. "You'll hold up your end of the deal and get the addersfork for them, now that I'm here?"

"Of course. Though the sprite I'd entrusted with that duty was Dorian Ingle."

Lottie blinked. "What?"

"He's one of the few sprites brave enough to have ventured into the Wilders, and one of fewer still to know where the addersfork grows."

"I wish we'd heard back already from your search party," Lottie said.

"I do, too," Rebel Gem said softly, surprising Lottie. "But worrying doesn't change a single tick on the clock. Better we focus our energies on what we *can* change."

"Wait. If you're a healer, then what's your keen?" Lottie tried not to sound overeager. "Is it like mine?"

"It's a touch keen," said Rebel Gem, "which I hear yours is, too?"

Lottie nodded.

"When I touch sprites," said Rebel Gem, "I can feel their mental distress. Over time, I learned to ease the burden of a fellow sprite's mind. You might say I'm a healer of troubled thoughts more than anything else."

"So, like a psychiatrist?"

"A what?"

"Never mind."

"I told Lyre to promise you sharpening lessons during your stay here," said Rebel Gem. "I thought, if you'd like, I could train you myself."

Lottie felt dizzy. "I—that is, well, that's very nice of you to offer. But, um. Well, this is a bit complicated, but I don't exactly want to stay in the Northerly Court."

Rebel Gem's calm expression did not change.

"The Tailor didn't even ask my permission about whether or not I wanted to come," said Lottie. "And if he *had* asked, I would've told him that my friend Eliot has to get back to Kemble Isle, and I promised to go with him. He needs me around, you see, to stay well. And Dorian said you have a silver-boughed tree here?"

Rebel Gem nodded.

"Well, and it was a horrible shock, when Iolanthe invaded Wisp Territory and chopped down their tree.

And then we *had* to come up north. But I wondered if, once I know Adelaide and Oliver are safe, I could take Eliot back to Kemble Isle. Just for a little while. Through Christmas, maybe. Which, um, is this holiday we celebrate back in—well, that's not important. I just mean, I'm not trying to be ungrateful, but I really need to get back to the human world."

Rebel Gem raised a single brow but still said nothing. Lottie was afraid she knew what this meant.

"You're not going to let me do that, are you?"

Rebel Gem placed her hand on Lottie's shoulder. Like her voice, the grip was kind but very firm. "You have important work to do here, Lottie. I'm not sure you realize how important."

"I'm not sure *you* realize how important it is for Eliot to get back!" Lottie cried, yanking herself from Rebel Gem's grip. "If you don't let us use that silver-boughed tree, then you're just—you're a terrible person! I don't care how nice you seem or how important you think I am to the Northerly Court. If you don't let us go, you might as well be holding us captive. And if you're holding us captive, you're no better than King Starkling."

Rebel Gem did not react in the way Lottie was expecting. She had thought that Rebel Gem would be angry, or that her face would at least turn sour. Instead, she remained as placid as always. She crossed her arms, thoughtful.

"I made a deal with Lyre Dulcet," she said. "And a deal that's been struck can't simply be *unstruck*. I asked for your presence in my court in return for addersfork. If the Dulcets were to learn I'd given you up to the human world, they would perceive me as weak, malleable."

"Well, *I'd* see you as *kind*," said Lottie. "Doesn't that count for anything? Anyway, why do you care what the Dulcets think?"

"I'm a ruler, Lottie," said Rebel Gem. "I have a reputation to guard. I cannot afford to be considered weak by the Dulcets or the Southerly King or my own people. Politics is a messy business, and I'm very sorry you've gotten tangled up in it. When I made that agreement with Lyre I had no idea there were . . . extenuating circumstances."

"So that's all Eliot is to you? An extenuating circumstance?"

"Of course not. But you must understand my position."

"*Why*?" cried Lottie. "Why must I understand yours when you won't understand *mine*?"

Rebel Gem stared at Lottie in a quiet, expressionless way that made Lottie tremble with anger. Then, at last, she spoke.

"Your Eliot can't return to the human world alone?"

Lottie shook her head. "He needs me by his side to keep him healthy. And even if you did let him go for a little while, by himself, how could I know you'd let him come back? Or that you'd let me follow later?"

"And if I let *you* go," said Rebel Gem, "how would I know that *you* would come back?"

Lottie frowned. "Oh. I guess I see what you mean."

"I have a proposal," said Rebel Gem. "A compromise. What if Eliot wrote a letter to his father?"

Lottie nodded slowly. "That's what we did in Wisp Territory. He sent letters back home every day."

"Then I will allow you to do so here," said Rebel Gem. "That way, Eliot's father will know you are safe and have merely been delayed. And if you really must return to the human world, I will grant passage to both of you, but *only* after the addersfork has been delivered to the wisps, and *only* under the condition that you return. I want your help here, Lottie, and whatever you may think, I'd rather not get it by turning you captive."

"Eliot and I still won't be back in time for the holidays," Lottie said glumly.

"And I will be letting you return to your world with no guarantee you'll ever come back to mine. That's the nature of a compromise, I'm afraid: neither party is fully satisfied, but both get what's most important to them."

"All right," Lottie said slowly. "But you have to *promise*."

"Of course. That's the nature of a deal."

Lottie stuck out her hand. "Then it's a deal."

Rebel Gem smiled at the gesture. Rather than shake Lottie's hand, she turned it palm up, then placed her own hand over it.

"We've struck the deal," she said. "Northerly style. I will grant you and Eliot passage back to Kemble Isle once the addersfork has been retrieved and given to the keeping of the wisps."

Lottie nodded. "Then someone had better get that addersfork soon."

CHAPTER TWELVE

Recoveries

THE FESTIVITIES on the supping lawn were still in full swing when Rebel Gem and Lottie returned, but Lottie headed straight back to the caves—the collection of bedrooms and common areas that Rebel Gem laughingly referred to as the "Slab of Mab" before bidding Lottie goodnight. Lottie found Fife asleep in his room. Eliot was by his side, sifting through a stack of letters—his father's letters.

"I wish I hadn't lost my sketchbook in the river," he said, once he'd followed Lottie back to her own room, where they wouldn't have to speak in whispers. "There's so much here I want to get down on paper."

"You'd do it justice, too," said Lottie. "I bet one day the sprites will have a whole gallery dedicated to the work of Eliot Walsch."

As they sat buried in the covers of Lottie's massive bed, Lottie told Eliot about her conversation with Rebel Gem, starting with their agreement about the silver-boughed tree. Eliot's shoulders slumped, but he didn't look too surprised.

"It makes sense," he said. "Now that you're here, why would Rebel Gem let you go?"

"But it isn't fair to you," said Lottie.

"At least I can let Dad know I'm okay. That's what's bothered me the most: we didn't show up when we said we would, and he's got to be so worried."

Lottie nodded tearfully. "I didn't mean for any of this to happen."

"Of course you didn't," said Eliot, circling his arm around her. "And anyway, it's been an adventure, just like you promised. It's been fun."

"Not *all* fun," said Lottie, clearing the tears from her face.

"Yeah, but nothing's *all* fun. Not even stuff like birthdays and Christmas."

Then Eliot told Lottie he had to fetch something from Fife's room. He reappeared at her doorway minutes later with a book in hand—the same book he'd been reading at Fife's bedside. Once he was back on the bed, he opened the book and tore out its front page in one swift movement.

"What are you doing?" Lottie asked, eyes huge.

"There's nothing else to write a letter on," said Eliot. "And I want to send one first thing in the morning."

He then produced a stubby pencil from his shirt pocket and began scribbling away, while Lottie looked on in silence. When Eliot was done, he folded the letter once and slipped it under the cover of the book.

"It's not home for the holidays," he said. "But it's something."

"It's something," Lottie agreed.

Then Eliot reminded Lottie of the first time Mrs. Yates had allowed Lottie to spend New Year's Eve at the Barmy Badger. Together, they recalled the caramel cocoa Mr. Walsch had made, and how it had snowed so hard that night that ye ol' porthole looked out on nothing but a sheet of white.

They talked so long that Lottie swore she could taste the liquid chocolate on her tongue and smell the wooden scent of the Barmy Badger's parlor and feel the soft wool of Eliot's favorite blanket on her toes.

She and Eliot fell asleep that way, led into dreams by memory.

❦

In the morning, no one demanded that Lottie return to the supping lawn for breakfast. She ate in Fife's room, with the boys. She asked first thing if there was any news about Oliver and Adelaide, but the reply was only sad headshakes.

The absence of their two friends had an effect on all their appetites. Though Lottie's tray was piled high with clusters of grapes and soft cheeses and buttered toasts, she ate very little. She did, however, drink a hot, spiced cranberry drink in slow sips and found she liked this much better than the ale from the night before.

The white-haired boy served them at Fife's bedside, and all the while he kept a sullen eye on Lottie. After he had left them to their food and Lottie was quite certain he would not return, she said, "I think he hates me, and I don't know why."

"Does he?" said Fife, scratching his tangled mess of hair. "Hadn't noticed."

"He keeps giving me nasty looks," said Lottie. "And last night, he was all gruff and snippy."

"Why do you care?" asked Fife.

"He's intimidated," said Eliot. "You being the Heir of Fiske and all, he probably just doesn't know how to behave."

"I don't think that's it," said Lottie, but she didn't have any other explanation for the white-haired boy's behavior, so instead she updated Fife on her news from the night before.

"Hear, hear," Fife said when she was through. "I can't believe you bargained with *Rebel Gem*. And got away with it, too!"

"You're an expert diplomat," said Eliot.

"This goes to show that Rebel Gem can't be all bad," said Fife. "I mean, it's rotten business about the silver-boughed tree, but at least she's reasonable."

"What about sharpening lessons?" asked Eliot. "Are you going to do it?"

"I don't know," said Lottie. She wanted to explain that, somehow, benefiting from Rebel Gem—the only one who stood between Eliot and his father—felt like a kind of betrayal. But she couldn't say that out loud. Not to Eliot.

"What do you mean, *you don't know*?" Fife asked, aghast. "Puck's ever-loving sake, Lottie, if you don't take her up on this, I will never speak to you again. Here I am, stuck in this stupid bed, forced to convalesce. Meanwhile, you've got the chance to sharpen your keen under Rebel Gem, and *you don't know*?"

"I don't see why you wouldn't," said Eliot. "Isn't that what you've wanted? To get better at healing?"

"Oh, I see," said Fife, crossing his arms. "She's only pulling our leg, Eliot. Well, aren't you, Lottie? Because you can't seriously be thinking of refusing sharpening lessons from the Healer of the Wolds. *The* Healer of the Wolds. She's the only legitimate healer left in the North!"

"But she's practically made us her prisoners," said Lottie. "I don't like being part of a deal. I can't explain it, but I don't want to—I don't know—give her the satisfaction."

"You can't think of it like that," said Fife. "You've got to think of it as benefiting from your captor during your captivity. That's how all the greats did it, in the old stories. They didn't just loll around woefully while they were imprisoned. In secret, they trained and strengthened themselves until the opportune time came to overpower their captor. They defeated their enemy using the very succor they'd found at their enemy's table, and, sweet Oberon, I sound just like Ollie."

"Fine," said Lottie. "If you put it like *that*."

She'd been watching closely to see if Fife's tongue emerged during any of this pretty speech, but it hadn't. Maybe, she reflected, Fife could be just as eloquent without the use of his keen.

"When do they say you can get out of that bed?" asked Lottie.

Fife's face darkened. "It'll be another two days at least," he said. "It's only one silly little gash, but they say the stitches will come loose if I move around too much."

"Luckily, we've come to the really good part in our book," said Eliot.

"Good part?" Fife snorted. "If you call mixed metaphors and a surplus of adjectives *good*. Good as a Northerly book can get, I guess. What I wouldn't give to get my hands on a novel."

"At least you've got something to keep you entertained," said Lottie, smiling at Eliot. He really was good to keep Fife company all this while.

"Eliot," she said, a thought occurring to her. "Where's your room, exactly?"

"Oh." Eliot shrugged. "I haven't got one. That is to say, I haven't needed one."

Lottie recalled how she'd first found Eliot, asleep in the chair by Fife's bedside, and realized he'd been here day and night. She turned to Fife. He looked a little sad, and a little guilty, too.

"Eliot insisted on staying here," he said.

"*Fiske.*"

Lottie turned to find the white-haired boy standing in the doorway.

"Rebel Gem wants to see you," he said.

"I haven't finished—"

"*Now.*"

Lottie cast Eliot and Fife a glance that said, *See? I'm not making it up.*

She grabbed a piece of toast to go.

"Fine," she said, deciding that she would walk very close to the white-haired boy the whole way there, eating with her mouth open, and let the crumbs fall where they pleased.

"Wait!" cried Eliot. "Here. For the apple tree."

He placed something in her hand. It was a folded piece of paper, ripped along its edge, with printed words on its back and Eliot's handwriting on the front. His letter home.

Lottie tucked the letter into her coat pocket. She nodded, and Eliot nodded back—a silent promise exchanged.

The white-haired boy led Lottie down a passageway she had not walked before. It required slipping behind a thick, brown tapestry marked with the emblem of a bird in flight—a genga, Lottie assumed. The ceilings here were low, and the ground sloped downward. Lottie tripped once on a loose rock and righted herself by grabbing hold of the wall. She swiped her hands off with a disgusted gasp. Something goopy was caked to her palms. She tried to clean it off as best she could, but her hands still felt dirtied the rest of the way.

At last, the cramped passageway led not into a throne room, as Lottie had been expecting, but outdoors. It was a gloomy, moss-covered space, bordered by pine trees. Lottie's boots squelched into a patch of mud, and while she was working to unstick them, a voice said, "Afraid of a little dirt?"

Lottie looked up. The boy had disappeared. In his place stood Rebel Gem, cloaked in green.

"No," Lottie said, abandoning her work and straightening to a prouder posture. She had a mind to tell Rebel Gem that she'd never been afraid of dirt, even as a kid. She and Eliot had gotten into all sorts of scrapes.

"Good," said Rebel Gem. "One can't afford to be prim in our line of work."

"Where are we?" asked Lottie, looking around at the pines, trying to sort out just what made this place special enough for Rebel Gem to be standing in it.

"We're outside."

"Yes, I can see that," said Lottie. "I just thought you'd be in your throne room."

"My throne room?" Rebel Gem pushed back her hood, laughing. "Merciful Titania, there aren't any *throne rooms* in this court."

"But," said Lottie, "you're basically a queen."

Rebel Gem looked suddenly serious. "We have no queens or kings here. And I hope we never will."

"But what about those crowns in the House of Fiske?"

"The Fiskes ruled before the Schism," said Rebel Gem. "Afterward, we Northerlies swore we'd never have a king or queen again. The Southerlies and wisps can have their pomp and ceremony. We prefer a simpler way of things in the North. Now, come on."

Rebel Gem placed her hand on Lottie's back and guided her to a bench in the middle of the clearing. It was wide across, and so high that Lottie had to hoist herself up. Once sitting, her feet dangled above the ground.

"I know you're new to this world," said Rebel Gem, "but sometimes I forget how new. If you have questions, Lottie, I want you to ask them. Better to hear the truth from a Northerly than believe that palaver from down south."

But, thought Lottie, *you haven't given me much reason to trust your word over theirs.*

"You do wish me to help, don't you?" asked Rebel Gem.

Lottie thought of Fife's irate expression back in the cave, when she'd said she wasn't sure about sharpening. She thought of Eliot's face turned pale with a cough.

"Yes," she said.

"Good," said Rebel Gem, and she really did look pleased about it. She seemed so much younger now than she had just seconds before, and Lottie wanted badly to ask her how old she was and how someone like her could come to rule the Northerlies, and if they didn't believe in queens and kings then what *was* she exactly, and—

"Are you listening to me, Lottie?"

Lottie started. "Sorry, no. I was thinking."

"I asked," said Rebel Gem, "what you've been taught already in the ways of sharpening."

"Not much," Lottie admitted. "Mr. Wilfer was very busy, so we didn't have a lot of time for lessons. And when we did . . . well, I wasn't good at them. We never got past me trying to clear my mind."

"Clear your mind?"

"Yes," said Lottie, wondering if perhaps Rebel Gem was tipsy again, as she had been last night. "You know, the very first step to sharpening."

Rebel Gem made an incredulous sound. "*Well*. That may be Moritasgus Wilfer's approach, but it certainly isn't mine."

Hope bubbled within Lottie. "Really? Because I'm awful at it."

"I've noticed," said Rebel Gem. "Tell me, how many times have you used your keen?"

"Twice now," said Lottie. "The first time, when I healed Eliot, and the second was just a few days ago, on the river. But I don't know exactly how I did that."

"Were you particularly clear-headed either of those times?"

Lottie thought about this. She thought of the anger and fear she'd felt by Eliot's bedside, when Mr. Wilfer had told her the truth about the Otherwise Incurable. She thought of the fear she'd felt on the boat, after Nash had attempted to kill her.

"No. Not at all."

"I didn't think so. Clearing your mind is an all right trick for Southerlies to teach their six-year-olds, but you're no Southerly, and you're well past the age a sprite ought to begin sharpening."

"You don't have to remind me," Lottie said miserably.

"Don't wallow in self-pity," said Rebel Gem. "To be honest, Lottie, I have no idea what you're capable of at full potential. But I do think that Mr. Wilfer—however good his intentions—was training you the wrong way. No disrespect, of course. I've heard nothing but good things about his talents. But *his* keen is about receiving—receiving signals about a sprite's well-being. That's it. He can't *give* healing like us. Calming one's mind is very fine if you're trying to listen, like he has to. But you and I aren't so much listeners as talkers. And if you're going to become any good, you've got to *talk*, and talk *loud*."

Rebel Gem crisscrossed her legs on the bench and dropped her chin into her hands. She squinted hard at Lottie.

"If your mind wasn't clear those times you used your keen, then what was it filled with?"

"Well," said Lottie, thinking back. "Anger, I guess. I was angry that Eliot was going to die. And I was angry that Nash had lied and tried to hurt me. I don't know if anger is the right word for it, though."

"It's enough to work with," said Rebel Gem. "Lottie Fiske, you and I are going to get angry."

They spent hours in the pine clearing. The sun rose above the treetops, then fell back down again. All the while, Rebel Gem gave Lottie orders, and Lottie obeyed—or at least tried her hardest to obey.

Together, she and Rebel Gem made a list in a blank-paged book Rebel Gem had brought along. They wrote down all the people and things that made Lottie angry. Pen Bloomfield was on the list, along with King Starkling and Iolanthe. So were smaller things, like people who spat on sidewalks or talked in movie theaters.

Then Rebel Gem read off the items one at a time. She told Lottie to think of the angriest she'd ever been about each person or thing.

"Then stop *thinking* about it," she told Lottie, "and start *feeling* it. Feel it here"—she pointed to her gut—"deep down. And once you feel it, *move* it."

Lottie tried. She thought of the night Iolanthe had cut down the silver-boughed tree in Wisp Territory. She thought of the sadness in Eliot's face and the anger in her own heart. Iolanthe hadn't just cut off Eliot from home; she'd destroyed something very precious. The more Lottie thought about it, the more she *felt* it—a hot, coiled thing in her stomach.

It was undoubtedly anger, and it felt similar to one of her bad spells. Similar, but not quite the same. And try as Lottie might to *move* the anger in her stomach through the rest of her body, she never could. She knew what Rebel Gem was after. She knew what it meant to *move* the anger, as strange as it sounded. She knew, because she'd moved her bad spells before, the two times she had healed.

"Think. Feel. Move," Rebel Gem instructed. "Think. Feel. *Move.*"

Lottie strained herself until her hair stuck to her sweaty skin and her arms shook. She thought of the anger, she felt the anger, but she could not *move* it.

"I'm doing something wrong!" she shouted after the tenth time she and Rebel Gem had worked through the exercise. "Why do we keep doing the same thing over and over again when it's not working?"

Rebel Gem looked untroubled.

"Who says it isn't working?" she said. "I told you to *try* moving. I didn't say you had to succeed. In fact, you probably never will. You were right before: anger isn't the best word for what you felt those times you used your keen. It's close, yes, and it's part of it, but it isn't *exactly* it. You can't properly move anger the way you can the *other thing*—the thing you can't quite name. And that's what's at the heart of your keen."

Lottie gaped at Rebel Gem. All the anger she'd been *thinking* and *feeling* for the past few hours swelled inside her, and she realized that she was hungry and thirsty and had a terrible headache, and this was *all Rebel Gem's fault.*

"Then what have we been doing any of this for?" she yelled. "It's just as worthless as trying to clear my head!"

"Someone's impatient," said Rebel Gem, which was the worst thing to say to Lottie Fiske. If Lottie were to make an exhaustive list of things that made her angry, one of those items would be the horrid set of people who used the word "someone" when, in fact, they really meant "you."

"We're just wasting time!" Lottie shouted louder, as though the loudness of her words would grant them more truth. "We've been at this for hours, and don't you have anything better to do? Aren't you supposed to be, I dunno, *ruling*?"

Rebel Gem remained unmoved by Lottie's shouting.

"The best way to rule the Northerlies right now," she said, "is to spend my time helping the Heir of Fiske with her sharpening. I don't think I'm wasting time. It's a pity you do."

"But I'm not sharpening," said Lottie. "I can't move anything inside of me, and I'm not healing anyone!"

"Lottie," said Rebel Gem in her infuriatingly calm way, "you seem to think that sharpening is the same as instantaneous progress."

"Well, I'd like to see a *little* progress. Right now, it just feels like I'm sharpening the wrong thing."

"Oh, you're sharpening the right thing. Believe me, you wouldn't be acting so anxious and tiresome if we weren't onto something. You just can't expect to be an expert healer after one lesson. That's unfair to me, and it's most unfair to yourself."

"Yeah, I guess," Lottie muttered, slumping into a sit on the ground. She didn't even care that the seat of her dress was getting damp and muddy.

"When you learned to read," said Rebel Gem, "you didn't start off by just picking up a copy of *In a Time of Schisms* by Ferdinand Ellard III, did you?"

"No," said Lottie grumpily, "because I've never heard of that book in my life."

"What I mean," said Rebel Gem, "is that you began by learning parts of words and then full words and then words put together into sentences and then paragraphs and chapters and *then* books. And even then, you didn't pick up any Ellard for some time, until you were ready."

Lottie studied her bootlaces with a pout. She knew what Rebel Gem was trying to say, but she didn't want to admit it. Rebel Gem was treating her like a child. Even now, as Rebel Gem knelt beside Lottie, placing a hand on her back, Lottie felt so *small*.

"I know it's frustrating to start sharpening so late," Rebel Gem said softly. "I know you feel you have a lot to make up for in a very short space of time. And it won't get easier. Sharpening is always hard, often painful. But it's worth it. I promise."

Lottie's mood began to change. The bitter barb in her throat dislodged. She felt the anger of the past few hours fizzle out. Rebel Gem wasn't trying to make her feel small, Lottie knew. She'd done that to herself. She looked up with wet eyes and a half scowl.

"Are you using your keen on me?" she said.

"It's helping, isn't it?"

Lottie sniffed and nodded. Then she asked, "How long did it take you to get any good at *your* keen?"

Rebel Gem's hand slipped from Lottie's back. She settled in the moss, opposite her. "My story's unusual. The exception, not the rule."

"That's all right," said Lottie. "Mine's unusual, too."

Rebel Gem nodded. "Well. I began sharpening very young, when I was three. I did it all on my own, for a long time without my parents' knowledge. By the time I was ten, I'd reached my limit. I'd sharpened as far as I could. My parents brought me down from the Northerly Wolds to court and presented me to the first Rebel Gem. He was already very old then, and neither he nor his council had found any sprite they considered worthy to take his place.

"Since I was a healer, my parents thought I would be an asset to the Northerly Court and its soldiers. But Rebel Gem saw something else in me. He thought I would make not just a good healer, but a good leader. He trained me to take on his position. In the meantime, I earned my reputation as the Healer of the Wolds. The people of court came to care for me, and I for them. When Rebel Gem lay on his deathbed, he nominated me as his successor, and the council unanimously voted for me to take his place." She shrugged, and the solemnity went out of her voice as she said, "So here I am. The new Rebel Gem."

"But you're not the *real* Rebel Gem?" Lottie asked. "Gem isn't even your name?"

"Does that matter?"

"I think it does. Everyone in the South still thinks you're an old man."

"That's just as I want it," said Rebel Gem. "As far as Starkling and his people know, I'm still the frail, cautious sprite I replaced. Many of my own people still think so, in fact, and any diplomats that come to the court—Lyre Dulcet included—are sworn to secrecy about my true identity."

"But *why*?" said Lottie. "Why try to cover it up? Why not use your own name?"

Rebel Gem tapped at something—a small locket clasped beneath her cloak.

"Did you know, Lottie," she said, "there hasn't been a single woman on the Southerly throne? Not since before the Great Schism, when the two courts were still united."

Lottie shook her head. "I didn't know."

"You see, Southerlies took it into their heads that women had no business sitting on thrones and giving orders."

"That's stupid."

"Stupid, yes," said Rebel Gem, "but a popular idea nonetheless. You may have caught wind of the fact that the Southerlies and Northerlies don't hold each other in high esteem. The Southerlies would only respect us less if they knew a woman led our people—especially a woman as young as I am."

"How old are you, exactly?" Lottie asked.

"How old do you think I am?"

"I don't know. Sometimes you don't seem much older than me. But other times, you act older than even Mr. Wilfer. I can't figure it out."

"I'm twenty-three," said Rebel Gem. "Which isn't a respectable age in any profession, and certainly not in the business of ruling."

"But that's so—so *stupid*," Lottie repeated, unable to come up with a better word. "You're good at what you do. In fact, I think you're the best ruler I've met in Limn. I don't see why the Southerlies wouldn't respect *that*."

"But you're seeing it from your perspective, Lottie, and not from the perspective of old men—and the old men are still the ones who make the decrees and write the newspapers down in the South. Starkling choosing Iolanthe as his new right-hand sprite is a very big deal. She's the first woman to hold that spot. The king's detractors are more upset about that fact than the rumor that Starkling is building a world gorge. It's unfortunate, but that's the way of it."

Lottie was starting to have a headache.

"How're you feeling now?" asked Rebel Gem after a moment of silence. "Less angry?"

"More, I think," Lottie muttered.

"It'll be suppertime soon. I'm sure you've worked up an appetite for it."

"Yes," Lottie said, "but can I eat with Fife and Eliot tonight?"

"Tired of my company?" Rebel Gem asked, smiling.

"No. It's just that I miss them. And it's not like I have much to do on the supping lawn. Everyone cheered for me and all, but afterward it was like I didn't exist."

Rebel Gem burst into laughter.

"What?" Lottie demanded.

"You have a bruised ego, Lottie Fiske, haven't you?"

"No, I don't! I just meant—well, for all their talk of the

Heir of Fiske, it's like they don't care I'm here. No one spoke to me all through supper but Roote and Crag. Nobody else even tried to ask me questions or—"

"Ask for your autograph, you mean?" said Rebel Gem. "Lottie, I thought you were more solid than that. I *told* you we're not like Southerlies. Much as the Northerlies respect the name of Fiske, it would be rude beyond belief to show any more interest toward you than toward our fellow sprites. That's the first rule of Northerly conduct: we treat everyone as equals here."

An autograph was not what Lottie had meant. "People treat *you* differently." But even as Lottie said it she recalled that she'd seen no crown upon Rebel Gem's head, nor heard a fanfare announce her presence. Rebel Gem's seat at the supping lawn was no different from anyone else's. More than that, she'd spent the good part of her day in the middle of the wood, sharpening Lottie's keen, and not one attendant had come trotting out to remind Rebel Gem of all the important appointments on her agenda.

"Don't take it personally," said Rebel Gem, touching Lottie's shoulder for the briefest moment. It was then that Lottie felt, *really* felt the full effect of Rebel Gem's keen. Peace, cool and sure, flowed through Lottie. She felt instant reassurance. Why *had* she taken it personally?

"There are some exceptions to that rule, of course," Rebel Gem continued as she and Lottie walked back into the caves.

"There are fanatics who live in the Wolds and the Wilders and believe a Fiske to be the answer to all their woes. *They'd* likely make a fuss over you. But as to the rest of us, we're a skeptical bunch. No one doubts you're a Fiske, but no one is under the impression that you're our great savior, either. Your name carries power with it in the rest of Albion Isle, and that's why I want you here. But you're just the same as any one of us, Lottie. Our heroes aren't determined based on blood but on merit."

"And I guess I haven't got a lot of merit yet," said Lottie.

"Not yet. But you're young. And despite what you think, you're a fast learner. I'd say there's hope for you yet."

"Rebel Gem?"

"Hm?"

"Does this mean we're done with training for today?"

Rebel Gem nodded.

"Good," said Lottie. "Because I've got a letter to send."

Rebel Gem led the way to the apple tree, and Lottie was grateful she did, because she was sure she would've gotten lost otherwise, even with the most detailed instructions. Unlike the wisps' apple tree, which had grown in the wood where anyone might happen to pass it, the Northerlies' tree was hidden away. Lottie followed Rebel Gem back into the caverns and down a winding series of stone hallways.

Torchlight lit their path, but all else was wet, dark shadows and the sounds of distant scuttling.

"Watch your head," Rebel Gem instructed as the roof grew lower—or was it the floor that had grown higher?—but the warning had not come in time; Lottie's forehead smacked into a slime-covered stalactite.

Rebel Gem made a sympathetic "ooh," and came back a few steps to examine Lottie.

"No damage done," she said after a moment, patting Lottie's head in a way that Lottie supposed should have offended her dignity but instead left her feeling much calmer than before.

From there on out, Lottie continued to duck often, crouching and scrambling, and wondering just how low the ceiling would get. Just when she'd begun to walk in a perpetual stoop, Rebel Gem led them into an adjoining hallway—this one far roomier and taller than before. And from the end of the hallways came a faint light that looked like—

"Sunlight?" Lottie shook her head. "But that can't be right. We've been heading downward for ages."

"Come on then, Lottie," said Rebel Gem. "Pick up the pace."

The light grew nearer and brighter until, in one moment, it burst all around Lottie. She blinked against the force of it, shielding her eyes and, on instinct, grabbing at Rebel Gem's hand, for Lottie had a sudden petrifying thought that this sunlight was not natural at all but something terribly magical that could very well blind her.

Rebel Gem gently shook off Lottie's grip, pointing ahead. "Don't be scared," she said. "Look."

Lottie lowered her hand. Slowly, her vision adjusted, and she strained her eyes to see into the light. They were standing in a large, circular room, hewn from gray stone. The ceiling was unthinkably high. The walls rose above Lottie for foot after foot after foot and were covered in square, glittering mirrors, all tilted toward a wide circle in the far distant ceiling—the source of the light. Lottie got the distinct impression she was standing at the bottom of a glittering wishing well.

And at the very center of this well stood an apple tree, its leaves a lush green and its apples deep yellow. Lottie let out a long breath.

"My sentiments precisely," said Rebel Gem. "It's rather magnificent, isn't it?"

"If Iolanthe ever visited *you*," said Lottie, "she'd have a much harder time chopping your tree down."

Rebel Gem's gaze darkened. "If Iolanthe ever visited us, we'd have a whole slew of other problems on our hands. Now, your letter."

"Oh. *Oh!*" Lottie couldn't believe she'd nearly forgotten her whole reason for paying a visit to the apple tree. She dug Eliot's letter from her pocket and walked toward the tree. There were six guards positioned around its trunk with drawn swords and stoic gazes. They carried shields, too, made of metal and engraved with black diamonds.

Lottie turned back to Rebel Gem. "The wisps only had one guard at theirs."

"I'm well aware of the fact," said Rebel Gem. "Upon receiving news of what happened to the wisp tree, I ordered this guard be doubled. Our tree is far less vulnerable than others, perhaps, but I won't take any chances."

"Good," said Lottie. She didn't want anything left to chance when it came to her and Eliot's one route home.

She took a few steps closer to the tree, gaze fixed on Eliot's letter, afraid to look any of the guards in the eye. Then she remembered something. She turned to Rebel Gem again. "I don't have a way to send it back. I used a copper box before, but Iolanthe and her soldiers stole it, or destroyed it, or— well, the point is, it's gone."

"I've thought of that," said Rebel Gem, motioning back to the tree.

One of the guards had set aside his shield and was holding a box, which he now offered to Lottie. She shrank with embarrassment, realizing that if she'd actually been brave enough to meet the gaze of the guards, she might have noticed the box sooner.

She took the box from the guard. It was far heavier than it looked; Lottie suspected it was made of pure silver. There was an engraving on its lid of a single apple, split in half so that its seeds—tiny inlaid rubies—were visible.

"Are you sure it's okay for me to use this?" Lottie asked.

Rebel Gem laughed. "I'm sure, Lottie. It's mine to give to whomever I'd like. And you have need of it. So *use* it."

Lottie opened the box and placed Eliot's letter inside. Then she drew closer to the apple tree. The two guards nearest her stepped aside, and Lottie set the box at the tree's base.

"All right, Trouble," she said, reaching into her pocket and finding, to her relief, that he was actually roosting there this time.

Trouble rustled in her hand, shivering out his wings with an annoyed squawk. A few moments later, once he found his bearings, he fluttered to a low branch and perched. Lottie walked up to the silver bough, jumped, and grabbed hold. Using all her weight, she tugged the branch down. Then came a deep groaning sound. The tree's bark splintered, and Lottie stepped back as a doorway formed in its trunk. With a satisfied nod, she retrieved the silver box from the ground. She walked straight up to the tree's threshold and placed the box inside. As she did, she felt certain she heard a faint hitch of breath behind her, from Rebel Gem.

"Mr. Walsch's house, Kemble Isle," she whispered into the tree.

Then she released the box, stepped back, and watched as the apple tree's bark whorled back in on itself, sealing up the doorway.

"There," Lottie said, holding up her hand for Trouble to return to. Though of course, Trouble did not wish to return immediately. He chirped obstinately and flew three wide circles around the tree, swooping quite close to some of the guards' heads. Lottie gave Trouble a look once he'd finally landed in her palm.

"Show-off," she muttered, tucking him into her pocket.

"Um, thank you for your service, guards," she said, hoping she sounded confident and mature. Then, she returned to Rebel Gem, who had remained at a distance from the apple tree and was watching Lottie with an apprehensive gaze Lottie had never seen on her before. As Lottie came closer, Rebel Gem shook off the strange look and smiled.

"All right?" she asked.

Lottie cast a glance back at the tree. It was strange to be so close to her route home and yet so very far away.

I could have gone back right then and there, she thought. *I could have, and no one would've been able to stop me in time.*

She wondered if Rebel Gem had thought about this, too. She wondered if this was why she had gasped as Lottie stepped so close to the tree's threshold.

But, of course, Lottie would never have stepped into that tree. For one thing, Eliot was not with her, and for another, she had made a promise to Rebel Gem—and Rebel Gem certainly seemed to be holding up her end of the deal.

"Soon we'll go home, Eliot," Lottie whispered on the long, dark journey back to the surface. "Soon."

There were guests in Fife's room. Even before Lottie stepped through the doorway, she heard peppery laughs and a deep voice shouting, "No fair, that! Eh! No fair!"

Roote and Crag were paying a visit. They and Eliot sat on the giant canopied bed, while Fife floated above a mound of pillows. Scattered on the bed were colored stones and octagonal pieces of paper that resembled playing cards.

"Greetings, Lottie!" cried Fife, flapping an arm at her. "The boys and I were just playing a game of skipping stone."

"Cheatin' is more like," said Crag, throwing down his cards. "That boy ain't allowed to float like that. 'E can see everything in our 'ands!"

Fife laughed loudly. "It was just a joke. Tell them, Eliot."

"It isn't funny," said Eliot, who was very white in the face. "You shouldn't be floating. Rebel Gem said you haven't fully recov—"

"Oh, who cares what *she* says. She hasn't checked on me in a full day."

Eliot broke into a cough and turned his face away.

"Eliot's right," Lottie said angrily. "You're supposed to be resting, Fife. There's no way you'll be able to explore the Northerly Court if you split your stitches back open."

"I'm *fine*." But even as Fife said it, an undeniable wince flickered across his face. He lowered back to the bed but added, "I'm only doing it because I *want* to sit back down."

The sound of a horn sang down the cave hall.

"Supping time," said Roote, collecting the stones and cards from the bed. "But this isn't over, young Dulcet. We'll be back for another game."

"Counting on it," said Fife.

They left, and Lottie glared at Fife.

"*What?*" he said. "I'm bored. Don't begrudge this sprite a little gambling to stave off the doldrums."

"You shouldn't be floating," Lottie said.

"What are you, my mother?"

Lottie, who didn't appreciate being compared to Silvia Dulcet, decided not to press the issue further.

Later, after the white-haired boy had cleared their supper away—all the while casting Lottie the stink eye—Lottie insisted that she take over Eliot's watch.

"Just tonight," she told Eliot in an appeasing way. "You should sleep on my bed. I want to stay up with Fife and talk."

Eliot looked prepared to argue, but his eyelids were already drooping. He gave way only after he secured Lottie's promise that she wouldn't let Fife read ahead in their book. When he'd gone, Lottie turned the book over. The cover read *In a Time of Schisms,* by Ferdinand Ellard III.

"Quick," said Fife. "Burn it. Burn it while you have the chance."

"I heard it's a classic," Lottie said.

"That doesn't mean anything up here. You could write the word 'mud' on a piece of paper, and the Northerlies would call it a classic."

"You're starting to sound like Adelaide."

Fife's face went stony. "Take that back."

"No," Lottie said, grinning.

Silence fell, and finally Fife spoke again.

"Don't you dare ever tell her this," he said, "but I miss her. A little."

Lottie made a show of dropping her jaw. "Fife *Dulcet*," she said, throwing her hand on her heart. "You miss *Adelaide*?"

"Ollie, too, of course. But I kind of miss her stupid nagging. In a *stupid* way, you know?"

"No," said Lottie, suddenly serious. "I know."

Fife shifted in his pillows, scooting closer to where Lottie sat. "Is everything okay with Eliot?"

"Why?" Lottie asked, ignoring the judder of her heart.

"It's only, he's been acting kind of sick today. And I didn't know if that was normal, if he just has his bad bouts every so often."

"No," Lottie whispered. "It isn't normal. I think he's getting sicker."

Fife licked his lower lip. "Lottie—"

"Don't use your keen. Please. You don't have to say a thing. It's just, I thought at first I'd made him better for good."

"He's human, Lottie. He isn't like you. He's full-blooded human, and he's been living in Limn for a while. That would make any human sick—even the healthiest, strongest one alive."

"Do you think that's all it is?" Lottie asked, drawing her knees up and burying her nose in them.

"Yeah, I do. I mean, it's what happened to your father, isn't it?"

Lottie went still.

Yes. That was what had happened to her father. He had stayed too long in Limn, and he had grown sick. By the time Lottie's mother brought him back to the human world, there was nothing to be done.

"Lottie?" She felt the press of a hand on her knee. "I'm sorry. I shouldn't have brought that up."

"No," said Lottie, dragging her face up. "You're right. It *is* what happened to my father. Which is why I won't let it happen to Eliot. I can't."

"That search party is going to find Ollie and Adelaide," said Fife. "And they'll find Dorian, too. They will, and then Dorian will get the addersfork for the wisps, and Rebel Gem will let you and Eliot use the silver-boughed tree, and everything will be okay again."

"Yes," said Lottie. "That's the deal anyway."

"You don't say that like you mean it."

Lottie met Fife's gaze. She forgot sometimes just how terrifyingly bright his eyes were.

"I've been thinking about the future," she said.

"Whoo boy. Why would you do something like that?"

"I'm *serious*, Fife. I've been thinking of where I belong. I know I'm half human, but there's nothing about the human world I ever liked much, except Eliot."

"You mean you prefer being chased around by wild beasts and the Southerly Guard and nearly getting assassinated by one of Iolanthe's spies, and, I dunno, almost drowning in a raging river of doom?"

"I didn't say things here were *easy*," said Lottie. "I just mean, in spite of all those terrible things, I really do love it here. I feel like I'm home when I'm in Limn, even though I don't have a proper home at all. I feel like I belong here. I want to stay. But—"

"Eliot can't."

"Eliot can't."

"Oberon," muttered Fife. "And I thought I had it bad."

"When I was talking to Rebel Gem and she promised she'd let me and Eliot go back to Kemble Isle, I realized: I don't *want* to go back to Kemble Isle, even though I know it's what's best for Eliot. Because I think of you all, and I think of the wisps dying and King Starkling and Iolanthe and the horrible things being done. And I think how, even if it's just a little thing on my part, I might be able to *do* something about all of it. So, who's more important: Eliot or the rest of you? I'll be miserable no matter what I choose."

"I think," said Fife, "you've been sharpening too hard today."

"No. I'm seeing things very clearly."

Fife sighed. "I don't know what to say. Usually, I'm pretty good at that."

"It's okay," whispered Lottie.

Then arms wrapped around her and held her close. Fife was hugging her. She felt his cool chest and the brush of his downy black hair, ducked against her neck. For a quiet moment, they stayed just like that.

Fife made a mumbling sound. A few mumbles later, his words became audible.

"Ummm, Lottie? I've never hugged anyone before. So I don't quite know, um, how to stop."

Lottie remained still. "You've never hugged *anyone*?"

"Well, the immediate family isn't exactly the warmest bunch, in case you hadn't noticed. And as for Ollie . . . *Well*."

Slowly, Lottie slipped out of the embrace.

"There. That's how you stop one. More or less."

Fife nodded, his eyes on the pillows. "Easy enough."

Lottie nudged Fife's knee with her own. "Thank you," she said.

"Yeah, well, I didn't want my cheese earlier, and I could see you eyeing it."

"No, Fife. Not for that."

He didn't look at her when he said, "I know."

CHAPTER THIRTEEN

Discoveries

"I WANT PAPER," Lottie said first thing the next morning, when Rebel Gem met her in the pine clearing. "Preferably a sketchbook, but loose-leaf will do. And I want charcoal, and I want a Southerly novel. A *good* Southerly novel."

Rebel Gem had been poking at something within the locket that hung around her neck. At Lottie's arrival, she clamped the locket shut and gave Lottie a long stare. Lottie marveled at Rebel Gem's ability to never—not once—look startled, even when Lottie did plenty of things she herself considered startle-worthy.

"That can be arranged," Rebel Gem said at last. "I'll have them delivered to your room this evening."

"Not my room. Fife's."

"Ah, I see."

Lottie had expected resistance. She'd expected Rebel Gem to say that Lottie was under her rule and had no right to make demands. Lottie wasn't sure how to behave now that she'd so easily gotten what she wanted.

"There are Southerly books up here, then?" she asked.

"In my own personal collection, yes. You know, they write *much* better novels than Northerlies do."

"So I've heard," Lottie said.

﹘

For the rest of the morning, and well past noon, they resumed Lottie's sharpening lessons. Only, today, Rebel Gem did not ask Lottie to think and feel things that made her angry but rather things that made her afraid. It was hard work at first, compiling a list—far harder than it had been to list things that made her mad. Lottie felt she had a right to be angry with someone like Starkling. But to admit that she was afraid of him, too, and afraid of Iolanthe and her soldiers—to admit that made Lottie feel weak.

Eventually, they came up with enough items for Lottie to begin thinking and feeling through. As she did, she discovered that fear felt different than anger. It wasn't the feverish burning sensation she'd endured the day before but a deep, nauseating ache in her gut.

Rebel Gem was relentless. *Think*, she told Lottie, and *Feel*, and *Move*. But no matter how much Lottie thought and felt the things that caused her fear, she still couldn't *move* the feeling, couldn't send it radiating to her hands. She went to bed exhausted that night, before suppertime.

There was still no word from the search party of soldiers and gengas that Rebel Gem had sent out. Lottie tried not to think about this and what it might mean. Her worry, like her training, became all-consuming, taking hold of her hours, her thoughts, and even her dreams. She told herself that Oliver and Adelaide had to be all right, and she refused to let herself consider the alternative explanations that flooded her nightmares.

The next morning, when she arrived at Fife's room, Eliot had received a thick, leather-bound sketchbook and a set of well-sharpened charcoal pencils, bound in twine. On the table at Fife's bedside sat a book entitled *Tales of a Fairwind Pauper*, which Lottie had of course never heard of but Fife was enraptured to possess.

But none of the new items compared to the letter the white-haired boy delivered along with breakfast. According to his report, it had arrived in the dead of night and been handed over to him straight from one of the yellow-apple-tree guards.

Lottie watched anxiously as Eliot read.

"Father says he's concerned," he said once he was through, handing the single sheet of folded paper to Lottie. "But he understands and is glad we're safe."

Lottie read over the letter twice, but she felt worse, not better. Mr. Walsch's worry bled across the page, and when Lottie looked up she saw Eliot sopping a tear into his wrist.

For that day's sharpening, Rebel Gem changed the target emotion yet again—this time to sadness.

"Why can't I think and feel *happy* thoughts?" Lottie asked, scowling. "Maybe I could actually move feelings if I felt good about them."

"Did you feel particularly happy when you healed Eliot?" asked Rebel Gem.

Lottie wanted to lie, but Rebel Gem already knew the truth: Lottie had been miserable the night she'd healed Eliot. She'd thought her best friend was going to die.

"It just seems wrong," said Lottie, "to feel all these horrible things *on purpose*. Does *everyone* have to torture themselves when they're sharpening? I mean, what, did Fife have to remember all his worst nightmares when he was first trying to taste people's words?"

"I imagine not. Everyone sharpens differently. But every approach is painful in its own way."

"I'm asking Fife," said Lottie. "I bet it wasn't as painful for him."

"You're not going to get anywhere if you keep comparing yourself to someone else," said Rebel Gem. "Focus on you. Focus on *your* emotions."

Again, Lottie made her list. She was sad whenever she heard a song that Mrs. Yates had liked to play back at the boarding house—an old Irish ballad called "Two Brothers."

The month of January made her sad, because everything was cold and dead, and there was no more Christmas to look forward to. Stray dogs and cats made her sad. So did the fact that she'd been separated from the Barghest on the journey north and that there was still no word from the creature. She made her list, and she *thought* and *felt* but still could not *move*. She left the pine grove well after sunset with heavy limbs and a heavier heart.

"It's no good," she told Fife and Eliot that night. "The whole thing's pointless. Maybe Rebel Gem is just torturing me for fun."

"Possible," said Fife. "You know that saying about Northerlies."

"Neither of us know the saying," said Eliot. He pointed at himself, then Lottie. "We are mere earthlings."

"Oh, right. Well, I don't remember it verbatim. Just something about them not being trustworthy and stuff."

"But *you're* half Northerly, aren't you?" said Eliot.

"Yup," Fife said proudly.

"How bad was sharpening for you?" Lottie asked him, trying to sound casual.

"Hm? Oh, plenty bad. I didn't have a fancy tutor like Ada and Ollie, so I had to figure it all out on my own. I went a whole year without being able to taste the sweet in anything. Chocolate tasted like dirt. It was brutal."

Lottie sighed. "It doesn't sound as bad as what I have to do."

"Oh, get over yourself. You wouldn't believe the stuff Ollie had to endure—all those experiments to see if his involuntary pigmentary transference was curable. And when she was eight, Ada overworked herself and went deaf for a spell. She was so scared she'd never hear again that she cried for weeks straight." Fife shuddered at the memory. "Point is, you're not special, Lottie. It's always painful one way or the other."

"I know I'm not special," Lottie mumbled.

"Do you?" Fife smirked. "I mean, you're the *Heir of Fiske*. That's got to be going to your head. I bet you think someone wrote a prophecy about you. I bet you think there are clans in the Wolds that *worship* you. I bet—"

Lottie shoved Fife against the pillows, laughing.

"Ow, ow, *hey*!" gasped Fife. "I'm the invalid here!"

"Not for long," said Lottie. "Aren't you allowed out of bed tomorrow?"

Fife's expression turned wicked. "This court won't know what hit 'em. Spool's been scouting all the best places for me to wreak havoc."

"We should go exploring together!" said Eliot, hopping excitedly on the bed. "Once you're through with lessons, Lottie, let's all look around. It'll be just like it was in Wisp

Territory, only better, 'cause we'll have daylight on our side, and we, um, won't have to avoid the plagued areas."

It occurred to Lottie then that Eliot hadn't yet seen anything outside the caves. She'd been so preoccupied with and exhausted by sharpening lessons that she hadn't once thought how bored he must be. She cast a glance at his sketchbook, which lay open on the floor, filled with drawings. The sketch visible was of a whorl-branched yew tree in Wisp Territory. The sight made her feel funny.

Disquiet had been growing inside of Lottie ever since her first lesson with Rebel Gem. It was something left unsaid, something she should have brought up every time she and Rebel Gem compiled their lists, but she hadn't. She'd never talked about the two things that made her the most angry, fearful, and sad.

She hadn't talked about Eliot.

She hadn't once mentioned her parents.

Those were people too real and feelings too leaden with hurt. But the more Lottie ignored them, and the more she told herself it didn't matter they weren't on her list, the more her heart thudded in protest. Perhaps, Lottie thought, as she stared at Eliot's charcoal drawing, nothing was hindering her keen but *her*.

That night, as she lay awake in bed, she took up what had become a nightly ritual. She removed her mother's lapis lazuli ring from the safekeeping of her coat pocket, and she turned it over in her fingers, careful of its sharp edges, marveling at the smoothness of the band and the intricate notches that made up the flowering bud.

My mother wore this once, she thought. *My father placed it on her finger, and there was love, so much love caught up between them in this ring, this ring I'm holding now.*

The thought made her ache in an old, familiar place she had been acquainted with ever since the day she'd learned what the word "orphan" meant. She ached, but atop that ache, spread like a balm, there was happiness, too. She knew more now about her parents than she'd known before. She owned something they had touched and treasured. For all the anger and fear and sadness Lottie had felt these past few days, there was also this single happy fact.

Lottie was the first to arrive for lessons the next morning. She didn't take her customary seat on the bench, but instead paced from one end of the clearing to the other while Trouble swooped overhead, following her steps with laps of his own, singing a minor-key melody. Lottie hadn't ventured into the House of Fiske since that night at the supping lawn, but Trouble didn't seem to mind. During her training sessions, he flitted from branch to branch, watching her in a quiet way. At night, he perched on her bedpost and roosted there contentedly. It seemed that, for now at least, Trouble had no more plans of his own. He was willing to sit by her side. For *now*.

Lottie was so lost in her pacing and in Trouble's song that she didn't see Rebel Gem arrive.

"Fine morning for wearing out the moss with your boot heels," she said, taking a seat on the bench.

Lottie started. She'd been repeating to herself what she intended to say when Rebel Gem arrived. She'd been reminding herself that if she did not speak first thing, she would lose the nerve. So now she marched up to Rebel Gem, building courage with each step.

"Oh dear," said Rebel Gem. "What new demands are we making today? Don't tell me your friends weren't happy with their gifts."

"It isn't about that," said Lottie. "I think I've been doing something wrong."

"We've talked this through, Lottie. You can't expect progress this early, when—"

"No, it isn't that," Lottie interrupted. "I know I'm not special. But there is something I could do to make sharpening better. I haven't been entirely honest on those lists. I haven't been telling you everything."

Rebel Gem's mouth parted with realization. Then she smiled and said, "I know that."

"What? But—but how could you?"

"Why wouldn't you hide things from me?" said Rebel Gem. "You barely know me. I didn't expect you'd tell me your deepest, darkest emotions straightaway. That takes time. To be honest, I thought it'd take far more time than this."

"But—but—" Lottie sputtered.

"I think," said Rebel Gem, "you've forgotten what I am. Sensing others' states of mind is my specialty."

"Well, do you think that's what's been holding me back?"

"Of course."

"Then why didn't you *tell* me?"

"You would've resisted," said Rebel Gem. "Your thoughts and feelings are your own, Lottie. You would've fought me tooth and claw had I tried to pry into them any deeper than I already have."

This was probably true, Lottie acknowledged. Her frustration, boiling before, settled into a simmer.

"I should say them out loud," she said. "I think it would help."

"If you'd like." Rebel Gem's air seemed almost indifferent; it was only her attentive brown eyes that made Lottie feel that what she was about to say was important.

"I'm most angry about my parents dying," Lottie said. "I'm most sad that I never even knew them, and I never will. All I have is a picture and a ring. And I'm most afraid that I'll lose Eliot like I lost them—only it'll be much worse, because I *know* Eliot, and I can't bear the thought of him *not being*. I'm afraid of that more than I am of anything else in this world."

Rebel Gem said nothing for a long while. Wind rattled through the pine needles and blew back the slack hair from Lottie's face.

"Yes," Rebel Gem said. "I do believe those are the deepest things within you, Lottie Fiske. The deepest you know about, anyway."

Lottie had expected to feel better. Instead, she felt laid bare, like she'd been curled beneath the shelter of a rock, and that rock had just been lifted and tossed aside, exposing her to the harsh light of the sun.

I shouldn't have told her, thought Lottie. *I shouldn't have said a thing.*

Rebel Gem fiddled with something at her neck, tugging it out from beneath her cloak. It was the locket Lottie had seen her touch so many times before. Rebel Gem now unclasped it and pooled its chain in her palm. She held it out toward Lottie.

"This was my father's," she said. "It was his father's before him, and his father's—tracing back to the days of the Schism, when the House of Vance moved northward into the Wolds. It was meant for his only son, but when I was your age, my brother was killed. He was posted as a lookout on the border, and one day he was ambushed by Southerly soldiers. The Southerlies took his body, so we could never give him a proper burial, never say a true goodbye. It killed my father. And on his deathbed, he gave me this."

Lottie was grateful to have something to look at other than Rebel Gem's saddened eyes. She stared at the locket. There was a black diamond carved upon it, and within that a golden *V.*

"I'm sorry," Lottie said. "I'm very sorry."

"My brother was my best friend," said Rebel Gem. "If he had lived, I would've wanted to rule with him as my most trusted counselor. He was far wiser than I was. Far calmer under pressure. He didn't wish to serve as a soldier on the border; it was my father who volunteered him for the post. And if I'm honest, Lottie, I never forgave my father for that. When I look at the pendant of Vance, I don't think of him, but of my brother—the one who should've worn it."

"Oh, *don't*," said Lottie, gasping for breath.

A searing pain cut across her chest. Lottie had been vividly picturing Rebel Gem's story. She saw an old man, proud and stooped, dressed in leather, sending his young son southward. She saw Rebel Gem waving goodbye to her brother with a tearstained face. She saw blood soaking the ground, a body thrown into an unmarked grave. Then the face of the body appeared in Lottie's mind, and it was no longer the vaguely filled-out features of Rebel Gem's unknown brother.

It was Eliot.

"Don't," Lottie repeated. "Don't say any more. It's terrible. I can't—I *can't breathe*."

She was having a bad spell.

Pain exploded in Lottie's chest. She felt like her lungs were shrinking and a black vacuum expanding in their place. She felt something else: Rebel Gem's hands on her shoulders.

"Move the pain, Lottie," she whispered.

Lottie had done this twice before. She knew what to do. The pain was already surging from her chest up into her throat, then through her shoulders in a spindling spasm, down her arms and into her hands. Lottie grabbed hold of Rebel Gem's elbows.

She felt the pain pooling in her palms like liquid, then draining away from her into Rebel Gem's skin. Lottie's eyes flew open as the bad spell subsided. Rebel Gem seemed utterly unaffected. Her face remained a calm veil as Lottie let go, chest heaving.

"Did I—" Lottie gasped, "did I do it? Did you feel anything?"

"Yes," said Rebel Gem. "You did it."

"My keen *worked*?"

"I'm afraid it was wasted on me," said Rebel Gem, "but had I been ill, it would be a different story."

Lottie stared at Rebel Gem's locket, dropped on the muddy ground between them.

"Did you do that on purpose?" Lottie asked. "Did you try to make me upset?"

Rebel Gem didn't respond, but she didn't have to.

"That was a mean thing to do!" Lottie cried, stumbling back. "Did you know I'd see Eliot when you told me that story?"

"I knew nothing about what was in your heart," said Rebel Gem, "save that you were experiencing three very strong emotions at once, and that all you lacked was the opportunity to empathize."

Lottie shook her head. "What does that mean?"

"When you told me about your parents, you felt anger *and* fear *and* sadness, and you felt something beyond that, too—the unnamable thing. But the only way you could move those feelings was to project them onto someone else's story: mine. You empathized with me, and as you did, all those emotions you'd felt for yourself suddenly reached out for me."

"I moved," Lottie murmured.

Rebel Gem nodded.

"Is that it?" asked Lottie, dumbfounded. "I just have to feel bad for someone else?"

"You have to *empathize* with someone else," Rebel Gem corrected. "And even then, sharpening isn't a science. It isn't something you can re-create again and again, the very same way. We're still learning, but at least we know now how to approach things. That's progress."

Lottie marched back to Rebel Gem with new resolve. "Then let's try it again. I want to see if I can still do it."

"That's not a good idea. You're a little delirious right now."

"I am not," Lottie retorted, just before her knees buckled.

Rebel Gem caught her, then helped her to sit on the bench. Even after Lottie had regained her balance, Rebel Gem did not let go. Lottie felt a cold sensation rush down her back, pronging out in many directions. The anxiety, the fear, and the anger that had been thrashing inside her now vanished, swept away by a whisper in the deepest place of her ear.

"*Everything will be set aright,*" it said. "*Don't fret so.*"

Lottie felt grounded, as though she'd been in a rocking boat all this time and had only now been placed safely upon the shore.

"W-what's happening?" she asked.

"I'm taking your cares away," said Rebel Gem. "I'm wrapping them up and setting them aside. Just for now. You deserve it. You're tired, and your heart needs rest."

"But I wanted to practice again," Lottie said weakly.

"You would only hurt yourself. It's dangerous to over-strain your keen, and it's already had more than enough strain for one day—for a whole week, really."

Lottie wanted to protest, but she was reminded of what Fife had said about Adelaide overworking herself and going deaf for weeks. She swallowed her retorts and nodded.

"But I did it," she said with satisfaction. "I *did* it."

"You did. Far sooner than I thought possible, too."

There was a long silence during which Lottie did nothing but grin.

Then Rebel Gem said, "There's something we need to talk about, Lottie. Something serious."

Lottie's grin vanished. "What?" Her thoughts immediately flew to Eliot.

"I'm hesitant to even bring it up. I don't want to scare you. But if you've progressed this far, then you need to know the . . . risks."

"Risks?" Lottie frowned. "You mean, overextending myself? I already know about that. That's why I'm resting, isn't it?"

"No, it's not that. It's about what you're capable of. What your keen can do. If it's anything like mine—and so far, it has been—then you don't just have the potential to heal. You could do the opposite, too."

Lottie stared at Rebel Gem. "You mean I could *hurt* people? Like Oliver can?"

"Not exactly like Oliver. His keen is something he can't control. You and I, Lottie, we can affect the insides of another person. That is a great advantage when it comes to making that person feel better. But if we were to channel our keen in a different direction, we could also use our power to harm someone. Harm them in the worst possible way. Do you understand what I'm saying?"

"You mean," said Lottie, "if I'd concentrated on hurting Nash back on that boat—if I'd wanted to make his bruises worse, rather than better . . . I could've?"

"You *could* have, but a true healer would never do such a thing. Healers help, we do not harm. It is not our place to play judge or to exact punishment. Our place is only to feel someone else's pain and do what we can to relieve it. I've only told you about this now so there's less chance of an . . . accident. I don't think you bear ill will toward any of your friends, but if you were purposefully trying to hurt them . . . I just need you to be aware of the danger."

"Fine. I'm aware."

Lottie couldn't keep the anger out of her words. She was upset with Rebel Gem, and she couldn't place why. Perhaps it was because Rebel Gem suddenly reminded her of Mr. Wilfer, cautioning Lottie to wait, treating her like she didn't know her own strength.

"Come on," Rebel Gem said softly. "I'll take you inside to your friends, and you can tell them the good news."

Lottie tried to push her irritation aside as they walked up the sharp incline of the cave passageway.

Rebel Gem isn't like Mr. Wilfer, she told herself. *She's actually helping you sharpen your keen. And you did it. You're not useless, you're powerful. You did it.*

"By the way," said Rebel Gem, "I've received some news I think you'll find most agreeable. My genga returned early this morning."

Lottie, who'd been turning heavy-lidded, snapped to attention.

Oliver, she thought. *Adelaide.*

"She encountered a party of three travelers on the widest of the wooded paths, headed here," Rebel Gem went on. "Your friends are both well, as is Dorian. I expect they'll arrive at court within a day."

Lottie cast Rebel Gem a sharp look. "If you knew all this earlier, why didn't you tell me?"

"I didn't want to distract you from your lesson."

"*Distract* me? I was already distracted. I've been worried sick about them!"

"All right. No need to—"

Lottie slapped away Rebel Gem's hand, which had been approaching her shoulder.

"Don't touch me," she said. Then, thinking better of it, "*Please*. I don't want any more of your keen, thanks."

"Beg your pardon. I didn't realize how quickly it wore off on halflings."

They emerged from the passageway into the blazing light of the great meeting room. The usual groups of sprites were huddled about the fireplaces, and Lottie recognized a few of the faces as ones she had seen at Rebel Gem's table, the night at the supping lawn. One of them noticed their entrance and waved both arms in their direction.

"Rebel Gem!" he cried. "Ey, ey! Over here, if you please!"

"Excuse me," said Rebel Gem.

Lottie wondered if she'd only imagined the bite in Rebel Gem's voice. She watched the swish of her green cloak as she joined a group of murmuring sprites. Lottie headed for Fife's room, trying to sort out all the fiery emotions boiling inside her.

She was angry with Rebel Gem, but grateful to her, too. She was nervous and excited and scared—all by what Rebel Gem had told her about the full scope of her keen. She was overwhelmed with happiness about the news of Keats, but now more impatient than ever to see her friends again. Muddled as her mind was, though, there was one clear thought that rose above the rest: she'd used her keen. She'd done it a third time. Soon, she would be able to use it on Eliot and dispel that horrible cough once and for all.

Her heart thumped in time with every step she took toward Fife's doorway, her tongue straining to let loose the exciting news. But as she stepped inside, every word she'd meant to speak fell back into her throat.

"Aha!" said Fife. "We were about to form another search party."

Adelaide laughed, actually laughed, and Oliver's eyes turned golden at the sight of Lottie.

For there Adelaide and Oliver were, sitting on Fife's bed as though it were the most natural thing in all of Albion Isle.

CHAPTER FOURTEEN

Unexpected Visitors

ALL WAS LAUGHTER and whoops and the creak of Fife's bed as the five of them sat piled atop the covers. Adelaide had thrown herself on Lottie first thing, squeezing her into so tight a hug that Lottie squeaked, sure her bones would snap.

"Titania's sake," Adelaide said. "Oh, *Titania's sake*, Lottie, we thought you were dead! Or else you'd all been captured by Northerlies and put in shackles and sent into the quarry mines. We worried for you every minute, didn't we, Oliver?"

Oliver's eyes dimmed to gray. "Slow, slow as the winter snow, the tears have drifted to mine eyes."

Lottie didn't have to ask how they'd arrived in Fife's bedroom. Adelaide launched into the story with vigor, barely stopping for breath in the pauses between.

The night of the ice crawler attack, Adelaide and Oliver had jumped from the boat and been dragged under by the current, just as Lottie had.

"I thought I was going to drown," said Adelaide. "Can you imagine a more unrefined way to go?"

"I can," began Fife, but Adelaide continued talking over him.

"There I was, thinking those might be the last moments of my life, when someone grabbed me by the collar and pulled me out of the water. It was a Northerly. He and his wife lived in a cottage nearby and had heard our shouts. They fetched Oliver out of the water, too, and then they helped out Dorian, who'd caught hold of a tree root farther down the river. When Fife came back looking for us, I tried to call him over, but then—"

"The ice crawler," said Lottie.

Adelaide nodded. "The Northerlies were afraid, so they dragged us away from the riverbank and to their cottage, where we dried and warmed up. We returned to the bank later that night. We tried calling for you, but there was no reply. We looked everywhere, up and down the bank. Oliver and I were so afraid."

"And we were just as worried about you," said Eliot.

A blush rose in Adelaide's cheeks, but she continued her story. "Oliver and I tried sending our gengas out, but they kept circling back to us. They didn't have any idea where we were, and they were too scared to leave our sides after the attack. And Dorian lost his genga."

"You mean, it flew away?" Lottie asked, thinking of Trouble's penchant for disappearing.

Adelaide's face darkened. "No. I mean he *lost* his."

Lottie blanched. "That's awful."

"Yes," said Adelaide. "Anyway, Dorian told us the best thing to do was head to the Northerly Court with the hope that you all had made it there safely. But first, he said, we should go to Gray Gully, which wasn't too far off our path, and where we could find supplies and transportation.

"And *guess* who we met there? Mr. Ingle! He owns a little house in the town center. If you can even call it a town center. It was so *primitive.* They didn't even have a florist there. I checked. But dear Mr. Ingle is just as kind as he ever was, and I think he's much better off in a house than that frightful inn of his, even if it *is* a house in Northerly territory. He didn't seem to understand just how uncivil a town Gray Gully is, though I tried to explain."

"What!" gasped Fife. "How *dare* he not care about incivility!"

Adelaide gave Fife a dirty look that made Lottie want to weep from happiness. She hadn't realized just how much she'd missed Adelaide until now—even the most irritating things about her.

"*As I was saying*," Adelaide went on, "Mr. Ingle was very kind and hospitable, but Oliver and I were still worried silly about the rest of you. We stayed two days longer than either of us wanted, but Dorian insisted it was worth it because of the type of transportation he was waiting on. And you'll never guess what it was: a cart drawn by *horses*."

"You're lying," said Fife. "Impossible."

"You can see them for yourself!" Adelaide said, ablaze with excitement. "They're tied up just outside the caverns. A gray one and a white one, and they're just as regal as I thought they would be. It seemed cruel to make them pull our weight."

"She's lying," Fife said to Oliver. "Isn't she?"

"It's true," said Oliver. "There are dozens of them in Gray Gully."

"What's the big deal?" said Eliot. "They're just horses."

"Are horses common in the human world?" asked Adelaide, astonished.

"Common enough," he said. "Though, come to think of it, I guess there aren't many on Kemble Isle."

"Then you've seen them before?" Adelaide looked impressed.

"Of course," said Eliot. Then, to Lottie, "They're talking about them like they're *unicorns*."

"Maybe that's what they're like to sprites," Lottie said, equally amused.

"Anyhow," said Adelaide, "on our way here, Rebel Gem's genga found us and carried the news ahead. We weren't far behind. And when we reached court, Dorian insisted we wait around for Rebel Gem to show up because she was liable to have questions for us, but then Oliver said Dorian would have to tie him up in a hundred knots if he intended to make us sit around rather than find our friends. So Dorian finally let us go, and we found Fife and Eliot, and now you, Lottie. And everyone's well, and we're all together, and surely things can't possibly be as bad as they've been these past few days."

"Fife told us about how you saved his life," Oliver said, turning dark green eyes to Lottie.

"It was Trouble who saved us, really," said Lottie.

"Lila's been in such a tizzy." Adelaide nodded to the violet finch roosting in the crook of her crossed ankles. "Her heart was beating so fast on our journey here, I thought she might burst from fear."

"I sent Keats down to Wisp Territory," said Oliver. "He reported back a few hours ago."

"And?"

"Lyre has ordered the entire Guard to fall back to the glass pergola in an attempt to keep the 'most important' wisps safe, should Iolanthe and her soldiers attack again. Father is well. He's still tending to the sick and working on his cure."

"Did you tell him our news?" asked Lottie. "About the ice crawler and the assassin?"

Oliver grimaced. "I wasn't sure I should worry him just yet. I'm sure you know how frustrating correspondence like that can be, even when it's good news. This told, I joy; but then no longer glad, I send them back again and straight grow sad."

"That's very martyr-like of you, Ollie," said Fife. "True to form."

There was a loud cough at the doorway. It was the white-haired boy.

"'Scuse me," he said. "Rebel Gem has requested an audience with the Heir of Fiske."

All eyes turned to Lottie. "Um," she said. "Just me?"

"Yes," said the boy, staring at his feet.

"*And* an audience with her most illustrious royal guest, Fife Dulcet," said Fife. "I think you forgot that part of the message."

"I—I didn't forget anything," said the white-haired boy, looking nervous.

"He's just joking," Eliot said kindly.

"You know what this means, Lottie," said Fife. "You're growing up, turning into an important public figure."

He dabbed at a fake tear, and Lottie rolled her eyes, though she was grateful for the joke. It gave her something else to focus on besides the nervous feeling in her stomach.

What did Rebel Gem want with just her? They hadn't parted on the best of terms.

"Rebel Gem said to come immediately," said the white-haired boy.

"All right, all right," said Lottie, getting down from the bed. She cast one look at the others. Eliot was giving her a thumbs-up. Oliver's eyes were a reassuring green. Fife and Adelaide were already arguing again.

"You'd think she could wait a little longer," Lottie told the boy as they walked the passageway. It wasn't that Lottie particularly wanted to talk to the white-haired boy, but she was desperate for something to stave off the jitters. "I only just got to see my friends. And half the time, I've been worried they'd drowned."

The white-haired boy glared ahead. "Some of 'em did," he said. "Or do you even care what happened to the others?"

Lottie slowed her pace. In all the excitement, she'd been forgetting something: Reeve. Nash. She hadn't asked what had happened to them. Now she wasn't sure she wanted to know.

"Guess those other Northerlies aren't worth your concern, Heir of Fiske."

Lottie flinched at the words. She hurried to fall back in step with the boy. He turned his face away from her, but it was too late. She'd seen. He was crying. She stopped walking altogether. He did, too, and scrubbed his face.

"You knew one of them, didn't you?" she asked quietly.

"Yes," he said after a long pause. "Nash was my brother."

Lottie felt faint. She didn't know what to say. All this while, she'd never once stopped to consider the white-haired boy's story. He had waited on her for days and nights, and Lottie hadn't even tried to learn his *name*. Nash was his brother. Nash, who had tried to murder her. Did the boy know that? If he didn't, Lottie couldn't possibly tell him now.

"He was very brave," she said at last. "A hero, really. He fought the ice crawler, trying to save the rest of us. He mentioned you, too. You could tell by the way he talked that he loved his brother very much and would do anything for him."

It wasn't the full truth, but Lottie didn't think the truth was what the white-haired boy needed right now.

"Really?" he whispered.

"Really."

The white-haired boy nodded limply.

"By the way," said Lottie, "I'm afraid I never learned your name. It's—?"

The boy's eyes darkened. "Thwaite," he said crisply.

Then he resumed his walking. Lottie followed in guilt-ridden silence until she noticed Thwaite leading her up a steep, narrow passageway she didn't recognize.

"Where are we going?" she asked.

Thwaite didn't give an answer, and Lottie didn't press for one. Thwaite shouldn't have been on duty at a time like this, she thought. He needed rest and to be around friends who loved him. Did he have friends like that?

The new passageway turned into a steep stairway, which they climbed all the way to an opening to the outside world. They passed two guards on their way out and then emerged at the crest of a hill. From this height, Lottie could see an orange sun kissing the horizon, its rays spread out over the swaying heads of pines and oaks. It was a beautiful sight, but Lottie felt uneasy.

"Where's Rebel Gem?" she asked, turning to Thwaite.

"Just a little farther this way."

They descended the hill and entered a thick wood. Lottie followed Thwaite's path through the trees until they reached the mouth of another cave. Lottie recognized the enchanted torch burning at the entrance, lighting the inscription inside: MOST REVERED HOUSE OF FISKE.

"She wants to meet me *here*?" Lottie asked. She was trying to right her disoriented sense of place.

"Yes," said Thwaite. He was shivering. "She's just inside."

Lottie peered into the shadows. She felt movement at her side, then heard the flap of wings. Trouble had emerged from her pocket and, without so much as a tweet, he soared out of sight.

"Trouble!" Lottie cried. "Trouble, come back here!"

It was no use. He had disappeared into the wood.

Lottie felt in her other pocket, for her mother's ring. It

was just a dark hallway. She'd been down it before. Why was she suddenly so afraid? She closed her fingers around the silk-covered ring and took a steady breath. She stepped inside. She hurried down the passageway, toward the enchanted torchlight at its end. She stepped into the room of statues and glass cases. She didn't realize that Thwaite hadn't followed her inside. She didn't see the two red-cloaked guards close in behind her. Not at first. She was too distracted by another sight.

A woman stood before her, dressed in a cloak. But it wasn't Rebel Gem.

She was tall. Her hair was as light as Rebel Gem's was dark. Her shoulders were broad and her eyes over-wide, and she shared Lottie's open stare. She stood behind one of the glass cases, its door ajar. It was the case that had contained the lapis lazuli ring.

"Hello, Lottie," she said.

Lottie knew that voice. She'd heard it in the dark woods of Wisp Territory.

When Lottie turned to run, she saw the two Southerly guards blocking her path. They stared ahead, impassive, heavy maces in hand.

Think, Lottie told herself. *Think.*

Slowly, she turned back around.

"Hello, Iolanthe," she said, trying her best to sound unafraid.

"Then you know who I am?" Iolanthe arched a brow.

"You're the king's new right-hand sprite," Lottie said. "You invaded Wisp Territory, and you cut down their apple tree. You sent out assassins to kill me."

Iolanthe's face was solemn. It looked like a face that had never, ever laughed.

"Do you know why I'm here now?" she asked.

Lottie swallowed hard. "Because you want to kill me."

"You've caused the Southerly King an inordinate amount of trouble, Lottie Fiske. We're going to put an end to that today."

Iolanthe stepped out from behind the glass case, and Lottie saw the thin sword in her hand, its blade drawn to a sharp point.

Do something! her mind shouted. *Remember what Rebel Gem told you: you could use your touch to hurt her. This is a last resort. It's your life on the line. So do* something, *before she turns you into a pincushion!*

But Lottie just took a step back. The guards reacted. One jabbed the end of his mace into her back. Lottie cried out from the pain.

"Don't," she said. "Please, *don't.*"

Iolanthe stepped closer, examining Lottie as though she were nothing more than a turkey in need of carving.

"Don't worry," she said. "It will be over soon."

Lottie shut her eyes.

She waited for the pain.

For a moment, the room was utterly silent. Then came the clatter of metal.

Lottie's eyes fluttered back open.

Iolanthe was reeling.

"I can't see," she said. Then, in a shout, "I can't see! *Get her.*"

But the guards weren't in a better position. They were feeling around blindly in the air, as though the room had been cast in darkness. One grazed Lottie's shoulder, but she shook free and ran. She ran as fast as her feet could take her down the passageway, only to stumble straight into Thwaite. Lottie yelped and hurtled away from him, but Thwaite ran after her into the wood.

"Wait!" he called, hard on her heels. "Not that way!"

He grabbed her arm, and Lottie tried to break free but instead fell to her knees.

"Don't touch me!" she yelled, still struggling. "You let Iolanthe into the court. You were going to let her kill me!"

Lottie understood it all now. Thwaite *had* known what his brother planned to do on that boat. He'd known, and now he was trying to finish the job.

But Thwaite was shaking his head.

"I'm sorry," he choked out. "I thought I was doing the right thing. Nash told me—"

There were shouts from the cave. Running footsteps. Whatever had blackened the vision of Iolanthe and her soldiers was now apparently gone. Whatever it had been . . .

"You," she said, staring at Thwaite. "Was that *you*? Your keen?"

"I changed my mind. I'm sorry. Now c'mon. We've got to run. *This* way."

He helped Lottie up, and together they ran deeper into the wood, where night was fast choking away the remaining sunlight. Already, it was colder out, and Lottie's face stung from the whipping wind. She saw lights glowing ahead, at the peak of the hill they were climbing. Lottie hurried her steps toward them. She emerged from the grip of the wood and ran still higher up the bank of the hill, toward the looming boulders that bordered the supping lawn.

She could hear shouts up ahead.

They've begun the supper festivities early tonight, she thought.

"We have to find Rebel Gem and warn her," said Lottie. "Do you know how many—"

But Thwaite was no longer by her side. He was nowhere to be seen.

"Thwaite?" Lottie whispered.

There was a whistling sound in the dark. Lottie's head was knocked sideways with sudden pain. She touched her ear. Something wet was trickling from its ridge: blood. She looked around, frantic. Then she spotted it, glinting in the moonlight, lodged in the muddy hillside. It was a silver arrow.

Lottie heard it again—that strange whistling sound, only this time fainter and farther off. Another arrow sailed through the air. Then another. She sank to a crouch and, keeping her eyes upward, scrambled up the hill, toward the shelter of one of the boulders.

She had been mistaken. The shouts she'd heard were not shouts of merriment, and the metal clangs were not that of chalice against chalice but of *sword against sword*. This wasn't a feast. This was a battle.

Lottie thought of Eliot, of Fife and Oliver and Adelaide. Her brain pounded with terrible images of what could be happening inside the cave. Her mind ordered her to move, to run, to search for the others, but her leg muscles had gone as stiff as hardened glue.

"Move," she said, a command she'd grown so used to in the past days. "*Move.*"

Life slowly returned to her joints, but just as Lottie was about to make a run for it, something yanked at her coat collar, sending her legs sprawling out under her. Lottie flailed, swatting at her captor, but a hot, sweat-coated hand clamped over her mouth.

"If you scream, Fiske, I swear to Oberon . . ."

It was Dorian Ingle.

Lottie shook her head, a promise to be quiet. Dorian removed his hand from her mouth.

"W-what's happening?" she asked.

"Southerlies" was the grunted reply. "Somehow they breached our defenses."

I know how, Lottie thought, wondering again where Thwaite could be.

"But they can't just do that," Lottie said. "That's basically declaring war, isn't it?"

"Look, Fiske, I'd love to delve into a discussion about the political ramifications, but what I'd like best is for us to get out of this alive. Agreed?"

"A-agreed."

Lottie found herself being raised to her feet with the help of strong arms beneath her own.

"Listen closely," Dorian said against her ear. "Stay with me. I can hear where the enemy is. We're going to follow the boulders until we reach the cave. Then we'll make a run for it."

"Why are we going *inside* the caves?" said Lottie.

"Do you want to join up with your friends, or not?"

"It just seems like—"

"Save it, Fiske. Do you understand what we're going to do?"

Lottie nodded doggedly.

"On second thought . . ." Dorian stooped. He motioned to his back.

"Climb up," he said. "I'll carry you."

Lottie felt the absurd urge to laugh. "You want me to *piggyback*?"

"Faster that way. And no chance of you running off. Get on."

Lottie climbed on Dorian's back and wrapped her arms about his neck. He rose to his full height, and Lottie felt a surge of adrenaline.

"Right," said Dorian. "Here goes. Sorry in advance if I get us killed."

He set off. They ran along the curved line of the boulders. The sounds of cries and clashing metal filled Lottie's ears. She soon felt her hands going slick with sweat. Then her vision blackened, and for a terrified moment Lottie thought she had fallen from Dorian's back and into unconscious oblivion.

But this wasn't oblivion, for Lottie could still hear sounds, now compounded by the echoes of stone walls. They'd made it inside the cave.

"Here, Dorian. *Here*."

Dorian veered a sharp left. Then he knelt. Lottie slipped from his back and blinked up in the dim light at Rebel Gem.

"Lottie!" cried Eliot.

He appeared from behind Rebel Gem and wrapped Lottie in a hug.

"No time for that," said Fife. "Come on."

Eliot grabbed Lottie's hand, and together they hurried after Rebel Gem, who was already striding deeper into the cave. Oliver and Adelaide walked and Fife floated just ahead. Dorian remained behind Lottie, his sword drawn.

Lottie recognized the route they were taking. Rebel Gem was leading them down the cramped tunnel that led to the pine clearing. Lottie was now well acquainted with the slope of the ground and where all the loose rocks and uneven places were. Eliot was not. He stumbled, nearly taking Lottie down. She righted him just in time.

"Stay close to me," she said. "I'll walk just a little ways ahead."

Though they moved quickly, the passageway seemed much longer than it ever had before. At last, they emerged into the dark outdoors. Rebel Gem took them to the edge of the clearing and turned abruptly, throwing her hood over her head.

"Dorian," she said. "They go with you. Don't let them out of your sight."

She said it calmly, as though she were reciting her two-times table.

Dorian shook his head. "I'm not going without—"

"That's an order," said Rebel Gem. "My place is here, protecting my people."

"Rebel Gem," panted Lottie. "Iolanthe's here. She tried to kill me."

"What?" cried several voices at once.

"I think she came here for me," said Lottie, "but she could also be here for your silver-boughed tree. You can't let her cut it down."

"I won't," said Rebel Gem. "But if Iolanthe is still looking for you, there isn't a second to spare. All of you, go. Dorian, you know what to do."

"She'll murder you, Cora," hissed Dorian. "You'd do your people a better service by protecting yourself."

Rebel Gem's expression did not change.

"Go," she said again.

It was a command that left no room for argument.

Dorian strode toward the wood, but rather than pass Rebel Gem, he pulled her into his arms. Then he kissed her firmly on the mouth.

"Whoa!" cried Fife. "Whoa, I did not see that—*ow!*"

Adelaide had silenced him, hitting him hard in the stomach. Lottie looked away. She'd never before seen two people she knew kiss, and, more than that, she felt this was something delicate and absolutely none of her business.

Just as suddenly as he'd kissed her, Dorian set Rebel Gem free again.

"Come on," he said roughly, to the rest of them.

He disappeared into the wood. Fife floated after him without hesitation, Oliver and Adelaide just behind. Though Rebel Gem's face was as calm as ever, there were tears streaming down it.

Lottie stayed where she was. There was so much she wanted to say.

Rebel Gem turned to her. "Run, Lottie," she said. "Now."

Lottie ran.

CHAPTER FIFTEEN

An Old Friend Returns

LOTTIE KEPT Eliot's hand clasped tightly in her own. Though Eliot ran hard, he and Lottie soon lagged far behind the others. Eventually Oliver noticed and called for the rest of the company to stop and wait up. Once Lottie and Eliot had closed the distance, they set out once more, but the space between them widened again as Eliot's stumbles grew more frequent and his breathing erratic. They had no lanterns to light their path, but a full moon cast its eerie white light on the wood. After a full hour of running, the air grew heady with a bittersweet scent.

"Frost plums!" cried Adelaide. "Oh, please let's stop. We're all aching, and no one's following us, and there are *frost plums*!"

To Lottie's relief, they did stop, and only then did she have the chance to take a good look at the forest surrounding them. There wasn't anything unusual about the trees themselves. Their bark was brown, and their branches fanned out in an ordinary way—nothing like the strange trees of Wisp Territory. It was what grew from the trees that startled Lottie.

The leaves, wide and heart-shaped, were completely transparent. The fruit, which hung in heavy clusters, was the size of Lottie's fist, plump and powdery, and colored light blue.

"Is it edible?" Lottie asked.

"Yef," Fife said through a mouthful. His lips were stained an alarming shade of red from the pulp of the fruit.

Lottie picked a plum from a branch so laden down with fruit that it nearly touched the ground.

"Gather what you can," said Dorian, "but we can't stay here. We'll need to find a more advantageous location to set up camp."

"What's more advantageous than a wood full of frost plums?" said Fife, who had cast away the pit of one plum and was already at work on another.

Dorian gave Fife a look that chilled Lottie's already cold body.

When he spoke, it was emphatic. "Get the food you want. Then we leave."

Fife shrugged. "Yeah, okay."

"I'm going to scout ahead," Dorian said. "Don't wander off."

He disappeared into the wood.

"Sheesh," said Fife. "Touchy, that one."

"He's worried about Rebel Gem," said Eliot, as though this were common knowledge.

Adelaide, who had been busy filling her coat pockets with plums, stopped short.

"Do you think they're *lovers*?" she whispered.

Fife fake-retched. "Oberon, Ada, never say that word again."

"I'll say whatever words I please." Adelaide turned her back on Fife and addressed the others. "Well, do you? I think it's very romantic."

"You aren't jealous, then?" asked Fife. "I thought you found him handsome."

Lottie thought Adelaide ignored the remark quite graciously.

"I hope she's all right," said Lottie. "And Roote and Crag, and all the rest."

Though what Lottie meant to say was, *I hope they aren't killed because of me.*

"What happened with Iolanthe?" Oliver asked her. "How did she find you? How did you escape?"

Lottie considered telling the others everything—that Thwaite must have been the one to grant Iolanthe access to the Northerly Court, that he was Nash's younger brother, and that he'd tried to get Lottie killed.

"Iolanthe kidnapped me on my way to see Rebel Gem," she said instead. "Thwaite used his keen to protect me."

"Huh," said Fife. "Didn't think he had it in him. Good for Thwaite. And he's . . . okay, right? I mean, she didn't . . ."

"I don't know. We got separated in the wood."

She thought of Thwaite's sorrowful face, cast in shadow. She hoped he'd escaped, that Iolanthe and her guards hadn't caught up to him.

"You don't need to worry about the rest," said Fife. "Iolanthe's only advantage was the element of surprise. The Northerly Court's got way more soldiers than she brought along, and she knows it. Northerlies might be disorganized, but they're tough fighters. They don't spend their time getting fat on puddings like in the Southerly Court. Did you see the muscle on some of that lot? They'll outmatch those idiot soldiers in no time at all."

Lottie hoped Fife was right. Rebel Gem was strong, and she was a leader, but Iolanthe was King Starkling's right-hand sprite. And if Rebel Gem was hurt and Iolanthe still on the move, then . . .

Lottie shuddered. She couldn't think that way. She busied herself with plucking plums and tucking them into her pockets. All the while, she kept a close eye on Eliot.

"I'm fine, you know," he finally said.

"What?" said Lottie, shifting her attention to a loose coat button.

"I see you watching me. I know you're worried, but I'm all right."

"I haven't told you yet about what happened this morning," she said, in a low voice that the others would not pick up. "I can *do* it now, Eliot. I think I know how to use my keen. *Really* use it."

Eliot's expression was unreadable. "Oh."

"That's good news. When we make camp, I can try—"

"No." Eliot backed away. "No, I'd rather not."

Lottie frowned in confusion. "What? But, Eliot, don't you understand what I'm—"

"No, I understand. I just don't need you to try your keen out on me."

"But I'm not *trying it out*. I'm trying to make you better."

"I—"

But Eliot's reply was cut short.

"Come on, all of you! I've found us a place."

Dorian had reappeared, cheeks red from exertion. He waved for them to follow. Now fully stocked with plums, they started up a rocky incline that led out of the tree line to a flat, stone plain. Up ahead, a large rock jutted from a towering cliff face. It was curved on its edges, like a canopy.

"We'll rest here," said Dorian, motioning under the rock.

"Did you check inside?" asked Adelaide. "What if there are wild animals living in there?"

"It's perfectly safe," said Dorian, ducking into the shallow cave. "See? Far better to have a roof over our heads and something solid at our backs. It won't be a comfortable sleep, but it'll be secure."

They settled inside as best they could, first kicking out stones and moldering leaves, then searching out the smoothest stretch of ground to lie upon.

"I'll keep watch," Dorian told them, "but you can't rest long. I don't trust that we're out of danger just yet. We'll leave at dawn."

"Where are we going?" asked Lottie.

"You lot are going to a town called Sharp Bend, where you're going to stay nicely tucked away at an inn. *I'm* going to the Wilders."

"What?" said Lottie. "You mean, you're going after the addersfork *now*?"

"Do you have a better idea, Fiske?" Dorian snapped. "You've just seen for yourself how far Starkling's hand has stretched. Iolanthe is in the Northerly Court, for Oberon's sake. It's not my place to speculate on whether addersfork can bring him down, but if fetching it means maintaining our alliance with the wisps, then that's what I'm going to do."

"But what about us?" said Fife. "You're just going to stash us in some inn?"

"Look," said Dorian. "There might be more assassins after Fiske here, and I don't like the idea of dragging you kids into the wilderness. I know Sharp Bend well. I have friends there, people who will take care of you."

"Like Reeve and Nash took care of us?" Adelaide huffed. "No thank you."

"This is different," Dorian said crossly. "I never said Reeve and Nash were friends. I'm talking about sprites I know and trust. And as a Northerly soldier, I can get you free lodging. Warm beds and food and—"

"No," said Lottie, crossing her arms and taking a step toward Dorian. "Not a chance. I'm going with you. It's because of this stupid addersfork we were sent up here in the first place. Anyway, from what I hear, the Wilders are really dangerous. You'll need help."

"I'll be fine."

"What if you get hurt?" Lottie demanded. "What will you do with no one to help you? It's better to have companions, and you know it. And don't try telling me we're just children. We're all very capable, thanks very much."

"Lottie's right," said Eliot. "We should stick together."

"I agree," Oliver said. "Strength in numbers. Two sturdy oaks, which side by side withstand the winter's storm, and spite of wind and tide grow up the meadow's pride, for both are strong."

"And just think," said Fife, "I'll be able to tell everyone I've been to the Wilders."

Adelaide remained conspicuously silent. Lottie wondered if she would've preferred staying in town but just wouldn't say so with everyone else opposed. And, really, Lottie herself had doubts. Rebel Gem had said that few sprites were brave enough to venture into the Wilders. It couldn't be an easy journey, and Lottie worried about Eliot making it.

"Fine," said Dorian, throwing his hands up. "It's not like I can stop all five of you. But I swear, I'm not slowing down for anyone. We keep to my pace and my schedule, is that clear?"

Everyone assured Dorian of how very clear his instructions were. Then they settled into tired silence.

At least we'll all be together, Lottie thought. *Even though one of Iolanthe's assassins or Iolanthe herself could be prowling nearby, at least I'm with my friends.*

When Lottie woke, it was without any memory of having closed her eyes. Their shelter was awash in pale light. Oliver and Eliot were already awake. They sat with their backs to Lottie, a pile of frost plum pits between them. Eliot's shoulders were shaking with laughter. Lottie smiled. Then she winced. As she sat up, she found she was unbearably stiff. Her head was pounding and her lips chapped. She struggled to comb her fingers through her knotted hair.

"Oh, here," said Adelaide, who sat nearby, a half-eaten plum in hand. "I'll fix it for you."

She set aside the fruit and pulled a violet finch from her pocket.

"Ribbon, Lila," she said, stroking her genga.

Lila tweeted obligingly, then made a delicate rumbling sound. She coughed once, then again, the opening in her beak growing larger and rounder until she coughed out a small wooden comb, followed by a strand of white ribbon.

"Thanks, dearest," said Adelaide, pressing a kiss on Lila's head. She carefully wiped the film from the comb and ribbon, as Lottie had seen Fife wipe film from the medical vials Spool stored. Lottie sat still as Adelaide combed a path through her hair less painfully and more efficiently than Lottie could have. Then, with practiced skill, she twirled back Lottie's hair into a neat braid, securely fastened at its tail by the ribbon Lila had supplied. When it was over, Lottie turned to Adelaide with a grateful smile.

"I really missed you," she said.

Adelaide smiled back. "I missed you, too. Dorian might be pretty to look at, but he and his father are as uncouth as wild dogs. The house was a mess, and the food . . . well, I don't blame Mr. Ingle, but you'd think for an innkeeper he'd have better cooking skills."

Though she'd been too afraid to try the frost plums the night before, Lottie's stomach now groaned from emptiness. She ate one plum, then another, and then three more. So *this* was why Adelaide had been raving about them. Their flesh was light and crisp, with the slightest bitter tinge at its edges. Though the rest of Lottie's body still ached, she felt more refreshed and capable as they set out on the morning's journey.

In the early afternoon, they stopped in the town called Sharp Bend to gather supplies. The town was little more than a single broad street bordered by houses, taverns, and shops. The buildings here were a far cry from the regal stone and brickwork of New Albion. They were constructed of wood and thatch, and all seemed in a general state of disrepair. Paint peeled from shutters, grime covered windowpanes, and Lottie heard the howl of a stray dog from a nearby alley.

"I'll wager there's no florist here, either, Ada," said Fife.

"I've begun to think they don't exist in the north," she replied.

They came to a stop outside the dirtiest building on the street: a tavern with a rotting front door and a sign that read REBEL'S SPRITES WELCOME. Even from outside, Lottie could hear shouts and slurred words.

"It's only noon," said Oliver, judgment in his narrowed, brown eyes.

"Best let me take care of this," said Dorian. "Look around if you want, but don't stray too far. We'll meet here in fifteen minutes."

"Look!" said Eliot, once Dorian was gone. He pointed across the street at a shop sign, which had come loose from one of its pegs and hung lopsided. Still, the red paint was readable:

QUIGLEY BOOKS

"Suppose they have anything worth reading?" Eliot asked Oliver.

"May as well look," Oliver answered, his muddy brown eyes turning gold with interest.

"I think I'll join," said Adelaide, and Lottie wondered if she was the only one to notice the shy way Adelaide looked at Eliot when she spoke.

"The more the merrier," said Eliot.

Lottie watched the three of them cross the street.

"What?" said Fife, who'd taken a seat on a wobbly bench outside the tavern. "You aren't curious as to what literary treasures await?"

Lottie sat beside him. "I'm just not much in the mood for reading. I think there are bigger problems to worry about."

Fife nodded. Then he breathed in sharply, his eyes closed.

Lottie frowned. "What's wrong?"

"Nothing."

"Is it your wound?"

"It's *nothing*."

Lottie gave Fife a hard look. Then she yanked at his sweater. He gave a cry of consternation, but it was too late: Lottie had revealed his injured stomach and the blood soaking through linen bandages.

Fife scrambled to push the sweater back down. "It's none of your business! I just popped open a few stitches is all. I could sew them up myself if they weren't in such an inconvenient location."

"*Fife*. You've got to get this taken care of! When did it even happen?"

"I said, it's *nothing*."

"Give me your hands," said Lottie.

Fife looked around, as though Lottie could possibly be talking to anyone other than him. "W-what?"

Lottie rolled her eyes and grabbed Fife's hands.

"What are you—"

"Shut up," she said. "I'm trying to concentrate."

Fife grunted as Lottie closed her eyes. She had to focus on her emotions, just as she had done with Rebel Gem in the pine clearing. She had to focus on what made her angry, fearful, and sad. She had to think of a worn photograph of her parents' freckled faces, and of the words "*Two, maybe three weeks to live.*"

A full minute passed.

"Erm. Lottie?"

"Shhh," she said. Then, opening her eyes, "I have to empathize with you. Tell me something about yourself."

"Um," said Fife. "I hate parsnips?"

"No," said Lottie, growing desperate. "Something more important than that. About your fears, or your parents—something personal."

Fife's face darkened. "My *parents*?"

"I have to know something about you that you might not want me to know. That's how it works. There has to be a connection between us."

Lottie wasn't sure how it happened. One moment, Fife was looking at her with large, watering eyes. The next, she felt a gentle pressure against her lips.

Fife was kissing her.

Lottie's mind went blank. She pulled away with a choked gasp and found Fife staring at her, bewildered, his face flooded with color.

"I—I—" he stammered.

"You kissed me," Lottie said stupidly, touching her lips.

"Um." The color in Fife's cheeks grew more vibrant. "You said something I might not want you to know. That's . . . one of them."

"You like me?" Lottie whispered.

"Uh." Fife's swallow was audible. "Well, yeah."

Lottie was silent, wide-eyed, uncomprehending.

Fife's expression transformed from embarrassment to something far worse: hurt.

"But if you don't like me back, that's—I mean, it was stupid of me to—"

"No!" Lottie said quickly. "No, I just—*ow*." Her chest tightened, squeezed in on all sides by invisible hands.

It was a bad spell. She doubled over in pain, gasping for breath.

"Lottie?" Fife said, panicked. "Lottie, are you okay?"

Lottie grabbed Fife's hands again. She clung to them tightly as the bad spell grew stronger, straining at her muscles and skin as though it might tug her to pieces from the outside in.

Move the pain, she told herself. *Move.*

And the pain moved. It burned out of her chest and down her arms, into her hands and out to Fife's. The bad spell surged from her, and though Fife jerked from the contact, he did not break away.

Then it stopped.

Lottie opened her eyes. Her hands went slack, and she removed them at last from Fife's.

"Are you—?" she started. "Are you all right?"

But Fife was too busy tugging at his bandages. There was no more blood beneath them. The scar on his side was healed. All that remained was the faintest outline of pink, puckered skin.

His gaze met hers.

"Y-you kissed me," Lottie repeated.

"Yeah," Fife said. "You *healed* me. How did you even do that?"

"It's . . . hard to explain."

"I bet." Fife looked distressed about something.

"What?" Lottie asked.

Fife said nothing at first. Then, very softly, "You didn't kiss me back."

A blush burned up Lottie's face. "I—I got distracted. I wasn't expecting it, and then I was busy—"

"Healing me," Fife finished. "I noticed. So . . ." He looked more uncomfortable than Lottie had ever seen him. "So, you didn't hate it?"

"*There* you are! Haven't moved an inch since we left you."

The others were heading toward them, Adelaide in the lead. Lottie hurriedly scooted away from Fife. He tossed the bloodied bandages behind the bench, into a mud-caked stream running beneath the tavern's doorstep. Adelaide didn't seem to notice.

"The sorriest excuse for a bookshop I've ever seen," she said, tromping up and taking a seat between the two of them. "The shop clerk didn't know where anything was. He thought Edna Hapshock was a *playwright.*"

"It's just as well," said Oliver, though his eyes were gray with disappointment. "It's not as though books are the priority. Or that we'd have anything to buy them with if they were."

"Books are always the priority!" said Eliot, the only cheerful one of the group. "At least there were some interesting covers. Like the one with the glittery lettering and all the locks?"

"I don't suppose you found anything on survival skills for the Wilders?" said Fife. He turned to Lottie with ease, as though nothing had passed between them only a minute earlier. "Not that I don't trust Dorian, but . . . Hmm. I *don't* trust Dorian. Seems a little preoccupied with his mission. Don't think it'd bother him much if one of us took a tumble off a cliff on the way north."

The tavern door burst open, and with it came a wave of boisterous singing. Dorian called back to someone inside, then shut the door soundly behind him. He carried a large, soot-covered bag.

"Right," he said. "Supplies acquired. Some food and a flagon, too. We've wasted enough time here. Last chance for you to stay behind."

"As you say," said Adelaide, "we've wasted enough time here."

"Yeah," said Eliot. "Let's find some addersfork."

They left the town of Sharp Bend behind, heading northward on a narrow dirt path that wound through trees and over brooks. Ahead, mountains—not the hills that surrounded the Northerly Court, but real *mountains*—rose in the distance, peaked with snow.

"Your boots better be sturdy," Dorian told them. "We'll be taking the pass. No climbing required, but it won't be easy on your soles."

They hadn't traveled long when Lottie began to hear rustling in the thickets bordering their path. Then she thought she saw a flash of black.

She stopped in the middle of the path.

"Did anyone else see that?" she asked.

Adelaide, who had been busy talking to Eliot, now perked to attention.

"You're right. There's something close by. I can hear it now." She turned to Lottie. "I think it's a *Barghest*."

Lottie stepped closer to the thicket.

"Barghest?" she called. "Is that you?"

There was a low growl. In the space just between tree and thicket, a hulking black creature appeared, its silver pinprick eyes alight. It was, indeed, a Barghest. And not just any Barghest—it was *Lottie's* Barghest.

Lottie wasn't the only ecstatic one. Eliot clapped his hands excitedly, and Fife gave a cheer.

"Where have you *been*?" Lottie asked, kneeling to throw her arms around the Barghest's mane. "I thought we'd lost you for good!"

The Barghest released a growl so deep it shook Lottie's ribs.

In its rough voice, it said, "There were complications."

"But you're okay?" asked Lottie.

She stood to get a better look at the creature, afraid now that she would find gashes or scrapes ripped through its beautiful coat of fur. But from what she could tell, the Barghest was unharmed.

"You are the one who has been in grave danger," said the Barghest. "I let harm come to you, Heir of Fiske. I did not fulfill my duty."

"Oh, that doesn't matter anymore," Lottie said. "I'm here, aren't I? And all the rest of us. We're just glad to have you back. And you know, even if you weren't able to protect us, other Barghest did."

"Tell us, Barghest," said Dorian, "have you heard anything about the state of the Northerly Court?"

The Barghest nodded. "The Southerlies are defeated," it said. "Fifty soldiers, all cut down by brave Northerly hands. Rebel Gem was wounded, but not mortally so."

"Then she's alive," whispered Dorian.

The Barghest barked in the affirmative.

Dorian nodded weakly and turned his back to the others.

"What about Iolanthe?" Lottie asked the Barghest.

The Barghest shook its head. "Hard to say. Her body was not found amongst the slain. It is believed that she escaped."

"Then she could still be on the hunt for us," said Oliver.

"Do you really think she's after *us*?" said Eliot.

"Who else?" said Fife. "She's tried to kill Lottie twice now—once by assassin, and once in person. It's not like she came up north to pick flowers and spread sunshine."

"I'm glad we have you with us now, Barghest," Lottie said. "I feel a lot safer with you around."

"Where are you traveling to now?" it asked.

"Dorian's taking us through the mountain pass to the Wilders," said Lottie.

The Barghest growled, its back arching.

"What?" said Oliver. "You don't think that's a good idea?"

"By my counsel," it said, "I would not travel that way."

Dorian turned around, pale-faced.

"Why is that?" he asked. "It's the best known route. I've taken it plenty of times before."

"That is precisely why it is not safe," said the Barghest. "It is the most obvious choice. Iolanthe has stationed more Southerly soldiers in the pass, just out of sight, high up on the mountain ledges. They lie in wait for an ambush, knowing full well you intend to take that route. It is by no means the safest path. Nor is it the only one."

Dorian bristled. "If you're suggesting the ferry, you're out of your mind, Barghest."

The Barghest pawed a step toward Dorian, its body tensed with challenge.

"You doubt my word?" it snarled.

"I've heard tales of that passage. I'd rather take my chances fighting off Southerly poltroons than entrust my life to a nix."

"Do *you* know what they're talking about?" Eliot asked Lottie. She shook her head.

"Why would I lead the Heir of Fiske astray?" said the Barghest. "I speak the truth. Far better to follow the flatlands and take the ferry."

Lottie stepped forward. "If Barghest says there are Southerly guards in the pass, then shouldn't we go the other way, Dorian?"

"No," he said, voice hard. "There is a curse on that coast and a strange magic at work in that part of the flatlands. I wouldn't advise it, not for all my lifeblood. I say we stay true to our current path."

"And what do you think, Barghest?" Lottie asked the creature, who was still glowering at Dorian. "Which path do you think is less dangerous?"

"This sprite fears riddles and old war stories," the Barghest said, nodding toward Dorian. "I do not. If you have a sharp mind, there is nothing to fear from the flatlands, and no threat of Southerly attack, either. Moreover, my route will take two days less than journeying through the pass."

Lottie looked back to Dorian. "If that's true, it seems like the flatlands really *are* the better way to go. And I trust the Barghest."

"You mean to say you don't trust me?"

"Sorry to bring up a sore spot," said Fife, "but she did almost get assassinated on your watch, Ingle."

Dorian squared his jaw. "Rebel Gem sent me north for a reason."

"'Cause she's your girlfriend?" Fife suggested.

Dorian moved swiftly, as though to grab hold of Fife, but Fife was too quick for him. He floated out of reach with a calm smirk plastered on his face.

"Just saying."

"I'm sorry, Dorian," said Lottie. "I know it wasn't your fault, but we have gotten into trouble before with you as our guide. Barghest was right the last time. It told us not to trust Nash, and it was right. And if Barghest thinks it's safer to travel by ferry, then I think we should take its advice."

Dorian dragged his hand across his face, looking at Lottie in a tired way.

"Shouldn't Lottie be the one to choose?" said Adelaide. "She's the one running for her life."

"It's a bad plan," said Dorian. "But I can't stop the six of you if you've all got your wills set against me."

"It's nothing personal, Dorian," said Lottie.

"Oh, certainly not. It's only that you *personally* trust the Barghest more than me."

"Then it is settled," growled the Barghest. "I will lead you to the ferry."

"Well go on, then, dog," said Dorian, though it was more like a snort than a sentence. "Lead on."

The Barghest brushed past Dorian, pupils thin slits in a sea of silver. It bounded ahead of them, turned back once, and gave an encouraging growl. They set down the path in the opposite direction.

Lottie hadn't spoken to Fife, *properly* spoken, since she had healed his wound. There hadn't been a chance. He floated alongside Eliot and Oliver, joining in their conversation about Vincent Van Gogh every so often with a laugh and, once, a joke about severed ears. Lottie was glad to see he was getting on better with Eliot, but she still felt a funny twist inside every time she looked at his bobbing mane of black hair.

"Did you hear me, Lottie?"

Lottie looked up, startled. Adelaide had fallen into step with her.

"I was saying," she said, "how well the boys seem to be getting on."

"Oh. Yes."

"I suppose they just needed a bit of adventure to bring them together, hm?"

"I guess."

"I think you made the right decision, too, siding with the Barghest. Dorian's very charming, but I *do* wonder sometimes if he's the best sprite for the job."

Lottie looked ahead at Dorian. His hand rested on the hilt of his sword.

"I don't know," she said. "Rebel Gem said he's one of the only sprites to have gone to the Wilders, so I think he must be very brave."

"Well, there's no doubting that. The stories one hears about the Wilders! Almost impassible, with pits and cliffs in every which direction. The soil there is poisoned, they say. Impossible to grow trees or vegetables or anything worth eating."

"But possible to grow addersfork?" asked Lottie.

"So we're told."

Their new route wound over hills, some steep and others gentle. Their walk became a rhythm—straining up and up, then skidding down and down, with the constant tip and turn of the earth. Lottie had seen many strange trees during her time on Albion Isle, but the ones that grew along this path were by far her favorite. Maybe, she reflected, they were her favorite because they reminded her of the human world. There was nothing unusual about them—no silver boughs or transparent leaves or white bark. They were perfectly ordinary oaks and aspens and ash, and their leaves were aglow with the fire of autumn.

They stopped once, very briefly, to eat and rest their legs. Then Dorian tapped his boot impatiently and said they'd better get moving again. He and the Barghest had fallen into a grim but manageable partnership where, though neither spoke to the other, they walked together.

They traveled hours more through the color-drenched wood, and when their path forked—as it did many times—they always veered right, right, and right again.

"We're nearing the coast," Adelaide told Lottie. "If I try very hard, I can hear the gulls."

When they forked right yet another time, the trees rapidly began to thin, and moments later the company was walking through a vast, open field. In the distance, Lottie made out the outline of mountains to her right and a row of cottages to her left.

"They call these the flatlands," said Adelaide. "Rather a dreary name for such a pretty place, isn't it?"

Lottie agreed. The green of the fields seemed to stretch on forever. The sky was cloudless. Here, the sun warmed

Lottie so thoroughly that she first took off her scarf, then unbuttoned her coat and hung it over her arm. Eliot, who'd been walking in time with the boys, hadn't coughed but once the entire journey, and Lottie began to wonder if maybe he wasn't getting sicker after all. Even if he was, Lottie knew what to do now. She'd used her keen three times since that night at the Barmy Badger. She just hadn't expected the last time to involve a kiss.

I'm doing something at last, Lottie thought. *Finally, I'm making progress. I healed Nash of his burns. I healed Fife's wound entirely, and if I can heal Fife, surely I can make Eliot better.* Completely *better.*

They walked toward a setting sun, and with growing night came the cold. Lottie wound her scarf back around her neck and fastened her coat to its top button.

They made camp under the shelter of a lone oak tree, just a little way off the path. Dorian removed blankets from the bag of supplies he'd obtained at the inn. They were coarse, but they were a welcome change from the rocky bed Lottie had slept on the night before.

Lottie felt restless as she watched the others. Oliver sat talking to Fife and Eliot. Adelaide had made herself a snug bed within two thick tree roots and was curled into a ball, already asleep. The Barghest prowled around the tree's perimeter in slow circles, its silver eyes ever alert. Farther off still, Dorian was crouched on his own, eyes toward the road, keeping watch. Lottie wrapped her blanket around her shoulders and walked out to join him.

"If you've come to apologize," he said, eyes still fixed ahead, "save your breath."

"I didn't," Lottie said.

Dorian snorted. "Ah. Well then."

"It *wasn't* personal," said Lottie. "I know Nash trying to kill me wasn't your fault, and I don't think you're a terrible guide or anything. It's just that Barghest has done so much for me. He helped me back when I was in a lot of trouble."

"I understand. If I were friends with a venomous beast who obeyed my every command, I'm sure I'd side with it, too."

Lottie didn't think Dorian was being fair, but then again, she hadn't been very fair to him, either.

"Do you think things are really all right back at the Northerly Court?" she asked.

"If Rebel Gem's genga is to be believed, then yes."

Lottie lit up. "What? Her genga found us?"

Dorian turned to Lottie to afford a better view of his hands. They had, until now, been cupped. He opened them to reveal a lark with plumage of the deepest blue.

"Oh," said Lottie. "She's beautiful."

"She is."

"What's her name?"

"Flame."

"Flame," Lottie repeated. "I think that's very appropriate for someone like Rebel Gem."

Dorian laughed hoarsely. "Yes. Very."

"Oh." Lottie sat straight with realization. "I've interrupted you, haven't I? You were talking to her. Sending a message back."

Dorian shrugged. He slipped the genga into his vest pocket.

"It's all right," he said. "I'd be happy to pass along your own message, if you'd like."

Lottie thought of all the things she'd like to tell Rebel Gem, all the questions she was dying to ask. But she couldn't ask them here, in front of Dorian.

"No," she said. "That is, you could just let her know I'm happy she's okay."

"Will do."

In the silence that followed, Lottie heard Eliot's loud laugh. It was a sound she would never grow tired of.

"I knew your parents, you know."

The voice was so soft that Lottie thought at first it couldn't possibly be Dorian's.

"You—you did?" she whispered.

Dorian nodded. "I was just a kid, but I remember. They were friends with my father, and they stayed at the inn sometimes, when I still lived in New Albion, before Father sent me north to sharpen. Your father made me laugh so hard once that I shot soup straight out my nose."

Lottie laughed. "Really?"

"Really. They were nothing but kind to me. That's what I remember. It isn't much, but there it is, for what it's worth."

"It's worth a lot," Lottie said. She sank her hand into her pocket and touched the silk-covered ring resting there. "Sometimes I feel so far away from them. They're my parents, but they're strangers, too. That probably doesn't make sense."

"At the risk of sounding like a sap," said Dorian, "I'd say you've done them proud."

Lottie gave Dorian a disbelieving stare. He just nudged the tip of his boot against hers. Then he shivered and tugged on the sleeves of his coat. As he did, Lottie saw the white circle imprinted on his wrist.

"I forget sometimes," said Lottie, "that you were born Southerly."

Dorian scoffed. "You're not *born* either way. Southerly, Northerly—they're just alliances, and alliances can shift. You should consider yourself lucky with that unbranded wrist of yours."

"So," said Lottie, "you don't think of yourself as a Northerly, either?"

"Not a chance. I just side with whoever is doing the least amount of damage."

"And, I guess, for now that's us?"

"Yeah," said Dorian. "For now, it is."

CHAPTER SIXTEEN

The Riddle on the Rock

"I THINK I'm coming down with a cold."

They had set out early that morning, with renewed
energy and stomachs full of breads and cheeses from the
Sharp Bend tavern. Everyone's spirits seemed high, but
Adelaide had begun sneezing around noon, and she
hadn't let up.

She now rubbed miserably at her runny nose and added,
under her breath, "This wouldn't be a problem in New
Albion. I would've just taken Father's medicine and be done
with it."

"You mean, Mr. Wilfer has a cure for the common cold?"
asked Lottie.

"Of course," said Adelaide. "Healers long before him first concocted it. Goodness, I mean, that's *primitive* medicine."

Adelaide paused to sneeze, then rubbed at her reddening nose. "Don't look," she said. "I'm sure I look a fright."

"You look fine," Lottie assured her. "Just as worn down as any of us."

For most of the day, they'd been plodding down a broad path across the open field. The flatlands, true to their name, stayed flat, and when the path sloped, it did so gently. Lottie found it nice not to have to strain her legs so much as she had in the Northerly Court, but she did miss the shade of trees. Nothing grew out here but grass, and occasionally a wide expanse of corn or grain. It was a pretty enough sight, but Lottie soon felt her skin burning under the glare of the sun. She felt, also, that she was in a perpetual state of squinting. She'd forgotten what it was like to spend so much time in unhindered daylight.

As they walked, Lottie found herself thinking often about Fife. They still hadn't spoken properly. Fife talked to Lottie in front of all the others, of course, but that wasn't the same. Several times, Lottie had tried to walk alone with him, alternatively falling behind or skipping ahead to where he floated. But every time she did so, Fife would float off as though he hadn't noticed and begin a new conversation with

Oliver or Eliot. After hours of this, Lottie gave up trying. It had been one thing when they'd been distracted by finding food, shelter, and the right path. Lottie hadn't expected Fife to talk to her then. But now, with nothing but hours of smooth walking on hand, Lottie realized that Fife was purposefully ignoring her.

Very well, she thought. *If he's got nothing to talk about, then neither do I.*

So, instead, she talked to Adelaide about her runny nose. And when she wasn't talking to Adelaide, she spent time spying barns and thatched cottages in the distance. In fact, Lottie grew so distracted by the sight of a weathervane atop a nearby barn, she did not notice the Barghest's presence until the creature released a deep growl.

"Oh!" Lottie found the Barghest slinking alongside her, his gray mane blowing in a gentle wind. The Barghest was a large animal, but it could move so softly, and Lottie wondered if she was not just impressed by this fact but also a little frightened.

"How fares the Heir of Fiske?" the Barghest asked.

"I'm all right. Just nervous."

"Why is that?"

"Well," said Lottie, "nothing bad has happened to us for a full day, which makes me think that something extra horrible is right around the corner."

The Barghest released a crunchy bark that Lottie took for a laugh.

"Not a cheery thought," it said.

"Guess not. But there's no reason for me *not* to think that way. It seems that just when we think we're safe, someone attacks. Nash on the boat, and Iolanthe in Wisp Territory *and* the Northerly Court. Why can't the Southerly King mind his own business and let me be?"

"You are a threat to him," said the Barghest.

Lottie frowned. "Well, yeah, but I'm not the one who's going to poison him. None of that was my idea. I wish he'd just give up already. It gets tiring, always running, never safe."

"That it does," said the Barghest, shaking its mane.

Something squelched under Lottie's foot. She stepped back to inspect it and immediately wished she hadn't. Brown slime coated the sole of her boot, and on the path lay the upturned body of a large, goo-covered toad.

"Ugh," she said, wiping her boot on the path.

The others looked back.

"What is it?" asked Eliot.

"Oberon," said Fife, spotting the dead toad. "That's disgusting."

"I didn't see it," said Lottie, swiping her foot all the more vigorously, desperate to rid it of blood.

But Adelaide was pointing to the ground, her eyes wide with horror. "Look," she said. "*Look.*"

The toad was moving again. Or rather, something was moving *inside* the toad. It bulged against the toad's skin until it burst free in an explosion of yet more brown slime. Everyone shrank back. Adelaide shrieked. Lottie shielded her eyes. When she looked again, she saw three filmy toads emerging from the first toad's body—each one just as big as the first. One let out a menacing *croak* and hopped straight for Fife.

"AAAH!" he screamed, leaving the ground just in time to avoid collision.

"There's something strange at work here," said Dorian. "Move out, quickly. And whatever you do, don't step on another one of them."

Eliot took a cautious step back. His heel landed squarely on the toad that had just missed Fife.

"Watch out!" said Lottie. "I think they *want* to be stepped on. That's how it works. Look!"

For just where Eliot had squished the creature, another three toads emerged from its corpse, their eyes dark and slitted.

"Run!" she shouted. "Run, but *watch your feet!*"

It took only a half minute's fleeing to confirm that Lottie's hypothesis was all too right: the toads threw themselves underfoot as though they desired nothing more than to be squished. And with each squishing came the arrival of three new toads. No matter how careful the company was to watch their footing, the toads were quicker and more cunning. In no time at all, the pathway was swarming with them. The sound of their awful croaks filled Lottie's ears. A stench like a mildewed rag began to clog up her nose. The toads where everywhere, piling atop one another and jumping high. Lottie gave up trying to be cautious; she began to run blindly.

Lottie wondered if she could die this way. She wondered if the toads would continue to pile and pile until she was dragged under their miry bodies, suffocated. And, just as she began to despair, she felt arms, firm and strong, wrap around her middle. Her feet left the ground, and she rose upward, out of the din.

"Steady on, Lottie," said a voice at her ear.

She knew Fife was using his keen, but she didn't care. She wanted to feel better. From where she floated, she could see the full stretch of the sea of toads, growing ever deeper and wider. She saw Dorian hacking away with his sword and the Barghest nipping at the toads with its fangs. She saw Eliot and Adelaide, close beside each other, arms covering their heads.

"We have to help them!" she said. "Drop me down some-place safe. Out there!"

As she pointed to the horizon, she saw for the first time that the shore was in view. There was a long bank of sand and the wink of blue waters.

"Set me down up ahead," she said, "and go back for the others."

"Are you crazy?" shouted Fife. "It could be a trap. This could be just what Iolanthe is after—to get you alone and kill you off. I'm not leaving you."

"But we've got to do *something!*"

She looked again at the terrible scene below. Something was different. The toads were still multiplying, and the others were still fighting them off. But the *color* of the toads had begun to change. What had once been a sea of brown was now filled with glimmers of red, blue, black, and purple. It took Lottie a hard moment to figure out what was happening. Then she spied Oliver in the midst of the colored sea, and she knew.

"Oliver's touching them," she said. "And look, Fife! I think they're dying for good."

Fife's float had sputtered to a low hover, close enough for them to see the action better. Oliver was grabbing at toads left and right. As his hands made contact with each one, their bodies bloomed with new color and fell away. One landed just beneath Lottie's floating feet, dead. It was stained as bright blue as the cloudless sky above. No new toads emerged from its lifeless body.

"He's stopping them," Lottie said. "Do you see? He's *really* stopping them."

"It must be killing him," Fife whispered

Oliver was red-eyed and red-faced, his movements frantic. But he didn't seem to be hurt, didn't seem to be incurring injures from the frogs he touched.

"I think he's okay," Lottie said.

"No," said Fife, lowering them to the ground, clear of the swarm. "No, I mean, it must be killing him *inside*."

On instinct, Lottie stepped forward, but Fife grabbed her by the elbow and held her back.

"You can't do anything," he said. "Not yet. Just wait it out."

Lottie knew Fife was right, but it was agony to watch the others bat off the remaining toads, to hear Adelaide's screams, to see the red of Oliver's eyes. The others had taken note of what Oliver was doing. They'd all come to a stop, crouching down with hands over their heads until the attack had subsided and the ground was littered in the discolored carcasses of dozens upon dozens of toads. The tide had turned. The remaining toads hopped away into the field and out of sight.

It was over.

Slowly, Adelaide and Eliot uncovered their heads. Dorian straightened to his full height, sword at his side, its blade coated in mud-colored blood. The Barghest pawed roughly at the bodies of several toads lying dead at its feet. And in the midst of it all stood Oliver, hands limp at his sides, his eyes a burnt-out black.

"Lottie!"

Arms swung around her. Eliot.

"Are you okay?" she asked him. "Are you hurt?"

"No," said Eliot, pulling away to get a good look at her. "You?"

"Fine," she said, just as Adelaide joined them. "Fife and I are fine."

"Just goes to show who your favorite is, Fife," said Adelaide. "Left the rest of us to our doom, did you?"

"I hardly call a bunch of hopping toads your *doom*," said Fife. "Anyway, Lottie is the Heir of Fiske. Top priority and all that."

"Everyone in possession of their limbs?" asked Dorian, crossing over the mound of toads with a sickening *squelch, squish, squash*.

Everyone confirmed that they were all right, just badly shaken. The Barghest joined them, panting.

"Well, we've had our scare for the day," said Dorian. "But the coast is in sight. We should journey on—and this time be more mindful of where we set our feet."

"Hold on," said Eliot. "Aren't we going to, I don't know, applaud Ollie for his bravery? If it wasn't for him, we'd all be drowned in frogs."

All eyes turned to Oliver, who was still standing in the pile of colored toads. His eyes turned pink under their gaze, and Lottie knew instantly that this was the very last thing Oliver wanted.

"Eliot," said Lottie, touching his hand, "Dorian's right. We should just move on."

Eliot didn't notice the warning in Lottie's voice.

"What's the matter with all of you?" he said. "We just got our lives saved! Ollie deserves a standing ovation!"

"*No.*" Oliver said it loudly, coldly—in a way that made Lottie squirm inside. His eyes turned back to black.

"No," he said again. "I don't want applause. I don't want to think about it. I don't want anyone to talk about this ever again."

Dorian sheathed his newly cleaned sword.

"Then come on," he said. "Let's move out."

They headed for the coast. If Lottie had been paying full attention, she might have noticed the fresh, salty taste the air had taken on; she might have heard the squawks of gulls overhead; she might have noted the way the sun glinted off the distant blue water. But Lottie wasn't paying full attention. She was too distracted by Oliver's mood and Eliot's guilt and, on top of all this, a nagging feeling about Fife.

"I don't understand," Eliot whispered to Lottie as they walked on. There were tears resting in his eyes. "Why is Ollie so angry? If I could fight off enemies with my bare hands, I'd be proud. He's basically a superhero."

"Oliver doesn't see it that way, though. He doesn't like hurting or killing anything."

"Ooh," said Eliot. "You mean, like, he's a pacifist?"

"It's more than that," said Lottie. "I don't think anyone knows how guilty he feels when he uses his hands like that."

"I feel rotten," said Eliot.

"Don't," said Lottie. "You didn't know."

But she could tell that Eliot was still feeling bad about it, and there was nothing she could do to stop it, just like there was nothing she could do to stop Oliver from feeling guilty or make Fife speak to her about what had happened in Sharp Bend.

The grass turned to heather, and the beach stretched before them—a narrow strip of white sand and black rocks, edging the coast as far as Lottie could see. Waves crashed on the surf in a gentle lull. Lottie's lips felt puckered and briny.

Lottie had visited the coast of Kemble Isle twice before. Once, Mrs. Yates had taken her to a fund-raising tea at a seaside resort, which might just as well have taken place in the middle of New Kemble, since Mrs. Yates refused to let Lottie venture out to the beach. The second time, Lottie and Eliot had concocted a bike trip to the beach that took four hours longer than they'd anticipated and ended with Mr. Walsch driving out to pick them up after dark.

Lottie had never seen a coast so pristine as this. The beaches she'd visited had been made of dirty sand, bordered by condominiums and hot dog stalls. But this beach was desolate. There were no houses or docks or people. As Lottie took her first step into the pillow-soft sand, she got the feeling she was trespassing on a very fine estate without the owner's knowledge.

Fife floated to Lottie's side, awe in his face.

"I didn't know it looked like *this*," he said.

"What?" said Lottie. "Have you never been to the beach? I thought you'd done *everything*, Fife Dulcet."

Fife smirked. "Practically everything."

"It's so empty," said Adelaide. "The Southerly beaches Father took us to growing up were much prettier than this. Weren't they, Oliver?"

Oliver, still black-eyed, said nothing.

Dorian stopped ahead and squinted at the horizon.

"What do we do now?" Lottie asked him. "Where's the ferry?"

Dorian turned to the Barghest. "Well? This was your route, dog. Where to now?"

But even the Barghest looked uncertain.

"I have never used the ferry," it growled. "I only know it is the safest route for the Heir of Fiske."

"Well, it's the *only* route now," said Dorian, "considering she can't cross the waters any other way."

"Why not?" asked Eliot. "I mean, isn't there a boat rental place or something?"

"Not on this part of the coast," said Dorian.

Lottie turned to Oliver. His face was painted with poetry.

"The poems say there was once a great naval battle here between Northerlies and Southerlies," he said. "It was the bloodiest confrontation in the Great Schism. Thousands lost their lives to the sword, and then a great squall splintered the remaining boats to pieces and drowned the soldiers. Many sprites said it was Nature's curse on all the bloodshed of war, and from then on, the western coast was considered cursed, from the tip of the Wilders to the Northerly Gate. It's said that the only seacraft Nature will not drag into the depths is the ferry, since it's not run by sprites proper, but by a nix."

Everyone had gone very quiet. Adelaide made a low, disgusted sound.

Oliver shrugged. "That's what the poems say, anyway."

"Sorry," said Eliot, "but what's a nix?"

"A sprite who has bound himself to the sea," said Dorian. "Legend has it they sacrifice their souls to know all the sea's secrets. They can never leave the water."

"You don't really believe that, do you?" asked Fife, snorting.

Dorian gave Fife a sharp look. "I've heard enough from fellow soldiers to keep me wary."

Lottie walked nearer the shore—so near that the water stained the tips of her boots.

"Well, there's no sign of a ferry here," she said. "We should send our gengas out in both directions and have them report back."

"Yup," said Fife, pulling Spool from his pocket.

The yellow kingfisher swooped down the shore. A lavender finch flapped in the opposite direction, sent off by Adelaide's hands.

"Barghest," said Lottie, turning to the creature. "Do you see that pile of rocks up the coast? Go inspect it, please. Maybe something's hidden behind it."

But the Barghest remained where it was.

"I would not advise that course of action," it said. "Better not break up our company."

"Hey!" cried Eliot, who stood a little way down the coast. "Look at this!"

Lottie and the others joined Eliot where he stood. He was pointing at one of the jagged rocks that dotted the sea. It was wide across, and words were carved into it in boxy script:

TO THOSE WHO SEEK THE WATER'S FAVOR

WHOSOEVER ROWS AGAINST THE FLOOD,

OF SORROW HE SHALL DRINK.

WHOSOEVER GIVES OF SORROW SHALL NOT SINK,

GRANTED PASSAGE TO THAT OTHER SHORE.

WHOSOEVER GIVES OF BLOOD SHALL BIND HIM EVER TO THE SEA

AND WALK THE LAND NO MORE.

"Oh, it's a riddle!" said Adelaide. "I'm very good at these. Let me think."

"Is this it?" Lottie asked Dorian and the Barghest. "It says 'granted passage to that other shore.' So, what, is it a ferry you can only take by solving the riddle?"

"Seems like," said Dorian. "The nix are known for their schemes and wiles."

"Um," said Fife. "So remind me why we're trusting them to carry us across the sea?"

"I never said *I* trusted them," said Dorian. "There's a reason I've never traveled this way. This was all the Barghest's doing. Direct your questions to *it*."

"Shush!" said Adelaide, waving them to be quiet. "We should be trying to figure out what it means."

Lottie, too, was staring intently at the rock, attempting to make sense of its words.

"*Gives of sorrow*," she said out loud. Then, "*Gives of blood*."

"It seems to me," said Adelaide, "that if you do the *first* thing, you will drown in the sea. No thank you. And if you do the *third* thing, you'll be bound to the water, same as the nix. How dreadful. So it's the *second* thing we want to do. If we 'give of sorrow,' whatever that means, we'll get safe passage on the ferry. Well. Don't you think?"

"Maybe," said Lottie, "'give of blood' literally means to drop your blood in the water."

"That would make sense," said Oliver. His eyes no longer shone black but dark yellow. "The whole curse started because of bloodshed. Many poems say that the wounded sailors didn't drown, but by bleeding into the sea became the first nix. Now, perhaps, anyone else who drops their blood in the water will become like them."

"Then what does the second line mean?" asked Eliot. "Instead of blood, you give what to the sea? Tears?"

Fife snickered. "You mean you've got to stand on the shore, crying into the sea? How melodramatic. Sounds like one of your Byron poems, Ollie."

"Do you have a better idea?" asked Adelaide.

Fife shrugged. "How're we supposed to get someone to cry, though? Tell them a sad story? Punch them in the stomach?"

"Honestly," said Adelaide. "Nothing so violent. I'm sure I could manage without any help."

"Oh, I'm sure you could, Miss Priss."

"Fife, cut it out, would you?" said Lottie, irritated. Then, to Adelaide, "Do you really think you could?"

Adelaide nodded stiffly and approached the water's edge. She placed both feet in the shallow water and closed her eyes, bunching her face into a contorted expression.

Fife was laughing. Dorian gave him a sound whack over the head, and he hushed up. The rest of them watched in rapt silence.

It took nearly a minute, but a teardrop finally appeared at the edge of Adelaide's right eye. Then another, at her left. Then yet another, and another. Slowly, they wound down her cheeks, and Adelaide tilted her chin toward the water so the drops could more easily fall into the sea. Each drop clung to her skin for several seconds, then plopped into the water. Lottie had lost count of how many tears Adelaide shed by the time she wiped her cheeks, opened her eyes, and looked up.

"Well?" she said. "Do you think that's enough?"

Dorian shook his head. "There's nothing left but to wait and see."

So they waited. They waited minute upon minute, watching the surface of the water. There were a couple times Lottie swore she saw something moving, but it only ever turned out to be the foaming roll of a new wave. They waited, and waited, but they saw nothing.

"I'm not sure tears is right."

Lottie was surprised to hear Eliot's timid voice break the silence.

"I have another idea," he continued. "What if 'gives of sorrow' doesn't mean tears at all? What if it just means that whatever you drop into the ocean has to *cause* you sorrow?"

"You mean, you have to sacrifice something to the sea," said Lottie. "Something that means a lot to you."

Eliot nodded.

"Well, what have any of us got that fits that description?" asked Fife, throwing his hands up. "We're traveling light here. There's nothing on me I care that much about. Definitely nothing that would cause me *sorrow*, or whatever."

Lottie dropped her hand into her coat pocket. Her fingertips touched the silk handkerchief and, beneath it, the solid form of her mother's ring. Sacrificing that would certainly cause her sorrow, but Lottie wasn't sure she could. The ring was all she had of her parents that she knew they had touched and cherished. But no one else here knew about the ring. She didn't have to tell them.

"We still don't even know that it's going to work," she said. "It might not be a riddle at all. Or maybe it used to be, and it doesn't work anymore."

But no one was listening to her. Their attention had shifted while she'd been weighing the worth of her ring. They were all staring at Eliot, who had approached the water's edge and was holding out a thick bundle of papers in his hands. Lottie realized immediately what they were: all the letters from his father.

"Here it is!" he shouted at the water. "Something precious. Something of myself. You'd better grant us passage now."

"Eliot, no!" Lottie cried.

It was too late. With great force, Eliot threw the letters out to sea. Lottie watched, aghast, as they fluttered down to the water. There, they bobbed on the rocking surface until, much sooner than Lottie expected, they slipped entirely from view.

All was silent. Moments passed, long and agonizing. Lottie scanned the surface of the water, looking for any sign of a disturbance, something out of the ordinary. But time crept on, and more time still, bringing with it restlessness.

Lottie ran to where Eliot stood, his gaze still fixed on the sea. She took his hand in hers.

"Eliot," she whispered. "You didn't have to do that."

He shook his head, eyes still focused on the water. "Yes, I did. For once, it's something I *could* do."

Silence hung about them for a minute more.

"W-w-what are we supposed to do now?" Adelaide finally whispered.

"Ask the dog," said Dorian. "It's the one that led us this far."

The Barghest snarled at Dorian.

"Does anyone else have an idea about what the riddle could mean?" asked Oliver.

Fife shook his head. "I really thought the sorrow thing was right."

"I guess we wait until Spool and Lila return," said Lottie, her face downcast. "We'll see if they were able to find any sign of the ferry and then—well, if they don't, I guess we'll just have to go back the way we came."

"You mean, take my route."

Lottie heard the triumph in Dorian's voice.

"I only chose what I thought was best," she said defensively. "You don't have to—"

"Lottie!"

She stopped short. Eliot was pointing at the sea. Lottie turned around.

Something was happening. Bubbles were rising in the water. The bubbles turned to froth, and the froth grew thick, and the water began to spiral around the froth in a magnificent way. Then something appeared at the very center of the spiral. It heaved out of the water in one great surge, and water sprayed in every direction, reaching all the way to the beach and spattering Lottie and the others. Lottie wiped the salt water from her eyes, transfixed.

The water began to settle. The spiral slowed, loosening its arms until it disappeared entirely. The froth faded away. All that remained was what had emerged from the water, now a solid and visible thing.

It was a boat, small in design. Its sail looked to be made of nothing more than gossamer. A single person stood inside—a man, dressed in a cape the color of sea foam. His face was turned to the sky, and he wore the oddest expression.

"Right, then, Dorian," said Fife. "Got that sword at the ready?"

"Is that one of them?" asked Eliot. "Is that a nix?"

"Don't know what else it could be," said Dorian. "Stay close, all of you. We still don't know if he's friendly."

Lottie didn't budge. She remained next to Eliot, her boots touching the water. She saw now the reason for the nix's odd expression and upturned face: he was *blowing at the sail*. With each heave of his shoulders, the boat moved more swiftly toward the shore. It was soon so very near them that the nix dropped something large and fork-shaped over the edge—an anchor, Lottie guessed. Then he jumped into the water, which came up to his knees, and sloshed toward them, hands on hips.

For a sprite rumored to have sold his soul to the waters, he looked remarkably unremarkable. His features were plain, his build not particularly fat or skinny, tall or short. The only thing even slightly out of the ordinary about him was the shimmering cape that covered him from neck to toe. Rather than pool about him in the water as a normal cape would do, the material stayed close about his legs, as though it were a part of them. He stopped when only his feet remained in the water. At least, Lottie *assumed* there were feet under that cape . . . .

"You!" he called, pointing at Eliot. "You have summoned me for passage, have you?"

"Um," said Eliot. "*Um.*"

Lottie squeezed his hand.

"Have you, or haven't you?" demanded the nix.

"I—I have," Eliot said. He shifted in what looked like an attempt to stand tall. "I want you to take me and my friends to this place called the Wilders. Have you heard of it?"

The nix took a good look at Eliot. He took a good look at the others. Then he laughed.

"Impossible," he said. "Have you seen my boat?"

Lottie had. It was small. Very small.

"Not a passenger more than three," said the nix, wagging his finger at Eliot. "Choose two companions, if you like, but no more than that will I allow. Too treacherous to carry all of you."

"But that's hardly fair!" Lottie cried.

"I made neither the riddle nor the boat," the nix told Lottie. Then, turning back to Eliot, "Choose your companions."

Eliot turned to the others and whispered, "What am I supposed to do?"

"You heard him," said Dorian. "If you don't want to have thrown away all those letters for nothing, I suggest you pick two companions. Me, because I'm the only one who knows where to find the addersfork. And I imagine you'd like the other one to be Lottie."

"Yes," Lottie said quickly. "I need to be near him. In case . . . anything happens."

To Lottie's surprise, Eliot looked annoyed. "It's not like my limbs are going to fall off in your absence, you know."

"I—I know," she stammered.

But—though Lottie didn't admit it out loud—she had her fears. She had known, ever since the boat capsized in the River Lissome, that something could easily separate her from Eliot. She didn't know what might happen once they reached the Wilders. She only knew that, so long as she could, she intended to keep Eliot by her side.

Eliot faced the nix again. "Dorian and Lottie," he said. "Those are my two companions."

"So be it," said the nix, making a low bow in their direction. Lottie got the feeling he was mocking them. "Thus the passengers will be: Dorian, Lottie, and—what was your name, little one?"

"Eliot Walsch, sir. And, um, what are we supposed to call you?"

"When I was called something," said the nix, "I went by the name of Sigeberht."

"And I thought Dorian was bad," muttered Fife.

"Tell us, Sigeberht," said Dorian, "how long will it take your boat to deposit us at the cove of the Wilders?"

"I'd wager three hours at most," said Sigeberht. "What you want there I shudder to think, but it's not my place to ask. Now, we've squandered enough time gabbing. Board my boat, and let's be on our way."

"This wasn't how I pictured things going," Lottie told the others. "I'm sorry. The whole point in heading to the Wilders was not splitting up, and now we're splitting anyway."

"There's a village called Darrow," said Dorian. "It's farther inland, but not more than a mile back. Find the inn marked with the black diamond and show them this." Here he handed Fife a circular pendant on a red cord, fished from his pocket. "That's your pass for free room and board. Don't expect frills. We'll be back within a day."

"What?" said Lottie. "That quickly? But I thought—"

"Within a day," Dorian repeated.

"Sounds like a good plan to me," said Fife. "We'll lounge about in bed while you all fight off dragons and goblins."

"Oh, stop it, Fife," said Adelaide. "You're making Lottie nervous. Look, she's positively *shaking*."

Lottie looked down to find that her arms were, indeed, trembling hard.

"It's nothing," she said. "Just the cold."

Oliver was staring at her with sharp green eyes.

"Exultation," he said, "is the going of an inland soul to sea. Bred as we, among the mountains, can the sailor understand the divine intoxication of the first league out from land?"

The shaking in Lottie's arms began to subside, but she now had the most horrendous urge to burst into tears. She knelt beside the Barghest to hide her face.

"You know we'd take you, too, if I could," she said. "But you'll protect the others while I'm gone?"

The Barghest bent its head and said, "I will do my duty."

Lottie rose to her feet. "Well then," she said, looking at no one in particular for fear that the urge to weep would come again, "we'll see you soon."

"Better take off our shoes," said Eliot, pointing out the distance between them and the boat, "unless we want to have wet feet the rest of the journey."

So Lottie, Eliot, and Dorian waded into the sea, shoes in hand. The water was frigid, and Lottie's bare feet stung. She sloshed as fast as she could to the boat's edge, where Dorian and Sigeberht helped her aboard.

Eliot waved to the shore, where the Barghest, Oliver, Adelaide, and Fife stood watching. Only Fife waved back.

Sigeberht raised anchor. Then he lifted his face toward the sail and blew. The boat lurched with tremendous force. Each of the nix's breaths packed the energy of a squalling wind, and the harder he puffed, the faster the shore sped from view until the others were nothing more than specks on the horizon.

Lottie couldn't help herself from staring at Sigeberht much longer than was polite. She wondered if this gift of his was a keen or if it was something beyond that—something he'd gained when he'd become a nix.

Then another thought came crashing into Lottie's mind. She frowned at the horizon.

"All right?" asked Dorian, taking notice.

"I just remembered something. Earlier, I gave the Barghest a command."

"What's wrong with that? If anyone should be commanding a Barghest, it's you."

"No, that's not it," said Lottie. "The thing is, I gave the Barghest a command, and . . . it didn't obey."

CHAPTER SEVENTEEN

Addersfork

SUNLIGHT HUNG heavy on the sea, glinting on the water in new ways with every bob of the boat. They glided along with a speed that Lottie couldn't quite get used to, even after an hour's worth of traveling. The wet wind blew Lottie's hair into her eyes and prickled at her neck. Sigeberht said nothing, only blew and blew, filling the sail and sending them on at a dizzying speed. They had reached a place where there was no land in sight, no matter which way Lottie turned. All was vast sea. It was beautiful, but it was frightening, too. Lottie tried not to think of what strange creatures were swimming below the surface. There was no telling in a place like Albion Isle.

"What did you mean, we'd be back within a day?" Lottie asked Dorian. "We've already been at sea at least an hour, and once we reach the Wilders, you'll have to blaze a trail to find the addersfork, won't you?"

Dorian didn't answer.

"*Hey*," she said, kicking his foot. "What did you mean, we'd be back in a day?"

"You heard Sigeberht," said Dorian. "It'll take three hours to get to the cove, three hours back. The addersfork grows on the cliffs of the cove, so our journey by land won't take long. All in all, it totals to less than a day."

"But if the addersfork is that close to us," Lottie said, "then the best way to get to it was by ferry all along!"

"The *shortest distance* was by ferry," said Dorian. "That's not the same as the best way."

"Nothing's gone wrong yet," said Lottie. "I still don't see why you wanted to go the long route, even after the Barghest said there'd be soldiers waiting for us."

Dorian cast a glance at Sigeberht, who was still busy filling the sail. He leaned in closer to Lottie, and Eliot, too, who had been attentively listening in.

"I told you," said Dorian, "the nix have a bad reputation. More than that, I've heard soldiers talking about strange goings-on near the western coast—talk of bad magic. I think it's better to face a known danger than an unknown one. I'm familiar with the Southerly Guard. I would've felt far safer fighting them off than I do now, crossing the sea with a nix."

Lottie looked nervously at Sigeberht, afraid he might overhear Dorian, but he seemed just as preoccupied as ever with his work.

"The Wilders," said Eliot, looking pensive. "It doesn't sound very friendly."

"There's nothing about the Wilders that's *friendly*," said Dorian. "Only the toughest or most desperate sprites choose to live there, and half who do don't make it through a winter."

"But you made it," Lottie pointed out. "Rebel Gem said you're one of the few sprites who has."

Dorian smiled sadly. "I did, yes. Back when I was very young and very stupid."

"Dorian," said Lottie. "Do you think it's worth it? Do *you* think the addersfork will work?"

"There's no way of knowing. I like to hope it's true. If I wasn't hoping that, this entire journey of ours would be unbearably depressing. It's thanks to my time as a spy in the Southerly Court that the wisps have hairs directly from Starkling's head. Once they've got the addersfork, they'll have all they need to attempt the poisoning. And when that day comes, I guess we'll all just have to cross our fingers."

"At least we're doing something," said Eliot. "At least we're trying."

Just then, a cry filled the air, whistling and melodic. Lottie looked up and saw a creature soaring overhead. It wasn't a bird—or at least, not any type of bird Lottie had seen before. Its wings were wide and flesh-like, its skin sandy brown. It looked, Lottie thought, a little like the manta rays she had seen on a Kemble School field trip to the aquarium, only rather than flap its fins through water, this creature flapped its wings through air. It had a tail, too, thin and long, feathered on its end.

"What *is* that?" asked Eliot.

"Look," said Lottie, pointing. "There's another one. Another *three*."

"They're flatrooks," said Dorian.

Lottie shook her head in wonder. "Those don't exist in the human world."

"No need to look scared stiff," Dorian said, laughing. "Sailors say they're friendly to sprites. A good omen. I've heard more than one tale of a shipwreck where flatrooks came to the rescue of the drowning passengers."

"So that makes them like albatrosses," said Eliot. "You know, those birds that are supposed to be good luck charms?"

"We have those, too," said Dorian. "But I'd say flatrooks are the better bird. An albatross can't carry you on its back to safety."

"Good point," said Eliot.

The flatrooks circled the boat twice, their high, pretty melodies piercing the air. Then they flapped westward, farther out to sea. Lottie was a little saddened to see them go.

They sailed on. Sigeberht did not once take a break from his work. Silence settled on the boat, but it was not uncomfortable. Lottie stole a glance at Eliot, who was looking out to sea. She was thinking of what he had said earlier, on the shore: *For once, it's something I could do.* All this time, she had been worried about Eliot's health, not his feelings. Now, for the first time, she wondered if he felt useless the same way she'd felt when she had first arrived in Albion Isle and everyone else seemed to know things she didn't and do things she couldn't. She thought of those letters fluttering down to the water, lost for all time. Sadness welled within her and puddled in her chest.

She was still looking furtively over at Eliot when he closed his eyes against the setting sun and shifted his grip on the boat's edge. His eyes fluttered back open, and he let out a soft hiss. He held up his hand to reveal a splinter of wood lodged at the fleshy base of his thumb. A drop of shining, crimson blood bubbled to the surface.

Lottie acted without thinking. She let out a shout and threw herself across the boat. Grabbing Eliot by the shoulders, she hauled him back with her to the boat's base.

"Ow! Lottie, *what?*"

Above her, Dorian was shouting a string of words Lottie did not recognize but took to be hearty swearing. She grabbed Eliot's hand and did not let go, even as he righted himself into a sit.

"You're bleeding," she gasped. "You were going to—it was going to drop into the water."

The boat was rocking violently, which Lottie realized was entirely her doing. It shifted even more as Dorian knelt beside them.

"By Puck," he said, coming closer. "Let's take care of that."

Lottie let go of Eliot's hand and moved over for Dorian to take her place. She watched as he swiftly removed one of the piercings from his nose and pocketed the backing in his vest. He pulled a match from the pocket and bent to strike its head against the edge of his boot. He held the needle of the piercing in the fire and then, just as the flame reached his pinched fingers, blew it out.

"Right," he said, grabbing Eliot's hand. "Here goes."

Eliot was utterly silent as Dorian squeezed his thumb in one hand and maneuvered the needle of the nose ring with the other. He managed to pull the splinter free in one clean movement. Another drop of blood trickled out, but after Eliot wiped his hand against his shirt, no more rose to the surface.

"You keep away from the boat's edge," Dorian instructed, "just in case."

He returned to his side of the boat, and Lottie crept beside Eliot, apology in her eyes.

"Sorry," she said. "I just saw the blood, and I thought of the riddle, and I—"

"Saved me, like always." There was something in Eliot's voice that sounded strained. But the next moment he said, "Thanks. I'd rather not turn into a nix. No offense, Sigeberht."

Sigeberht did not reply. He was still blowing wind into the sail, seemingly unaffected by this entire episode. Though Lottie did think she saw a change in his pale eyes—a slight shift, nothing more than a glint really, but it gave her a chill.

The sea turned amber with sunset and then, as the last rays of sun slipped away, deep blue. It grew colder. Lottie kept her hands in her coat pockets, one wrapped around Trouble, the other around her mother's ring.

"How much farther is it?" she asked Dorian.

"Can't you see the coast?" said Dorian, pointing.

Lottie screwed up her eyes. In the distance, she made out a silhouette stretched over the sea, jagged and pointed, not unlike the Barghest's teeth.

"That's it?" she said. "The Wilders?"

"When we get to the cove," said Dorian, "you and Eliot both stay close, understand? I've only got one lantern and one sword, and I can't be expected to protect you if you go wandering off."

"We won't," Lottie promised, now fixed on the sight of land as it grew more defined with every puff of Sigeberht's lungs.

The jagged shapes soon loomed straight above them. Moonlight touched their edges, revealing a rocky cliff face, curved toward them in a half circle. All was darkness and shadows, and as the boat drew closer to the sandy cove, Lottie wondered if there were other things on this beach she could not see—creatures in the dark.

Dorian lit his lantern.

"Just do what I said," Dorian ordered, "and stick with me. If things go according to plan, we should be off this foul land by sunrise."

"And if they *don't* go according to plan?" asked Eliot.

"Aren't you a right little optimist" was Dorian's reply.

At long last, Sigeberht stopped his puffing and hurled the anchor overboard. The boat drifted close to shore, then lurched away again in the lapping water.

"Can't come any closer," said Sigeberht. "Too close to land."

Lottie wasn't sure if Sigeberht was talking about the boat or himself.

"Shoes off," Dorian instructed. "We'll wade to shore. Expect us back by dawn, nix."

Sigeberht smiled. "I wouldn't make a habit of *expecting* in these parts. Can't count on a thing when you're in the Wilders."

"Just be here when we return," said Dorian.

He jumped into the shallow water. Lottie and Eliot followed, though at a far slower pace. They put their socks and boots back on while Dorian stood over them, lantern aloft, turning his head one way, then the other, toward the shadows. Try as she might, Lottie couldn't completely rid her wet feet of sand, so even after her boots were laced, she felt the tickle of loose grains in her socks. Her eyes were droopy with sleep, but she strained to keep them wide open in front of Dorian. Eliot did not. He yawned loudly.

"We can sleep once we've found the addersfork," said Dorian. "This way."

He led them the only direction Lottie supposed they could go—into the dark unknown of an opening cut into the cliff. There had been no need for Dorian to worry about them wandering off; Lottie and Eliot could do nothing but stay close to him and his light. All else in the cave was skin-clenching cold and solid darkness. They were heading up an incline, from what Lottie could tell.

"What's that?" Eliot said, grabbing Lottie's hand so hard she felt sure he'd pushed all the blood out of it. "Did you hear something over there?"

"No," Lottie lied.

She could hear all types of somethings—scuttling and skittering and a constant *drip-drip-drip*. She'd been trying to convince herself that these sounds came from her imagination, not the reality of the cave. But if Eliot could hear them, too . . .

Just when Lottie felt sure she couldn't take another step without screaming or laughing or otherwise releasing the fear within her, she saw light ahead. Not bright light, but rather the smoky blue of moonlight. All the same, it was *light*, and it meant that they were close to the outdoor world again.

The incline had grown so steep that, once Dorian was free of the cave, he offered a hand to Lottie, then Eliot, and hoisted them up to the level land. They had climbed the cliff underground, Lottie realized. The sea was now far below them, and they stood on a rocky plain, bordered by the same jagged rocks she'd seen from Sigeberht's ferry.

"Well!" said Eliot. "If we've climbed a cliff, I guess we can do anything."

Dorian led them on. The wind was sharper here than it had been below, and though Lottie was as well bundled as she could be, she still felt cold in the deepest parts of her bones. There were no trees here, no shrubs, no chatter of birds. All was rock, in every which direction. Lottie wondered if this was all the Wilders were: stony bareness and no life save the unseen things in the caves.

She could not say how long they traveled on that way, over rock, in howling wind. Her mind frosted over, stilling all extraneous thought. She thought in terms of action only—of moving her feet and keeping Dorian's lantern in her sights.

Then something changed. Lottie heard the trickle of water. A few steps more brought her to its source. A stream of black water flowed ahead of them, cutting through the rock face like an open wound. It was narrow enough to leap over, but Dorian made no effort to do so. Instead, he changed directions and began to walk along the bank, studying the ground as though looking for something he had lost. Then he seemed to find it. He stopped, knelt by the stream, and motioned for Lottie and Eliot to do the same.

"Don't touch the water," he said. "I'll be the one to do it."

Dorian rolled back his sleeve and, without further warning, plunged his hand into the stream. His arm shook violently, but he kept it submerged. Then, with a sudden heave, he removed it. In his grip were three thick, green stalks. They drooped limp like seaweed. At the end of each stalk was a blue bulb, no larger than a marble.

So this was addersfork. Lottie was a little unimpressed. She didn't know what she'd anticipated—for it to be growing in a golden urn, placed upon a pedestal?—but this was not it. She hadn't thought that addersfork was a plant that grew in a place so inconspicuous as this, or a plant that grew *underwater*.

"That's it?" she asked.

Dorian nodded. His face was pinched, as though he was in pain. He removed a thick towel from his satchel and placed the addersfork inside, blotting at the excess water, then carefully wrapping the bundle until it looked like nothing more than a lumpy, used washrag. Then he laid it inside the satchel with tender care. He was just getting to his feet when he let out a strangled cry.

"What?" said Lottie, jumping up. "What's wrong?"

She tried to make sense of what she saw in the lantern light: Dorian's right hand was covered in a dozen thin lines, the color of blood.

"It isn't fatal," he said. "I'll be fine."

"Did the addersfork do that?"

Dorian shook his head. "Just a wildereel."

"What's a—um, what's *that*?" asked Eliot.

Dorian breathed sharply, shook his head again. "They guard the addersfork."

Lottie now understood why Dorian had told them not to touch the water. Her chest warmed with appreciation.

"You knew that all along, didn't you?" she said. "You knew you were going to get hurt."

"It was the quickest way to do it," Dorian said. "And the stinging will fade in a few hours' time. It's nothing to worry about."

"I could help," Lottie said softly. "If you let me—"

"*No*. We don't have time for you to waste fiddling with your keen. We've got to get back to Sigeberht."

Lottie shrank back. Dorian's words doused the warmth that had been growing within her.

"I'm not *fiddling*," she said angrily.

"This isn't the time," Dorian said, "and I don't have endless lantern oil."

He set out the way they'd come. Lottie and Eliot had no choice but to follow.

"Don't take it personally," Eliot told Lottie minutes later. He kept his voice in a whisper, but Lottie knew that would do no good; Dorian would be able to hear everything they said. "It's just because he got hurt back there. Dad always says, 'Hurt people *hurt* people.' I'm sure it doesn't have to do with your keen."

"Doesn't it?" said Lottie. "*You* don't even want me to use my keen on you."

Eliot cleared his throat. After a moment, he said, "Maybe I'm not as sick as you think. I've hardly coughed at all the past day. Haven't you noticed?"

Lottie thought back. Now that Eliot brought it up, she couldn't remember him coughing nearly so much, even on their grueling walk through the Wilders.

"Maybe the air here is good for me," he said. "Maybe I've just got allergies, and Wisp Territory had terrible pollen."

"You know it's not that," Lottie said. "You're still sick."

"But I'm not *helpless*. You don't have to fix me every time I get something in my lungs. When I cough, you don't have to look at me like I'm a wounded animal. Like I'm weak. I can take care of myself."

Eliot was angry, Lottie realized in shock. He was *angry* with her, when all Lottie had done was offer to help him.

"Fine," she said. "Then take care of yourself. Go ahead."

They did not speak after that. In silence, they followed Dorian across the windy, barren plain. Lottie tried not to think. She willed for her mind to fall once more into a muddied stupor, but it was no use. Eliot's words clattered around in her head, repeating themselves again and again: *I can take care of myself.*

Didn't Eliot understand he *needed* help? How, after all the time she'd spent searching and sharpening, could Eliot say a thing like that? Out of habit, Lottie stuck her hand into her pocket and felt for Trouble. She found him shivering.

"I'm sorry," she said, bringing him out. "If I could warm you up better, I would."

Trouble brushed his head against Lottie's fingers. He sang a melody, sweet and good, and Lottie's thoughts finally drifted from Eliot and the cold into a far happier place, where she could remember what it felt like to sleep in a proper bed and eat hot, well-cooked food.

Only when they reached the cliff face cave did Lottie reluctantly pocket Trouble and concentrate her efforts on scrambling down the steep, underground path. She struggled to keep her balance, worried at every moment that she might go toppling headfirst the whole rest of the way down. Eliot stumbled once, slid five feet down, and righted himself. Lottie said nothing, did nothing. After all, Eliot could take care of himself, couldn't he?

When they emerged onto the beach, new light shone upon the water, coming from over the cliffs: dawn. Lottie's weary eyes felt wearier still under the light of the breaking sun. She wanted nothing more than to plop down in the sand, curl her knees in, and sleep for uninterrupted hours. But sleep would have to wait. They'd retrieved the adders-fork, but they had yet to place it in the right hands. There was now another journey ahead of them, back to Wisp Territory.

And after that . . .

Lottie thought of Rebel Gem's promise. She thought of Iolanthe's attack on Northerly Territory. Would the Northerlies declare war on the Southerly Court? And if so, would Rebel Gem still uphold her promise to Lottie? Would she finally allow her and Eliot passage back to Kemble Isle? And if that moment came, would Lottie even *want* to go back? Lottie shook her head, scolding herself for the thought. *Of course* she wanted to go back. How could she think otherwise? She blamed it on her tiredness.

Sigeberht's boat was still moored in the cove, though farther from the shore than Lottie remembered—so far out that they couldn't possibly wade the distance.

"Maybe he hasn't seen us yet," she said, waving her hands over her head to signal the nix.

"No," said Dorian. "He's seen us."

There was a grim edge to his words that made Lottie lower her arms.

"Sigeberht!" Dorian yelled to the boat. "You promised us passage. Your summoner sacrificed to the waters, in keeping with the terms of the riddle!"

Lottie couldn't clearly make out Sigeberht's face from this distance, but she could hear his laugh.

"I promised passage," the nix yelled back, "not a return journey!"

Lottie remembered something Dorian had said earlier: *The nix are known for their wiles.*

"What's he doing?" asked Eliot, panicked. "Is he not going to take us back?"

"A curse on you, Sigeberht!" Dorian shouted.

"Oh, but a curse is *already* on me. Haven't much to lose, have I?"

"The boy already gave you his letters!" Dorian yelled back. "What more do you want?"

There was a long silence. Then Sigeberht said, "A little of his blood would be nice."

Lottie balked. "*What?*"

"It wouldn't be painful," the nix continued. "The life of a nix isn't nearly so bad as you cowardly sprites think."

Lottie turned to Eliot. All anger she'd been feeling toward him now vanished, replaced by horror.

"No one's going to touch you," she said fiercely. Then to Dorian, "We're not going to touch him."

"Of course we're not," said Dorian. "What do you take me for, Lottie, a savage? We're not about to play a nix's game."

"Then what *are* we going to do?" asked Eliot.

"Trouble," said Lottie.

Of course. Eliot had no genga, and Dorian had lost his, but Lottie still had a way to find the others and get help.

She dug into her coat and removed Trouble. He emerged in a tumble of black feathers.

"You know what to do," she said, cupping Trouble in her hands. "Go back to the flatlands, to the inn in the town called Darrow. Find the others. Tell them we're stranded here at the cove. They'll find a way to help us."

Trouble didn't argue. He didn't squawk or refuse to budge. Without a moment's hesitation, he swooped from Lottie's hands and out to sea.

"But that could take hours, couldn't it?" Lottie asked Dorian.

"Days, possibly," he replied.

Eliot made a whimpering sound. He wasn't crying, but he didn't look particularly well. He sat in the sand, his breathing shallow.

"Eliot?" Lottie knelt beside him. "You okay?"

"Just tired," he wheezed. "I'm tired is all."

"Go on, then!" Dorian shouted toward the sea. "Blow yourself away, you soulless beast!"

Lottie looked to the horizon. Sigeberht was sailing from the cove so quickly that, in just a few seconds' time, there was no sign he had been there at all—not even the slightest disturbance in the water.

"There has to be something else we can do," said Lottie.

Dorian crossed his arms and gave Lottie a look. It was a look that reminded her she'd been the one to insist they take the ferry, that Dorian had warned against the dangers, and that Lottie didn't have any right now to complain. Dorian had been right: they shouldn't have trusted Sigeberht. But Dorian being right didn't make Lottie any less restless.

There had to be *something* else they could do.

The music was distant. Lottie thought at first it was only a ringing in her tired ears. But the longer she remained still, the clearer and louder the notes became. She looked to the sky, shielding her eyes from the sun's glare.

They circled overhead in a lazy circle, flapping their wings far less often than Lottie thought necessary to stay aloft. They were more beautiful now in the dawn than Lottie remembered from earlier. They continued to sing their glassy melody.

Flatrooks.

"Dorian," Lottie said excitedly. "The flatrooks! You said they helped sailors, didn't you?"

But Dorian looked far less enthused. He stared warily at the circling birds.

"That's what the stories say. But—"

"Then maybe they'll help us!" said Lottie, throwing her arms above her head. "Hey, flatrooks! We need you! We're in trouble! Help! *Help!* Hel—*emrph!*"

Dorian had slapped his hand over her mouth. Lottie struggled against his hold, but without success.

"What are you doing?" he hissed. "I only said there were stories. There's no way of knowing what they'll *really* do."

Lottie ignored him and instead squinted at the sky, trying to make out what was happening, if anything, in the circle of spinning flatrooks.

They had stopped singing their melody. Their spinning had grown slower. Then, abruptly, the flatrooks stopped flapping their wings.

And they dove.

They headed straight for the beach at an alarming speed.

Dorian removed his hand from Lottie's mouth just in time for her to shriek.

"Run for the cave!" Dorian shouted.

"Eliot, come on!" Lottie grabbed Eliot by the hand, dragging him up, and they piled into the cave after Dorian. Breathing heavily, they stared at the scene outside the cave's shelter.

Five flatrooks had landed on the beach. They stood on long legs, their claws sunken into the sand. Their feather-ended tails, which measured the full length of the rest of their bodies, dragged behind them. Lottie could see their heads now that the birds were not flying overhead. They were just small, round protrusions at the front of their flat bodies, fitted with three black, bulbous eyes, and one squat, hooked beak. If Lottie wasn't so terrified that she could soon be torn apart by those beaks, she might have found them comical.

"Aren't they supposed to help?" Lottie whispered to Dorian. "You said they were the best birds around."

"I've never actually met one for myself!" he snapped.

"Well, who's to say they aren't nice?" asked Eliot. "We won't know if we keep hiding in the dark like little kids."

He walked out so quickly that Lottie did not have the chance to stop him. Eliot stepped into the morning light, in plain view of the flatrooks. He held his hands out, palms up, as he walked toward them, one slow step at a time. The flatrooks gathered closer at his appearance, fixing fifteen solid black eyes upon him.

"Eliot, no!" Lottie screamed, running to his side.

But the flatrooks had not attacked. They did not look half so sinister as they had when they were diving toward the earth. They looked *curious*. Lottie wondered if she could talk to them the same as the Barghest. She decided there was only one way to find out.

"Will you all help us?" she asked them. "We need to get back to the flatlands. Back to the riddle rock. It's a very important matter. I don't know if you have allegiances or anything, but if you care a thing about Albion Isle, you'll want to help, I promise."

The closest of the flatrooks stepped forward. It opened its beak and released an airy, voiceless sound, like a yawn.

"Do you think that means 'yes'?" said Eliot.

Three more flatrooks bent their legs and stretched their fleshy wings to full length. Lottie thought she knew what this meant: the flatrooks wanted them to climb atop.

"Dorian?"

Lottie turned to find Dorian standing by her side.

"Forgive me," he said. "That was cowardice, just then. Pure cowardice. I'm ashamed."

Lottie smiled at how serious Dorian sounded.

"I think it turned out all right," she said. "Though do you know how we're supposed to, um, travel on them?"

"Not the slightest idea," said Dorian. Lottie looked at the flatrook nearest her, trying to sort out how she could possibly hold on to its wings and not slide off, mid-flight.

"Well," she said. "I guess the most important thing is just getting on."

She climbed onto the flatrook the same as she might climb onto a bed—hands first, then knees. She scooted as close to the center of the flatrook's wings as she could without drawing too near its head. It was an awkward position, but she had at least made progress. Eliot and Dorian did the same. It was a clumsy process, and they didn't look particularly secure, either. How were they supposed to *fly* like this?

But they did not fly. The flatrooks stretched their legs back to their full height, then walked to the water's edge.

"Can they swim, too?" Lottie asked Dorian.

Dorian did not have to answer the question, for just then, Lottie's flatrook splashed into the water and gracefully coasted out to sea.

"They *can* swim!" she cried.

Lottie had never seen anything like it. The flatrooks glided on the water as though skating upon a solid surface. Two of them—the ones without the weight of a passenger— swam ahead. Lottie watched as their feathered tails splashed in the water, propelling them forward. It was a mesmerizing sight, but not so mesmerizing that Lottie forgot to keep a sturdy grip on the front edges of the flatrook's wings. Or fins. She really wasn't sure what to call them now.

Beside her, Eliot let out a *whoop*.

"This is *awesome*!" he called to her. Then he *whoop*ed again, but this time the cry ended in a round of hoarse coughs, and the joy Lottie had felt only moments before disappeared.

They moved even faster than Sigeberht's ferry. Lottie couldn't look too long at the water flashing by without getting woozy. The wind smacked against her face, so relentless that it felt like a solid block of ice.

So things carried on, minute after minute, until Lottie was once again lost in threadbare thought. Her nose grew numb, and her hands, too, and she began to look down every minute or so just to be sure her fingers were still clutching at the flatrook, keeping her in place.

At this rate, she thought, *I could let go entirely and not feel the difference until I had fallen into the sea.*

That's when she saw land in the distance. It began, like the Wilders had, as a thin break between sea and sky. Then it grew wider and more solid, a sure thing.

Lottie looked over at Dorian with a hopeful smile. Dorian, however, was scowling.

"What?" she shouted over the sea spray.

"I hear something," Dorian called. "From the shore. The Barghest is there. Something's wrong."

Lottie sat up straighter, straining her eyes toward the shore as though this might help her better see whatever it was that was disturbing Dorian. For a long while, she could see nothing but a line of brown sand. Then, a solitary figure became visible. It stood at the water's edge, ears perked high. It was the Barghest. A minute later, the flatrooks had brought them within shouting distance.

"Barghest!" Lottie called. "What's the matter?"

But the Barghest only perked its ears higher and began trotting along the water's edge in a nervous jaunt. Why wouldn't the Barghest say something? Or—and here a truly terrible fear gripped Lottie—what if whatever the Barghest had to say was too awful to shout?

Lottie's grip tightened as her flatrook skated to the shore and, at last, came to a stop in the shallows.

"Thank you," she said, though it came out hoarse and hurried.

She jumped into the water, no longer concerned with saving her boots or staying warm. She could only think that something had happened, something was *wrong*—and the Barghest knew what it was. She tripped and sloshed to the shore until she was stooped before the Barghest, trembling from cold.

"What is it?" she said. "Barghest, tell us what's wrong!"

But the Barghest did not obey Lottie's command. It paid her no mind whatsoever. Dorian and Eliot, like Lottie, had thrown themselves into the water and now stood dripping by her side. It was Dorian that the Barghest fixed its pinprick eyes upon with vicious precision.

Then, in a single bound, the Barghest threw itself on Dorian—claws extended, fangs bared.

CHAPTER EIGHTEEN

The World Gorge

"BARGHEST, NO!"

The Barghest did not heed Lottie's shout. It pinned Dorian beneath its heavy paws and ripped its teeth into his shoulder. The sound, wet and grisly, turned Lottie's stomach. Dorian screamed. Blood stained the sand beneath him, blooming out from his arm and soaking into the Barghest's paws.

"Where is it?" the Barghest barked. "Where is the addersfork?"

"No!" Lottie shrieked. "I *command* you, Barghest. Don't you dare hurt him!"

At last, the Barghest turned to Lottie. It tilted its head down, as though in reverence. It flattened its ears, as though in remorse. Lottie felt her senses return to her. She shivered, but with relief as well as chill. Whatever horrible thing had just happened, at least Lottie still had command over the Barghest. Now she just had to think this through, come up with a plan. She had to save Dorian, had to—

Fingers gripped Lottie's shoulder. A heavy weight pressed against her back. The Barghest lifted its head, lips pulled back from its bloodied teeth. It was *smiling* at her.

"Take her," it said. "The boy, too."

The grip on Lottie's shoulder grew tighter. She wrenched away.

"Eliot, run!" she screamed.

It was too late. Eliot had already been thrown to the ground, face-first. His glasses lay broken in the sand, next to his bloodied chin. A red-cloaked sprite leaned with her knee pressed into Eliot's spine and was binding his hands with rope. Then hands were back on Lottie, harder than before. They jerked her arms so roughly, Lottie felt sure they'd been ripped clean off her body. She cried out in pain. Something wound about her wrists, cold as metal. Lottie fought against the hold, but it only grew stronger. Then she saw it on her captor's wrist: a white circle. She recognized it as well as she had the red cloak of Eliot's captor. These were Southerly soldiers.

The soldier at Lottie's back turned her to face the Barghest once more.

Only what Lottie saw before her now was no longer the Barghest she knew. Its fur was changing color from black to lightest gray. The fur itself was different, too— smoother and far less textured. The Barghest leaned back on its hind legs, and for a moment it looked like a strange circus animal, performing for a crowd. It was an unnatural sight, so unfitting for a creature as majestic as the Barghest. Still, it remained on its legs, fur transforming until it was most certainly not fur but *fabric*—the fabric of a long, gray cloak. The Barghest's front paws were no longer clawed, but fingered. Its arms turned smooth with skin. Where there had once been a muzzle was now a set of pale lips. Where there had once been ears hung a mane of a different sort, long and blond. The pinprick eyes were gone entirely, replaced by over-wide ones—*a woman's eyes.*

Only one feature remained unchanged: Iolanthe still wore the same bloody smile.

They say she's a splinter of the worst kind, Reeve had said. *The absolute worst.*

"What did you do to the others?" Lottie said. "It's me you're after, so just take *me.*"

Iolanthe ignored Lottie. She was watching a third Southerly soldier, who had pulled the satchel from Dorian's writhing, gasping body. The solider sifted through the satchel's contents.

"Here," he said, pulling out a linen-wrapped bundle. "This, m'lady. I can taste its potency from here."

"Careful with it." Iolanthe's words still came out like the bark of the Barghest. "Put it back. Carry the satchel. Follow me. You two, bring her and the boy."

Iolanthe turned her back to Lottie and strode down the beach. The one soldier scurried after her with satchel in hand, leaving Dorian in the red-stained sand.

"Move, you," Lottie's soldier grunted, pushing her forward.

But Lottie's legs felt as moveable as two bricks. She stared at Dorian's bloodied body. He was no longer writhing. He wasn't moving at all.

"Dorian," she said. "Dorian, hold on!"

She knew how stupid the words were, even as she said them. Hold on for *what*? Who would save Dorian? Who would save any of them? Who possibly could?

"*Move*," said the soldier, jabbing his mace into her back.

Lottie cried out. She placed one foot in front of the other, but not fast enough to match the soldier's pace. She stumbled again and again.

"That's it," said the soldier, stopping.

For one ridiculous moment, Lottie thought he might have given up trying to make her walk and decided to just let her be. Instead, he grabbed Lottie about the waist and hauled her over his shoulder. Lottie wanted to beat against his back, but she could not. She wanted to scream again, but what good would it do? There was no one to hear her but Iolanthe ahead and a dying Dorian behind and, beyond that, the unfeeling waves crashing upon the shore.

She watched the sand pass beneath her, watched the soldier's footprints form, then quickly shift away. And at the very edge of her sights were the buckled boots of the soldier in charge of Eliot. Lottie strained her neck just once to see that this soldier, too, had resorted to throwing Eliot over her shoulder. Weak with exhaustion, she dropped her cheek to the soldier's back and closed her eyes, listening to the slip of boots on sand, to the jostle of metal latches and buckles on the soldier's uniform, to the drag of the tide, and to the frantic *thud-thud-thud* of her own heart.

The sounds carried on for minutes piled upon minutes. The slip of boots, the jostle of metal, the drag of the tide, the thud of her heart. The noises bled together. Lottie's feet had gone numb from cold. Strange pains and thoughts dragged across her mind.

How much farther? Where was Iolanthe taking her? Where were the others? Was Dorian still alive?

Then the jostling stopped. Lottie felt the world slip from under her, felt earth at her back. She opened her eyes to a cloudless sky above. She heard labored breaths beside her. *Eliot.* Lottie wanted so badly to reach out and take his hand in hers.

"It's going to be okay," she whispered, even though she had begun to believe less and less, with each passing minute, that things would ever be okay again.

"Lottie!" shouted a voice, not Eliot's. "Puck's sake, don't tell him anything! Don't *give* him anything. We're all right. Let him do what he wants but don't—"

"I thought I told you to gag the wisp."

Lottie's joy at hearing Fife—he was alive!—turned sour at the sound of the second voice. She had not heard it in more than a month, but she recognized it instantly. It had haunted her dreams in Wisp Territory and still sat pungent on the back of her memories.

"Lottie!" yelled Fife. "Don't—"

Fife's warning was muffled. Lottie strained hard to see around her, but she could make out nothing save sky and sand.

"What's the meaning of bringing her here, Iolanthe? I told you—"

"I thought—I led her this way to bring her to you—" Iolanthe took a breath. "I think she may yet know something, Your Majesty. Something the others do not. She has now been to the Wilders. She has seen—"

"*Excuses!*" roared the Southerly King. "I gave you one simple task. Weeks it's been. *Weeks*, and still you've failed me. I'd do better to throw you to the Northerly Vines, same as I did Grissom."

"Most excellent sire, if you'd only—"

"All it took was a slip of a knife, an arrow properly nocked, a sword to the heart. Now, fifty of my finest soldiers slaughtered, and you dare approach me with your own neck unharmed, dragging that abomination behind, still breathing? I told you I wanted her dead. I told you I wanted her before me *in pieces*."

Lottie shook so hard that her teeth knocked against each other.

"She's as good as dead, sire. Look at her. Wouldn't you rather she suffer?"

Starkling's voice, so wild before, now took a horribly soft turn. "I would rather she be a corpse, buried beneath my feet, no longer a nuisance biting my heels at every turn. She started as a gnat, Iolanthe, and you have let her turn into a snake. And you bring her to me *now*, of all possible times. You bring her just at the start of my war."

"I thought you would consider it a bounty, sire. I thought you would be glad to have her underfoot once and for all. A celebratory gift, if you will, to commemorate the dawning of a new age. The age of your people."

There was the sound of movement, slight but rough.

"My people," said the youthful voice of the Southerly King. "Do you presume to know anything about *my people*?"

"Forgive me, my king. I only meant—"

The sounds, the sights, the sensations came in a flurry. Lottie found herself hoisted to her feet, held up by a vicious grip.

"Stand up, you. *Stand.*"

Starkling held her by the coat collar, as though Lottie were nothing more than a worm caught in his talon. She struggled to find her footing, but the sand slipped under her toes, and she kept lurching forward, unbalanced. Then came a slice at her wrists, and scalding pain. Starkling had cut her bonds, but he had cut into her skin, too. The hot blood felt strange on her frigid skin. At last, Lottie found her balance. She turned, arms raised, ready to beat against the king's chest, to inflict whatever pain she could. Starkling didn't give her the chance. He grabbed her by the elbow and dragged her after him. As he did, Lottie got her first good look at the Southerly King.

The damage Lottie had seen working on Starkling's skin the last time she'd stood before him, in the throne room of the Southerly Palace, was now far more advanced. Gone was the king's unblemished face. In its place was a bony, sallow complexion. His arms were scaled like a fish's and covered in sludge-filled boils. His eyes were reddened and murky. His grip on her, Lottie now saw, was the grip of five fingers rotted down to nothing but bare, black bone.

"Stop it! *Stop!*"

Lottie's attention snapped away from Starkling to those he was dragging her past. Fife, Adelaide, and Oliver all sat in a circle, backs to each other, wrists bound. Fife had been gagged. Two Southerly soldiers stood guard over them, maces in hand. Adelaide was watching Lottie with wet eyes.

"I'm so sorry, Lottie," she cried. "We didn't know it wasn't the real Barghest. We swear, we didn't know until it was too late."

"It isn't your fault," Lottie said, and though she meant for the words to come out strong, they fell flat from her lips, papery and barely audible. She was too preoccupied with whatever Starkling had in store for her.

The king dragged her on, past the others, past Oliver's grim, slate-green stare. Lottie wanted to say something. Goodbye, perhaps, or her own apology. But before she could form words, Starkling threw her to the ground. Lottie's bloodied hands caught the fall, her open wounds filling with sand. Lottie shrank against the pain. Then, pushing past it, she looked ahead.

She found herself staring at a sight unlike anything she'd seen before on Kemble Isle or in all her journeys through Limn. She was kneeling at the edge of a vast chasm. Its edges were not composed of sand, but silver—a strange shifting color that seemed almost liquid. And deep down, at the pit of the chasm, was blackness—utter blackness.

As Lottie stared, she was overcome by the sensation that the chasm was *growing*, yawning out even as she watched.

But that was impossible.

Wasn't it?

Lottie blinked. She took another look. But the illusion had not vanished. The gulf really was growing. Its walls were pushing outward in both directions—one down the coast and one toward Lottie. Sand shifted under her boots and began to pour forward, disappearing into the silvery dark. Lottie scrambled backward, but her back rammed into Starkling's knees. He stood directly over her, grinning a red, toothy smile.

"One hundred apple trees," he said. "One hundred silver boughs. Can you imagine the time it took? The things I had to do? But now all the silver has been extracted and placed in just the right positions. A hundred silver boughs, laid end on end, to rend the world."

"A world gorge," Lottie whispered.

"Never before has there been one of such magnitude—a gorge that will conduct the passage not just of a single soul, but of an *army*." Starkling's smile disappeared. "And you've ruined the big moment. I asked Iolanthe to deliver your corpse. But they say if you want something done right . . ."

Starkling yanked Lottie to her feet. Fear rattled down her spine as the king leaned his rotting face toward her. Dark spittle flew from his lips as he spoke.

"Iolanthe believes that you and your friends have information I'd be interested in. But do you know what I think? I think dear Iolanthe's had a moment of weakness, just as Grissom did before her. I really ought to choose my right-hand sprites with better care."

Lottie could hear sand sifting behind her, could hear the chasm groaning from new growth. Her fear grew, but so did her anger.

"My friends never did a thing to you," she said. "Just let them go. You don't have any right to hurt them."

"I haven't the *right*?" The smile returned to Starkling's face. "Oh *my*."

He shoved Lottie, hard. She stumbled back, and a gust of wind warmed her bare neck. *Warmed* her, for it was a hot breeze, blown as though fresh off a desert plain. It was coming from the gorge, the edge of which was only a pace away from her boots. Lottie thought of the gaping blackness she'd seen below. When Starkling pushed her in, how long would it take her to fall? How long would she be aware of the end coming?

Lottie thought of Eliot, and of Dorian. She thought of ragged coughs and bloodstained sand. Her grief was suffocating her, but she couldn't *reach* them. She couldn't breathe—

"Feel that?" said Starkling, his skeletal fingers ripping

into her coat. "Can you *feel* it? It's the heat of Dim. The heat of my world, coming up for air. I'll be here to witness it in all its glory. But you *won't*."

Lottie knew. This was the moment. Now came the final shove. Now came the fall.

The agonizing pain she felt for Eliot, for all her friends— the fear of what would happen to them—caught up her remaining breaths. Lottie raised her bloodied hands. Weak though they were, she wrapped them around Starkling's arms. She closed her eyes, concentrating. She gathered all her clamoring feelings and focused on Starkling alone. Strength returned to her fingers, and she dug them into his wet, peeling skin.

Starkling picked Lottie up by the lapels of her periwinkle coat. Her feet left the ground. She was aware of someone somewhere screaming her name.

The tightening sensation began, as it always did, in the very center of her chest. It squeezed on her ribs, the pain compact, like a spring pressed under a weight of iron. Lottie fought for breath.

"No," she choked out. "*No*."

Her hands had not left Starkling's arms. She clenched them into the oily scales. She closed her eyes. The bad spell swelled within her, then shot through her arms with more force than it ever had before. It seeped out her fingers and into Starkling's arms.

He screamed.

It was a scream of agony, of pain beyond what even Lottie was experiencing.

Starkling released his grip on Lottie. She fell. Her back hit the ground—the blessed, sandy ground. The world gorge had not yet reached them. She was safe.

Then she looked up.

Starkling had fallen to his knees. His skin bubbled like boiling water. Scales sagged from his arms and dropped into the sand like melted wax. Lottie scrambled away in horror, out of reach of the expanding gorge. Still, she could not take her eyes off the Southerly King. His jaw had turned loose like taffy. His eyes bulged crimson in their sockets. What remained of his once blond hair now dropped to the sand in clumps.

No words came from his mouth, only the screams. And then there were no screams, only a melting face with no mouth. Then no nose. Then no eyes. All turned to dark, bubbling liquid. King Starkling had disintegrated before her eyes.

Lottie had never seen a sight so horrible, and yet she could not turn her face away.

For she had done this.

She had used her keen.

Only this time, Lottie had not healed.

She had destroyed.

All that remained of the Southerly King was a simmering puddle being fast absorbed into the sand.

Lottie scrambled to her feet. She blinked again and again, trying to understand what had just occurred. But no amount of blinking or head shaking removed the sight of the puddle at her feet. Slowly, she looked up, beyond it. Iolanthe stood nearby. Her face was painted in shock, her eyes wide with disbelief. At her side stood Southerly soldiers, lost in a similar trance. Eliot sat at their feet, looking ashen. Farther off, the three soldiers guarding Adelaide, Oliver, and Fife, looked equally stunned. Everyone was staring at Lottie. Everyone was silent. The quiet closed in on her from all sides, heavy with its sheer *un-noise.*

Lottie turned to Iolanthe.

"Do you see what I can do?" she called, hiding her trembling, bloody hands behind her back. "Let my friends go. Let them go *now.*"

At that, Iolanthe's glazed eyes snapped into focus with purpose.

"Guards," she said. "Release the children."

The Southerly soldiers fumbled to undo the bonds of their prisoners. Iolanthe strode toward Lottie, arms outstretched, though not in a menacing way at all, but rather like she meant to embrace her. Lottie didn't dare step back, for to do so would mean stepping in the stained sand that had once been King Starkling.

"What a change of events," said Iolanthe. She stopped her approach and lowered her hands. "I went to all that trouble to get ahold of your addersfork, yet you were capable of destroying him all along. And to think, I nearly cut your head clean off, when you were capable of accomplishing the thing I most desired."

Lottie struggled to make sense of what she was hearing. "You *wanted* Starkling dead?"

"Same as you and yours," said Iolanthe. "There's no need to threaten me, Lottie. You and I are on the same team. I was going to use the addersfork to kill Starkling. But on my own terms, you understand. In my own way."

Lottie opened her mouth. She looked around. She understood. These sprites were no soldiers of the Southerly King. They had been loyal to Iolanthe all along. Now finished with their task of setting their prisoners free, they gathered around Iolanthe in reverent postures.

"My queen," said one, kneeling before her. "We are at your command." Then he cast a glance at Lottie, and the look in his eyes turned her blood cold. He looked horrified. He looked disgusted. He was horrified and disgusted by *her*. "Do you wish us to subdue the girl?"

Iolanthe shook her head. "That won't be necessary. She and I are reaching an understanding, aren't we, Lottie?" She took another step closer. "You see, Starkling had his own ideas about what to do with the world gorge.

My plan is better. And if you and your friends are willing to go along with it, I'm sure I could make good use of your talents in my court. I could elevate you all to respectable positions. Your rainbow-eyed friend would prove an especially valuable asset."

"But you've been hunting us! You tried to kill me. And you tried to kill . . . *Dorian*." Lottie whipped toward the others, who were just getting to their feet. "Dorian. He's been hurt. He could be dying."

Fife, now free of his gag and bonds, floated forward. "Where?" he asked.

Lottie pointed down the coast. "By the water's edge. Oh, please, Fife. *Hurry*."

Fife sped away, zipping over the heads of the soldiers.

"Attacking Dorian was necessary," said Iolanthe, watching Fife's departure. "There was no getting around it."

"I guess not," said Lottie. "Just like there was no getting around killing innocent wisps. Or destroying their only silver-boughed tree. Or invading the Northerly Court. I guess there was no getting around murdering *me* in the Revered House of Fiske. Is that what you mean?"

Iolanthe smiled thinly. "I was under orders. Even rebels must obey orders when the circumstances demand it."

Lottie did not voice the reply jumping on her tongue. She couldn't say everything that came to her head right now. She had to think. Iolanthe was smart. She was now the most powerful Southerly sprite in all of Albion Isle, and she was offering Lottie and her friends protection.

Or she could still be planning to kill them.

A magnificent groaning sound interrupted Lottie's thoughts. She turned to find that the world gorge was still growing—slower now than before, but growing just the same. Sand continued to pour down its walls, and little by little the distance between Lottie and the ravine's edge grew shorter.

"How—how do we stop it?" she asked.

"Why would I want to stop it?" said Iolanthe, looking shocked. "Though I can promise you, if you and your friends are willing to lend me your keens, I can protect you from what's to come."

Lottie's mind was ablaze with half-formed plans. She'd already written out several in her mind's eye, then discarded them, one after the other. And then a plan stuck.

Lottie sank her hands into her pockets. In one, she felt the absence of Trouble, and for a moment her worries caught on the panic of where he could possibly be. Then her attention shifted to the item resting in her other pocket: her mother's ring.

She had to be careful. She had to remove the ring from her pocket, still in its silk covering, and once it was uncovered, she could not cut her own hand.

I'm sorry, Mother, she thought.

Tears stung her eyes as she pulled out the handkerchief, then cautiously but quickly unwrapped and discarded it from the delicate circle of lapis lazuli.

"What do you have there?" asked Iolanthe, eyes narrowing at the ring Lottie held pinched between her thumb and forefinger.

Lottie did not hesitate. She lunged forward, plunging the sharp diamond edge of the ring into Iolanthe's arm and dragging it down her skin, leaving a wet, crimson cut in its wake. Then she pulled away, bloodied ring in hand, and ran.

She heard Iolanthe's enraged shrieks and the sound of heavy footsteps behind her. Still, she ran. She ran in spite of pain, in spite of fear, in spite of deafening thoughts. She ran to the water, into the crashing waves, and threw the ring with all her might. It soared through the air in a high arc, glinted once in the burning sun, and then disappeared into the sea.

Lottie's heart hammered.

"Please work," she whispered to the water. "*Please.*"

When Lottie turned, she found herself face-to-face with Iolanthe. She stood shin-deep in the water. Her expression was livid.

"What have you done?" she demanded.

She made a grab at Lottie, who flung herself toward the shore. She tripped, but recovered fast enough to avoid

Iolanthe's grasp. When she reached dry sand, she tripped again and landed on her battered hands. She felt so weak. She felt she couldn't move again. She closed her eyes against the wet sand and waited for Iolanthe to reach her.

But she never did. With difficulty, Lottie rolled onto her back and saw Iolanthe standing at the water's edge. Her forehead was creased in concentration, her arms outstretched, fingers splayed. But she could move no farther. It was as though an invisible wall had been constructed on the edge of the tide, blocking her in.

It had worked, just as the riddle promised. Lottie had thrown Iolanthe's blood into the water, and now Iolanthe was bound to the sea.

Lottie laughed. It was the worst possible time for a laugh, and yet clunky giggles emerged from her throat. Iolanthe had finally realized what was happening. She beat her hands against the air.

"Soldiers!" she screamed. "Help me!"

Four red-cloaked sprites hurtled into the waves. Two took Iolanthe by the arms, two by the waist, attempting to hoist her forward. But it was of no use. Though the soldiers could set foot on dry land, Iolanthe could not.

"Stop it!" she shouted. "Stop it, you idiots! You'll pull my arms straight from their sockets. Try it this way. You, take me by my legs . . ."

Lottie did not stay to watch. She had to get to the others.

She lumbered up the bank to where Adelaide, Oliver, and Eliot stood, as fixated on the sight of Iolanthe's predicament as the remaining soldiers.

"Lottie!" Eliot cried, pulling her into his arms. "What did you *do*? What happened?"

"She used the riddle," said Oliver. "She bound Iolanthe to the waters, the same as the nix."

Eliot backed away, face turned down. "No, I don't mean that," he said. "I mean . . ."

He trailed off, but there was no question as to what Eliot meant. Lottie had not let herself think of it until now. She still didn't want to. She looked to the sand where King Starkling had once stood, but even the stain had disappeared, swallowed up by the growing world gorge.

Oliver's eyes were a troubled yellow. "So wrap up care in a cobweb," he said, "and drop it down the well, into that world inverted where—"

Oliver stopped quoting. An awful sound had ripped through the air like thunder, turning them all silent and wide-eyed. Then the ground shook beneath their feet, and Lottie saw the source of the terrible noise: the world gorge was still expanding. It was splitting down the coast. A crack, wide across as a river, drove through the sand, opening wide and speeding straight toward—

"Oliver!"

His eyes met Lottie's. They were a bright shade of gold that Lottie had never seen before. Then the chasm was beneath him, and Lottie stared in numb horror as Oliver lost his footing, wavered once, and fell.

"Oliver!" Lottie screamed again, running toward the newly formed fissure.

He had fallen in, but with one hand, he'd grabbed hold of a silvery edge jutting from the ravine wall.

Lottie dropped to her knees beside the chasm, where Oliver struggled to regain his grip. He tried swinging his free hand to the surface, but his fingers merely slipped through the sifting sand. He could not pull himself out.

"Stand back!" Lottie shouted to Adelaide and Eliot. "Grab my legs, both of you!"

She saw the fear in Adelaide's face; she knew what Lottie was going to do. Still, Adelaide nodded. Lottie steeled herself. Adelaide grabbed her by one ankle, Eliot by the other. Then Lottie stretched out flat on her stomach and reached her arms over the edge.

"Grab hold of me!" she shouted to Oliver.

He looked up with black eyes. He shook his head.

Despite the chaos surrounding them, despite the ongoing roar of the world gorge expanding, Oliver said the words softly, like he might if he and Lottie were sitting together in a quiet park. "Lottie, *no*."

"It doesn't matter!" she yelled at him. "I can heal myself. Oliver, just *grab hold*."

Oliver shook his head.

Lottie lunged forward. She wrapped both her hands around Oliver's wrist.

"Don't!" Oliver said. "Let go, Lottie. I'll—"

"If you won't grab me, I'll grab you!" she shouted. "But it'd make things a lot easier if you just held my hand."

"I *can't*." Oliver's voice was broken.

But even as he said it, Lottie slipped one hand through his, threading their fingers and locking them tight. The pain was instantaneous. It was an overwhelming, unrelenting burning that felt like Lottie had stuck her hand into a roaring fire. A green pigment washed up her fingers, her knuckles, her wrist. Still, Lottie held tight. She didn't cry out. She gritted her teeth and worked up the will to say, "Give me your other hand!"

This time, Oliver did not argue. He swung his hand up, and Lottie caught hold. The pain doubled, searing through her skin and coloring her other hand deep blue.

"It's okay," she gasped out. "We've got you now." Then she called back to Adelaide and Eliot, "Pull us up!"

She felt a jolt on both legs. Her stomach dragged across the ground, and Oliver rose from the gorge by a foot. His hands and Lottie's now rested in the sand.

"Good!" she said. "Nearly there. Just—"

The awful booming sound came again. The ground rumbled. A great crash echoed from somewhere nearby. The earth Oliver was resting on crumbled.

Lottie screamed. She lost her grip on Oliver's left hand. A heavy weight pulled on her arm. Hot wind blasted into her face. She could no longer feel solid earth beneath her. She was falling into the darkness below.

She heard Eliot's scream very near her ear. Adelaide's shrieks came after, though higher up, at the surface. All was shouts and warm air and the rush of silver.

Then, all was darkness.

—

Then . . .

A light in the darkness.

And a voice that said, "My, *my*. Visitors."

Quotations in order of appearance

p. 39 "As 't were a spur upon the soul, / A fear will urge it where / To go without the spectre's aid" (Emily Dickinson, "I Lived on Dread")

p. 54 "Home-keeping hearts are happiest, / For those that wander they know not where / Are full of trouble and full of care;" (Henry Wadsworth Longfellow, "Song")

p. 83 "I am the master of my fate, / I am the captain of my soul." (William Ernest Henley, "Invictus")

p. 95 "I, now thirty-seven years old in perfect health begin, / Hoping to cease not till death." (Walt Whitman, "Song of Myself")

p. 111 "What though on hamely fare we dine, / Wear hoddin grey, an' a' that; / Gie fools their silks, and knaves their wine; / A Man's a Man for a' that: / For a' that, and a' that, / Their tinsel show, an' a' that; / The honest man, tho' e'er sae poor, / Is king o' men for a' that." (Robert Burns, "A Man's A Man For A' That")

p. 118 "God help me! save I take my part / Of danger on the roaring sea, / A devil rises in my heart, / Far worse than any death to me." (Alfred, Lord Tennyson, "The Sailor Boy")

p. 145 "Yet, love and hate me too; / So, these extremes shall neither's office do;" (John Donne, "The Prohibition")

p. 286 "Slow, slow as the winter snow / The tears have drifted to mine eyes;" (Elizabeth Barrett Browning, "Change upon Change")

p. 291 "This told, I joy; but then no longer glad, / I send them back again and straight grow sad." (William Shakespeare, "Sonnet 45")

p. 311–312 "Two sturdy oaks I mean, which side by side, / Withstand the winter's storm, / And spite of wind and tide, / Grow up the meadow's pride, / For both are strong." (Henry David Thoreau, "Friendship")

p. 357 "Exultation is the going / Of an inland soul to sea, / Past the houses—past the headlands— / Into deep Eternity! / Bred as we, among the mountains, / Can the sailor understand / The divine intoxication / Of the first league out from land?" (Emily Dickinson, "Exultation Is the Going")

p. 404 "So wrap up care in a cobweb / and drop it down the well / into that world inverted / where left is always right, / where the shadows are really the body, / where we stay awake all night," (Elizabeth Bishop, "Insomnia")